HONOR THY FATHER

A Legal Thriller

JASON HOLLAND

Amber House Books

Cover design by Control Freak Productions
Cover Photo © Fer Gregory and Elwynn (via license Shutterstock.com)

Published by Amber House Books, LLC
http://www.amberhousebooks.com

For more information, contact publisher@amberhousebooks.com

For Porter…

The moving finger writes and, having writ, moves on.
Nor all thy piety nor wit shall lure it back
to cancel half a line
nor all thy tears wash out a word of it.

Omar Khayyam

Now

_____

June 2018

Chapter One

Cassandra Warren felt nothing but exhilaration as she stepped out of the shower and dried herself with a plush towel. She tousled her stylishly-trimmed, freshly high-lighted locks with her fingers. Even damp, her hair looked perfect. She took her time applying lotion to every reachable part of her body. It was her most prized possession, tanned and toned in a way that belonged only to the extremely disciplined or the extremely wealthy. Cassandra was both.

She donned his favorite nightgown, then dabbed her favorite scent on the pulse at the side of her throat, a jasmine that she ordered custom-made. She wandered into the spacious master bedroom and draped herself over the chaise. The candle was lit, the wine already chilling in the ice bucket. Sliding glass doors along the opposite wall offered a moonlit panoramic view of Lake Barkley. Through the open windows she could hear the lake's waters gently lapping against the shore below.

She was taking a sip of the wine when she heard him come in. She had never felt this sort of anticipation for anything or anyone, but it was this way every time they met. She heard his steps as he walked across the hardwood floor toward her. Her breath hitched in her throat as she waited for him to touch her. The first touch from him was always her favorite—a harbinger of things to come. No man could do for her what he did. She sensed him—no, she *felt* him —standing silently just inches behind her, and sighed.

He was everything she wanted.

His fingers grazed her bare shoulder and eased up her neck. Cassandra turned her head to press her lips to his hand. She couldn't see his other hand, nor the silver instrument it held, gleaming in the moonlight.

In that moment of anticipation, Cassandra Warren did not realize she had only seconds to live.

He felt her skin prickle beneath his touch. Cassandra Warren was so aroused by who and what she thought he was. It would be her final mistake.

Still, he played along.

His hand moved up the side of her neck and cupped her jaw. "Mmm…" she purred, closing her eyes and nuzzling her face against his hand. "I've been waiting for you."

"No," he replied in a hoarse whisper, "you haven't."

Before she could react, he seized her jaw in his left hand. She didn't have time to react or resist. The straight razor gleamed in his other hand. He planted the blade a few inches below her left ear. Feeling it catch in her tender flesh, he pulled the razor back to his right in a surprisingly smooth and easy motion.

He watched as she spewed and choked on her own blood until the considerable fight within her was gone. He picked her up from the chair, carried her to the king-sized bed and gently laid her down so that her head dangled over the edge. Blood pulsed through the canal gashed across her throat and dripped to the floor, where it began to pool. It was the very spot where the house's last mistress had died. It gave Cassandra a view of the lake, albeit upside down. He wondered if in these, her final seconds, she would still admire that view. After all, she had worked so hard to get it.

He knew he should run, but he lingered to watch the light fade from her eyes for the last time. He unconsciously fidgeted with the blade, twirling it between his fingers, flicking it in the air, and then catching it safely by the handle. A groundswell of emotions began to stir inside of him. He felt a sob catch in his throat, but he choked it back, remembering why he had come here.

Why he had come here the last time.

It had begun. Again.

He snapped the knife shut and pocketed it. With the look of resignation that comes with mourning the very life you just took, Cassandra Warren's killer simply turned and walked away.

Chapter Two

Hunter Cameron's long, rangy frame rose easily from the solid oak table traditionally used by the defense. He doffed his jacket and ambled toward the twelve jurors seated in the middle of the courtroom.

During this trial, now in its third—and God willing—final day, more than one juror had been struck by the strong resemblance between Hunter and the subject of one of the judicial portraits hanging to the right of the judge's bench. The portrait was of Hunter's late father James, whose humility had prevented him from allowing anyone to call him "Judge" anywhere except inside this courtroom during his distinguished twenty-two years on the bench. Just like his father, Hunter's once-dark hair was frosted with a silver that only served to highlight his green eyes. High cheekbones and a straight nose complimented his striking face and made him look a decade younger than his fifty-seven years.

Hunter had grown up within these walls. And when he began his closing argument, speaking in a rich, southern baritone hued with whiskey and honey, there was no doubt among the jurors as to whom the courtroom belonged. The room's acoustics seemed to greet his words with a warmth not reserved for other voices, as though it was welcoming an old friend.

Sheriff Thomas Dooley was familiar with the allure of Hunter's words. In his thirteen years with the department, he had heard them countless times. Until now, however, his seat had not been *behind* the defense table.

Late last summer Sheriff Dooley had developed an interest in his neighbor's bosomy daughter, Dorothea. To his surprise and as a profound testament to the theory that some women couldn't resist a man in uniform, *any* uniform, Dorothea had welcomed his advances. Unfortunately for Dooley, he was so busy shaking off his resulting disbelief that he failed to note an important fact about Dorothea before they began their two-week affair—her age.

In Kentucky the age of consent was sixteen. Although Dorothea had been a willing participant in their acts—including sex atop the hood of his squad car, which she affectionately termed as doing it *Dooley-style* —she was six months shy of sixteen and thus, *not* of consenting age.

When the indictment was returned by the Christian County Grand Jury, the disgraced sheriff turned to the man he knew to be the best criminal defense lawyer in western Kentucky. Hell, the best defense lawyer in the Commonwealth, some said.

Robert Galusha, the Commonwealth's Attorney from Todd County, had been appointed as special prosecutor in the case. Galusha had brawled his way through the trial, lacing the Sheriff with layer upon layer of salty and lurid accusations, leaving little to the imagination. No matter how minute the detail, Galusha jack-hammered it into the jurors' minds. However lacking in subtlety his approach may have been, Galusha had nonetheless been effective. During the Commonwealth's case, some onlookers in the court-house swore that they could actually feel the weight of the jurors' disgusted scowls aimed at Dooley. Others in the County Clerk's office were positive they had heard hissing from the jury box.

And then it was Hunter's turn.

His approach was, as it always had been, one of understated grace. He wasn't interested in brawling with Galusha, or in dazzling the jury with his intelligence. He simply wanted to connect with them. And connect with them he did.

From the beginning of the trial, Hunter had followed the same routine when he came into the courtroom. He'd make the obligatory handshakes, go to his table, and unload his battered briefcase. He would display the contents prominently on the defense table— the binders of notes, a law book or two, and his trusty pouch of Red Man tobacco. Not dip. Chewing tobacco. Never mind the fact that he'd never had a chaw in his life and had been bringing the very same pouch of the very same tobacco to trials for years. Silly though it may have seemed to an outsider, that bag resonated with a jury in this rural community with traditionally strong tobacco ties. *I'm not like that prosecutor over there*, it said. *I'm one of you.*

But props weren't the only way Hunter connected with the jury. Careful not to attack Dorothea while she was on the stand and risk offending the jury, Hunter gently prodded her to acknowledge that she routinely drove a car to her rendezvous with Dooley. She also admitted, without a trace of embarrassment, that due largely to her indisputably mature appearance, she was regularly able to purchase alcohol for her friends. Finally, she admitted—over Galusha's vehement objection that the testimony asked for speculation by Dorothea —that under those circumstances, ol' Dooley probably *did* think she was over sixteen.

This evidence, he argued, was consistent with Dooley's claim from the outset that he had believed Dorothea to be of consenting age. If that was the case—and he reminded them, Dorothea testified under oath that it was—then it was their sworn duty, under Kentucky law, to find Dooley not guilty. Of course, Hunter was far too seasoned to put Dooley on the stand to ask him whether or not he had known about her age. Frankly, he had no desire to learn the answer to that question himself.

Now, during his closing argument, Hunter subtly, but repeatedly, reminded the jury of this evidence. The look on their faces would later be described by onlookers—the very same onlookers who had predicted imminent conviction and perhaps a hanging at the court square—as that of a church body, anxiously receiving and accepting the words of their preacher. Hunter knew that the only real question to be answered by the jury was which one of them would be elected as foreperson, not what their verdict would be.

———

SHORTLY AFTER THE jury acquitted Sheriff Dooley and before the starved western Kentucky media could grab him for a much-needed shot of adrenaline for their otherwise sleepy headlines, Hunter Cameron breezed down Highway 68 toward the lake home he shared with his wife Katherine. The convertible top of the burgundy BMW was down and the warm summer air rippled the waves in his hair. Instinctively, he felt the pocket of his shirt, checking as he had just seconds before and would do again, that the folded piece of paper was still there. He left it in his shirt pocket, breathing a sigh of relief. The directions, written in his own hand, were there.

Thank God.

The directions weren't another prop to impress a jury. On the contrary, he'd gone to great lengths to prevent anyone from knowing that he needed them and that he had needed them for several months now. He didn't need them every day, he assured himself. But when he did, his shame was palpable, even though no one knew his secret. After all, these were the directions to the home in which he had lived for the last twenty-six years.

Chapter Three

The smells of country breakfast awoke Hunter from his deep sleep. He yawned, rose from his bed and, donning his robe, wearily wandered down the hall, following his nose each step of the way.

He paused in the doorway of the kitchen to revel in the view of his wife of thirty years. Covered with one of Hunter's oversized oxford shirts, her long, lean figure was more the by-product of good genes than of strict diet and exercise. Her once-porcelain facial features had developed more character with the age lines, producing a lived-in, comfortable beauty, much like the antiques she sold from her parlor in town. Her still-dark auburn hair was tied back and her hazel eyes made him think of leaves descending from trees, cooler weather, and all things autumn.

Snapping out of his spell, he approached her from behind, wrapped his arms around her waist, and nudged the morning stubble of his chin down the nape of her neck.

"Mornin' love," she said in a wispy voice indicative of the early morning hour.

"No more low-fat diet? Who do I owe for the reprieve?"

Katherine flipped the eggs and gently broke from his embrace to check the biscuits in the hearth-style oven. "A reprieve is all it is. Enjoy the sunset of your freedom while it lasts," she said, grinning.

"Shit."

Hunter sat at the kitchen table and gazed through the large glass door that opened onto the deck, affording a spectacular view of the lake. The sun glistened sharply off the water, blazing a broad streak of light across the bay and the main channel.

Lake Barkley and its adjoining sister, Kentucky Lake, comprised one of the world's largest man-made bodies of water. The land mass located between the lakes, creatively titled "The Land Between the Lakes", was a haven for campers and anglers alike. Each summer both locals and tourists would pour in to enjoy the tranquility and hospitality of the area. Although it was only seven-thirty, the lake was already well populated by fishermen trolling Barkley for the bountiful catfish, bass, and crappie for which it was nationally known. Within a couple of hours, the fishermen would retreat to their campsites and be replaced by weekenders and tourists, cutting across the waters in houseboats, pontoons, and runabouts. Hunter and Katherine enjoyed watching the droves arrive each spring, but were happy to wave goodbye when they left in August. Though they both worked in Hopkinsville, the twenty-minute morning drive was a sacrifice worth making. Neither of them could imagine not living on the lake.

The table, typically set for four, held only two place settings. Their daughters, Payton and Alexandria, were away at college. Payton, the eldest at twenty years of age, was a junior accounting major at her father's alma mater, Centre College, some three hours away. Alexandria, the more outgoing, creative one, had just enrolled at Northwestern University in its acclaimed drama department. Not yet eighteen, she had left for college a month early to become acclimated to life at the university's home in Evanston, Illinois. The quiet from the girls' absence had been unsettling at first. However, the appeal of not having to sneak around after some twenty years of being careful not to be caught in a compromising position by one of the girls, was welcomed by the Camerons.

The morning newspaper lay on the table, still bound snugly in its blue cellophane wrapping. Hunter was typically unimpressed both by his courtroom victories and by the press's consistent inability to correctly detail what had occurred, so there was a great likelihood that the morning's headlines regarding Sheriff Dooley's acquittal would not be read.

He poured his first cup of coffee as Katherine placed breakfast on the table. Plates full of fried eggs, bacon, sausage, grits, and gravy flanked a pyramid of homemade biscuits. Several condiments, including three flavors of preserves, rounded out a feast that Hunter and Katherine, and four other couples, could never consume in one sitting. However, Katherine knew that during the week Hunter was often in a hurry and would eat anything in the refrigerator. So she wasn't concerned about wasting leftovers.

"I take it Sheriff Dooley is happy," Katherine said as she sipped her coffee.

"Relieved maybe," Hunter replied, "but I don't know about happy." He took a bite of his bacon before continuing. "He's resigned from his position, with little or no benefits. Been publicly humiliated. Now that the need for the public illusion of a united family front is gone, Janey told him that he'll be served with divorce papers on Monday. When she gets sole custody of their kids, which she will in light of his admission that he indeed had sex with a girl not much older than they are, he'll be reduced to getting them every other weekend. All in all, I don't expect he's out kicking up his heels."

"You know what they say, Hunter. Maybe the good Sheriff should've thought about that before he decided to use his squad car to go parking with high-schoolers. I mean, really, Hunter. *Dooley-style?*" Her face contorted with disgust.

"He didn't know she was underage," he mumbled.

"Didn't know, my ass," she replied, sitting up a little straighter in her chair. "He's in the high school all the time. He doesn't miss a ball game. You're going to tell me he didn't have any idea how old that girl was?"

"The jury didn't think so." Hunter blinked innocently at her.

Katherine offered him a curt smile, then leaned over and patted him on the shoulder. "And he has a brilliant lawyer to thank for that. And I'll remind his brilliant lawyer that this Dorothea isn't *that* much younger than the brilliant lawyer's own two girls." She leaned back in her chair and crossed her legs, silently daring him to rebut her.

Wisely, he refrained.

Hunter sensed it was time to move on to a different, potentially more rewarding topic. "So, I was wondering," he said, feigning the voice of a nervous teenager, "do you have any plans for tonight — y'know, with your folks or something?"

Catching her cue, Katherine slowly laid down her coffee cup, adjusted her posture and rested her chin on her clasped fingers. She arched an eyebrow and with an exaggerated drawl said, "I don't know. Why do you ask?"

This was one of the routines that made their relationship not just a marriage, but a living, breathing romance. Mindful of marriages that had collapsed once the glue of rearing children was gone, Hunter and Katherine went out of their way to not take any aspect of their marriage for granted. In that vein, dates were not to be assumed. Hunter would always *ask* if she would join him for dinner, picnics, movies—whatever the plans were. Katherine, not wanting to place the entire burden on Hunter, would occasionally do likewise. The result was a marriage that remained unusually fresh.

"Well, I thought—if you were interested—I might commandeer the grill tonight for those pork chops you like so well. Dinner on the deck, overlooking the water, without the girls…"

Katherine rose from her seat and positioned herself in Hunter's lap. She wrapped her arms around his neck and gave him a mischievous look. "I think it was dinner on the deck overlooking the water that brought us the girls in the first place."

Hunter cocked his head, still savoring his role. "I see. What will it take then?"

With a gentle pull, she brought his face within inches of hers. Her hands moved to the sides of his face. She closed her eyes and, with the most seductive voice she could muster, whispered "You'll have to get me drunk first."

Hunter rolled his eyes. *Damn. The wine.* He had forgotten to pick it up. *This just cannot be happening.* He had traditionally brought a bottle of their favorite Chardonnay home on the last day of every trial. *What is it with me lately,* he wondered. It wasn't just the getting lost while driving home, either. His episodes of confusion were becoming more frequent. Although his mind had always tended to wander, he could not get over how he was having difficulty remembering even the most mundane things. He found himself using landmarks to drive to places where he had traveled his whole life. He constantly struggled to remember someone's name. Or left something at the office that he needed in court. His secretary had started double-checking before he left to make sure he had everything and to spare herself an emergency trip to court.

Perhaps he was just getting older and more susceptible to the rigors of the practice of law, particularly a solo practice. Maybe Katherine was right. She had been encouraging him to slow down, perhaps even retire. His lucrative practice had long ago made them wealthy, so there was no financial need to continue. He could scale back and begin to enjoy the comforts of the life he and Katherine had made. This was probably his body's way of telling him he needed to set course in another direction.

"...so if you'll make certain we have gas in the grill, I have fresh corn and can make the baked potatoes and the salad." Katherine's voice broke his train of thought.

"Sure, honey," he said, patting her leg. He had to go back into town to get the wine and didn't want to alarm her the way he had himself with the knowledge that he had, for the first time, forgotten to pick up the post-trial wine.

"I've got to run back to the office, I forgot to sign some orders that need to go out."

Her grin turned southward. "Why do you need to go back in today? It's Saturday. The office is closed and so's the courthouse. What could you possibly hope to accomplish today that can't wait until Monday?"

Katherine knew him, she knew his schedule. She was largely cooperative with the demands of his career, but when it was her time, then, by God, it was *her* time. However, Hunter had anticipated this objection from her and had a response fashioned and ready.

"Well, I need to sign the orders and I wasn't planning on going in to the office on Monday."

Her disapproval immediately changed to surprise. "You're not?"

Hunter managed to keep a straight face. "Nope," he said, "or Tuesday, either." He could feel her hope, the sense of anticipation rising from within her. "In fact," he added, "I think we need to take some time and just run off together."

This type of talk was just plain heresy coming from her husband. She looked as if she was expecting some belated April Fool's joke.

"Where?"

"I don't know. How about we decide when we get to the airport? Let's just wing it." They had often talked of doing such a thing many years ago, before careers and children had drained their sense of adventure, leaving them with only the mundane and the practical.

"What about your clients?" she asked. He could tell he had her hooked now, but she was going to make certain the water was safe before she dove in.

"They'll be here when I get back. And if they're not, the hell with 'em."

"What about the girls..." She cut herself off, realizing the silliness of the question.

Hunter laughed out loud. "*Oh, please*. They're in college. I refilled their bank accounts last week. So long as we let them both know where we are once we get there, they won't give a shit what we do."

He was face to face with her now, his hands on her hips. He gazed down at her, giving her his warmest smile. "No excuses. We'll pack tomorrow and head for destinations unknown."

Finally accepting that one of her dreams was about to come

true, Katherine nuzzled her face against his chest. His hands slowly raised the oxford shirt from above her thighs. With little effort, he picked her up and felt her legs quickly wrap around his waist. Careful not to knock over any of the plates still on the table, he placed her on top of it. Her head fell back as the buttons of the oxford, one by one, slowly came undone.

———

THREE HOURS LATER, Hunter was on his way back from Hopkinsville. He had stopped by his office on Main Street, the one opened by his father fifty years earlier, signed the orders, and managed this time, to remember the wine. At the subdivision's security gate, he looked at the card he never used to carry and carefully entered his code. The iron gates swung open with the speed of a drawbridge. He was navigating the winding roads that came part and parcel with lakefront development, when he first spotted the police blockade. As he approached, the deputy sheriff held Hunter's car at bay with his outstretched hand. Hunter leaned out the window of the BMW to peer at the scene. The Warren house was the largest, most majestic home on the lake. The police cars and equipment vans parked in front of it looked like peasants' wagons hunkered down in the shadow of their lord's castle.

He knew the home well.

The tragedy that had occurred there forty-five years earlier had affected many lives, few more so than his own. But he had eventually taken those memories, boxed them up, and stashed them neatly away in the back of his mind. Now released, they came crashing down upon him like a tidal wave on an unsuspecting shore, leaving only debris in its wake. Sharp, bladed debris that must be sorted through before it can be cleaned up and thrown away.

The problem with waves is that they eventually come back to shore.

As if on cue, a stretcher flanked by a pair of hefty paramedics was pushed through the house's massive solid oak double-doors. Although the body was draped in the standard-issue white sheet, strands of the corpse's dark hair were visible at the head of the stretcher. Hunter instantly recognized the victim and felt the tide rising again, preparing to crash against the shore. Lost in those memories, he never heard the tremble in his own voice.

"Not again," he whispered. *"Dear God…not again."*

Then

Part One

**Commonwealth of Kentucky
v. Javier Vazquez**

July, 1972

Chapter Four

Twelve-year-old Hunter Cameron slouched in one of the leather chairs adorning the lobby of his father's law office. The late afternoon sun peeked through the partially pulled blinds, casting streaks of light across the dark hardwood floors. The bill of the St. Louis Cardinals baseball cap pulled low over his forehead did little to mask his impatience or frustration.

Thwap. Thwap. Thwap. Time after time, he smacked the scuffed baseball into the weathered baseball glove. His clear green eyes focused on the wood-framed clock on the paneled wall to his left. As the minutes ticked by, the ball hit Hunter's glove more frequently and a little bit harder. *Thwap! Thwap! Thwap!*

James Cameron's secretary, Pauline Story, occasionally looked up from the legal brief she was typing to cast a quick glance at her employer's only child. The boy was normally very friendly. Downright charming, in fact. Without children of her own, she knew that she had quickly become easy prey for the boy's wiles. He seemed to instinctively know, as beautiful children often did, precisely how to use his blessings to his advantage.

He had his father's dark hair and lanky build. His gait seemed to exude an air of quiet confidence. He might have been mistaken as aloof were it not for his warm personality. And that smile. Oh, that smile. With a simple grin, it was as though the young man could open any door. Pauline was relatively certain that, even at his age, no girl to whom the smile was directed would ever fail to return it.

Virtually none of these characteristics were present now, however. Pauline, or Ms. Polly as he called her, could have looked at the calendar months ago when the trip was planned and known what Hunter's mood would be on the day he and his father were to depart. This was an annual event, the same as a holiday or a parade.

Each year James and Hunter made a late season trip to Busch Stadium in St. Louis to watch their beloved Cardinals play a weekend series. For Hunter, the annual trek to St. Louis was much more than simply a father-son trip. It was an opportunity to see his idol, Ted Simmons.

Unfortunately for Hunter, the battle to get his father to leave his busy law office on time was as much a ritual as the trip itself. It wasn't that James wasn't an attentive and loving father. On the contrary, he doted on his son. Hunter's mother, Elizabeth, had died when Hunter was two, leaving James to raise their only child. Although he knew he could never completely make up for the loss of Hunter's mother, James did everything in his power to make certain his son knew how much he was loved. Still, the practice of law was a jealous mistress and far too often Hunter found himself competing with the profession for his father's time.

Hunter had declared long ago that he would never, *ever*, be a lawyer.

Shaking her head, Pauline went back to her work. Another hour passed. Then another. It was nearly two o'clock, just five hours from the first pitch, and James was still in his office with his door closed. Hunter continued to simmer. The ball hit the glove again and again. *Thwap! Thwap!* His father was, no doubt, sitting behind the scratched oak desk with his feet propped up and the phone stuck to his ear, idly trading words for the pitches they could be watching in St. Louis.

Thwap! Finally, Hunter heard the heavy door to his father's office creak open and saw James step out into the hallway. Hunter stood up anxiously as his father approached, waiting to hear the words, "OK, let's go." However, as James walked into the lobby, the stunned expression on his ashen face made it clear that they would not be on time for the game. In fact, they would not be going to the game at all.

Chapter Five

His son had not taken the news well.

James Cameron sat in the small concrete-walled lobby of the Christian County Jail, waiting to introduce himself to the client who had already changed his life. The jail was old and, by necessity, had one of the more peculiar methods for prisoners to meet with their attorneys. The jail cells were located in the basement, creating, as intended, a dungeon-type feel. The building was barren of private meeting areas, so when a lawyer came to meet with an imprisoned client, the prisoner would be summoned to the top of the narrow stairs, where he would be separated from his counsel by a door of thick iron bars. As James waited for what was sure to be a lengthy and difficult meeting with Sgt. First Class Javier Vazquez, his thoughts strayed to the disappointed young boy he had left an hour before in his office.

James often felt like the rope in a never-ending game of tug-of-war—one end in the hand of his demanding career and the other end in the hand of his precocious young son. Most of the time he believed he held his own as a single father. Many days after long hours at work, James would loosen his tie, roll up his shirtsleeves, and don a catcher's mitt so he could be peppered by Hunter's wild pitches. He carefully walked the line between helping Hunter with his homework and doing the work for him. He answered every question the boy asked about his mother and encouraged him to ask more.

He knew how much Hunter looked forward to their annual trip to St. Louis. Although they invariably left James's office later than Hunter liked, Hunter's irritation would vanish once they left behind the Hopkinsville city limits. However, this was the first time James had been forced to cancel the trip altogether. The tears that had rolled down his son's face were streaked with bitterness, making James feel like the tug-of-war rope had become a noose around his neck. Oh, he had promised that there would be another weekend. But he had been careful to avoid promise of a trip for the rest of this season. He didn't want to completely lose his son's faith in him. And by all appearances, Javier Vazquez would be occupying a large portion of his time for the foreseeable future.

Javier's company commander had contacted James. James maintained a very good relationship with the Judge Advocate General's office at Ft. Campbell, the U.S. Army base located fifteen miles away. Consequently, he often received referrals for soldiers who faced criminal charges off-post. The captain had little information to give James, only that the military police had come during a drill and had taken Javier to the MP station. Apparently, a Christian County judge had issued a warrant for Javier's arrest.

The charge was first-degree murder.

James sat back in the cheaply-upholstered chair. The news that Eleanor Warren, wife of the tobacco magnate Charles Warren, had been found murdered in the Warren family's lakefront estate had already began to filter through western Kentucky like a stream of water through the rock of a gravel road. After all, the Warren name was synonymous in the Commonwealth with money and power.

Kentucky had, along with Virginia and North Carolina, taken the early lead in the growing and processing of tobacco in the mid-to-late 1800's. In 1864, a revolutionary strain of tobacco was discovered. This strain was strange looking—its leaves were finely textured, with a light, golden color. Its sweet taste was preferred for smoking, but it soon became extremely marketable for both plug and twist tobacco. It was also easier for farmers to grow and process. The sweet tobacco leaf exploded upon the already expanding tobacco market, and by the 1870's, the leaf was one of Kentucky's economic mainstays.

In the decade following the Civil War, Copeland Warren, a widowed father of two small children, had returned to his small family farm and saw a wasteland, barren of crops and depleted of food and livestock. All the Yankee soldiers had left behind was a barn full of the previous year's tobacco. Desperate to feed his family, Copeland hauled the tobacco into his wagon pulled by mules, gathered his children, blankets, and food, and traveled from town to town, attempting to peddle the tobacco. He could never have imagined that he was on the brink of creating an empire.

Although Copeland had recognized the bright future of the new strain of tobacco, he also recognized the fickle nature of growing tobacco. The process was long and any profit depended on quality. Quality, unfortunately, required an element beyond skill and expertise—it required a good share of luck as well. A bad drought, a heavy rain—any of it could ruin a tobacco crop. Copeland wanted to limit the element of luck as much as possible. As he sold more and more of his tobacco, driving his mule-drawn cart across the rural landscape, his plan for the future materialized—let someone else grow the tobacco; he would sell it.

With his initial earnings, Copeland sought out other tobacco farmers, going to their homes and offering to purchase their crops. The farmers, amazed at their good fortune in not having to find a buyer, quickly agreed. Copeland, who had always had personality to spare, soon realized that he had an aptitude for sales. His fortune rapidly grew, as did his ambitions. He began to process the tobacco before selling it. When his barn became too small for his enterprise, he purchased an old log factory in Christian County, where the tobacco could be granulated and packed. The Warren family business was flourishing, and Copeland's young son, Kirkland, watched with eyes brimming with anticipation, looking to the day when he would run the business.

Kirkland inherited his father's ability to look ahead and to recognize future trends. When he realized the potential popularity of cigarettes, he struck quickly. He began to hire expert cigarette rollers to manufacture cigarettes on a large scale. The Warrens expanded their market west—first to St. Louis, then to Kansas City, and even further west. By the close of the nineteenth century, the Warren Tobacco Company was an industry empire, surpassed only by the Dukes of North Carolina. However, while the Dukes globalized, the Warrens were content to maintain their North American niche.

Kirkland and his young wife would sire only one child, a son named Charles. Before he had taken his first step, Kirkland had his son in the office, intent on giving him a lifelong education in the family business. Young Charles became consumed with the family business, even more so than his father and grandfather before him. While he shared their ambition, his seemed unbridled. Perhaps because he was born into wealth rather than growing into it, Charles, unlike his ancestors, lacked any sensitivity toward others. He seemed to enjoy buying out bankrupt farms and capitalizing on the economic climate after the Depression.

Charles Warren wielded his power broadly throughout the Commonwealth. Governors were known to spend weekends lounging at the Warren's lakefront estate, enjoying lavish parties hosted by his young trophy wife. A new building constructed by Warren dollars at the University of Kentucky bore their name. He kept seats, seldom used, next to the University president for UK basketball games, and had Coach Adolph Rupp's home phone number, though it was usually the legendary coach who called him. He and his beautiful wife were regulars in the luxury boxes at the Kentucky Derby. The Warren power and influence was unparalleled in the Commonwealth.

James's thoughts were interrupted by the coarse voice of the guard. "It's your turn, Counselor."

James forced a smile, grabbed his briefcase, and rose, offering a polite, "Thanks," as he passed the guard. As he headed toward the jail's stairway, James was unsure whether his gratitude was for his wait coming to an end or for the guard interrupting him before he could change his mind about taking the case.

———

THE LIGHT SHINING behind James provided little illumination for the cellblock located at the bottom of the stairs. He blinked down into the blackness as he waited patiently at the iron-barred door to meet with his client. When the face of SFC Javier Vazquez appeared at the bottom of the stairs and began a slow ascent up the stairs toward James, it was as though the man was emerging from the dark waters of a deep sea.

Vazquez's physical appearance confirmed his Hispanic heritage. He was at least two or three inches taller than James's own six-foot frame. Though outfitted in standard baggy orange prison garb, it was evident the twenty-nine-year-old was in excellent condition, at least physically. His skin was naturally a sandy brown, with his face a shade darker due to the sun. His cheekbones were like glaciers, sleekly carved and settled perfectly on each side of a full mouth. His eyes were rich and brown, the hue of mahogany stain. James surmised that Javier Vazquez was, by any standard, an extraordinarily handsome man.

When Javier reached the top of the steps, James already had his hand extended through the bars. This was typical. He'd learned that most criminal defendants were full of nervous energy by the time they had their first meeting with their attorney. He often got his hand back very sore after the very eager shake by his new client. They always saw him as their only hope—the handshake, the actual, physical touching of their savior, was often a source of great relief to them. Relief meant calm and calm meant rational thinking, or at least a better shot at obtaining it. It was obvious to James, however, that this client, Javier Vazquez, charged with the murder of the wife of the most powerful tobacco magnate in the Commonwealth, was not in need of the reassurance of his lawyer's handshake.

"Sgt. Vazquez?" James asked politely, as though it could be someone else.

"Yes sir."

"My name is James Cameron. I'm an attorney, a criminal defense attorney. Your company commander contacted me. Do you understand why you've been arrested?" James hated the awkwardness of these questions, but they were ice-breakers and he was never surprised at a client's lack of an even basic knowledge of why they might be spending time in the dank cells downstairs.

"Yes, sir." Vazquez's words were clipped, force of habit after many years in the military. But his voice was calm and sounded intelligent. "They think that I killed Ellie."

Ellie? James was surprised by the young soldier's knowledge of a casual nickname of the mistress to a fortune, but managed to hide it. "Yes. Eleanor Warren. You have been charged with the first degree murder of Eleanor Warren."

He paused, waiting for the obligatory denials. It was the one aspect of practicing criminal defense that rarely failed: his clients would almost never admit that they had done anything wrong. The stories were many, the explanations were varied, but the song remained the same—they hadn't done it.

Vazquez bypassed this ritual, as though he knew that he should. He was already proving to be full of surprises.

"Will I go to court on Monday?" he asked.

"Monday afternoon. For arraignment." It wasn't unusual for the police to arrest a suspect on a Friday afternoon. The judges, after all, did not work on weekends. That ensured Javier and others like him would spend at least a couple of days in jail.

"That's when I'll enter my 'not guilty' plea, correct, sir?"

"That's right." Javier must have talked with some of the other prisoners, many of whom were more familiar with criminal procedure than were some of the lawyers in town.

"They won't give me bail, will they sir?" It was more a statement than a question. Vazquez's accent was more New York than Hispanic, although not strongly so. Perhaps the soldier had traveled enough to form a melting pot of a dialect, staying nowhere long enough to develop any distinction.

The case was being treated by the Commonwealth as a death

penalty case. In such cases, the clear rule was that bail was not offered. James saw no point in sidestepping candor at this point. "Not unless you can give me some sort of information that would make it obvious to the world that you didn't do this."

"Sir, on the lives of my wife and children, I did not kill her." There it was. Old reliable.

James opened his leather-bound notebook, placing it on a raised knee to begin taking notes. He looked up between scribbles. "That's a good start."

"I loved her."

Slapping the notebook shut, James jerked up his head and met Vazquez's gaze. "That wasn't quite what I was looking for, Sergeant."

In the brief time James had to consider the case, he had not pondered what motive his client would possibly have had to commit such a heinous offense. It was too early for that. But had he considered motives, an affair between the wealthy, elegant Eleanor Warren and this relatively lowly, though very handsome, soldier would not have been among them.

He regained his composure and reopened the notebook. "You're married, aren't you?"

The first discernible look of emotion—shame—came over Vazquez's face. He visibly stiffened, as though answering a superior officer. "Yes, sir."

Things weren't getting better. "How many children and how old?"

"Two, sir. A five-year old son and a two-year old daughter."

James felt himself sinking into the abyss as he continued with his curt questions and his notes. He learned Vazquez was originally born in New York, but was a military brat, moving from state to state, base to base, wherever his father's career had taken them. When his father had retired, the family moved back to New York, where Vazquez graduated from high school. Vazquez immediately enlisted in the Army, as if there had never been any other option. He was first stationed in North Carolina and then Arkansas. He found his bride in Texas—a pretty eighteen-year old Hispanic girl named Teresa. Their first child, Michael, was born a year later at Ft. Bedford, Oregon. They had been stationed at Fort Campbell about sixteen months ago. Shortly thereafter, their daughter Mia was born. Vazquez's military service record was excellent, no disciplinary problems. He swore that he had no criminal record whatsoever.

Wading back into the troubled waters, James asked, "So how did you know Mrs. Warren?"

"We were"—he paused sheepishly for a moment—"We were involved, sir."

"And when was the last time you saw her?"

"This morning, about oh-six hundred, sir."

It was getting worse. "Where was she?"

"In her bedroom, sir."

James pursed his lips. In the twenty minutes he had spent with this client, he had heard admissions, however unlikely, of adultery by this soldier who stood accused of murdering his paramour. And the victim was not just any murder victim—she was the young, beautiful wife of the state's most powerful man, a man not known to have a propensity for forgiveness. And now, instead of providing some—hell, *any* sort of alibi, his client admitted to having slept with the victim just hours, maybe less, before she was found brutally murdered. James removed his wire-rimmed eyeglasses and ran his fingers through his wavy hair. At least, he thought, it couldn't get any worse.

Until Javier, clearly sensing his exasperation, turned away and said quietly, "They must have found my letters."

Chapter Six

Hunter squinted, his gaze boring in on the husky boy standing on the mound, twisting the baseball in his hand. The boy's name was Chad and he went to school in Illinois. But he spent summers with family here and was allowed to play in Hopkinsville's Little League program, much to the chagrin of the local boys. "Big Chad", as most people called him, was at least three inches taller than any of the boys on either Hunter's team or his own. His shoulders were easily the broadest on the field and his legs seemed far too developed for someone who allegedly would not see the age of thirteen until January. His size was imposing, but his hellacious fastball, called *Ol' Rumor*, made him the most feared pitcher his age. An opposing coach had coined the nickname, stating that, like its namesake, it was never seen, only heard.

Hunter had never batted against Big Chad before today. His first two at-bats had been embarrassing. He had been an All-Star every year since he had started playing three years ago and was generally considered to be the best player in Christian County. This year had been his best. Until this game, he had not struck out a single time all season. But it had taken Big Chad a total of only eight pitches to dispatch Hunter, striking him out both times. The fact that his team was being no-hit and that no one had even put the ball into play against Big Chad, did nothing to soothe Hunter's jangling nerves.

Still, with his team winning by the scant margin of 1-0, Big Chad had started this, the final inning, by walking the first batter. *Maybe he was human*, Hunter thought. Then Big Chad breezed through two batters like wind through a screen, striking each of them out on three pitches.

Maybe not, Hunter reckoned as he walked to the batter's box, his team's season resting like an anvil on his reed-thin shoulders.

He dug in his feet and tapped the barrel of the bat on the far side of home plate. Chad's gigantic figure eclipsed the afternoon sun as he stood atop the mound. His shadow cast itself through the batter's box.

"Come on Hunter!"

"Just watch the ball Hunter!"

"Let's go Hunter! You can do it!"

The yells from his coach and teammates were meant, he knew, as encouragement. But he couldn't help but think how empty the words were. They couldn't really be dumb enough to actually believe what they were saying, could they? After all, Big Chad had struck out everyone he had faced in the game. Hunter could not remember ever actually being scared to face a pitcher before. But nobody else threw the ball as hard as Big Chad.

Big Chad wound up and threw the ball. Hunter saw what looked like an explosion leave Chad's hand. He heard something dash through the middle of the plate and pop hard inside the catcher's mitt.

Ol' Rumor.

"Strike one," bellowed the umpire.

Hunter stepped back from the plate and looked over at the bench. His teammates continued to cheer him on, more from a sense of duty than actual belief.

He put one foot into the box, then the second. He took two slow-motion practice swings, then resumed his stance. Chad was in his delivery.

Hunter started his swing early—"cheating" as his Dad, who had taught him the concept, had called it. When someone had a really good fastball, start your swing early to catch up with the ball. The drawback, Hunter knew, was that if the pitch was outside the strike zone, there was no way to stop the swing.

Whhhooossshhh!

Ol' Rumor whizzed by. It sounded as though it had been at about shoulder level for Hunter and it missed Hunter's bat entirely. His hat spun off his head, propelled by the torque of his mighty, yet empty, swing. Even if he had cheated his swing early enough, which he hadn't, the ball was too high to hit. He could not have made contact on the same pitch in another hundred swings.

Hunter slowly walked over to his now-dusty navy cap, beat it against his leg, and placed it back on his head. He looked not at his dugout, where the volume of the cheers was fading, but instead peered out at the mound. Chad had just received the call back from the catcher and had turned his back to home plate, rubbing the ball with both hands. As Chad turned away, Hunter could have sworn he saw a grin briefly cross his face.

The look, real or imagined by Hunter, would have gone unnoticed by most adults, much less a twelve-year-old. However, it flew all over him. He felt a burning sensation go up the back of his neck, like hot water poured into a tall glass. Had they been close enough to him, his teammates and coaches would have noticed Hunter's ears turning beet-red. It was the only way anyone could ever detect anger in him. It was a reaction, his father often said, given him at birth by his mother.

Hunter glared at Chad beneath the brim of his cap. He slammed each foot into the box and dug in again. Chad didn't notice; he was too busy preparing to strike him out.

The big windup came and Ol' Rumor shot toward the middle of the plate. Big Chad's massive jaw dropped when the pitch was not met with the familiar thud of the catcher's mitt.

CRACK!

A hush followed the sharp sound as the crowd watched the ball arching out to right field. Big Chad followed its flight with disbelieving eyes.

Hunter had felt a familiar rush when he struck the ball. He had hit home runs before and knew immediately that he had just hit another. But this one was different somehow. Perfect, in fact. So perfect that he ignored a rule drilled into him by his father and slowed his running pace around the bases so he could watch the flight of the ball. He had not yet reached first base when the ball loudly thudded off the wooden scoreboard, twenty feet beyond the right field fence.

As he rounded first base and looked out beyond the outfield, he noticed just how bright the afternoon sun had become. As he looked into the sun, the over-powering glare forced him to squint, resulting in a brief "sun grin" as he had heard it called. He caught himself, as he headed for third base, realizing that Big Chad had been gazing into the same sun when he had "smiled" before the fateful pitch.

Hunter crossed home plate, only to be enveloped by his jubilant teammates. The congratulatory smacks on his back might have hurt, but Hunter, the resident David victorious over Goliath, did not feel a thing. Hoisted onto their shoulders, his eyes broke from the celebration long enough to scan the crowd, all of whom were standing and clapping. He was certain, even before he was carried away toward the dugout, that he had not seen his father's face.

James was, he knew, still squirreled away in his office, working on the soldier's case.

Chapter Seven

J ames stood in the doorway of his son's room. Hunter was sitting upright in his bed, listening to the Cardinals broadcast over the small transistor radio on his nightstand. According to Jack Buck's throaty narration, Joe Torre had just doubled into right field to score a run and had brought the Cardinals within a run of the Dodgers at 4–3.

It was nearly nine o'clock and the small lamp next to the radio provided just enough light to make out some of the Cardinals memorabilia spread throughout the small room. Pennants, baseball hats, and cards decorated walls, dressers, and shelves. The items were arranged neatly with attention to detail that was uncharacteristic for any boy, let alone one Hunter's age.

A framed picture of Hunter's mother stood alone on the modest desk in the far corner of the room. Although everyone said Hunter was the spitting image of his father, James had always seen more than a passing resemblance between the boy and his mother. Granted, Hunter's dark coloring and lanky build were his own, but the boy's cool green eyes belonged to his mother. Even now, when James saw a picture of her, his body would ache with need.

"Dad?"

James jerked his startled gaze from mother to son, giving thanks as always that she had left such a beautiful reminder of herself on this earth. "What's the score?" he asked, not wanting to reveal just how long he had been standing in the doorway, drinking in the sight of his boy.

"4-3 Dodgers. Steve Garvey doubled in two in the fourth," Hunter replied, his sullen gaze flicking back to the paperback copy of *The Yearling* in his hands. School wasn't in session, so this wasn't a school assignment. For a twelve-year old, the boy read hard.

"Where are you in the book?"

"Jody just found the yearling and named him Flag." The stubborn set of Hunter's jaw did not relax.

James was not easily dissuaded. "You enjoying the book?"

"Jody's pa seems to like his son."

James hesitated, torn between irritation at his son's tone and admiration at the boy's pluck. "Yeah, that's true," he replied, treading carefully. "Penny Baxter was a good father. His wife was kind of tough so I guess he had to be."

"My mother's dead." Hunter's tone was sharp, his head still buried in the book.

"Yes. Yes, she is."

Hunter sighed and lowered the book to his lap. He slowly lifted his eyes to James's face. "Do you ever miss her?"

"Every day, Hunter. Every single day."

"What about me? Do you ever miss seeing me?"

"I do see you, son." James frowned. "Why would you ask me that?"

"It sure doesn't seem like you ever see me anymore." Hunter slid his legs off the bed, turning to face his father. "You don't even come to my games."

"Son, I was working." The words tasted sour coming out of James's mouth.

"You worked before, but you never missed my games."

"Hunter, I know you don't understand, but this case is different. That soldier's life is at stake. I'm the *only* one who can help him."

"I understand," Hunter snapped. "You think I don't, but I do. I understand that you want to help that soldier more than you want to spend time with me."

"That's just not true, Hunter!" James moved closer to the bed. As he approached, Hunter sat upright, his arms folded across his chest, steely and resolute.

James knew he had to defend himself. Even though he wasn't certain he was right. "Hunter, I wish I could be with you all the time. You know that, don't you?"

No answer.

"Don't you? Hunter, I'm talking to you. Hunter?"

Hunter was glaring at the wall, studying the five-year old Cardinal pennant hanging there as if he had never seen it before.

James could feel his anger growing. It was bad enough getting his ass chewed by his own kid. But now, the boy was ignoring him. The instinct to yank the him up and paddle his willful ass came shooting up. But something stopped him. Maybe he was just being too soft. He didn't spank Hunter often and when he did, he wasn't sure whom it hurt more.

Or maybe it was just that he knew he was wrong.

He sat on the edge of the bed. He put his hand on his son's leg, hoping to reassure him. Hunter flinched away. He didn't want to be touched. James felt himself swimming upstream.

"Hunter, please look at me." After a couple of seconds, the boy finally turned his gaze from the pennant and toward his father.

"I wish that I could be with you every day. All day. You know that. I know you know that. Now, I should've been at your game. I owe you an apology for that. And I'm sorry."

James felt the taut muscles of Hunter's leg relax beneath his hand. It was a start.

James raised his right hand, taking a solemn oath in this pennant-and-trophy filled room. "It won't happen again. You've got my word."

Hunter turned away, nodding slightly.

"Well, since I missed it, tell me about the game. Did you really hit a home run off Big Chad?"

Hunter grinned involuntarily and blushed. It was that so-rare combination of ego and embarrassment. "Yep," he replied. "It was *Ol' Rumor* too."

"*Ol' Rumor*? How fast was it?"

Hunter shook his head, the sparkle returning to his eyes. He still seemed amazed by what he had done. "Dad, I ain't seen nothin' like that before. Shoot, he struck me out the first two times."

James nodded. "Did it scare you to be up there against him for the third time?"

"Nope," Hunter said, trying to sound convincing.

"Did you start your swing early, like I showed you?"

"Yes, sir." Hunter paused for a second. "I never thought that I'd have to start it that early, though."

"Yeah, well, one day you'll learn that you can't always do that. Pitchers figure out that you're cheatin' on the fastball like that, they'll throw you a curveball or something slower and you'll look like a fool swinging at it." As James spoke, he was reminded how much he loved teaching his son. About baseball and life.

"Dad?"

"Yeah, bud."

"What is your soldier case about?"

The question took James by surprise. It was the first time he could remember Hunter asking him about a case.

"The police think that he killed a woman."

"Who was she?" Hunter asked.

"Her name was Eleanor Warren. Folks called her Ellie."

"Was the soldier married to her?" Hunter was sitting up now, fully engaged.

"No, not exactly," James replied, choosing his words carefully. "They were kind of…well…they were kind of *going* together."

"But I thought she was married."

Shit, James thought. *How the hell do I explain this?* "Well son, she *was* married to someone, but she was kind of going with the soldier, too." James regretted the words the second they were out of his mouth, but was too sheepish to look at Hunter after he said them.

Hunter took in this information, visibly struggling to process it.

He looked as though he was trying a food for the first time. Surprisingly, however, he recovered quickly.

"Did she have any kids?" he asked.

James sighed, then immediately hoped that Hunter wouldn't understand his relief. This question he could handle. "She had a son. His name is Charles, but he goes by his middle name, Kirk. Or so I'm told."

"How old is he?"

"Let me think for a minute." James had taken in so much information recently that it took a moment or two for him to recall the answer. "Come to think of it," he said "I think he would be about your age. Yeah, about twelve years old."

Hunter furrowed his brow at the answer. "There's nobody in our class named Kirk," he said.

"No, he wouldn't be. He goes to a private school up near Louisville."

"Why?" Hunter asked. Though he was awfully inquisitive, James was happy the questioning had taken such a decidedly more innocuous turn.

"Well," he said, "sometimes rich people want to send their kids off to a private school because they think they can get a better education there."

Hunter's brow did not release. "Why don't you send me there?"

"Well, number one, we're not rich. Number two, I think you get a fine education right here in Hopkinsville."

"Do *you* think the soldier killed her?"

James hesitated, studying his son's thoughtful face with a pang of regret. He was a boy already asking a man's question.

"No, son. I really don't believe that he did." James only hoped he could convince a jury of that; it wouldn't be as easy as convincing his son.

Hunter finally shook his head, then said matter-of-factly, "I was thinking. You're so busy with this trial. Maybe I could help."

His son's offer knocked him off balance yet again. "What do you mean?"

"Well, I could start comin' to the office after school and help you with the law."

James bit back a smile. His son was full of surprises tonight. "Well, I don't know. You have to go to school for quite a while to know the law. And you have school starting here soon."

"I could come to the office after school."

"You already come down to the office after school."

Hunter lurched forward in exasperation. "*No*," he said. "I want to come there and *help.*"

"With what?"

"With that soldier's case."

James was proud that Hunter wanted to help. But he had to ask, "And what would you do to help?"

Hunter scowled. "I don't know. You're supposed to be the lawyer."

James couldn't help but laugh at this. There was precious little that Hunter could help him with in the law office. Plus getting ready for a murder trial was far from the ideal time to have his son running around the office, even under the auspice of "helping." But there was no way he could was going to tell the boy no.

"Scoot over," he said.

Hunter shuffled over on the small bed. James followed him in, resting his back against the headboard and stretching out his long legs until his shoes hung well off the end of the bed.

The radio seemed to flicker with each syllable as Jack Buck announced that Ted Simmons had hit a grand slam to give the Cardinals the lead. Father and son, lost in their plans for the upcoming weeks, never heard a word.

Chapter Eight

Summer grew restless and tiptoed into a particularly cool fall. Despite their best intentions, it was the only real change that occurred for James and Hunter Cameron.

They were together more, at least in a sense. James made good on his word and tried to give the boy odd jobs to do around the office. And Hunter applied himself diligently to every task assigned him. He picked up the mail at the post office a couple of blocks up the street. He swept the sidewalk in front of the office. He even made the bank deposits after Ms. Polly filled out the slip and placed both it and the day's earnings into the worn leather bag. But despite Hunter's best efforts and his obvious intellectual gifts, there was only so much a boy his age could do to help around a law office. James quickly discovered that figuring out a daily task list for Hunter was taking a great deal of time, time he frankly didn't have. The trial of Javier Vazquez for the murder of Eleanor Warren was set to begin the first week of November, just a few weeks away.

Pauline assumed the delegation of tasks for Hunter and proved to be more creative than James. She learned that the boy was adept at collating paperwork, and with the trial so close and motions and briefs being filed daily, that particular aptitude came in handy. She and Hunter grew closer every day and she would find herself watching the clock, looking forward to 3:15 when school let out and he would race the six blocks to the office.

One such afternoon, an umbrella-less and thus rain-soaked Hunter dripped his way into the office. With wet bangs falling into his eyes, jeans rolled up over the top of his canvas sneakers and his once-red tote-bag now a well-drenched burgundy, he looked like a Norman Rockwell portrait. Pauline quickly grabbed a towel from the office bathroom and attempted to dry him off. Once done, she retreated to the office's kitchen and began heating hot water for hot chocolate.

Minutes later, she was back by the counter, organizing and labeling an exhibit folder for the trial and Hunter was sitting atop a stool, the now-damp towel wrapped around his shoulders, a steaming cup of chocolate in his hands. He was eager to help out, but a child's priorities being what they are, he had decided to finish his hot chocolate first.

"Ms. Polly," he asked between sips.

"Yes, honey," she replied as she wrote on a file.

"Are you married?"

She struggled to contain a smile. "No, sweetheart. I'm not."

"Why not?"

Ah, the inhibition of youth, she thought. It was a question she heard from her family on a routine basis. She was, after all, twenty-nine years old. And, with her fair-haired good looks, it wasn't as though she lacked for suitors.

"Well, honey," she said. "I guess I haven't found the right person yet." It was *cliché*, she thought. And not entirely accurate. She turned to the boy and smiled. "Or maybe," she said with a wink, "the right person hasn't found me."

Hunter pondered this for a moment. "Well, I think you're really pretty. Prettier than any of the girls at school."

"Why, Hunter Cameron, thank you very much. That's a real nice thing for you to say."

"You smell better than they do, too," he continued, his tone unabashed. "If I was older, I would marry you."

Ms. Polly walked over, placed a hand on his face, and took his now-empty mug with the other. "Well, that's just my loss then. I'll have to hope I can find someone my age who's as nice and well-mannered as you are."

She returned the mug to the kitchen and then came back to the front counter. Hunter had moved the stool next to the counter, where he could sit next to her and help organize the papers. It quickly became apparent, however, that work wasn't the only thing on his mind.

"My dad is older than me, you know."

"Yes, I had kind of figured that one out."

"He's older than you, too, isn't he?"

"That's right, Hunter. He is."

"Well," the boy said, shuffling a small stack of papers until the edges were perfectly even. "I think that *he* should marry you."

"You do, do you?" The answer was reflexive. Pauline didn't know what else to say.

"Yes, ma'am." Hunter's voice was casual, particularly given that he was proposing to someone on his father's behalf.

Pauline could feel herself blushing, but luckily, her head was turned. While most kids his age wouldn't notice, Hunter definitely would. She was fumbling for a way to change the subject when he did it for her.

"Do you ever want to be a momma?"

It wasn't the first time Pauline had heard that question. "Yes, honey. At some point, I would love to have children."

"One like me?"

"Of course, I would love to have a boy like you," she said, meaning every word.

"I miss my momma," he said.

"I'm sure you do."

"Sometimes I wonder if that makes sense."

"What do you mean, hon?"

"Well my momma went to Heaven when I was little—too little

for me to remember her. If I can't remember her, then how can I miss her?"

Pauline took a deep breath. She was stunned that a child, no matter how bright, could ask such a poignant question. "Sometimes, baby," she said, struggling to get the words out, "we just know. Even though you don't remember seeing her, or her taking care of you, you still just know somewhere inside of you how much she loved you. And you wish she was still here so you could actually see her loving you. And so she could see you loving her."

She watched Hunter for a reaction, hoping the explanation didn't sound as awkward as it had felt. Thankfully, the look on his face assured her he was either satisfied with her answer, or he had moved on to something else.

"This soldier that my dad is the lawyer for...he has kids, doesn't he?"

"Yes, he does."

"How old are they?"

"He has a little girl, maybe two years old. And his son, I believe, is about five years old."

Hunter digested this for a moment. "You know what I think?"

"What's that?" she replied. Her paperwork, for better or worse, was temporarily forgotten.

"I think I know why my dad is working so hard to get this soldier out of jail."

Jail may be the least of it, Pauline thought. But she knew better than to tell Hunter that, if convicted, Vazquez would potentially be facing the electric chair in Eddyville.

"And why's that?" she asked, legitimately curious as to what the precocious boy was thinking now.

"I think it's because he knows that if he loses, that soldier's kids might not ever get to see him again, like I'll never get to see my momma again. He doesn't want them to lose their dad the way I lost my momma."

With that, Pauline walked over to the stool where he sat. She took the boy in her arms as if he were her own. She wasn't his mother, but at that moment—and not for the first time—she wished that she was.

Hunter stayed in her embrace for more than a short moment before gently pulling away. He gazed up into her face with his striking green eyes, seeking the same reassurance he might have sought from his mother had she lived.

"Dad'll win his trial, won't he, Ms. Polly?"

Chapter Nine

Teresa Vazquez, wife of the accused, sat rod-straight in the wooden chair, the well-worn oak desk the only physical thing separating her from James Cameron.

She was petite, no more than five feet tall and a hundred pounds, if that. Her straight dark hair was pulled back in a neat knot at the nape of her neck. Her make-up was evenly applied in modest amounts, perhaps just enough to hide small marks likely left from teenage acne, and her features were soft and not unattractive. The net effect was that of a quiet dignity, unusual for a woman of just twenty-four.

During their first meetings, James had simply taken her for a strong-willed woman. But in this, their final meeting to prepare her testimony for her husband's murder trial, he was beginning to realize the true measure of her resolve. He wanted to compliment her on this, but he also realized she would not be impressed by empty praise for what she believed were duties given her by God.

They had been reviewing her testimony for the better part of two hours. In clipped English, she had described how she had met Javier when he was stationed in Texas, married him, bore his children, and followed him to Fort Campbell. She discussed how excited and, at alternate moments, frightened she had been at the news that they would be stationed in Kentucky. It was the first time she had ever crossed the Texas state line to go anywhere other than her family's native Mexico.

She talked at length about how her husband was a dedicated soldier. How he had quickly risen in the ranks, despite his relative youth. She talked about how gentle and loving he had always been with their children, how proud he was to be a father. How he was an affectionate and loving husband, a good provider, and…

"Do you know where your husband was on the night of July 13, 1972," James interrupted.

She paused immediately and gave him a curious look, as though he had asked her a completely inappropriate question. Her reaction would have been much less troubling had this been the first time he had asked her the question. However, he had asked it several times before and each time she gave the same wary look and the same unlikely response.

"He spent the night at home," she said after a moment.

James patiently set down his notepad. They had been through this before. He forced himself to remember that, for all the stress he was currently under, she was under more. But he had to have her testimony. He had precious little else.

Granted, the case against his client was circumstantial. The murder weapon had never been found, but Eleanor Warren's throat had been slit by what appeared to be a garden-variety sharp-edged instrument, likely a straight-razor. Such an instrument could easily be rinsed off and discarded without ever being found.

There were no witnesses to tie Javier to the scene, but, shortly after his arrest, he had confessed to the police that he was having an affair with Eleanor Warren and that he had been to the house that night. His fingerprints and body hair were all over the house, in particular in the bedroom where she was found. He acknowledged that she had recently discussed ending the affair with him because she was afraid of losing her young son, as she surely would, if her husband found out. He admitted that he had written her several letters begging her not to break it off with him.

James had seen the letters. They looked like nothing less than correspondence written by the hand of a desperate man.

Finally, Javier admitted that as he was getting dressed in her bedroom that night, Eleanor told him she had decided once and for all that they could no longer see one another. In short, Javier had motive, opportunity, the means, and had admitted to being with the victim at nearly the precise time at which she was murdered.

And despite his best efforts, James really had nothing more than a series of character witnesses for Javier. Members of his command unit would testify what a conscientious and diligent soldier he was. But none of that testimony would address the circumstantial evidence against him. And in a small southern town such as Hopkinsville, all it made him was a good Hispanic soldier who was screwing a rich white man's wife.

Jesus...

"Teresa," he said, "we've discussed this a number of times." He was trying to measure his tone. "On the night he was arrested, Javier admitted to the police that he had spent the night with Eleanor Warren at the Warren's lake home in Cadiz."

He watched Teresa closely as she winced at this notion and as her face became a sheet of defiance.

"They forced him to say that," she said. "My husband is a good man, a good soldier. He could never do that to me or his children."

James momentarily struggled with the urge to literally pull his hair out. It wasn't that she was lying, that much he knew. Rather, as he had known others to do, she had simply convinced herself beyond any doubt that what had, in fact, happened did not really happen. He had once heard that denial was a safe place to be, but in this instance, Teresa's denial, in the face of her husband's admissions, made any other possibly valuable testimony she might offer totally worthless.

James had even resorted to asking Javier to talk to Teresa during their visits. He hoped that hearing it from Javier would somehow

convince her to acknowledge the obvious. The soldier had obediently done as instructed, but to no avail. He told James that whenever he tried to discuss the matter with her, she would smile
painfully at him for a moment. Then, it as was though he could
actually see the machinations of her mind as it rejected the notion.
She would regain her composure and tell him that he was just tired
and wasn't remembering things correctly. And how much the children missed him and how glad they would be when he came home
next month. Even the husband whom she continued to worship,
however naively, could not get through to her.

James decided to try a different approach. "Okay. If he was at
home with you that night, what did the two of you do?"

The question stumped her for a moment, as James had thought
it would. After all, Javier hadn't really been with her that night.
Perhaps by questioning her as though it was a cross-examination, he
might be able to get her turned around.

"He was working that night," she said.

"He told you that?"

"Yes, he said that he would be in the field late, probably into the
early morning hours."

James knew that the prosecution had already obtained Javier's
military records, which would confirm that he did *not* work that
evening. He had them, too. He showed them to her and then gently
said "Do you recognize that, according to the military records,
Javier wasn't at work that evening?"

Teresa stared blankly at the page, another fact designed to shake
her core belief in her husband. After a second, she looked up at
James. "The military has made a mistake. Javier was at work that
night."

Had this sad sequence not long ago passed into the absurd,
James might have given up. But he was determined, obsessed. He
was going to save Javier. He was going to save him, dammit, no
matter what his wife inadvertently did to prevent it.

He continued with his questioning. "Did you see him come in
that night?"

"No, sir," she said. "I must have fallen asleep before he came home."

"After he left for 'work'," he said, making air quotes with his fingers, "when was the next time you saw Javier in your home?"

"The next morning. I woke up to get the baby, but when I went into the kitchen, Javier was already in there feeding her."

"And what time was that?"

"About six…about six-thirty, I think."

"What was he wearing when you saw him?"

She didn't hesitate. "His combat uniform."

James gazed straight at her, hoping he could make his point without saying anything further. After a few moments of silence, he realized that he couldn't.

"His combat uniform?"

"Yes."

"Was the uniform dirty or clean?"

"It was clean. He never wears a dirty uniform."

"So what you're saying is that he worked most of the night, came home from work in the early morning hours after you were already asleep, slept in his still-clean work clothes, and was still wearing them when he was feeding your daughter the next morning."

She paused for a moment. When she finally spoke, it was with slightly less conviction. "Yes."

"Does your husband usually sleep in his uniform?"

No answer. Just a blank stare.

"Teresa, please look at me." James was focused intently on her now, hoping in quiet desperation that she was finally seeing the light of the inevitable. If so, then he could get her to acknowledge the reality that everyone else could see and not risk her credibility on the stand. He got up, walked around his desk, and sat in the wooden chair next to hers. He took her hand, and in a soft voice, asked again.

"Does your husband usually sleep in his work clothes?"

Teresa finally looked at him. For the first time since he'd known her, large tears began to well up in her small brown eyes. She took a deep breath, tilted her head for a moment, and then sat up again, never removing her gaze from him.

"My husband is a good man and a good soldier. He would never do something like that to me or to his children."

Jesus…

Chapter Ten

J ames Cameron strategically organized the contents of his
file in several thin piles across the heavy counsel table of the
Christian County Circuit Courtroom. He had organized
them umpteen times already, but dammit, he was nervous
and they needed shuffling again.

He had arrived in the courtroom by twenty minutes after seven
that morning. Whenever he was in trial, by design, he would always
be the first person in the courtroom. He wanted to be alone with it,
to get the feel of it again. Like putting on a coat he hadn't worn
since the previous winter.

He imagined himself walking from his counsel table to the front
of the jury. He paced the courtroom floor, trying to settle on a pace
to use whenever he crossed it to approach a witness or the bench or
to stand before the jury box, which was dead-center of the courtroom. He didn't want to appear too anxious or too laconic for the
jury. He knew that his strength was a chaste earnestness, that he was
credible and made people *want* to believe him. And he would need
every ounce of that quality to keep Javier Vazquez from a date with
the electric chair.

By eight-fifteen, others began to trickle into the courtroom. At first, it was a couple of local newspaper writers and a few other nosy souls, looking to get a good seat for what would surely be the event of the fall, people's tastes for the macabre being what they were. Around eight-thirty, Teresa Vazquez entered with five-year old Michael. The baby, Mia, was back at the Vazquez's home on post, being watched by a neighbor. Hunter had had several discussions with both Javier and Teresa regarding whether or not to bring one, both, or neither of the children. The practical problems of having a two-year-old in the courtroom aside, there were pros and cons to having the children present in front of the jury.

On the positive side, it could be argued that the picture of the doting wife and small, pretty children would humanize Javier, who, under the circumstances, needed all the humanizing he could get. On the other hand, a jury could easily look at the walking family portrait and bristle at the notion that, by his own admission, he had forsaken them for the love of another woman. *Why should we allow him to lean on them now when he was ready to shove them aside?*

In the end, the three of them decided to opt for moderation and only bring Michael. If the jury found Javier guilty and the case proceeded to sentencing, they could pull out all the stops and have the baby in the courtroom. Until then, they would just go with Michael.

The boy was a miniature version of his father, preposterously handsome with dark features and an innocent face still untouched by the fault lines of life. He sat unattended on the front row bench, skinny legs hanging off its edge, hands folded in his lap. He was quiet and dignified in a manner that James seldom saw in a child that age. It was easy to tell that this kid had spent his early life under the influence of the military.

James and Teresa were huddled quietly at the table when the holding cell doors opened. An immediate hush fell over the courtroom. Sgt. Javier Vazquez, accused murderer of Eleanor Warren, was led in handcuffs past the front row of the audience and to the counsel table, where James held out a chair for him.

Javier was, as planned, dressed in full military regalia. It was vital to present the image of Javier as the *good soldier* to the jury.

Javier patiently waited for the bailiff to release him from his handcuffs. Once that was done, he shook hands with James and
embraced his wife for the first time since his arrest five months
earlier.

Though Javier was still a handsome man, the strain of the past
few months was taking its toll. Dark circles rimmed the once-perfect
skin under his eyes. Lines had formed creases in his brow where
once there were none. James guessed that Javier had lost close to
twenty pounds while in jail. The uniform he was wearing, though
impressive, now hung loosely on his tall frame.

Still, Javier seemed a little more alive than he had been in weeks.
Though he knew the odds against him were long, he was anxious to
finally assert his innocence. He had done wrong by engaging in an
adulterous relationship. He had betrayed his wife, his children, and
himself. At best, his military career was over, likely with a forced
resignation and a dishonorable discharge. But he was willing to
acknowledge his mistakes and move forward. And he planned to
apologize to his family, and even Eleanor's husband, if need be. He
would use the trial as a springboard to make amends and to rebuild
the rest of his life with his wife and children.

James heard some rustling in the back of the courtroom and
turned to the double doors to see Charles Kirkland Warren step
briskly through them. Although they both lived in this same small
town, James had never seen Warren in person before. It was as
though Warren existed on a higher plane, not *in* Christian County,
but rather, hovering *above* it.

Warren was a tree-trunk of a man, well over six feet tall and way
north of two-hundred pounds. A handmade suit and silk tie hung
expertly off of him, gold cufflinks exposed at the bottom of the
sleeves. His head was large and spit-shined-bald on top, with a
wreath of closely-clipped brownish-gray hair stretching like a hedge
from one ear to the other. His face was broadly square-jawed and
clean-shaven. He was more indomitable than attractive and it wasn't
hard to tell that, when he walked into a room, he was the one for
whom the seat at the head of the table was reserved.

Without prompting, those still milling around the center aisle of the courtroom parted with each step that Charles Warren took, creating an alley to the front row of seats reserved for the family of the victim. It was there that Warren sat, but only after fixing his gaze upon James, rather than Javier, for every step of the twenty-yard walk. While James had been stared down and even threatened before, the look he received from Warren was unlike any he could recall. It was a look of sheer *power* in its purest form and James could feel that power radiating from Warren in waves.

Warren slowly took a seat on the bench. He was promptly joined by a well-dressed, but painfully skinny, older man carrying a legal briefcase. James took the man to be Warren's private attorney, probably from Lexington or Louisville, though he couldn't be sure. They appeared to be the only members of Eleanor's family who would be present. James had assumed the prosecution would want to have the Warren's young son present, but apparently, Charles Warren had decided against it. James doubted that Charles Warren would give a damn about what the prosecutor thought about his decision to leave the boy in school. Still, James knew the boy's absence from the sight of the jury would be considered a plus for the defense.

Beginning to feel a glimmer of confidence, James was turning back to the counsel table to whisper a word of encouragement to Javier and Teresa when a small crusty bailiff, whose name he couldn't remember, opened the courtroom's front door and spoke in a gruff tone.

"Hear ye, hear ye. All rise. This honorable court is now in session. The Honorable Judge J. Phillip Frazier presiding. God save the Commonwealth and this honorable court."

With that atypically formal introduction, Circuit Judge Phil Frazier briskly walked through the opened chamber doorway and toward the bench, where he had sat for the last twenty-one years. Frazier was nearing seventy years of age and was generally regarded as being a prudent jurist, but cold and detached from those around him. He offered nothing in the way of friendly or casual conversation to members of the local bar, let alone lay people. No one ever ran against him, so he didn't require charm to stay on the bench. Had James Cameron not practiced many cases in front of Judge

Frazier, he likely would not have noticed, let alone thought anything about what happened next.

As the judge neared the bench, but before he took his seat, he turned to the crowd in the back of the courtroom and asked in a thin, reedy voice that everyone be seated. As the rest of the court-room scurried to obey, James saw that Charles Warren was still standing. Although it was fleeting, James was almost certain that he saw Judge Frazier, otherwise so devoid of personality and warmth that the local practitioners questioned the existence of his pulse, nod and give a brief smile to Warren.

And then, in an unprecedented move, the judge subtly waited for Warren to take his seat before he took his own seat at the bench. When James glanced back at Warren, he was surprised to find the man glaring straight at him, his eyes narrowed in a look that might have been a warning...or a threat. Without breaking that gaze, Warren flashed the tiniest of grins at James. Taken aback, James looked back up at the judge, who was now staring intently at him as well.

It was at that moment, for the first time in his professional career, James felt a surge of bile rise in the back of his throat.

Chapter Eleven

Phillip McIntosh was a beloved figure in Christian County. He was very active in the community, never missing the opportunity to serve on boards dedicated to the social good. He was a Jaycee, a Kiwanian, a Rotarian, an Eagle, a Commissioner, a Director, a Chairman and a Deacon.

James Cameron thought he was an ass. And a smug one at that.

McIntosh had served as Commonwealth Attorney for Christian County for the last seven years. Unlike in the larger counties, his position was part-time. So a lawyer like McIntosh could be the county prosecutor, but wouldn't have to sacrifice his own private practice to do so.

When the position had come open, no one else had wanted it, figuring it would take away from their other, more lucrative, legal work. McIntosh had seen it differently. Since he wanted his practice to consist mainly of business and corporate clients, he saw the position as being something of a pulpit. If he could crack down on crime and let the businesses know what he was doing, then they would be more likely to come to him for work when they needed a lawyer. The plan, however simple, had worked brilliantly.

McIntosh's corporate practice had nearly tripled in the past few years and he had all he could say grace over. He had even hired a young attorney who did most of the grunt work associated with being the county prosecutor. These days, it was only in instances of a spotlight-grabbing case, such as *Commonwealth v. Vazquez*, that McIntosh would demean himself by stepping back into the office he was sworn to uphold.

James despised practicing against McIntosh, not because of his opponent's vast legal skill, but because of his arrogance and over-bearing manner. McIntosh was tall, at least a couple of inches taller than most of the other lawyers with whom he dealt and he liked to use his size to his advantage. He made it a habit to invade people's personal space, keeping his large melon-shaped face just inches away from whomever he was greeting, speaking, or otherwise glad-handing, while concealing the dagger he had targeted for their back. James had experienced the invasion so often he was confident he could identify which of McIntosh's molars had fillings.

This particular tic aside, the chief complaint by James and his fellow members of the local bar was McIntosh's absolute refusal to acknowledge even a scratch of wrongdoing by any of his clients. The bank was never wrong. The insurance company was never wrong. When he did this in his civil cases, most of his colleagues knew it was just a way to keep solvable cases unresolved so McIntosh could keep his considerable meter running. When he did it in his criminal cases, he was clearly doing it to court the press and to be a sanctimonious prick.

True to form, from the moment Eleanor Warren's body had been found, McIntosh had locked in on Javier Vazquez as her killer and had steadfastly refused to budge. When James had encouraged the man to at least *look* at other suspects, he had been unceremoniously rebuked.

"Have you looked at Warren?" James had asked during a July meeting in McIntosh's office, shortly following Javier's arrest.

"*Charles* Warren? You're kidding me, aren't you James?" McIntosh's voice was, as always, patronizing. He had leaned back in his expensive leather chair and began studying his well-manicured fingernails. James might have refused the meeting, since he had a feeling where it would go. But McIntosh liked meetings. He enjoyed the opportunity to let other lawyers know just how stupid he thought they were.

James fought to keep his temper. He had no leverage—the Commonwealth Attorney could investigate whomever he wanted. Still, *you catch more flies with honey than you will vinegar*, his mother used to say.

"Yes," he said. "Charles Warren."

"And why in the world would I do that?"

"Well, gee, Phil. I don't know. His wife was screwing a damned soldier. He's the richest guy in the state. A guy not renowned for his kindness and gentle spirit." James heard his voice growing louder, his efforts at self-control no more successful than plugging a dam leak with your pinky finger. "I doubt men like Charles Warren are used to being crossed in such a manner—especially not by their own wives."

McIntosh was unimpressed. "So?"

"So," James replied, "it sounds like a hell of a motive for murder to me."

McIntosh made little effort to contain an arrogant smirk. "You're bullshitting me, right?" Before James could open his mouth to reply, McIntosh decided to respond to his own question. "Let me get this straight. You think that Charles Warren, the tobacco magnate, the most prominent man in the state…"

"I know that *you're* impressed by him, Phil," James interrupted. "I don't need you to tell me."

The insult flew around McIntosh like a bowling alley gutter ball, missing him completely. "…you think that he would risk everything he has to get even with his wife?"

"Granted," McIntosh continued, "his wife *was* whoring around with that soldier. But the truth is, she was doing a damned-fine job of keeping it quiet because Charles knew nothing about it."

James chuckled. "I'm sure that's what he told you and you being his biggest fan and all, I'm sure you bought it at face value."

McIntosh's eyes narrowed a bit. Like most bullies, he was far better at levying sarcasm than he was at receiving it. "Tell you what,

James. I probably shouldn't do this. I should probably just let you walk your happy ass in front of that jury and begin pointing your finger at a grieving husband for the murder of his wife. They'll love you for it. And I'd love to watch it."

"Let me guess," James interjected. "Just to show me how magnanimous you can be, you're going to offer Javier life without parole on a guilty plea." He was being facetious. There was no more chance of getting Javier to plead than there was of McIntosh dropping the charges altogether. That said, since nothing was going to be gained here today, James figured he'd get in a couple of digs while he could.

"I'm not that magnanimous," McIntosh replied. "No, your boy is going to fry, all right. There's no getting around that. It's inevitable. But here's what I'm going to do for you, James. This trial is going to take enough time as it is. I'm going to save you—and therefore, me—some time. And I'm going to save you a hell of a lot of embarrassment.

"You see, we did ask Mr. Warren where he was on the night in question. Turns out, he was in Frankfort the entire day, looking at tobacco warehouses."

James considered that for a moment. Though Frankfort was about four hours away by car, there still would have been plenty of time for Warren to have driven back to the lake house and murdered his wife. There had to be more.

"And that night?" he asked.

On cue, a broad smile crossed McIntosh's face. He lived for moments like these.

"He spent the night at the governor's mansion as a guest. The Governor called me and verified it himself."

In spite of himself, James grimaced. He would later kick himself for giving that bastard McIntosh the pleasure of seeing it. But his best option for Javier's defense—pointing the finger at another viable suspect—had just disappeared.

"So, unless you want to impugn the governor and his entire staff in order to smear the state's richest man, I'd recommend keeping that club in the bag. On the other hand," McIntosh continued, never one to leave well enough alone, "maybe you can say that the Warren boy—he's about your boy's age, isn't he? Maybe you can say that *he* did it. After all, he was the only other person in the house…other than *your* client, that is. Maybe the jury will buy that one," he said, his grin spreading.

Now, four months later, James watched as McIntosh rose and addressed the jury the two of them had spent the last day choosing through the *voir dire* selection process.

Though it made James sick to admit it, Phillip McIntosh *was* effective in front of a jury. It was like the guy flicked a switch. His veneer of arrogance was immediately stripped away and the humble, folksy charm of the country politician and the Sunday school teacher deftly took its place. Witness by witness, question by question, McIntosh built his case gradually and methodically, the way all lawyers are taught to do.

Charley Betts, or "Chewin' Gum Charley" as he was better known in the county, had been sheriff for more years than many people could remember. The only thing that wasn't absolute gravel about the man was, per the nickname, his incessant smacking and chewing of gum. He was short and paunchy with a thick mustache that tried its level best to cover both his top and bottom lips. He spoke with a guttural twang and was an abomination to proper grammar. Chewin' Gum was a colorful character and James knew that the jury would take to him. Hell, James liked him, too.

Once on the stand, Chewin' Gum described how he was just having his morning coffee on that day last June when a rather frantic call came into the sheriff's office. It was from the maid at the Warrens' home on the lake, claiming she had found Mrs. Warren's body. He testified that he had immediately called the state police, grabbed his coffee, and took off with a couple of deputies for the Warren home.

Once they got to the home, Chewin' Gum and the deputies made a protective sweep. The only people present were the housekeeper and the Warren's son, Kirk, who was still in his bed asleep. The deputies woke him up and took both him and the housekeeper outside to their cars for their safety.

The housekeeper had said she found the body in the master bedroom. When he entered the room, the sheriff continued, with hat in hand, well, he was hardly prepared for what he was about to see. Of course, he'd seen dead bodies before. Several times, in fact. He'd seen drownings pulled out of the lake. He'd seen occasions where a couple of ol' boys had a few too many nips at the bottle and had shot one another. But, in twenty years of upholdin' the law, he had never seen anything like this.

Eleanor Warren was lying on her back, flat across the bed, still dressed in what had once been a white nightgown. The nightgown was now soaked with blood, blood that had flowed from the gaping cavern that stretched nearly ear-to-ear across her throat. That was bad enough, he said, but it was the eyes that got him. They were still open. With a look of the worst kind of fear in them.

"It was like she was lookin' at someone she knew and couldn't believe they would do somethin' like that to her…"

"*Objection!*" James shot out of his chair. "This is entirely speculative and irrelevant. No one, not even the sheriff here, can look into the eyes of a deceased person and know what that person was thinking when that person died. This testimony should be stricken from the record."

"Sustained," the judge said. He turned to the jury. "The jury shall disregard the sheriff's last statement about the deceased knowing the identity of the person who killed her."

Thanks a lot, James thought. *If you're going to repeat it, why don't you just have the court reporter read the whole damned thing back to them?* He was pissed at himself, though, for not objecting sooner, before Chewin' Gum got the whole statement out. He might have suspected McIntosh had scripted the statement, but he seriously doubted the ability of Chewin' Gum to remember his lines. That was the worst part about it. He knew that, whether or not he was correct, the sheriff was actually describing what he believed he saw. It was bloodcurdling testimony and James knew the jury had heard every last word. They were no more likely to disregard it than he was, instructions to the contrary be damned.

The Commonwealth's next witness was the county medical

examiner, Dr. Joseph Ellis. He was tall and extremely lanky, skinny to the point of being emaciated. His face and features were likewise long and narrow, with the exception of large blue eyes that seemed charged and appeared to never blink. His frizzled hair was mostly gray and it was apparent that any efforts he made to comb it down were, at best, half-hearted. He looked like an aging scarecrow in a tie. To look at him, James would have expected a sparse, twiggy voice, but when Ellis spoke, it was in a baritone so low that it was almost cryptic.

Under McIntosh's questioning, Ellis methodically explained his background, his undergraduate studies at Western Kentucky University and his time in medical school at the University of Kentucky. James probably would have stipulated to his qualifications, but McIntosh wouldn't have agreed. He thought it better for the jury to hear it. It was just another opportunity for McIntosh to hear himself talk in the courtroom.

Once he had been qualified, Ellis explained how he had been called to the murder scene. He had pronounced Mrs. Warren dead at about 8:15, though given the gruesome circumstances, the pronouncement was anti-climactic.

"What did you do next?" McIntosh asked him.

"I had the body taken to the county morgue and I conducted an autopsy later that evening."

"And what were your findings as to the cause of death?"

"Her carotid artery was completely severed, causing a severe and very quick loss of blood. She suffered a tremendous amount of hemorrhaging. I would say that she was dead in less than three minutes."

McIntosh looked stunned, as though this was news to him. He was really playing it up. "Dr. Ellis," he continued, "based on your medical expertise and upon your examination of the victim's body, do you have an opinion as to the type of instrument used to inflict these injuries upon her?"

Ellis nodded. "Yes," he said. "The wound was cut very evenly without indentions of any kind. In my opinion, it was with a very sharp object, one with a non-serrated blade."

"Would a straight razor be consistent or inconsistent with the type of injury suffered by the victim?" McIntosh asked. It was a leading question, James thought, but he knew the answer and figured he only wanted the jury to hear it once.

"Yes, it would be," Ellis said. "In fact," he said as he looked toward first the judge and then the jury, "it's my opinion that's exactly what was used to kill her."

Chapter Twelve

Phillip McIntosh next called John Palmer to the stand. Palmer had been a homicide detective with the state police for about ten years, but if the rigors of the job were getting to him, he was doing a good job of camouflaging it. Just shy of forty, Palmer appeared to be not much over twenty-five and looked more like a paper delivery boy than he did a detective. His brown hair didn't reveal even a hint of gray and he had retained his boyish looks. These traits unsettled James because he could imagine the two older ladies of the jury panel wanting to take the man home and feed him.

McIntosh first led Palmer through his credentials, then had the detective explain how he had responded to the scene. He described how, shortly after his arrival, the medical examiner had declared Mrs. Warren dead at the scene. Because most people who committed suicide didn't do it by slitting their own throat, it was quickly determined that this was a murder case and it was treated as such.

"How did you proceed?" McIntosh asked.

"Well, we looked through the house for a murder weapon. Based on the type of wound the victim had, we were looking for a sharp object with a slightly rounded blade."

"Did you find anything?"

"We didn't find the murder weapon, no."

"Did you find anything else?"

"We found a wooden box, located in a jewelry cabinet. We were checking to see if any valuables were missing so we could determine whether this was a burglary or something else."

"Were any valuables missing?"

"No, sir. Our preliminary investigation, as well as follow-up inventory with the victim's husband determined that no items were missing."

"Okay, Detective," McIntosh said, sweeping a look over the jury. "You mentioned the wooden box. Was there anything pertinent to your investigation found in the box?"

"Yes, there was."

McIntosh waved his left hand toward the jury. "Would you please tell these good ladies and gentlemen of the jury just what you found in the victim's wooden jewelry box?"

Palmer nodded, then adjusted his seat slightly so he could face the jury box. He had obviously spent some time on the stand before.

"Inside the box, we found several handwritten letters. There were approximately eight of them, all in the same handwriting. They were addressed to 'Ellie', which was the name most people called the victim, short for 'Eleanor'."

"Who were the letters from?" McIntosh asked.

"They were signed by the Defendant."

James watched as the letters were, one by one, entered into evidence and then read aloud. He had known about them and had read them. There wasn't any point in questioning their validity. Since Javier had confessed to writing them, both to the police and to James, James believed the best tact would be to treat the letters as being insignificant in front of the jury.

Read chronologically, the first letters, written in February and March, were almost like that of a lovestruck schoolboy. They described at great length, and with somewhat surprising sensitivity, how beautiful Javier had believed Eleanor Warren to be. How, one day, he would take her away from the unhappiness in which she now found herself.

However, the more recent letters took on a different, harder tone. It quickly became evident Eleanor was battling feelings of guilt over their affair. Javier had apparently been trying to convince her that, as wrong as their affair was, it was at least as wrong for them to stay in marriages in which they were both so unhappy. He even asked her to marry him—repeatedly.

James watched the eyes of the jurors, who periodically peered over at Teresa Vazquez and young Michael, and then turned their gaze to Javier. One might have expected Javier, or any man in such a situation, to wish for a giant hole to open up beneath his seat and swallow him up, if only to rescue him from his own shame. Instead, Javier's head was upright, his jaw jutted out, his gaze even. Just as he had been trained, even in the face of stark adversity, to be.

After the letters had been read, McIntosh continued on with Palmer's investigation. The state police had immediately contacted the Defendant, whose identity as a soldier at Ft. Campbell was easily discernible from his letters, and brought him in for questioning. During the questioning, Vazquez, after initially denying even knowing Eleanor Warren, owned up to the affair and to having been there during the night in question. They also obtained a search warrant for his home on post.

"During your search of his home, did you find any evidence tying the Defendant to the murder of Eleanor Warren," McIntosh inquired.

"We didn't find any more letters, nor any blood-marked clothes. However, we did find one item of interest."

"And what was that?"

"A stainless steel, black-handled straight razor."

"And what was suspicious about that razor?"

"It was our belief, based upon information from the medical examiner, that quite possibly, the murder weapon would have been a straight razor."

Chapter Thirteen

J ames walked eagerly to the podium next to the defense table. He had been getting his ass kicked up between his shoulders for nearly two days. There was little that he could do to the testimony of Sheriff Chewin' Gum and Dr. Ellis. He had known that in advance. He had also known that Detective Palmer would be his moment to do some kicking of his own.

"Detective, you patiently read the content of the letters written by my client to the decedent. At any point, was there any threat of danger or harm made by Mr. Vazquez against Eleanor Warren?"

Palmer was coolly indifferent, likely prepared by McIntosh for such a line of questioning. "No, there isn't."

"And, you stated earlier that you found no murder weapon at the scene, correct?"

"That's correct."

"And as we've seen from the crime scene pictures you placed into evidence, there was a lot of blood in that bedroom, wasn't there Detective?"

"Yes," Palmer replied. "There certainly was."

"And the only item you took from Sgt. Vazquez's home was the straight-razor that you placed into evidence, correct?"

"That's correct."

James furrowed his brow, looking intently at the detective. "Did you have the straight razor tested?"

"We did."

"Did you find any trace of Mrs. Warren's blood on the knife?"

"No, sir."

"Did you find any clothes in Mr. Vazquez's home with Eleanor Warren's blood on them?"

Palmer shook his head matter-of-factly. "No, we didn't."

"In your experience, isn't it very unusual to have such a gruesome and bloody murder and not find evidence of blood-splattering on clothes or the alleged weapon?"

"Well, the weapon can easily be wiped off…"

"And the clothes?" James interrupted.

"It would be unusual, yes. But not impossible."

"And you found no bloody clothes, correct?"

"That's true, sir."

"In fact, the only thing you have tying my client to the Warrens' home on the night in question was his admission that he had been there. Had he not told you that, you never would have known he was there, would you?"

"I suppose that's true."

"So what you're telling me, Detective, is that your chief suspect has nothing more tying him to the murder than eight, non-threatening love letters and a voluntary admission that he was at the victim's home on the night in question. To this very day, have you ever even *looked* for another suspect?"

"No, sir. We didn't need to."

James stood firm at the podium, but allowed himself a brief smile. "I guess then, Detective, that you and I reckon the phrase 'need to' very differently."

Chapter Fourteen

On the trial's fourth day, Charles Warren was called to the stand. Upon hearing his name, he rose slowly from his seat, paused as if to be noted by those around him, then strode confidently to the witness stand at the front of the courtroom. The bailiff's knees shook noticeably as he dared to approach Warren with a Bible. As the magnate touched the Good Book with his left hand and raised his right, James wondered just how much Warren resented pledging his oath to any God besides himself.

As usual, Warren was dressed for the boardroom. Black suit, a plasma-red tie, gold cuff-links. James was quite certain that any efforts McIntosh had made to get Warren to tone down his clothes in order to relate to the blue-collar quotient of the jury had fallen on deaf ears. When Warren took his seat on the witness stand, it was evident that he couldn't give a damn what the people on the jury thought about him.

The purpose of calling Warren as a witness was clear. Though he likely had nothing to offer from a pure evidentiary standpoint, he was the best, and probably the *only* way, to personalize the victim. If they hoped to get the death penalty for Javier, the Commonwealth would have to present his alleged victim, Eleanor Warren, as a wife and a loving mother, rather than as merely a corpse who had cheated on her husband.

Still, it was apparent that Warren's presence in the courtroom put everyone on edge, the prosecutor included. McIntosh smiled and nodded and basically did everything except bow before his own witness. Once he completed his groveling, McIntosh led Warren through a series of introductory questions, attempting to humanize him for the jury—no small task given Warren's regal aura. Only then did he begin to focus on the man's dead wife.

"Mr. Warren, how long had you been married to Eleanor?" McIntosh asked.

"We had been married eleven years and ten months at the time she was murdered. Our twelfth anniversary would have been in August." Warren turned to the jury before he answered his questions, using the opportunity to remind them that this wife had been brutally murdered. McIntosh had schooled him well, James thought.

"Did you have any children?"

"Yes," Warren replied, "we have a son named Charles Kirkland Warren. Eleanor doesn't want to be calling two people in the house 'Charles', so she insists that we call him by his middle name. We call him 'Kirk' for short." Warren was, James knew, intentionally speaking of his wife in the present tense as he had been instructed to do. A husband still in denial over his loss. He could have objected to the answer since Warren was going well outside the boundary of the question with his answers. But it would have been a technical objection and the jury would have hated him for it. Best to endure it for now.

"Please tell the ladies and gentlemen of the jury what kind of mother Eleanor was to young Kirk," McIntosh asked, gesturing toward the jury as he spoke.

Surprisingly dutiful, Warren turned to the jury and explained, in no small detail, what a kind and loving mother Eleanor had been to their only child. In this, he wasn't exaggerating. James had done a thorough check, and by all accounts, she was about as dutiful as dutiful got when it came to her son. Hers had been a difficult pregnancy and it had quickly become apparent to them, Warren said, that Kirk would be her one and only. And that was exactly how she had treated him.

"Mr. Warren, I don't mean to pry, but I'm afraid that I have to ask this question," McIntosh said, his tone all but dripping with regret. "Did you and your wife have any marital difficulties?"

Warren glared at the prosecutor for a moment, then ducked his chin, as if overcome by sudden humility.

"Yes. Our marriage was…troubled," he acknowledged. "Unfortunately, it took this rather tragic turn of events to force me to realize just how troubled."

McIntosh nodded, now every inch the sympathetic father confessor. "If you don't mind," he said "would you mind explaining to the jury and the court what those troubles were?"

Warren hung his head and then cast a long look toward the jury, a true penitent. It was apparent, rehearsed or not, that the man despised the indignity inherent in what he was about to say.

"I am and have always been a driven man. I'm driven by work and by success. And in work, I've had great success." He paused, careful not to give the impression he was bragging.

"But, as I've recently learned, my professional success has come at an unimaginable price." He paused for a moment, as though to collect himself.

"At the same time I learned that I had lost my wife, the mother of my only child, I also discovered she was having an affair. With *that* man." About twenty yards directly from the end of Warren's trembling finger sat Javier Vazquez.

"I was just so blind. Too blinded by my own ambition to see that I was turning my back on what was important. On *who* was important.

"I neglected my wife. I was gone days, even weeks at a time on business. She was so good, so accepting. She never said a word. I never…" He hesitated as if forced to swallow back a swell of genuine emotion. "She never complained and I never stopped thinking about myself long enough to realize I was too busy running my businesses to bother with being a husband and father.

"Obviously," he continued, "she needed more than I was giving her. Maybe she sent signs to me and I just didn't see them. I don't know. I honestly don't know." He dropped his head; his shoulders slumped. James wondered if this was the first time Warren's body had ever assumed such a position.

"And when I didn't give her what she needed, that man," Warren said, pointing once again at Vazquez, "was there to capitalize on my mistake."

James rose from his chair, but did so with reservation. "Objection, your Honor," he said. "While I admire Mr. Warren's candor regarding his mistakes in his marriage, I don't believe that any of this is relevant to this case." Even as he said the words, James wondered if the jury would resent him for speaking them, interrupting as he was, a man in the midst of baring his soul. Or at least, what was left of it. Still, the objection was certainly appropriate legally. More importantly, he couldn't allow Warren's diatribe to continue.

"I think the jury should hear what Mr. Warren has to say. He deserves this much," Judge Frazier said. "Overruled."

McIntosh then turned briefly to the jury and shook his head, feigning surprise that his opponent would dare to object at a moment such as this. The prosecutor then stole a triumphant look at James, silently warning him that the worst was yet to come.

Chapter Fifteen

cIntosh reached into a file on the prosecution table and pulled out what appeared to be two pages of notebook paper. The papers, heavily creased, had clearly been folded into a small square at some point in time. He then approached Charles Warren, in the witness chair. James and Javier both leaned forward across their table in an effort to discern exactly what it was that was about to be presented to the witness.

"Do you recognize these papers?" McIntosh asked as he handed them to Warren.

Warren took out his bifocals and placed them on his stout nose. He then took the pages and looked at them very briefly before answering, "Yes, I do."

"How do you recognize them?"

"This past week, I was sorting through and boxing up my wife's clothes. I've only now been able to force myself to do it. I could have had an employee do it, but I knew that I should do it myself. Yesterday, as I was going through her dresser, I found what I thought was a piece of folded paper, taped to the bottom of a top drawer. With a little bit of effort, I was able to pull it loose. This is the letter that I found in her dresser."

"To whom is the letter addressed?" McIntosh asked.

"It is addressed to my wife."

McIntosh flipped the first page and directed Warren to the second. "And whose signature is at the bottom of this page?"

Warren squinted at the bottom of the page, then turned again to the jury. "The letter is signed, 'With my love, Javier.'" He turned back to McIntosh, a look of raw hatred forming like storm clouds on his face.

"Your Honor," James interrupted. "May I see that letter for a moment?"

"You may," Frazier replied.

James rose and approached McIntosh, who handed him the letter. James began reading the letter, which was clearly written in Javier's hand. Before he had reached the end of the first paragraph, he consciously turned his back to the jury, not wanting them to catch a glimpse of the horror on his face.

After he had finished reading, James cleared his throat and stepped toward the Bench, where McIntosh was still standing. He wanted to be out of the jury's collective earshot.

"Your Honor," he said under his breath, "I object to the use of this letter. The defense is entitled to review in advance any such item that the Commonwealth intends to use at trial and we are just now seeing this letter for the first time."

McIntosh smiled patiently, as though he was tolerating a solicitor at his door. "Your Honor, Mr. Warren testified that he just found this letter yesterday. The defense has had just as much time to plan for it as we've had. I can personally assure you that the Commonwealth has made no efforts to hide evidence in this case."

Bullshit, James thought. *You love this kind of blind-side attack. It suits your chicken-shit personality.*

Struggling for composure, he said, "Your Honor, a man's life is at stake here. We simply cannot take the Commonwealth's word for how this last-minute evidence was obtained. The interests of justice dictate that, at the very least, this trial be continued for a week so we can review the letter, determine its veracity, and—"

"A *week*," interrupted McIntosh, ripe with indignation. "You need a week to have your murdering client tell you that he wrote that letter? Let me guess, he never told you before now, did he?"

"My defense is none of your damned business, Phil." *Even if you are right, you corrupt prick,* James thought.

"Take it easy, gentlemen," Frazier croaked. He was now studying the letter.

"Mr. Cameron, I see your point," he continued. He glanced at his watch. "It's eleven fifteen, but close enough to break for lunch. We will recess until one-thirty this afternoon. That should give you plenty of time to review the letter with your client."

James was flabbergasted. "*Two hours,*" he said. "But, your honor, I cannot prepare an adequate defense to newly-received evidence such as this in a two-hour lunch period during the middle of a capital murder trial."

Frazier gave James a condescending smile. "Oh, Mr. Cameron, you're a *fine* lawyer. I've always known you to be very resourceful. I'm sure you'll come up with something."

"Your Honor, I respectfully request that this trial be continued for at least a few days, so I can discuss this letter with my…"

"The court has ruled on your objection, Mr. Cameron. You have two hours."

"Your Honor, again, this time period is completely ridiculous."

"Are you alleging that this Court is ridiculous?" Frazier's smile faded. He wasn't used to having his decisions openly questioned.

"Well, your Honor, in all candor…"

"*Mr. Cameron,*" Frazier said, "I'm not accustomed to this type of behavior from you. While I am uncertain whether it is the rigors of this case that have caused you to act in such a fashion, or if it's just a new style you're developing, I don't find it at all becoming. In either event," he continued, "let me, once again, make myself clear. You have *two* hours to review this letter with your client. And if you attempt to argue this point with me again, not only will I seriously consider holding you in contempt of court, but I will reduce the two-hour window I have given you." Frazier leaned back in his chair, his glare boring a hole through James.

"Now, Mr. Cameron," he continued. "Do you understand my ruling, or do you need me to simplify it further for you?"

With that, James felt himself snap. It was as if he had become a third person and was watching himself from a distance, unable, and perhaps unwilling, to stop what he was about to do.

His face a mask of disgust, he turned to McIntosh. "Bought and paid for, right Phil?"

"What did you say to me, you pissant?" McIntosh retorted.

"You heard me," James said, the venom in his voice rising with each syllable. Their faces were inches apart, only now it was James who was invading the notorious McIntosh's personal space, rather than the other way around. "God knows how long you've been holding that letter, knowing that *your* judge here would let it in, even though it was blind-siding the defense."

Frazier was stunned and was only now realizing what was being said. With no small degree of force, his hammer struck the gavel. Both lawyers flinched, and when they faced the judge, the gavel was pointed directly at James.

"Mr. Cameron," he said. "You are in contempt of court. You may purge yourself of contempt by paying the sum of two-hundred fifty dollars to the Circuit Court Clerk by the end of the day today."

James took his admonition in silent stride. *Great,* he thought. *It was worth it.*

"And," Frazier continued "you can expect to receive a copy of a letter I will be forwarding to the Bar Association regarding your conduct in this trial."

Only then did James remember the jury was still in the court-room. Even though they couldn't hear the gory details, the gist of the meeting was clear—he was getting his ass chewed by the judge. Realizing he might have made a mistake that could actually hurt his client's case, he lowered his head to hide his grimace and said softly, "Understood, your Honor."

Frazier was still pissed. As pissed as James had ever seen him—or any other judge—for that matter.

"*I'm glad you finally do, Mr. Cameron.* Court is recessed until one-thirty. And Mr. Cameron," Frazier continued, just loud enough for the jury to hear. "I suggest that when we reconvene, you find a way to control yourself." With that final, and very public, rebuke, Frazier banged the gavel and stormed out of the courtroom.

As they were walking back to their tables, McIntosh sidled up next to James. Taking advantage of the commotion of the jury leaving, he leaned close and murmured, "Nice work, Cameron. You're really playing to the jury. Very impressive."

James wheeled on him. His voice was equally low. "Phil, unlike Frazier, you're not protected by the sanctity of a robe. I don't know how you and Warren got to him, but remember this: you pull another stunt like that on me again and I'll stick my foot about three feet up your pompous ass. Got it?"

James strode back toward his counsel table, where his ashen-faced client was waiting. McIntosh gathered his things and began walking out of the courtroom.

"You're through in this town, Cameron," he said as he passed.

Yeah, yeah, yeah, James thought. The future of his career was the last thing on his mind at the moment.

He waited until the courtroom had emptied out before presenting the letter to Javier. Javier did not have to read more than the first sentence. He dropped the letter in his lap and put his face in his hands.

James had not only been sandbagged by the prosecutor, but by his own client as well.

"Javier," he said, fighting to smooth the jagged edge in his voice, "why didn't you tell me there was another letter? Why didn't you tell me about *this* letter?"

"When you showed me the letters," the soldier replied, "I noticed this one was missing. I figured she'd thrown it away or they hadn't found it. I didn't see any point in bringing it up."

"You didn't see any point," James repeated, shaking his head. "He didn't see the point," he repeated to himself as he turned away and ran his hand through his thick hair. With his back still turned to his client, he asked again. "Why didn't you tell me?"

When Javier spoke, his voice was barely audible. "Because I wanted you to believe me."

Chapter Sixteen

Dear Ellie,

As I sit and write this letter, I am consumed with thoughts of things I would rather be doing with you. I would rather be lying next to you. I would rather be holding your hand. I would rather be talking to you. I would rather be telling you how much I love you. Unfortunately, letters are all we have now. All you've left me.

I don't understand why you can't admit what should be obvious to both of us. Isn't it obvious to you? Don't you realize I would be willing to give up everything in my life—my wife, my family, everything—to be with you? Of course you realize it. You must. You know I can make you happy like no one else can. But in spite of that, you refuse to make the same commitment to me. You just want to sit back and deny to yourself the reality of what we are.

Well, I can't take it anymore. I won't let you live in denial. I won't let you deny yourself or me. I feel you with every fiber of my being. Don't you see that what we have is beyond being a matter of choice? What we have isn't something that one person just decides to have for another. You can't simply sweep it away, like you would a gnat in your face. You can't and even if you *could, do you really think I would let you? No, of course not. I will make you see. I will make you understand.*

I cannot have a life without you. You may think that you can have one without me. But, I can assure you I will not allow that to happen. We will be together one day, whether it is in this world or in another.

I'm going to give you one more chance to agree to see me. One more chance to open your arms and embrace something greater than each of us. If you still refuse, then you will leave me no other choice. And I will do what I need to do to make sure nothing and no one will keep us apart.

My love always,
  Javier

By the time Charles Warren had finished reading the letter, a hush had fallen over the courtroom. The members of the jury were unsure what to do with the words they had just heard. They looked first at Warren, who was standing with head lowered, as if reading the letter had drained every bit of strength from him. Then they turned their stunned gazes to Teresa Vazquez and young Michael, the family that the Defendant had vowed in the letter to discard.

Teresa sat open-mouthed, a stream of tears flowing down her cheeks. Her silent weeping was somehow more damning than loud sobs would have been. Michael was patting her leg, trying to comfort her, but she was oblivious to her son's efforts.

Then, and only then, did the jury look at Javier. James, caught between the jury and his client, felt as though he had jumped between a firing squad and its intended target. He had always been amazed at the jury process—that twelve people from distinctly different areas of a community could agree on anything. But it was apparent that, at this very moment, there was solemn unity among them.

McIntosh lifted his head and surveyed the room. He looked to the jury, and in turn, they looked to him. One by one, he looked into each of their faces. Had they taken their gaze off of him, they would have seen that Charles Warren was similarly looking to them. As was Judge Frazier. But their attention was focused only on McIntosh. His expression, though outwardly blank, told them what had really happened that grim night at the lake and what they must do about it. In turn, their collective expression told him exactly what would be done.

After twenty interminable seconds of silence, McIntosh turned back to the bench and exhaled a deep breath. When he spoke, it was, for once, in a quiet, understated tone, as though he didn't want to disturb a resting soul.

"The Commonwealth rests, your Honor."

Chapter Seventeen

J avier Vazquez sat in the witness chair, the cool look on his face belying
the turbulence inside him. He had seen combat on multiple occasions
and had spent lengthy deployments in Korea and Egypt. He had been
trained to show courage in the face of enemy fire. And yet, in a room
surrounded by mostly middle-class Americans, many of whom did nothing more
violent than hunt or fish, he was so nervous that he felt like he was about to be
wrenched in two.

Putting Javier on the stand had not been an easy decision for
James, at least not at first. In fact, a day earlier, he had all but
decided his client should not testify. After all, as James had pointed
out under the cross-examination of Detective Palmer, there was only
circumstantial evidence against his client—and precious little of
that. James was convinced he had punched enough holes in the
prosecution case to, at worst, hang the jury.

But that was before the letter.

The letter had changed everything. Though it was just another
piece of circumstantial evidence, its practical effects were deep and
far-reaching. While the earlier letters had merely evidenced the
affair, this new letter had cast Javier in a vastly different light, made
him look desperate and out of control. Threatening even…

And now he sat in front of a judge who hated him, a prosecutor who was demanding he get the electric chair, and a jury that stood ready to show him to his seat.

James stood at the lectern, shocked to realize his normally steady knees were trembling. The next few hours of testimony would determine whether or not his client would live or die. Still, he kept a solid outward resolve, and began step by step to rebuild Javier's image for the jury. To pick up the shattered pieces of Javier Vazquez's life so he could try and save it.

They began by discussing Javier's upbringing in New York and how he had known from early childhood that he would one day enlist in the Army, as his father had done before him. He discussed how quickly he had bonded with the rigor and discipline offered in the armed forces. How, with each promotion in rank he received, his sense of duty and pride in fulfilling that duty grew. Unlike so many, he had not joined the military to escape from anything, or because he was forced to. He had enlisted and excelled because he wanted the military to be his life. As Javier testified, James periodically glanced over the jury in an effort to read their reactions to this testimony. Their expressions ranged from thoughtful to wary to outright distrust. With each face he studied, James felt the onerous weight on his shoulders get a little heavier.

He next moved to the subject of Javier's family. Her resolve tested, but not broken by the reading of the letter, Teresa sat in her now standard seat in the first pew with Michael, quiet and well-mannered as always, sitting at her side. Javier talked about meeting Teresa when he was stationed in Texas and quickly falling in love with her. For perhaps the first time since the trial began, pride beamed from Javier's eyes as he spoke about becoming a father, first with Michael's birth, and then with Mia's. It was at this point that James, after much consideration, decided to ask Javier where it had all gone wrong.

"Javier," he said, calling his client by his first name in an effort to personalize him for the jury. "You seemed to have it all. You had an excellent career with the military. You had a wonderful wife and two beautiful children. And yet you sit here today, charged with murder.

Can you please explain to the ladies and gentlemen of this jury how you got here today?"

The question might have seemed unusual, even dangerous, but to James it was a critical segue into the rest of his case. There was no undoing the actual wrongs that his client—an admitted adulterer —had committed. However, James was a firm believer that the first step to forgiveness was the admission of wrongdoing. Given the jury's understandable hostility toward Javier as crafted by the prose-cution, James believed it was imperative for Javier to acknowledge the sins he actually *had* committed and show contrition for them before denying those he hadn't. The two of them had gone over this question with painstaking care at least a dozen times. James hoped it had not been time spent in vain.

Javier took a deep breath and straightened his shoulders, ready to take his medicine. "Yes, sir," he said. "My life was good, sir. Very good. But even happy people make bad decisions. The bad decision I made was getting involved with Ellie."

"Are you referring to the deceased, Eleanor Warren?"

"Yes, sir."

"Please tell the ladies and gentlemen of this courtroom how you met Mrs. Warren and how your relationship grew from there." James was deliberately asking open-ended questions. He wanted Javier to talk to the jury without his defense lawyer getting in the way. If Javier could establish a rapport with them, they would be less likely to resent him for his looks, his ethnicity, and most importantly, for the fact that he had betrayed his own wife and children.

Before responding, Javier turned to them, as James had drilled into him to do. When he spoke, it was in quiet, measured tones. "I met Ellie at a Chamber of Commerce meeting in February. They had hosted an event at the Community Center for officers at Fort Campbell. Several unit commanders were asked to speak regarding the day-to-day activities of the military. I was one of the speakers." Javier paused for a moment, as though it was his first brush with a pleasant memory.

"Ellie was a member of the Chamber and approached me after the event. She shook my hand and told me she had enjoyed hearing me speak. I admitted that I had been nervous...that I'd never spoken at a civilian event before.

"I was sort of embarrassed the minute the words came out of my mouth," he continued. "I mean, I never really said things like that to people. You know, admitting that I was scared by something. But she smiled at me and it was, I don't know, it was just *different* than the smiles I was used to seeing. It was like, in just a couple of minutes, I was comfortable telling her things that I'd never really known I felt myself, much less told to someone else."

James stole another glance at the jury. Their faces were still drawn with skepticism, but he could see that Javier had also piqued their curiosity. He had to be careful not to overdo it, however. Just go slowly, he thought. One step at a time.

"What happened next?" he asked.

Javier shrugged. "I went back to post. A few days later, I was called to the phone at work. I assumed it was Teresa calling from home. When I answered the phone, it was Ellie. I...I didn't know what to say when I heard her voice." His voice was earnest, as though he was a young boy, recalling the first time he'd spoken to the girl who was the object of the neighborhood's crush.

"She told me that she would like to meet with me to discuss another Chamber event. She thought that I could be of help to her. I told her that there were people on post who handled public-type events for the Army. They would be much better than I would at that sort of thing and that I was very busy."

"And what was her reply?"

"She said to call her Ellie." A wistful note colored his voice as he recalled the moment. Having spent the vast majority of the last five months with his client, James knew that whatever shame the man felt for his part in this sordid tale, this particular memory was a fond one for him.

"So, did you meet with her?" James asked.

"Yes," Javier replied. "I tried to tell her no at first, but I guess I didn't try hard enough. She knew that I wanted to see her just as badly as she wanted to see me. I couldn't say exactly *why*, although maybe I should have known. I told myself it was just a lunch meeting. For the Chamber. That I wasn't doing anything wrong."

Careful, James thought.

"That was when it happened."

"That's when what happened?" James asked, legitimately confused.

As if forgetting all about the jury, Javier lifted his helpless gaze to James. "That's when I realized that no matter what happened, I would never be able to tell her no."

Chapter Eighteen

J avier continued before James even asked the next question. They had reviewed his testimony to the point where he knew what was coming next anyway. He was eager, almost desperate to let the world know what had happened between them. To get it out, once and for all.

If there ever really was a Chamber project Eleanor Warren had wanted to discuss with Javier Vazquez over lunch in a casual diner that first day, it was quickly forgotten, Javier told the jury and James. Instead, they lost themselves. First in flirty, friendly banter, the tension between them simmering like thin broth over stove heat. And afterward, in an afternoon spent between the cheap sheets of the nearest hotel.

She was interested in him, he explained. She wanted to know everything about him—where he had come from, what he was now, and what he wanted to do. "I had never met anyone like that," he said. "Someone so beautiful and privileged, but still so interested in *my* life. It was as if getting to know me was the most important thing in the world to her."

Javier glanced at Teresa. Her gaze immediately darted toward the floor. She clearly couldn't watch him admit what she had been resolutely denying for nearly five months.

"Then," he continued, "she began talking about her life."

This was yet another minefield that would have to be navigated carefully. Despite his powerful aura, it was apparent Charles Warren had been accepted by the jury as the grieving widower. If Javier was too frank in revealing Eleanor's criticisms of him as a husband, they would risk further alienating the jury. They had mutually decided not to delve into the murky waters of the Warren marriage. Besides being hearsay, Charles Warren had already acknowledged difficulties in the marriage. And it was fruitless to point the finger at Warren for the murder, since he had an alibi avowed by the governor.

James glanced down at his notes. He felt as awkward as the jury did. Taking the sting out of the ugly testimony of your own witness was a painful process, but it had to be done.

"We began meeting more and more," Javier confessed. "At first it was once every week or two. Then it was every week. At one point we met almost every day." He looked up again at Teresa, whose wide-eyed gaze was still glued to the floor.

"It was getting harder and harder for me to find ways to meet. I couldn't just leave the base whenever I wanted to. I told my wife I was working late. But she didn't mind. She always said that she understood." He was still staring at Teresa, clearly willing her to look up and meet his remorseful gaze. "I always hated it when she said that. I could almost deny to myself that I was doing anything wrong. That it was somehow okay. I could almost live with it, until she said that." He was talking directly to his wife now, confessing his sins. The jury might as well have disappeared.

"When did your relationship with Mrs. Warren begin to have trouble?" James asked.

Javier seemed to grab hold of himself again, refocusing on the matter at hand. "It was a month, maybe six weeks before she died." He once again dutifully turned to the jury. "Despite how unhappy she was," he said, "Ellie was a really good mother. She said that was the reason she didn't leave her husband. Because she didn't want to risk losing her son.

"After a couple of months, she got kind of...I don't know...I thought she was being paranoid. She thought maybe she was being followed. I told her I didn't think she had anything to worry about. That no one knew about us. But she was always scared."

Javier stopped for a second, and for the first time, looked toward Charles Warren in the back of the courtroom. Holding the man's gaze, he continued. "She said I didn't know how powerful her husband was and that he could easily have her trailed by a private eye."

"What happened next?" James asked, redirecting his client's attention.

"At first," Javier responded, "she cut down on her calls. Where she might have called once or twice a day, it became just a couple of times a week. Then we started meeting less and less."

"Did you say anything to her about this?"

"Yes, sir. I did."

"What did you tell her?"

"I wanted to know what the problem was."

"Were you angry?"

"No...yes, well. Yes," Javier stuttered. "I mean, it was like a switch got turned off. She went from wanting to be with me all the time to barely wanting to see me. She just seemed so scared we were going to get caught."

"What did you do?"

"I began calling her at home, even though I knew it was stupid. Her husband, a maid, even her son, could have answered the phone. But I was getting desperate. I just had to talk to her. Had to see her."

Careful, James thought again. *Don't let them see that side of you.*

"You saw the letter, Javier. Not the early letters that you wrote to her, but that last letter."

"Yes, sir."

"Did you write that letter?"

Still gazing at him, Javier nodded. "Yes, sir. I'm ashamed to say that I did."

"Why are you ashamed?"

"Because I'm ashamed of what I said in it. I was just at my wit's end," Javier admitted, his head hunkered down like an anchor was fastened to his chin. "It's hard to say what it's like. To have someone who is so desperate to be with you, who wants to know everything about you. That was how she treated me. I had...I had just never had anyone who seemed to want to be with me in the way that she did. I don't know. I got used to it. And when she pulled away...it was hard."

"So," James asked, "why did you write the letter?"

Javier pursed his lips in resignation. "Like I said, I was desperate. Ellie basically fell off the face of the Earth. I couldn't figure out what I'd done wrong. I've never been a drinker, but on the way home from work one night, I bought a bottle of whiskey. It was late, the middle of the night. Teresa and the children were asleep, but I didn't go to bed. I stayed up, drinking and simmering, both way too much." He stopped and appeared to be struggling to recollect exactly what happened next.

"All I wanted to do was tell her how hurt and angry I was. Only she wouldn't see me and I couldn't talk to her on the phone."

"So I decided I would write her a letter, like I had before. Only this time, I would let her know just how badly I was hurting. I found a pen and paper and wrote just as fast as I could. Everything that I was feeling at that moment just came out of me and spilled on to that paper."

"When I was done, even though it was the middle of the night, I put it in an envelope and went to the post office on the base and mailed it. I was so drunk that I was proud of myself. Like I had really shown her." Javier briefly shook his head, clearly disgusted with himself.

James nodded his head, pondering as though this was the first time he'd heard this story from Javier.

"But when I woke up the next morning," Javier continued, "I realized what a terrible mistake I'd made."

"I went to the post office, but I couldn't get the letter back. It was already gone."

"A couple of days later, Ellie called me at work. She had gotten the letter. I apologized immediately for what I'd said, but she was quiet—distant, really—on the other end of the phone. She said her husband was going out of town for business and she wanted to meet with me."

"At first," he admitted, "I was happy. She had seen the letter and wanted to meet with me. I really believed that maybe we could fix what was wrong and be together again."

"Did she say anything else?"

Javier shook his head. "She just told me where she wanted to meet."

"And where was that?"

"At her home. The one on the lake."

Chapter Nineteen

James stole another look at the jury. Javier's earnest testimony had them on the edge of their seats.

"Ellie said her husband was out of town on business and wouldn't be back until the next night," Javier said. "Her son was staying at a friend's house and she had sent the maid home."

Both his voice and gaze were distant now. It was as if he was reading the story of his own life for the first time and was wondering why the main character was making the decisions he made.

"She said that it would be just the two of us there."

"Did you know what she wanted," James asked.

"She didn't say. I didn't ask. I was just happy to hear her voice."

"When did you go there?"

"July 13th, sir," Javier replied as he shifted his gaze to James. "The night she died."

James nodded with approval at his client's show of candor. "What time did you arrive that night?"

"She said to get there at twenty-two hundred…I'm sorry," Javier said, catching himself in his usage of military time. "She said to get there at ten. She wanted to make sure no one would see me drive up. She only had a few neighbors and they usually went to bed early."

"Is that the time you arrived?"

"Actually, I got there at about nine-thirty. But I didn't go up to the house until ten, like she said. I parked my car on the gravel road a couple of hundred yards from her driveway, with my lights turned off."

"Why did you arrive so early?"

"No good reason, really," he said. "I guess I just wanted to be near her."

James looked over at the jury, particularly at the men. He wondered if any of them had ever been so desperate to be with a woman. For his client's sake, he hoped that at least one of them had.

"Okay, you went to the house at ten. What happened after you got there?"

Javier turned to the jury and drew a deep breath. "I remember seeing her face through the door…"

———

JAVIER HAD NOT FORGOTTEN a single detail from that night after Ellie had opened the door. When he first saw her face, he had felt a rush of warmth and smiled for the first time in weeks. He had leaned down to kiss her, but she had turned her face away, offering only her cheek. She quickly pulled him inside, but it wasn't because she was eager to have him there. She shoved him inside the entrance hall and then turned her back on him as she searched nervously for car lights driving past her driveway at the top of the hill. Clearly, she was less concerned about seeing him herself than the possibility that someone else would.

Her slender frame was wrapped in a white silk nightgown, which surprised him. Despite their numerous rendezvous in the last few months, it occurred to him that he had never seen her in attire of that sort. Maybe it was her shoulder-length dark hair, twisted into an elegant knot. Maybe it was her eyes, large and brown like a doe's, and how they looked at him in a way no one else's ever could.

Maybe it was the fact that he had just missed her so damned much. Whatever it was, Javier didn't think he had ever been so happy to see someone in his life.

"You look beautiful," he said, speaking from the heart.

She offered him a reluctant smile. "Thank you."

She led him to an expansive living area and asked him to sit on the plush sofa. She sat across from him, careful not to get too close. "I got your letter," she said. "We...we need to talk." Her voice was timid, awkward. She was obviously uncomfortable.

"I want to apologize," Javier interrupted. "I didn't mean what I said. I..."

"No, no..." She raised her hand to his face, covering his lips with her fingertips. "I'm not upset by the letter. I mean, I was upset at first." Withdrawing her hand, she rose from her seat and began to pace, clearly struggling to wring out the difficult words. "But then I realized from the letter what I was doing to you. I could live with what I was doing to my husband. For God's sake, I *wanted* to hurt him for everything he's done to me. But I *never* wanted to hurt you, and when I read that letter, I realized just how much damage I'd already done."

Javier sat in silence, uncertain of what to say. This was unfolding *very* differently from what he had imagined. So he held his tongue, waiting for her to finish.

She turned back to face him, but did not come closer. "What's even worse is that the hurt won't stop with you. I mean, what about your wife? I finally stopped, for the first time since I met you and thought about what we...what *I*...was doing to her. And to your children.

"I realized that by hurting you and turning you into something you weren't, I was hurting them as well."

She sank down beside him on the sofa. Her leg brushed against his, but it was the first time Javier could remember touching her and not feeling a surge of heat run through him. Seeing his own selfishness and guilt through her eyes seemed to have extinguished even that potent flame.

She took his hand. "We can't do this anymore, Javier. *I* can't do this anymore. Not to you. Not to them."

He gazed down at her, his sense of helplessness growing. "But it's not like that," he said, his voice a ragged whisper. "I...I'll leave Teresa and the children."

Eleanor smiled at him with tender condescension, like an adult admiring the stubbornness of a flailing child. "Could you really do that to them?"

"Yes," he said. "Yes. I can. I will," he said, his voice rising despite his best attempts to control it. "Don't you see? I'm no good for Teresa now." He surged to his feet, but Ellie remained seated. "I was good for her once, I loved her once. I *still* love her. But I met you and you changed all that. You changed everything. What we have is so different...it's so much more than what I have with Teresa. I can't just go back to her and pretend this never happened. That *we* never happened.

"Do you really think that's what's best for her? Having a husband who spends every moment longing for another woman? I deserve better. *She* deserves better."

Javier stood in the middle of the room, waiting for her to contradict him. Instead, she leveled him with the one blow he had no defense for.

"I'm sorry, but I can't risk *my* son either. I'm not willing to make that sacrifice...not even for you."

He gazed at her in pained silence. After a moment, he spoke, each word stinging him as it left his mouth. "How would you be losing him? You're the mother. You said that your husband almost never sees your son. No court would give the boy to him."

Ellie shook her head, her first sign of frustration. "You just don't get it, do you? You can't win; I can't win. If Charles found out about the two of us, he'd divorce me in a heartbeat and that would only be the beginning of it.

"You have no idea how powerful he is," she continued. "The man can get anything he wants with just a phone call. Politicians, judges—you name it. This isn't small-town rumor and innuendo. I've seen him do it.

"I wouldn't have a chance. Not a chance in this world. The law just doesn't apply to Charles. It's just another thing he can use to get whatever he wants."

The relief Javier had felt when he had first seen her that evening had now all but evaporated. In its place was a freshly-dug reservoir of hopelessness, greater even than that he had endured for the last several weeks.

"I don't understand how you can stay in a loveless marriage when the opportunity for something so much better is standing right in front of you."

Ellie rose from the couch and walked over to him. She put her small hands on each side of his face and then brought them to his shoulders. "I do see what is in front of me. You've made me feel things I didn't even know I could feel." She paused briefly, arching her graceful eyebrows. "Or at least could ever feel again. You didn't imagine anything that happened between us.

"And you're right, I know you're right," she said. "You're right about all of it. Except for one thing—my marriage isn't loveless. I love my son. He is part of my marriage. He's the part that won't let me walk away. Not even for the man I love."

Javier felt her words tear through his soul. He wrenched himself away from her, wanting to escape her touch for the first time since they'd met. Now, standing a few feet away from her, he felt a different sort of burn rising within him. He didn't even recognize the hurt and rage consuming him. His hands began to shake, and then his whole body. He was outside of himself now and he watched himself take the first step toward her...

———

"DID YOU MURDER HER?" James interrupted, as Javier recounted the details of his final meeting with Eleanor Warren.

Javier blinked up at his attorney, feeling as if he had just been brought out from under hypnosis. He was dizzy, out of sorts. He was still trying to get his bearings back when his attorney spoke again, this time more firmly.

"Javier," James repeated, "did you murder Eleanor Warren?"

His attorney's words were like sharp pellets striking him, piercing his skin. He could feel tears welling in his eyes. Teresa gasped and he knew she could see them, too. In all of the years they had been together, she had only seen him cry twice—those precious moments when he had held each of their children for the first time. He knew in his heart that this was the moment his wife's last hope died.

Javier didn't look at the jury this time, despite having been instructed by James to do so. This was no longer between just him and the jury. From the time he had met Eleanor Warren, something bigger, more encompassing than he could ever describe had taken hold of him. He was nothing more than an instrument in its hand. He had been willing to sacrifice everything for it. His wife, his family...even his soul. Now, finally, he felt free. He knew it was time to let it go. To let Ellie go, too.

"Mr. Cameron, I loved Ellie...I loved Eleanor Warren with everything in me. With God as my witness and on the lives of my children," he said, *"I did not murder her."*

Chapter Twenty

P hillip McIntosh strode toward the witness stand. He stopped
five feet in front of the stand, drawing a perfect visual
triangle between himself, the jury, and the stand. He held no
notebook, no papers, nothing from which to ask his questions. He
didn't need them. To him, the questions were open and obvious, like
a wound that would never heal.

"Mr. Vazquez," he said, sounding like a southern man struggling
with a foreign name, just as he intended. His arms were folded and
his index finger tapped on his lips. "Now it's your story, let me see,
that you began your affair with the victim back in May, correct?"

"Yes, sir."

"And you were married to another woman, correct?"

"Objection, your Honor," James interjected, rising from his seat.
"This territory has been well-covered through previous testimony.
Both parties were married. There's nothing to be gained by delving
back into this."

McIntosh smiled at the judge. "Your Honor," he said "I can
understand why Mr. Cameron would not want to hear again about
his client's *many* transgressions, but the Commonwealth has the right
to question Mr. *Vazquez* regarding his relationship with the victim. It

goes to motive and state of mind of the Defendant at the time he murdered the…"

"Objection!" James shouted. He glared at McIntosh as he addressed the court. "Your Honor, please instruct the Common-wealth Attorney that until he bothers to put up proof that my client committed any illegal act, let alone a murder, he keep his conjecture of what happened that night to himself."

With great reluctance, Judge Frazier nodded to McIntosh. "Move along, Mr. McIntosh."

He was probably getting concerned that this farce he was presiding over would get overturned on appeal, James thought, as he took his seat.

McIntosh returned to the matter at hand. "Isn't it true that it was the victim who ended the relationship with you, rather than the other way around?"

"Yes, sir."

"And that made you angry, didn't it?"

"It upset me, yes sir."

McIntosh walked over to the clerk, was handed a familiar piece of paper, and returned to his original spot. He briefly held up the letter and asked Javier to identify it.

"Yes, sir. That is the last note that I wrote to Ellie before she died."

"And you have admitted that you wrote it, correct?"

"I'm ashamed to say that is correct, sir."

"I'm sure you are," McIntosh responded. With a trace of a smirk, he turned toward the jury, offering his back to Javier. He pulled his glasses out of his jacket pocket and put them on. It was clear that he was about to begin reading from the letter.

Here we go, James thought. But he knew there was nothing he could do about it. The stage belonged to McIntosh and he was every inch the actor, savoring his moment in the spotlight.

"In your letter to the victim, did you write the words, and I quote: 'I won't let you turn your back on what we have'?"

Javier straightened again and lifted his chin, his face a portrait of strained dignity in the face of enemy fire. "Yes, sir."

McIntosh was undeterred. "And in your letter, did you not also write, quote: 'I will show you'?"

"Yes, sir."

"And did you not write, quote 'we are meant to be together, whether it's in this world or another'?"

"Yes, I did." Javier's eyes flickered as he answered. James could tell that the questioning was beginning to wear him down, as McIntosh had surely anticipated.

The prosecutor raised his bushy eyebrows in feigned disgust and returned the letter to the clerk. He then walked to the podium next to his counsel table and removed his glasses, gripping them in his left hand. He stared quizzically at Javier.

"On the night of July 13, 1972, you said that you sat in your car outside the victim's house for thirty minutes before going inside. Did anyone drive by the house while you sat in your car on the main road?"

Javier shook his head. "No, sir."

"And you admit that you were inside the victim's home from about ten o'clock until about eleven-thirty. Isn't that correct?"

"That's correct."

"And during that time, was there anyone else in the house?"

"No, sir."

"And did you see anyone else outside the house?"

"No." Javier's tone was becoming more cautious, as though he knew a trap was being laid. A trap that was about to be sprung on him.

"While you were inside the home, did anyone call the victim on the telephone?"

"No."

"And so, now let me get this straight—you were in love with the victim. She broke it off with you. You admit that you were angry and wrote that letter, in which—and I think we all can say this," he said, stretching out his arms to embrace the rest of the courtroom, "you made very clear just how angry you were."

"I already explained…" Javier tried to interrupt, but McIntosh would have no part of it.

"And," he said, his voice booming through the courtroom, "you admit that you were in the house, the *only* person in the victim's house, at just about the time the coroner set as the time of death. Isn't that all true, Mr. Vazquez?"

"Yes, b-b-but…" Javier was clearly shaken, his voice faltering for the first time that James could remember.

McIntosh didn't wait for him to finish. Instead, he walked right up to the witness stand and propped one arm on the railing of the box. With his face no more than a foot from the soldier's, James couldn't help but notice the difference between the two men. McIntosh might be nearly twenty years older, but his expression was vibrant, triumphant. Javier looked more like a dazed boxer caught on the ropes in the last round of a heavyweight fight. His legs were wobbling and his opponent was about to finish him off with a final blow.

When McIntosh spoke, his tone was softer, almost gentle, forcing the jury to strain to hear his every word.

"Mr. Vazquez, this has been going on for several months now. We're nearing the end. Why don't you just square up your end for me, for the judge and for the good folks here on this jury?" McIntosh gestured toward the jury. Javier, his expression still glazed, blindly followed the direction of McIntosh's hand and found himself looking directly into the eyes of those who were about to stand in judgment of him.

"Why don't you just tell them?" McIntosh asked. "Why don't you just tell them how you loved that poor woman and when she broke it off with you, you just couldn't take it? Tell them that you snapped. That you took your straight razor with you to her house that night and you…"

"*Objection!*" James catapulted from his chair.

"Sit *down*, Mr. Cameron," the judge snapped.

Javier continued to gaze at the jury. The jury waited for what he had to say.

Finally, he shook his head. "No," he said. "On the lives of my children and with God as my witness, I did not kill her."

McIntosh slowly exhaled and meandered back to his lectern.

"Yes, your children," he said. His voice was louder now, more authoritative. He turned to the back of the courtroom, spotted his target, and pointed a finger. Not at Teresa, but rather at young Michael, who sat quietly and peacefully, seemingly oblivious to all that was occurring around him.

"Is that boy, your son—Michael, I think his name is?—is Michael one of those very same children whom you claim to love?" Before allowing Javier the chance to answer, McIntosh attacked again. "And, in spite of how much you *love* him," he continued, his voice rising, "you were ready to turn your back on him, his baby sister, and his mother, all so you could sleep with a woman who was married to another man? Isn't that what you admitted to this jury earlier?"

McIntosh glared fiercely at Javier for a moment before continuing. "Is that the same child upon whose life you now swear your innocence?"

Javier winced, as did James. For once, there was no denying the prosecutor's words. Javier couldn't answer. He simply had no words left. Unfortunately for him, McIntosh was not quite so spent.

"As a God-fearing Christian," he said, "I can only hope for the sake of your eternal soul that you cannot forsake your God so easily as you can the lives of your children."

Chapter Twenty-One

I t took the Christian County jury all of one hour and seventeen minutes to find Sgt. Vazquez guilty of the murder of Eleanor Warren. Word had it that approximately thirty-one minutes was spent deciding who would be the jury foreman and would have the pleasure of announcing the verdict in open court. Another twenty-nine minutes was spent talking over local gossip, just enough time to get to the official lunch, which was provided by a local diner, courtesy of the taxpayers.

In Kentucky, following a conviction on the charge of murder, the convicted Defendant is entitled to a separate hearing for sentencing. The Defendant could call witnesses to testify why he or she should receive a sentence lower than the maximum. The Commonwealth could call witnesses, typically the victim or, in the case of a homicide, family members of the victim, to testify on why the Defendant should receive a heavy sentence, if not the maximum.

The Commonwealth had already rested its case on sentencing. Other than her husband and son, Eleanor Warren had no immediate family. A few well-known society women testified about her extensive involvement in the community and her dedication to her son. Wisely, they omitted any references to her being the proverbial loving wife. James could do little with them. Her infidelity aside, their testimony regarding Eleanor Warren was true.

Charles Warren was the last witness called by the Commonwealth. With the conviction of Javier already in hand, his conceit was much more apparent than it had been in the trial's guilt phase. Even so, he was still able to make a compelling case that, in spite of his considerable wealth, he was now left to raise his son all on his own. Javier had seduced his wife and then murdered her. It wasn't exactly a hard sell for the Commonwealth.

Who would be called for the defense at the sentencing had been an issue of much debate in Javier's camp. Juries sought contrition from the convicted Defendant, and in spite of the resounding conviction, Javier was not ready to admit anything, let alone express remorse for it. If anything, his attitude had deteriorated rapidly in the last twenty-four hours. If he confessed now, it would appear insincere since he had spent the last five months professing his innocence. It was clear the jury had no use for him anyway. He could only make things worse. So James decided to keep Javier off the stand.

Instead, James called several of his military commanders. Decked out in their dress blues, each of the officers testified that Javier had always been an honorable man and soldier. Their testimony went well, but it was the final character witness who had caused James the most consternation.

Teresa Vazquez had taken the conviction even worse than her husband. Since the jury had rendered its verdict, she had lapsed into a near-catatonic state. She had not been called as a witness during the trial simply because James knew she would continue her stubborn insistence that her husband had been home the night of the murder. He could not risk what little credibility the defense had.

The evening following the verdict, he had gone to the Vazquez home—a three bedroom townhouse on post at Fort Campbell. Despite all of the recent turmoil, the home was absolutely immaculate. James's heart ached when he entered the small dining area to discover the table freshly set for four.

Accepting a drink from Teresa's hand, he sat down in the living room with her. A neighbor was upstairs with baby Mia, but Michael, even at the tender age of five, seemed to sense the gravity of the situation. He sat on the couch next to his mother, his shoulders straight, his big brown eyes somber. James could not help but notice it was the boy who was holding his mother's hand rather than the other way around.

"Teresa," he said, breaking the tense silence between them. "We need to talk about tomorrow."

James's words hung unanswered in the room. Teresa was staring at a family photo hanging on the opposite wall. Michael looked up at his mother and squeezed her hand, clearly hoping to prompt an answer from her.

"Teresa," James said again, "I need your help. I need you to testify tomorrow."

She finally turned to him. Tears were streaking silently down her cheeks and James thought, not for the first time, what a relief it would be if she would just sob aloud.

"Javier is fighting for…" he paused for a moment, uncertain of whether or not to use the words in front of Michael. Then he remembered everything else the boy had heard in the courtroom during the last two weeks. "Javier is fighting for his life tomorrow."

If Teresa was moved by the words, it was impossible for James to tell. She just stared at him, saying nothing. He glanced at Michael, desperately seeking any ally, even a five-year-old boy. "Teresa," he said "you've got to try…for the sake of your children. Please help me help *them.*"

She flinched at the words, her flow of tears increasing. Finally, she turned to gaze down into the eyes of her son. There was no denying those eyes were a mirror of her husband's.

"You've got to try…"

They both flinched this time. The words hadn't come from James.

They had come from Michael.

AS TERESA VAZQUEZ took the stand, she appeared frail, but dignified. She was dressed conservatively in her best church dress. Her hair was pulled back and tied in a small bun. James had attempted to prep her for her testimony, but he was not at all confident about what her answers would be. She was still his best chance—his *only* chance—of keeping Javier out of the chair.

James stepped over to the lectern and nodded at Teresa. "Good morning, Mrs. Vazquez."

Teresa stared blankly at him.

"Would you state your name, please?"

Teresa tilted her head. James was getting ready to repeat the question when she finally spoke. "Teresa," she said. "My name is Teresa. Teresa Vazquez." Her voice was faint, but she was close enough to the jury for them to make out the words.

Thank God, James thought. At this point, he was willing to take even the smallest of victories.

"You are married to Javier Vazquez, correct?" It was leading as hell, but even that jackass McIntosh seemed willing to show an uncharacteristic bit of professional courtesy under the circumstances.

Teresa paused again before answering. "Yes."

"How long have you been married?"

"For seven…for seven years."

"And do you have children?"

"Yes."

"What are their names?"

Silence.

"Teresa," James asked again, his growing.

Her eyes were focused toward the counsel table, on Javier. She was studying him intently now, the sharpest focus James had seen from her in weeks. Javier gave James an uncertain glance. Teresa turned that same focused gaze on Michael, who was sitting politely as usual in the front pew. Fresh tears began to spill from her eyes.

And then, as though she had suddenly received a startling revelation, she turned away from her husband and her son.

She turned toward the jury, her voice ringing through the courtroom. "My husband is a good man, a good soldier. He would never do something like that to me or to his children."

Jesus...

Chapter Twenty-Two

Hunter Cameron had been kept away from the action long enough. He had been helping out in his father's office every day after school, just like he had promised. But it wasn't fun anymore. All the excitement was going on across the street at the courthouse. But his dad had told him the courtroom was no place for a boy.

But today there was no school. It was a teacher day or something like that. He had come to the office with Ms. Polly, who had been staying with him at night while his dad worked. His dad had come in briefly, washed up, and immediately headed off to court without a word to either Hunter or Ms. Polly. Hunter had watched out the window as his dad walked down the street toward the courthouse.

As his dad approached the front door, he was met by a small dark-haired woman, who was maybe Ms. Polly's age. Hunter recognized the woman. She was the soldier's wife. But it was the boy holding her hand that captured Hunter's attention. The boy looked a lot smaller than Hunter. Hunter remembered Ms. Polly saying the soldier's son was just five. Just a little kid, he thought. But then, when his dad and the woman went inside the courthouse, the little boy went inside with them.

Hunter scowled. He was in the sixth grade. Why should a little kid get to go into the courtroom with the adults, but he couldn't? He turned away from the window, but spent the rest of the day stewing about the injustice of it all.

Hunter finally decided he'd had enough. He wasn't in the habit of disobeying his dad, but he'd had all day to think about it. Maybe his dad had meant to tell him he could go to the trial today, but was just so busy that he forgot. Yeah, he thought. That had to be what it was.

As soon as three o'clock came, Hunter rushed up to Ms. Polly, who was busily typing a letter. He was barely able to contain his excitement.

"Ms. Polly," he said "I'd better be goin' to get the mail now."

Fortunately for him, Ms. Polly was focused intently on her dictation and didn't pick up on his unusual enthusiasm for the mundane task. She reached into the desk drawer and handed Hunter the key to the post office box. It was as if a member of a relay team had handed him a baton. He was out the door in a flash.

"Be careful!" Ms. Polly called after him, but he was already gone.

He sprinted down the street to the crosswalk, looked both ways, then darted across the street and ran to the courthouse steps. He took them two at a time until he got to the door.

Once he was inside, Hunter quickly found the steps that led to the big courtrooms upstairs. At the top of the stairs, he paused just long enough to remember exactly where the circuit courtroom was. He hurried down the long hall until he reached a set of large double-doors that had a sign above them saying *Christian Circuit Court*. Carefully, he pushed the doors open.

Hunter was stunned at how many people were inside. The few times he had been in this room with his dad, there had been maybe ten people sitting on the benches in the back. And his dad had explained that they were just other lawyers, waiting for some case or another to be called. But today the pews were full with onlookers crammed in shoulder to shoulder. He saw several people scribbling on notepads, like they were taking notes for school or something.

He walked slowly up the aisle toward the front of the court-room. Ordinarily, he might have been scared his dad would see him, but a bunch of adults were standing in the aisles. He was able to ease around them like a garter snake slithering through tall grass.

When Hunter reached a middle aisle, an older lady saw him and motioned to see if he wanted to sit next to her. Hunter nodded and the lady asked the people next to her to move down a little so he could squeeze in next to her. It was a good thing he was thin, he thought, since the other people on the aisle didn't seem too happy about it.

A tall man with slicked-back hair and a bald spot in the back was standing up in front of the people sitting in the box, talking to them about something. After a couple of minutes, Hunter realized the man was the prosecutor—the lawyer who was trying to send the soldier to the electric chair. He remembered hearing his dad talking, and not too fondly, about the man.

Hunter watched and listened intently. The prosecutor was talking very loudly, talking about all the hurt the soldier had caused. Because of him, the lady's son would have to grow up without his momma. And the lady's husband would never see his wife again. The prosecutor had a funny walk, a hitch like the circus clowns with big feet, and really seemed impressed with himself. No wonder Dad didn't like him, Hunter thought.

Finally, the prosecutor sat down. The judge said something to Hunter's dad. Apparently, it was his turn to talk. Hunter slid forward to the edge of the pew, his stomach tightening into an anxious knot. This wasn't how he felt when he was batting in a ball game. It was more like when he and his dad were at a Cardinal game and Lou Brock was getting ready to bat.

His dad stood in front of them all and talked about the soldier. He said that the soldier's bosses had already been there and talked about what a good soldier he was. What a hard worker. Then he talked about the soldier's wife. He said she had obviously been through a tremendous ordeal with all that had happened to her husband. He talked about her having to raise their kids alone. Hunter guessed his dad was trying to get the people not to send the soldier to jail. Finally, his dad asked the people to think about those kids. The soldier's kids. He told them to think about what they would be doing to the soldier's kids if they completely took their dad away from them for the rest of their lives.

As Hunter listened, he could not help but feel a rush of pride. He was beginning to feel guilty for being mad at his dad for not paying enough attention to him for the last several months. He realized now what his father had been doing all that time—trying to save another man's kids from never seeing their daddy again. He thought his dad was much better at talking to the people in that box than the prosecutor had been. He suddenly realized that maybe *he* wouldn't mind being a lawyer, too. Just like his dad. When he was done playing for the Cardinals, that was.

When his dad finished talking, the judge said something to the people in the box, and the old man in the police uniform—the judge called him a *bailiff*—led them out of the courtroom. Then the judge banged his hammer on the bench and told everyone that the court was in recess. *Recess like school?* Hunter wondered.

All of the adults in the room suddenly stood up and began to mill around, trying to get out the double doors at the same time. Hunter decided it was best to stay in his seat. He didn't want to get trampled.

As the adults thinned out in the courtroom, Hunter glanced over to his left. Across the aisle and just a couple of rows ahead of him was the soldier's son. He was sitting by himself on the front pew. His momma was standing up near the table where Hunter's dad and the soldier were sitting. The soldier was holding her hand and trying to talk to her, but it didn't look like she was saying anything back.

Hunter returned his attention to the soldier's son. The boy was small, even smaller than he had looked on the street. Hunter wondered if the boy understood that his dad might be going to jail. At that exact moment, he turned around and innocently returned Hunter's stare. He had dark hair and big brown eyes, just like his dad. Hunter nodded, but the boy just gazed at him for a minute, then turned back around toward his momma and dad.

"Hunter, what are you doing here?"

Hunter started guiltily at the sound of his dad's voice. There was no time for escape. His dad was already making his way down the aisle toward him. He did not look happy.

"What are you doing here, son?" his dad demanded. "I told you that this wasn't the place for kids."

"Well, um...D-Dad, I..." Hunter was still struggling for a response when the old bailiff rescued him. The man came up to his dad and whispered something in his ear. Hunter couldn't hear what it was, but his dad looked really surprised.

"You're kidding," his dad said. He looked at his watch. "After only twenty-seven minutes?"

The old man nodded and his dad bowed his head. After a second, he turned to Hunter. "We'll talk about this later," he said grimly, before walking back over to where the soldier and his wife were standing. Hunter frowned, his stomach tightening again. *His dad must really be worried about something,* Hunter thought. *He didn't even tell me to go back to the office.*

Word must have traveled fast. Within minutes, the prosecutor was standing at his table and the judge was back on the bench. All of the adults were crowding back into the courtroom when the people who had been sitting in the box emerged from a door at the front of the courtroom and took their seats.

The judge counted all of them and then asked them if they had agreed on a sentence. A heavy-set man, dressed in overalls and holding a piece of paper, stood up and told the judge they had agreed on a sentence. The judge instructed the old bailiff to get the piece of paper from the old man and bring it to him. Once the judge had the piece of paper in his hand, he took his time reading it. After a second, he took the glasses off of his long nose and asked the lawyers and the soldier to stand.

When the judge read from the paper, it was like he was using a different voice, Hunter thought. Like he had just gotten finished with a chore and was proud of his work. Weird, Hunter thought, as the judge began to read:

> *We, the jury, having found the Defendant guilty of the charge of Murder in the First Degree, this matter having come before us for sentencing, and having now considered the testimony of all of the witnesses in the case at bar, and the range of penalties available under Kentucky law to set for the Defendant, and the jury otherwise being fully and sufficiently advised...*
>
> *It is our finding that, in committing the offense of murder in the first degree, the Defendant acted in such a matter as to support a finding by this jury that aggravating circumstances existed at the time the Defendant committed the act. Accordingly, we fix punishment for the Defendant at death by electrocution at the Kentucky State Penitentiary at Eddyville.*

The judge brought his hammer down and it was as though the room exploded. Everyone who had been sitting surged to their feet at the same time. Some of them were happy, shaking hands and slapping backs like the home ball team had just won a game. The prosecutor was shaking hands, too—first with the sheriff and then with a thick, bald-headed guy wearing a suit with a dark tie. The man had a beard and looked like he was really, really strong. Though the man wasn't even looking at him, Hunter felt a trace of fear shoot through him.

Over at his dad's table, the reaction was very different. His dad and the soldier were both leaning over the table and his dad had his hand on the soldier's back. He had done the same thing to Hunter more than once after a losing ballgame. But as bad as the soldier looked, his wife looked even worse.

Sitting next to her young son, the soldier's wife was crying as hard as anyone Hunter had ever seen. The boy was just sitting there, not really doing anything. All of a sudden, the soldier's wife let out a piercing scream. Hunter clapped his hands over his ears and saw other people doing the same thing. She jumped from her seat and ran really fast toward the people who had been sitting in the box in the front of the courtroom. Hunter's dad lunged to grab her, but only managed to slow her down. The old bailiff immediately grabbed her and wrestled her down to the ground, but she quickly proved to be more than he could handle alone.

Her screaming continued, getting louder and louder, as she fought frantically to escape the bailiff's grip. His dad ran over to where they were and tried to help the bailiff. The soldier, seeing his wife tackled by the officer, tried to run to help her, but the other two bailiffs quickly grabbed him. The soldier tried to fight and get away from them, but one of them hit him in the back of his head with the butt of his pistol. The soldier collapsed on top of the table. The bailiffs handcuffed his hands behind his back and quickly dragged him, unconscious, out of the courtroom.

Hunter slowly lowered his hands from his ears, stunned by what he had just seen. He wanted to help, to do something, anything at all, but he didn't know what to do. As his helpless gaze scanned the courtroom, he noticed the adults were scrambling everywhere. And then, amidst all of the commotion, he noticed the soldier's son had swiveled around on his bench. The lost look Hunter had seen in the first-grader's dark-lashed eyes before had vanished. Instead, they had narrowed and Hunter would have almost sworn they were focused with almost eerie intensity on one thing and one thing only.

On him.

Part Two

Danville, Kentucky
August, 1978

Centre College

Chapter Twenty-Three

Hunter Cameron trudged up the steps at Wiseman Hall with yet another heavy box, his goal a small dorm room to be shared with a stranger. At eighteen, he had already developed a skeptical feel for the unknown. An unknown school. An unknown roommate. An unknown world. Such was life for a college freshman, even in rural Danville, Kentucky.

Centre College was a small liberal arts school, but also an up-and-comer in the hierarchy of U.S. colleges. Centre's alumni already included two Vice-Presidents, two U.S. Supreme Court Justices, and five Rhodes Scholars. That academic history was all well and good, but Hunter Cameron had come there to play baseball and get away from Hopkinsville.

Hunter pushed his way through the propped-open aluminum door and staggered over to the twin bed beside the window. *I've got dibs on the window,* he thought. Hopefully, Hunter mused, his roommate would be smaller than he was or have a healthy respect for his short-lived seniority. Or both.

His dad staggered through the open doorway with a similarly-sized box. The trip up the single flight of stairs had taken more toll on the father than it had the son. James lugged the box over to the empty bed and dropped it onto the bare twin mattress. As James bent over at the waist, raking back what remained of his hair with one hand, Hunter found himself studying the man he loved more than anything and calculating the effect of what the Javier Vazquez years had wrought.

In the years since the trial, James had aged at a stunning rate. His once-youthful appearance had vanished, leaving behind only a threadbare trace of the man he had been. A noticeable paunch circled his formerly trim waist like a small innertube. His eyes, once clear and blue, were saddled with well-hung bags, and his pupils were bloodshot, earned from the extra drink or two he indulged in every night just so he could sleep. His thick head of hair had thinned considerably, leaving a large patch of scalp in the back of his head.

In the aftermath of the conviction, James had launched a desperate series of appeals in an effort to save his client. Through sheer will, he had managed to prolong the tendered death sentence for five years. Still, he had lost at every turn and now the end hung squarely in sight. The appellate process was virtually exhausted, with little hope of further extensions. If Javier saw the end of 1978, it would be a legal miracle of epic proportions. As Hunter looked at the physical wreck that remained of his father, he couldn't help but wonder if the soldier's sentence would ultimately claim both client and lawyer.

After catching his breath, James meandered over and plopped down on Hunter's bed. Looking up at his son, he patted the mattress with his hand. Seeing each tap in what seemed to be slow-motion, Hunter felt the ominous signs of the last-ditch, coming-of-age, father-to-son talk that he had been taught by his peers to dread. He sat down next to his father, as much out of obligation as anything else. James draped his arm around Hunter's still-slender shoulders.

"This is a big day for you, son," he said. "I just wanted you to know how proud I am of you. Your mother would certainly be proud, too."

"I know," Hunter said sheepishly, eager to be done with this embarrassing ritual.

As though he was tiring of his own *clichés,* James stood up and paced a couple of steps away before turning back to Hunter. "I've got something I want to talk to you about."

"Okay," Hunter said, as though he had any other choice.

"I found out a few days ago that Judge Frazier is going to be retiring from the bench at the end of the year. Heart problems of some sort." James hesitated, clearing his throat awkwardly. "I think I'm going to try to get the appointment."

Hunter was shocked by his father's words. He had never before heard his father express any interest in being a judge. More significantly, the Vazquez trial had done more harm than good to James's career. Some of his clients had turned up their noses and left, not wanting to be associated with the lawyer who had defended the man who had murdered Charles Warren's wife. James had still managed to secure enough work for them to live comfortably, but his practice had definitely taken a hit. The thought of his father being politically well-heeled enough to get a judicial appointment seemed to Hunter to be nothing more than a pipe dream.

It was Hunter's turn to clear his throat. "How do you think you can get the governor to appoint you?"

James didn't appear to be offended. In fact, he seemed to appreciate his son's candor. "To be honest, if anyone else wanted it, I wouldn't stand a chance of getting the appointment."

"Nobody else wants to be the judge?"

"Nope."

"Why not? What about McIntosh?" Hunter was having a hard time believing that *nobody* would want the position, not even the blowhard prosecutor he had come to despise even more after witnessing the effects of the Vazquez conviction on his father.

"You would have thought he would have wanted it, but he doesn't. His private practice is just too good, I guess." James shrugged. "So, that leaves me."

Hunter pondered his father's words for a moment. Finally, he decided to ask the question that was burning inside of him. *May as well,* he figured. This felt like the first real discussion he and his father had had in years.

Oh, his father had still gone to all of the ball games, attended the school functions, made all the superfluous rounds. He had been attentive enough, but Hunter had sensed deep inside that he no longer had his father's *attention*. Not in the way he needed it. Not in the way he deserved it.

He could not help but resent all of the nights his dad had spent sitting in their darkened living room, a glass of bourbon in his hand, silently replaying every aspect of the trial, what he could have done differently or not done at all.

That's why Hunter had chosen a school so far away from home. At least now the distance between them would be physical, not just emotional.

He lifted his chin. "Do you think you're up to the job?"

James's flinch was almost imperceptible. He sank back down on the bed next to Hunter.

"I think I am, son," he replied. "I think I'm up to doing a lot of things I haven't let myself do in years. I let the Vazquez case take things away from me. Things that…that I shouldn't have allowed to be taken. I pushed people away. Not because I wanted to, but because I didn't know how to stop."

"But I've come to realize what I lost. And I'm ready to do everything I can to salvage what I can. I think becoming a judge will help me heal a little bit."

"You mean, *to right the wrongs of society*," Hunter said with a reluctant smile.

James smiled back. "Yeah, something like that I suppose."

Hunter was genuinely glad to see his father excited about something again. He might never be the man he was, but Hunter could finally see a glimmer of that man in his father's eyes.

"My classes on Friday will be over by ten," Hunter said. "I was thinking I might come home every couple of weeks or so. Maybe we could go fishing. Play catch in the yard. I don't want you getting old on me, your being a judge and all."

"I'd like that," James said. They both stood up and for the first time in five years, it felt natural for Hunter to step into his father's embrace. As James clapped him awkwardly on the back, Hunter

was a little shocked to discover that at well over six feet he'd
outgrown his dad by a couple of inches.

"Well," James said as he let Hunter go, "we'd better get going on
this moving if we want to be done before dark."

"I'll be right down," Hunter said as his dad moved to the door, a
fresh spring in his step. "I want to unpack these boxes before we
bring up more."

He was turning to hang some clothes in the small makeshift
closet when he heard footsteps behind him. His father must not have
heard him. "Dad," he said turning around, "I said I'll be down
there in just a…"

It wasn't his father in the doorway, but a small figure struggling
with an enormous suitcase in which he could easily have fit with
room to spare. He was probably Hunter's age, but about half the
size. His shoulders were narrow, his legs spindly. His thin curly hair
was a cinnamon color and sticking up in several spots. Thick glasses
stood out from his face like a billboard on a rural road.

"Here," Hunter said, "let me help you with that."

The two of them dragged the suitcase into the room and heaved
it on the bed against the far wall. Gasping for breath, they each
straightened and stretched their backs.

"Thanks for your help," the young man said in a squeaky voice.
"I can't believe they don't have elevators here. It's 1978, for God's
sake."

"Well, there are only three floors," Hunter said.

"But still," the little guy said, removing his glasses and wiping his
brow. "I heard they have elevators at U.K. This is supposed to be a
progressive school."

"I guess we're going to be roommates," Hunter said, extending
his hand. "My name is Hunter Cameron."

The kid pushed the glasses back on his small head and then
shook Hunter's hand in a tepid grasp. "Nice to meet you," he said.
"My name is Charles Warren…"

Chapter Twenty-Four

"...**B**ut I go by Kirk," Hunter's new roommate finished.

Hunter stared at the boy for a moment, remembering every fancy literary quote about irony he had ever read.

"Did you say that your last name is *Cameron?*" Kirk finally asked, frowning as if the word had just sunk in.

"Yeah," Hunter said faintly, reluctant to admit it for the first time in his life. They stood facing one another, arms dropped awkwardly to their sides.

"I'm not certain what we're supposed to do," Hunter finally said.

Kirk shook his head slightly. "Me, either."

"We can talk to housing if you want," Hunter said. "I'd bet they'd give us other roommates."

Kirk blinked at him from behind his glasses. "Is that what you want?"

Hunter shrugged. "I don't know."

Several seconds of silence passed between them as they both glanced around the dorm room to avoid looking at each other.

"Do you hate my dad?" Hunter finally asked. Though he had sometimes asked himself the very same question in the last few years, it still stung to hear the words spoken aloud. He braced himself for Warren's reply.

Kirk shrugged. "I never really thought about it."

Hunter couldn't help but be a little surprised. He would have assumed the son of a murdered woman would automatically hate the lawyer who had defended her accused killer.

"My *father* hates your dad," Kirk continued, "but my father hates a lot of people." Kirk sank down on the edge of the bed, propping his feet on top of that enormous suitcase. "I don't know. I guess that...I guess your dad was hired to do a job and he did it the best that he could. I can't say I ever held it against him."

Hunter nodded and the silence fell between them again.

Hunter sensed the decision was his. He studied Kirk out of the corner of his eye. Despite the awkwardness of their situation, he found himself liking the little runt. Perhaps, he thought, that was the only thing that mattered.

He finally asked, "You got a lot of stuff to bring up?"

"Not really," Kirk replied. "Most of my clothes are in this damned thing." He pointed to the giant suitcase. "I hope you won't mind one thing, though."

"What's that?"

"I'm a pretty big baseball fan. I bought the best radio I could find so I could listen to the Cardinal games in the room. I hope that won't be a problem."

Hunter grinned.

At just that moment his dad staggered back into the room and dropped another heavy box in the floor. He was wiping the sweat from his brow when Hunter tapped him on his back. "Dad, I'd like you to meet my roommate—Kirk Warren." There was a note of pride in his voice that he hadn't heard from himself for a very long time. "Kirk, this is my dad, James Cameron."

As James lifted his head, a sheet of white flashed over his face, replacing the flush that had preceded it. He gingerly extended his hand to Kirk, who embraced it warmly, clasping it in both of his small hands. Hunter's grin deepened.

Maybe, he thought, the healing had finally begun for all of them.

Chapter Twenty-Five

Summer was taking its time in passing to the fall and the temperatures remained unusually warm in Danville. Like most of his teammates on the Centre College baseball team, Hunter wondered why mother nature had chosen this particular time of year to have the sun bear down on them as they toiled on the dusty infield and scorched grass outfield, performing mundane hitting and fielding drills.

Hunter had already distinguished himself during the early weeks of practice. From the first day, he had lined hit after hit over the diamond. Unlike most freshman, he had also shown a discerning batting eye, unwilling to swing at anything that was even an inch or two off of the plate. He carried that same maturity to the pitcher's mound. Though lacking an overpowering fastball or a sharp breaking ball, he seemed to have a certain feel, a sixth sense, about pitching. His pitches were consistently on the corners of the strike zone—too close for batters to ignore, yet too far or tight for them to get in a healthy swing. He didn't strike out many, but no one seemed to ever hit a ball hard off of him, either. His sessions produced nothing but easy ground balls and lazy fly-outs. His coaches were duly impressed.

Hunter was toweling off in front of his small locker after practice when he felt the tap on his shoulder. "Hey, Cameron."

Hunter turned around and saw the burly figure of Dax Handley,
the slugging right fielder, towering over him. Dax was a senior and
the star of the team. Like most of the older players, Dax had little
use for the freshmen. Unless they were carrying his equipment bag
or bringing him water during practice or picking up his sweat-
stained jock straps and cups in the locker room. Those freshman
hazing methods had become a ritual for most college athletic teams.

"Yeah?" Hunter replied as he stood up slowly, trying to fake
nonchalance. Dax had him by at least three inches and forty
pounds.

"You threw the ball okay out there today."

Hunter didn't really know what to say. If he were as comfortable
talking to Dax as he was pitching to him, he probably wouldn't look
like such an idiot.

"Thanks," he croaked.

"You throw the ball okay all the time," Dax continued, "especially for a freshman. Hell, you may even turn out to be useful." If
Dax was trying to make a joke, Hunter thought, it wasn't apparent
from the look on the senior's face.

"Thanks."

"Listen up—we got some people coming over to the Kappa Sig
house tonight."

Hunter stared blankly at him.

"Several of the guys on the team, we're Kappas. We thought
you might want to come over and hang with us. See what we're all
about."

Hunter didn't know what to say. He didn't expect the seniors to
speak to him, let alone invite him to one of their parties. He
couldn't help but wonder why he was getting this invitation.

"Well?"

Hunter snapped to attention and began nodding. Not so much
because he wanted to accept the invitation, but because he didn't
know what else to do.

"Good," Dax said. "Just come over around eight or so. Someone will be watching the door when you get there. Just tell them you're my guest. They'll let you in. We throw the best parties on campus. There'll be plenty of girls, some music. And,"—his smile broadened as he grabbed Hunter's shoulder in one of his beefy hands—"there will be plenty of hooch."

Hunter's head was spinning, but it quickly stopped when Dax planted a friendly but heavy slap squarely between his shoulder blades as he turned to walk away. Now, only one thought was in his mind.

What in the world was *hooch*?

Hunter was still pondering that question when he heard Dax bellow again, this time from the locker room exit.

"Hey, Cameron," he said. "Bring a friend if you want."

———

"*YOU'VE* BEEN INVITED to a Kappa Sig party?"

Kirk jumped up off his bed, dropping the book he had been reading. He began to pace frantically around the dorm room, a habit Hunter alternately found humorous and irritating.

"But, how?" Kirk asked. "I mean, the semester just started. It's not even Rush week yet."

"I don't know," Hunter replied. "One of the senior players asked me if I wanted to come over." He was sitting at his desk, huddled over his biology book, simultaneously trying to make sense of it and the words being spewed by his hyperactive roommate.

"You know that Kappa Sig is the best fraternity on campus, don't you?"

"No, Kirk. I hadn't gotten the chance to brush up on the official rankings."

"Well, it is," Kirk said, unaffected by Hunter's sarcasm. "All of the campus big shots—the athletes, the class presidents—all of them are Kappas. Hell, their parties are the stuff of legend. I hear that the girls at UK drive here from Lexington so they can go."

Hunter buried his nose deeper in the textbook. "Well, I'm not a big shot."

Behind him, he heard Kirk's footsteps pause. "Don't tell me you're not going."

"Okay, I won't bother telling you I'm not going."

"But you're not?"

"Nope."

"You're crazy! Why aren't you?"

Hunter silently pondered the question for a moment, just as he had been doing ever since Dax had first offered the invitation. The truth was that he had thought of college as a time for his studies and baseball. As far as he was concerned, he was at Centre to study, pitch, and hit. Though he had been relatively popular in high school, he hadn't given much thought to the social part of college. Perhaps it was because social acceptance had always come easily to him, which was more than he could say for his roommate. Given Kirk's awkward appearance and quirky nature, attention and envy from his peers was the one thing that, even with his family's enormous wealth, he could not buy—no matter how badly he wanted it.

"Kirk, I'm pretty worn out from practice. I've got this biology quiz tomorrow and I don't understand *any* of this stuff. I just don't have the time."

Kirk stared incredulously at Hunter. "*Time?* You don't have the *time?* You've been invited to a party at the best fraternity on campus and you don't have the *time?*"

Though he was trying to be patient with his friend, Hunter felt his irritation building. He was sensitive to Kirk's need to be part of the in-crowd, but he just didn't share that need. He was on the verge of explaining that to Kirk when he glanced out the window next to him and caught a glimpse of something that completely erased the subject from his mind.

She was petite with hair the color of chestnuts. Her curls were tied back from her face, but a dark strand or two had made a successful escape, tumbling down to frame her cheeks. She was dressed in a Centre cheerleader outfit. Hunter immediately wondered if it was what the outfit did for her or what she did for the outfit. She was with another girl, who, though cute herself, simply paled in comparison. She was, Hunter was certain, the most beautiful thing he'd ever laid eyes on.

The two girls were talking to a preppy, athletic-looking guy who looked a couple of years older than either of them. The girls smiled as he talked to them and periodically nodded their heads in response to whatever he was saying. Finally, he opened up a notebook and scribbled something inside. The guy tore the piece of paper out and handed it to the dark-haired girl. He saw her look at the paper for a moment and then turn to her girlfriend. In unison, they both smiled and nodded at the guy. Hunter felt his heart sink as the guy turned and walked away. It was then that he saw the insignia on the guy's shirt. Though he wasn't familiar with the Greek alphabet, he knew the insignia's two letters.

"*Kappa Sigma*," he muttered to himself.

"Are you even listening to me?" Kirk's voice had risen until it sounded like the chirp of small bird. A small, *annoying* bird.

"About what?" Hunter replied, snapping out of his haze.

Kirk rolled his eyes in what was rapidly becoming a familiar gesture. "You know about what," he said. "I can't believe it. I just can't believe it. You've been invited to a Kappa Sig party and you're not going to go." He shook his head in exasperation, resting his hands on his hips.

Hunter let him suffer for a moment before finally saying, "All right, all right. You win. I'll go."

Kirk threw his arms up in the air, heaving a sigh of relief.

"But I do have a problem."

"And that is?" Kirk snapped, clearly still miffed he'd had to convince Hunter to do what was so obvious to him.

"Well, the thing is, they said I could bring a friend." Wanting to draw this out as long as possible, Hunter said slowly, "I don't know that many people and I don't really want to show up by myself." Hunter tilted his head, watching Kirk began to twitch. He began a silent count in his head, waiting to see how long his roommate could hold up.

He hadn't gotten to five when Kirk said, "Well…I guess *I* could go with you."

Hunter feigned surprise. "You'd do that? For me?"

Kirk pursed his lips and shook his head slowly. "Yeah. I don't really have anything else to do tonight."

"Okay," Hunter said, finally releasing the grin he'd been biting back. "We're supposed to get there around eight,"

"Eight?" Kirk shouted. *"Eight?* Why, that's only three hours away!" Kirk shot over to his small closet and began rifling through it, muttering to himself all the while. "What do you wear to these things? I need a shower! Where is my good cologne? I wonder how many girls will be there?"

Through sheer force of habit, Hunter tuned out his friend and turned his thoughts toward the auburn-haired girl. Dax had said that there would be plenty of girls at the party, but there was only one girl who interested Hunter. One question occurred to him, though. It was one that had crossed his mind more than once that afternoon, but one he had been afraid to ask. Still, he just had to know the answer.

"Hey, Kirk," he said to his friend, who was now vigorously brushing his teeth in the room's small sink.

Kirk looked up at Hunter, a large toothbrush protruding from his mouth. "Mmmm?"

"Can you tell me just what in the hell *hooch* is?"

Chapter Twenty-Six

The Kappa Sig house was one of five fraternity houses neatly aligned along Walnut Drive, better known as *Fraternity Row*. The houses were all spacious, two-story Victorians with multiple, dorm-style suites on both floors. There were fenced courtyards behind the houses and some of the houses, including the Kappa Sig house, had large, separate garage-style buildings, which usually doubled as game rooms. The week before Rush Week was a wildly popular social period at Centre College. The Inter-fraternity Council strictly forbade the presence of any alcohol at any formal fraternity or sorority function, which encompassed all activities during Rush Week. As a result, the industrious minds of the various Greek organizations had long ago made it a tradition to host *informal* functions the week before Rush. On this night, every house on fraternity row was rocking. And none more so than the Kappa Sig house.

As Hunter and Kirk approached their first fraternity party, Hunter did his best to keep his nerves comfortably tucked beneath his neatly pressed khakis and shirt. In contrast, Kirk kept fidgeting with his keys and the buttons on the sleeves of his wrinkled blue shirt.

When they reached the doorway of the Kappa Sig house, a tall, well-dressed member was waiting to welcome them. He exchanged handshakes and names with both of them and asked them to sign the register with both their names and the name of their inviter.

Inside, the house was marvelously congested. The Kappa Sig men were everywhere, wearing jackets boasting their Greek letters. The place was packed with beautiful girls of all shapes and sizes. Hunter and Kirk worked their way carefully through the crowded hallways, trying their best to conceal their amazement and act as cool as their hosts.

Hunter was relieved to find Dax leaning against a wall, a bronze-skinned brunette hanging on his arm. He approached Dax with Kirk in tow. To his surprise, the slugging star actually remembered him.

"Hey, the Rookie!" Dax yelled, his voice easily carrying over the blaring music. Temporarily extricating himself from the brunette, Dax slapped Hunter on the back in welcome, nearly making him stagger. Still, Hunter was grateful for the warm reception.

"Dax," Hunter managed, once his Adam's Apple has stopped swaying, "this is my friend and roommate, Kirk Warren."

Kirk barely came up to the baseball player's breastbone. The enthusiasm drained from Dax's face as Kirk pumped his hand eagerly. Dax nodded curtly and mumbled, "How ya doin'," before quickly turning his attention back to Hunter.

"Let me show you around," he offered, putting an arm around Hunter's shoulders and guiding him toward a glassed-in area that appeared to be a living room. Hunter dared a glance over his shoulder to find both Kirk and the brunette staring forlornly after them. Recovering first, Kirk offered the brunette his hand, but she just rolled her eyes and walked away, leaving him standing all alone.

Hunter's view was blocked by a parade of boisterous partygoers. Dax continued to lead through the house, stopping to introduce him to several Kappa Sigs. Each one of them greeted him warmly with a couple of the Kappa baseball players recognizing him as their new teammate. They eventually ended up in the courtyard where a large number of people were gathered around a large, round plastic garbage can.

"What's going on out here?" Hunter asked.

Dax grinned like a proud mentor instructing his protégé. "*That*, rookie, is the hooch."

The can was filled with what appeared to be grape Kool-Aid. A stack of cups sat on a small table next to it. Dax grabbed a cup, expertly scooped it through the mystery liquid, and handed it to Hunter.

Hunter gazed down at the innocent-looking brew. "But what exactly is it?"

"I told you. It's hooch," Dax replied, his toothy grin growing even larger.

Hunter took a tentative sip. "It tastes like grape Kool-Aid."

"Grape Kool-Aid with a *kick*, Rookie," Dax replied as he held up his own freshly-refilled cup and tipped it to his lips.

Hunter took another sip, stealing a surreptitious glance around as he did so. He hadn't spotted the cheerleader in the crowd. Yet.

"Say, Dax," he said. "I saw this girl today. I was wondering if she was here."

"What's her name?"

Hunter shook his head. "That's the problem. I don't know."

"What's she look like?"

"A cheerleader. Small. Really pretty. Do you know her?"

Dax chuckled. "Sorry, Rook. You just described most of the squad."

Dumb question number two, Hunter thought.

Hunter was taking another sip of his rather tasty hooch when, as luck—or fate as he would later deem it—intervened. A drunken Kappa Sig staggered aside and he saw her.

The cheerleader. *His* cheerleader.

She was standing on the steps just off the back porch, accompanied by the same girl she'd been talking to when Hunter had first seen her. She was wearing a pink shirt and denim skirt and looked even more beautiful than she had that afternoon. He could not help staring.

Dax was yelling something in his ear when Hunter turned up his cup and drained the rest of his hooch. Still gazing at the girl, he blindly handed the cup to Dax.

"Can you excuse me for a minute?" Before Dax had a chance to reply, Hunter took off in the girl's direction.

He approached her quickly, scared she would disappear again. "There any room on this step?" he asked her, hoping his face wasn't as flushed as the rest of him felt.

She looked at him oddly. "I don't know. I guess that depends."

"On what?"

"Are you a Kappa Sig?"

"Why? Does it help my chances of getting to stand on the step with you? I mean, what if I say that I am?"

Her response was quick. "Then I can tell you I hope you're better than the guy who asked me here."

Biting back a sigh of relief, Hunter nodded. She hadn't given him the boot—yet.

"And if I say I'm not a Kappa Sig?"

She flashed a grin that temporarily caused him to lose track of his senses. He scrambled to recover them, hoping she hadn't noticed.

"If you're not a Kappa Sig, then I won't have to worry about offending you by telling you that your fraternity brother who asked me here is a total bore."

They continued to gaze into each other's eyes as the crowd around them seemed to disappear.

––––––––

INSIDE THE HOUSE Kirk was having much less luck than Hunter. He made his way through the first floor and then to the second, desperate to find a friendly—or at least non-hostile—face. Despite his best efforts, he kept bumping into people in the tightly packed corridors. The nicer ones simply looked down their noses at him in disgust. Others pushed back and told him to watch where he was going.

Finally, after wandering back downstairs, he stumbled onto a garbage can full of hooch in the kitchen of the house. He grabbed a cup and quickly drank it down. The alcohol—pure grain, vodka, or whatever it was—quickly soothed his nerves. He refilled his cup and walked out of the kitchen toward one of the suites on the main floor.

Someone lightly touched his arm. "Excuse me. Where did you get that?"

He turned only to discover a girl blinking up at him. She was small, even smaller than he was. Her hair was straight and dark, her eyes brown. She wasn't beautiful, but she was cute. *Very* cute. And the fact that she was talking to him bumped her up to the status of a goddess. Kirk wasted a moment struggling to remember if a pretty girl had *ever* initiated a conversation with him for *any* reason.

"Your drink," she repeated. "Could you tell me where you got it?"

"Yeah, sure," Kirk said. "It's in the kitchen. Just down the hallway," he added, jerking a thumb back toward the way he had come.

"Thanks," she said earnestly. Then she did something that surprised him even more than speaking to him. She didn't immediately leave.

"I'm sorry," she said with a grin. "I'm just a guest. I've never been here before."

"Me either," he replied. "I just got invited by a friend who got invited."

"To be honest," she added, "I'm only a freshman. I've never even been to a college party before."

"It's a small world," he said. His inhibitions tempered by the alcohol, he was desperate to keep the conversation going. "Can I get you a drink?"

"Are you sure you don't mind?"

"Not at all," he replied. "It's too crowded for us both to go. Why don't I run down there and grab a cup for you?"

She smiled at him. "Only if you tell me your name first."

"Kirk," he said. "My name is Kirk."

"It's nice to meet you, Kirk," she said as she held out her hand. "My name is Alicia."

For the first time all evening, and maybe for the first time he could remember, Kirk didn't feel awkward. "Well, Alicia," he said, "let me get you that drink."

As he hurried toward the kitchen, eager to get back to her, Kirk was daring to dream. He was a college man, now. He had *arrived*.

He quickly grabbed a second cup, filled it with hooch, and began to make his way back to Alicia. But as soon as he looked down the hall, he realized she was no longer alone.

The Kappa Sig stood a foot taller than Kirk and was way over two-hundred pounds, probably closer to two-fifty. He had an enormous square jaw, his eyes were red, and his voice loud and slurred. He towered over Alicia, his mass preventing Kirk from being able to tell whether or not she actually welcomed his company.

Kirk continued to walk toward them, not quite knowing what to do. He came up to them and started to hand Alicia her hooch. For a second, he would have sworn he saw a glimpse of relief in her eyes. It was then that the giant turned on him.

"Excuse me there, buddy. Just what the hell do you think you're doing?"

Kirk tried to look around him, toward Alicia. The giant would have none of it.

"I asked you a question, *boy*." His voice was growing louder. People at both ends of the hallway began to stop what they were doing and crane their necks to see what the fuss was about.

"What do you think you're doing, bringing her a drink? Can't you see that she's with me? *Can't you?*"

Kirk heard Alicia yelling from what seemed like the other side of a mountain. "I'm not *with* you, you asshole. I'm not here with anyone. Leave him alone!"

But her rebuff only fueled the giant's anger. He took a couple of threatening steps toward Kirk, backing him against the wall.

"I asked you a question, twerp…now, *answer me!*" And with that, the Kappa Sig threw his enormous hand upward, slapping both of

Kirk's cups into his face. Grape hooch splattered all over Kirk's face and clothes.

The Kappa Sig grabbed him by his shirt collar and lifted him off the ground, pinning him against the wall.

"Now, see what you've done? You get invited into this house, twerp, hit on someone else's date, and then you get drunk and throw hooch all over our wall?" The giant's broad face was now as red as his eyes.

Kirk was shaking all over. He could hear Alicia screaming. Through the roaring in his ears, he thought he heard a couple of male voices telling his attacker to calm down, but no one was stepping forward to do anything.

"Got nothing to say for yourself, punk? Well, that's fine. I'll do the talking for both of us." The Kappa Sig held Kirk up with one hand and reared his huge fist back. Kirk tugged frantically at the meaty fingers closing around his throat, but it didn't budge. He squeezed his eyes shut as he heard several girls begin to scream. And then he heard the unmistakable thud of a fist hitting a jaw. But he felt nothing. Nothing at all. *Was he already dead?*

A stunned hush fell over the crowd. The pressure against his windpipe vanished and he slid down the wall to the floor in a crumpled heap, gasping for breath.

———

THE KAPPA SIGMA never saw the punch coming. He lay on his back in the floor for a full minute before slowly lifting his head. He shook his gigantic jaw a couple of times, then shifted his stunned gaze to his attacker.

Hunter Cameron stood between Kirk and the huge Kappa Sig. His right hand—his pitching hand—was broken. Hunter had heard it snap when his fist had connected with the giant's beefy jaw. Ignoring the searing pain, he clenched his other hand into a fist and raised it, prepared to defend himself and Kirk the best that he could.

Although he made no move to rise beyond propping himself on

one elbow, an ugly sneer curled the giant's lip. "You're a little too skinny to be playing the hero, ain't you, boy? I guess I'm just going to have to snap your scrawny neck."

Hunter knew full well that the overgrown mountain was entirely capable of making good on his threat. "That's exactly what you're going to have to do," he replied coolly, "if you plan to lay another hand on my friend."

Suddenly, Dax and a couple of other Kappa Sigs burst through the crowd and jumped in between the two of them. They yanked their grumbling fraternity brother to his feet and herded him away from the hallway.

Hunter turned around and offered Kirk his good hand. As Kirk staggered to his feet, still looking dazed in his rumpled, hooch-stained shirt, Dax yelled over his shoulder, "*Get the hell out of here, Cameron. I mean it! Now!*"

Hunter slowly nodded. Cradling his broken hand against his chest, he hustled Kirk out of the house. It had been a fabulous evening, he thought dryly. His roommate had been roughed up by a frat guy. His pitching hand was broken. Neither one of them would be allowed to join Kappa Sig, or perhaps any other fraternity.

But none of those things bothered him as much as his remaining thought. It was about the cheerleader...

He still hadn't gotten her name.

Chapter Twenty-Seven

Hunter was in the Christian County courtroom again. The soldier's courtroom.

He saw his father arguing with the prosecutor in front of the judge. He saw the judge banging his gavel. He saw the fat man in the overalls standing up in the jury box, reading from the piece of paper. He saw the soldier hang his head. He saw the soldier's wife jump from her seat and run screaming toward the front of the courtroom, where she was hauled down by the bailiffs.

The soldier's son was still seated in the front pew, with his back to Hunter. As the events were once again unfolding in front of them, the boy turned around and looked straight at Hunter as if they were the only two people in the courtroom.

Suddenly, Hunter looked away from the boy and down at himself, sitting in the pew next to the nice old lady. He wasn't twelve years old as he had been at the trial. His own body was taller, more mature. More adult than it had been six years ago.

He was eighteen years old. But how?

Stunned, Hunter looked up again at the soldier's son, but the little boy had turned back around and was politely watching the systematic destruction of his parents played out right in front of him.

Hunter wanted to go to the boy, to help him somehow. He started to stand, but something stopped him. He felt a hand on his shoulder forcing him back down. He struggled against the powerful grip, but to no avail. Finally, he tipped back his head to look directly into the face of his tormentor.

The man was huge, his dark suit straining to stretch across his thick chest and broad shoulders. His head was enormous, covered completely in fair skin mottled red. A tonsure of close-clipped red hair ran from ear-to-ear in the back. His eyes were too small for his head and their effect was unmistakably sinister. Hunter's terror coaxed a rare smile to the man's face. He knew Hunter had recognized him.

The man was Charles Warren. Kirk's father.

Hunter? The hand on his shoulder began to shake him.

Hunter? He was trying to pull away from the hand, but it wouldn't let go. The shaking became stronger, more violent.

Hunter!

His eyes flew open a split-second after he screamed. The first thing they saw was the bespectacled face of Kirk Warren, the son of his tormentor.

Kirk let go of Hunter's shoulder and stepped back from the bed. "You were having a bad dream," he whispered, the room behind him draped in shadows.

Hunter sat up in the bed. His heart was pounding, the t-shirt he slept in soaked through with sweat. He climbed out of the bed and trudged over to the sink. As Kirk returned to his own bed, Hunter flipped on the light and turned on the faucet. Careful not to get the plaster cast on his broken right hand wet, he used his left to splash cold water on his face, all the while hoping that Kirk wouldn't notice how badly both of his hands were shaking.

"You've been having them a lot, you know," Kirk said softly.

"Having what?"

"The nightmares. That's the third one this week."

Hunter lifted his dripping face to meet Kirk's gaze in the mirror. "How the hell do you know what I'm dreaming about?"

"My bed is ten feet away from yours," Kirk pointed out. "I don't sleep much to begin with and when you're tossing and turning and talking in your sleep all night, the odds are pretty decent that I'm going to notice."

Hunter grabbed a towel off a nearby shelf and dabbed at his face. He turned out the light and climbed back into his bed, then lay gazing wide-eyed into the darkness.

"They're about that soldier, aren't they?"

"What?"

"Your dreams—they're about the soldier?"

"What soldier?"

"Don't mess with me, Hunter. It's not becoming, particularly at two-thirty in the morning."

"What makes you think that I'm dreaming about him?"

"Just the things you mumble in your sleep. It's not too hard to guess."

"Why would I dream about him?"

"You'll have to answer that one for yourself, buddy. But I'd say the fact that he's supposed to be executed in three days has something to do with it."

This, Hunter knew, was the truth. The state appellate courts had affirmed the decision of the trial court. Appeals through the federal courts had ended with the U.S. Supreme Court refusing to hear the case. The soldier's only hope was a reprieve granted by the governor, an unlikely scenario made almost unimaginable given the manner in which the state's highest ranking official was indebted, both financially and politically, to the Warren family.

He turned toward Kirk's bed, propping himself up on one elbow. His friend was nothing more than a deeper shadow in the darkness. "I've never heard you mention him before."

Kirk pondered his words for a moment. "I guess I didn't really have anything to say about it."

"The man was convicted of murdering your mother. Surely you have some opinion on it."

"Not really."

Hunter felt an irrational surge of anger at Kirk's indifference. Kirk had lost his mother and the Vazquez case had all but ruined Hunter's own father, yet Kirk sounded as if were discussing something that had happened on television—maybe on some late-night soap or murder mystery. "How can you feel that way?" he demanded.

"I don't know," Kirk replied. "I never really thought about him as being responsible for it."

Hunter snorted, unable to believe what he was hearing. "That jury sure seemed to disagree with you."

"No, no. That's not what I meant." There was silence for another minute before Kirk's voice came drifting out of the darkness. "I guess I've always thought it was her fault."

"How could it have been her fault? She didn't kill herself."

"Yes, she did. To me, she did. To my father, she did. She did it by taking up with that soldier. She put herself in that situation. If she hadn't done that, she'd be alive today. It's that simple, really."

Hunter wondered for a moment if he was still dreaming. "So, you don't care whether or not he gets executed?"

"It's not up to me. None of my business, really."

The silence fell somewhere in the darkness between them. Hunter briefly wondered if Kirk had fallen back to sleep.

"So, your dad's not representing him anymore?"

"Nope," Hunter replied. "It apparently happens all the time on death penalty appeals. The new lawyer claims that the accused's lawyer screwed up at trial. 'Ineffective assistance of counsel' I think they call it."

"You don't think your old man screwed up the trial, do you?"

"No way. My dad's a great lawyer."

"Going to be a judge, soon, from what I hear."

"Yeah, looks that way. I hope he gets it. It can't be any worse than what his last few years of practicing law have been."

"Let me ask you something," Kirk said. "If your dad being a lawyer has been so hard on the two of you, why do you want to be one yourself?"

So I can make the dreams stop, Hunter thought.

"Because with my broken hand, which I got saving your ass, I won't be pitching or hitting my way into the Major Leagues anytime soon."

They both laughed then, though it was a little too forced to be anything other than awkward.

"Well," Hunter said, "I guess I'd better try to get to sleep. I've got to go meet with Coach Gates tomorrow to discuss my punishment for the fight."

"Wasn't breaking your hand punishment enough?" Kirk asked.

"Apparently not."

With that, their first and last conversation regarding the murder of Eleanor Warren was over.

Chapter Twenty-Eight

Hunter walked slowly out of his baseball coach's office, carefully shutting the door behind him. Their discussion had been decidedly one-sided. Predictably, the coach had not been sympathetic to the plight which had led to Hunter's broken hand. After all, the notion of a fight over a girl at a drunken frat party was not on par with rescuing orphaned kittens from a burning building. The fact that Hunter was defending his roommate was completely lost on his coach. The man's final words, spoken at an extremely high volume, still rang in Hunter's ears.

You'd better give your soul to God, boy...cause once that cast comes off, your ass is mine!

Fortunately, Hunter thought, fall practice was pretty much over. His hand would be fully healed and ready by spring. His ass, on the other hand, was apparently another matter altogether.

Hunter was deep in thought when he looked up. He was stunned to see the burly figure of Dax Handley standing at his locker.

"Hey, rookie," Dax offered.

"Dax."

"Listen," Dax said, "a lot of the guys were pissed at what you did. But a lot of other guys were glad that you did it, including me."

"The guy you hit is a real asshole. He's got that football player mentality and he doesn't know how to leave it on the field. A lot of us have wanted to do what you did, but nobody had the guts to do it. Until you." Dax reached into his jacket pocket, pulled out a small, card-sized envelope, and handed it to Hunter.

As Hunter gazed down at the envelope, baffled, Dax continued. "There's enough of us who think you're the kind of guy we want in Kappa Sigma Alpha."

Hunter had not considered even the possibility of such a gesture, let alone what his response to it would be.

"Well? What's it gonna be?"

Hunter pondered Dax's words. He liked Dax. He liked many of the other Kappa Sigs he had met before the fight had occurred. He liked the idea of being in a fraternity. Of being a big man on a small campus. Finally, and most importantly, he thought of the cheerleader whose name he had neglected to get in all of the excitement. Joining the fraternity would surely lead to another opportunity to see her again.

But his spirits sank as he remembered someone else. "What about Kirk?" he asked.

Dax frowned. "Who?"

"Kirk Warren. You know, my roommate. The guy I brought to the party."

Dax was perplexed. "What about him?"

Hunter held up the card. "Do you have one of these invitations for him?"

"No," Dax replied, his voice curt. "Why would I?"

"First," Hunter said, "he's a good guy. From what I saw the other night, he's better than several that you already have. Second," he continued, "he's my friend. The first one I had here and probably the best one I've got now."

"So?"

"So," Hunter continued, "I'm afraid we're a package deal." He kept his voice polite, but firm. "If there's no bid for him, there's no bid for me." Struggling to hide his own disappointment, he held out the card for Dax to take.

Dax stared at it, but made no effort to accept it from Hunter's outstretched hand. "Listen, rookie, you need to think this over. I mean *really* think this over." Dax's expression was stern, like that of an instructor lecturing a cadet. "I was able to pull some strings and get a bid for you. But there's a limit to what I can do."

"I know the feeling," Hunter replied. He turned around to resume cleaning out his locker.

Dax watched in stunned silence as Hunter stuffed the last of his things into the large duffel bag. He'd probably never had a prospective pledge turn down a bid for any reason, let alone one such as this.

Hunter zipped the bag shut and turned to face his teammate. "Listen," he said, "I appreciate everything that you've tried to do for me, Dax. I really do. But I'm just going to have to say 'no'."

"You know that there won't be another bid, don't you Rookie? Not next semester. Not next year. Not ever."

Hunter nodded. "I know." He gently patted his teammate on the shoulder as he passed.

He was walking out of the locker room when Dax's voice stopped him. "You always going to be there to fight other people's battles, Rookie?"

Hunter stopped. He thought about the question. About his father. And finally, about what he wanted to do with his life. He had liked standing up for Kirk. For someone who, for all of his wealth, had needed him. It had felt right—like something he'd been born to do.

Slowly, he turned to back to Dax. "Only if I'm lucky," he said, before he opened the door and walked out, allowing himself to be swallowed by the afternoon sun.

Chapter Twenty-Nine

A s Hunter strolled into the lobby of his dormitory, he was still thinking about the rueful expression on Dax's face after Hunter had rejected his invitation. Then he heard a familiar voice. A voice that had haunted him since the first time he had heard it.

Her voice.

She was standing at the front desk talking to a resident advisor. She wore a t-shirt and jeans as if they were a formal ballgown. Her thick, flowing hair was expertly tied back with a navy ribbon. The tan of the long-since-gone summer still clung to her shapely legs like a stowaway to a life raft. Hunter was too entranced by the sight of her to realize he was walking toward her.

She was talking in excited tones. "You don't understand," she said to the R.A., "I have to find him." She placed her small hands on the front desk, accentuating her desperation. "I've been to all the other dorms and they say that he doesn't live in any of them."

The R.A. was the short, stocky sort who wore glasses too small for his face. "That's all well and good," the boy said with an indignant sniff, "but you can't expect me to know if he lives here if you can't tell me his name."

Hunter waited for her reaction. He'd known from that first night that she wasn't like the other girls he had been with. She didn't suffer fools, particularly condescending ones, very easily.

She pointed a finger and blessed out the R.A. in a manner Hunter had never witnessed before. Wilting beneath the withering assault, the R.A. simply gave up, his shoulders slumping in defeat. Hunter felt a smile curve his lips. Had he not been so smitten, Hunter might have felt sorry for the kid.

There he was, Hunter realized, an eighteen-year old college freshman, fresh off of an ass-chewing of similarly epic proportion from his baseball coach, a nerve-racking rejection of a bid from the best fraternity on campus, a plaster cast hiding a broken, sweaty and rather itchy pitching hand. And in spite of all of this, he knew—by God, he just *knew*—that everything he had ever wanted was standing just a few feet away.

"Now, I'm going to ask you again,"—she paused just long enough to read the R.A.'s name tag—"*Johnny*…do you happen to know the name of a tall, dark-headed freshman baseball player who lives here? One of his hands may be hurt."

Johnny's face had flip-flopped from white to red and back again several times in the last few minutes. He desperately wanted out of the line of fire so when he peered over her shoulder and saw his means of escape, he heaved a sigh of relief.

"You mean *him*," he said, pointing a chubby finger.

The girl turned around and stared at Hunter. When he saw her face, for a moment—for one fleeting moment—his first thought was that he now understood exactly what it meant when the heavens smiled down at someone. But there was only one problem.

She wasn't smiling at him. She was glaring.

Hunter felt like he was in an interrogation room with the light directed right into his eyes. She strode toward him, cutting the distance between them down to a couple of feet.

"Hey, what are you doing—"

"You didn't tell me your name," she interrupted. She crossed her arms and arched one eyebrow. "Before you ran off to play Sir Lancelot, don't you think you could have told me your name?"

Hunter was so nervous he wasn't sure he could remember it. "I'm Hunter," he finally said. "Hunter Cameron." He started to extend his right hand, but was brought up short by the cast.

"Well, *Hunter Cameron,* if you'd shared that little bit of knowledge with me at the party, it would have saved me a lot of time, you know. I've been looking all over this campus for you."

"Why were you d-doing that?" he managed to ask.

She tapped her small foot. "Because I think you were about to ask me out on a date before you so *rudely* ran out on me."

Hunter felt his blood pressure begin to drop back down to a normal level. Catching on to her game, he said, "Oh, I was, was I? And just how was I supposed to ask you for a date when you never told me *your* name?"

Her lips were beginning to twitch at the corners. "You think I just give out my name to anyone who asks?"

"Maybe not. But," he said, his confidence growing by the second, "if you went to all this trouble to find me, including terror-izing this fine young gentleman here," he added, jerking a thumb toward the wide-eyed R.A., "I'd say that my chances are fair."

She laughed out loud then, a wonderful, husky, full-throated laugh unlike those he was used to hearing from the demure women in his hometown.

"Katherine," she said, no longer trying to stifle her laughter. "My name is Katherine."

Chapter Thirty

Having witnessed firsthand the effects of hooch on the brain of the average college athlete, Hunter and Kirk decided to take advantage of their newfound legality to buy their own beer.

Riding in Kirk's shiny new Camaro, they stopped at a store on the edge of town and bought a case of Budweiser. They drove to an old rural road a few miles from campus and found a spot where a local affiliate's broadcast of the Cardinal game was coming in clearly over the car radio. They each cracked open their first beers and took a swig. Both were ashamed to admit that they had liked the taste of the hooch better.

"So," Kirk said, "when's the big date?"

Hunter took another sip of his beer, struggling to hide his grimace. It tasted even more bitter than the first swig. "Thursday night, after I get out of science lab."

"Glad to see that the night at the Kappa Sig house wasn't a total loss," Kirk said. "At least for one of us. Did that Dax guy ever say anything to you about the party?" he asked, unable to completely disguise the hopeful note in his voice.

Hunter thought for a second and then shook his head. "No," he lied, taking another swig of his beer.

Kirk sighed. "Sorry I cost you that chance. Those guys were dying to give you a bid."

Hunter shook his head. "Nah. They're a bunch of assholes. Besides, I just don't think I'm a fraternity sort of guy."

"Apparently, neither am I," Kirk said, tapping his can against Hunter's in an impromptu toast. Kirk finished off his beer and leaned his head back against the seat, gazing out the window. "Neither am I," he repeated softly.

Hunter knew that the rejection by the Kappa Sigs had wounded Kirk badly. Some people went to college merely for the education. Others used college as a vehicle to start over. A fresh chance at all of the social opportunities lost because of being an awkward teen in high school. Hunter knew that Kirk had come to Centre College with the hope of reinventing himself, perhaps into something even he realized he could never be.

For a long time, they both sat without speaking. They continued to work on their beer, listening intently to the car radio as Jack Buck did his customarily brilliant job of calling the game. The game had made it through four innings—and four beers—when Kirk finally said, "You decided what you want to do?"

"Do with what?" Hunter asked as he struggled, cast and all, to pull back the top on number five.

"With your life." Kirk was still gazing out the window, as if he could see their future approaching in the distance.

"What makes you ask?"

"Isn't that what college is supposed to be about? Figuring out what you're going to do with the rest of your life?"

"I suppose."

"A lawyer," Kirk said.

Hunter would have sworn he heard a note of bitterness in Kirk's words. "What's that supposed to mean?"

"You said the other night you were going to be a lawyer, just like your dad. I think it's…I don't know…*ingrained* in you, somehow. I'm not sure you'd be good at anything else."

Hunter considered his friend's words, feeling unaccountably

annoyed. Kirk was right. He *was* going to be a lawyer. Just like his dad. It was almost as if he had never truly been master of his own fate. The realization made him feel both angry and exhilarated.

"I guess you're right," he finally admitted.

"Oh, I'm right," Kirk continued. "I'm just as sure of that as I am about what I'll be doing." He paused, prompting Hunter to ask the obligatory question.

"And that is?"

"What do you think, dumbass? I'll be running my father's company."

Kirk was right, Hunter thought. It was a dumb question.

"Yep," Kirk continued, "my dad decided my career path a long time ago, just like your dad did yours."

Had Hunter's head not been swimming from the beer, he would have taken offense to Kirk's notion that his father had pushed him to follow in his footsteps, which had definitely not been the case.

"But you're not going to be just *any* lawyer," Kirk said. "No sirree. You're going to be *my* lawyer." Kirk's voice had grown louder and its slurred cadences were making Hunter's head begin to ache. His eyelids were growing very heavy and all he wanted to do was steal a quick nap. "*My* lawyer," Kirk crowed again.

"Yeah, yeah, yeah," Hunter replied, his eyes drifting shut. He was irritated that he couldn't hear the game over Kirk's drunken rambling. "I'll be *your* lawyer."

And then there was silence. Blissful silence.

————

HUNTER WASN'T sure what woke him up. It could have been the sunlight beaming in through the car's windshield or the sound of the radio, which had continued to play all through the night after he and Kirk had passed out. Hunter was sure of only one thing.

He felt like hell. In fact, he wasn't sure hell could feel this bad.

Peeling his eyelids apart, Hunter squinted and struggled to determine exactly where they were parked. They were surrounded by rows of corn that seemed to extend to the ends of the earth.

They were definitely out in the boonies. Hunter just hoped they could make it back to Danville, since the route they had taken to get here was hazy at best.

Hunter nudged Kirk, who was snoring so profoundly Hunter feared it might continue even after he was awake. Kirk's head rested against the driver's side door. His glasses were dangling from one ear and a trickle of drool had dried at the corner of his mouth.

Hunter recoiled as Kirk snapped straight up to attention. He quickly paid the price, grabbing his head with both hands and groaning loudly. "Where are we?" he croaked.

"Beats the hell out of me," Hunter managed. "You're the one who drove us here."

Kirk smacked his lips. His mouth must feel just like Hunter's—as if it had been lined with wool. "Do we have anything to drink?"

"Yeah," Hunter replied dryly. "Beer."

Kirk was groaning again when a familiar tone sounded on the radio, heralding the morning newscast to follow. The sound of it seemed to pierce Hunter's aching skull. He reached to turn off the radio, but froze as the words delivered in the newscaster's nasal voice penetrated the beer-fueled fog still enveloping him.

At approximately 12:01 this morning, at the State Penitentiary in Eddyville, convicted murderer Javier Vazquez was put to death by means of electrocution.

Hunter slowly lifted his head to meet Kirk's wide-eyed gaze.

Vazquez was convicted nearly six years ago of the brutal murder of socialite Eleanor Warren, wife of prominent businessman Charles Warren...

———

HUNTER WENT OUT on his first date with Katherine the following Thursday. And on another one after that. And another one after that one. The dates continued through four years at Centre and then three more while Hunter was in law school at UK. They continued after Hunter and Katherine married and found their way back to Hopkinsville. And then, after they had their girls.

Kirk never did reinvent himself—not in college, nor in the years that followed. After his father passed away in 1995, he ascended to the leadership of his family's company. And there, he finally found his niche. The business, which he operated from his father's corporate office in Hopkinsville, was expanded into a more imposing empire than any of his predecessors could have envisioned. Kirk may have never been a social success, but he didn't suffer much rejection, either. After all, as he liked to say, it's awfully difficult to slam the door in the face of the guy who owns the house.

Bound together by the very circumstances that should have town them apart, Hunter and Kirk somehow managed to remain friends. True to his drunken pledge, Kirk hired Hunter to be his legal counsel, a relationship which helped to turn Hunter's fledgling law practice into a lucrative one. They ate lunch together twice a week, every week. Each stood for the other at their respective weddings. And Kirk was the first to hold each of Hunter and Katherine's girls after their births.

After the morning of his execution, Hunter and Kirk never again discussed Javier Vazquez or the murder of Kirk's mother. At least not for nearly forty years.

Not until Cassandra Warren, Kirk's wife, was murdered in the same bedroom in which his mother had been found.

Not until now…

Now
___

Part Three

Commonwealth v. Charles Kirkland Warren

Chapter Thirty-One

Looking across the carefully manicured lawn, Hunter saw Kirk's slight figure. His hands were cuffed behind his back and two burly state troopers flanked him on both sides, making him look even smaller. Hunter quickly pulled his car to the side of the narrow road and parked. He got out and made his way down the steep embankment and toward what was, he already knew, a murder scene.

Aside from the cuffs, Kirk looked almost exactly the same as he had when Hunter had first met him in that dorm room all those years ago. His expensive golf shirt and khakis were rumpled and looked as if he'd just fished them out the bottom of a laundry hamper. His narrow shoulders were positioned in their usual slump. The wisps of his thin, graying hair curled out and over his large ears, tossed by the midday lake breeze. Small eyes and thin lips did nothing to add character to his face. His vast family fortune and worldly success aside, he was what he'd always been—the last kid picked for every team at recess.

As Hunter made his way to the front lawn, a stocky young sheriff's deputy stepped in his path. He had on a pair of cheap gaudy sunglasses, no doubt chosen from the fine selection sitting atop the checkout counter at some convenience mart. He wore a no-nonsense crew-cut.

He folded his thick arms across a puffed-out powerlifter's chest. "And just where the hell you think you're goin'?"

Great, Hunter thought. *Lynyrd Skynryd on 'roids.*

Hunter knew the type well. In one fluid motion, he sidestepped the eager young deputy like a motorist ignoring a stop sign and expertly flipped the kid his card.

"I'm Hunter Cameron," he said. "Mr. Warren is my client." He didn't wait for a reply.

When he saw Hunter approaching, Kirk wrenched himself from the troopers' grips and awkwardly began to scramble toward Hunter. Caught off guard, the two troopers reached to restrain him, but quickly realized Kirk was not trying to flee.

"Cassandra's dead, Hunter! She's dead!" Kirk's voice, at best a high and jumpy tenor, was now an octave higher. Snickering, the troopers exchanged a glance.

"I found her and called 911. And now they think I did it! Just look at this!" He wheeled around, displaying his shackled hands to Hunter.

Hunter laid a hand on his friend's shoulder, hoping to calm him. He turned to one of the troopers, a man in his early forties whose slight paunch was only exaggerated by the form-fitting gray uniform issued by the KSP. Removing his hand from Kirk's shoulder, he offered it to the trooper, using that as his opportunity to guide the man out of earshot of Kirk and the second trooper.

"Hunter Cameron," he said with a smile, as though he was making the rounds at a dinner party.

The trooper reluctantly accepted Hunter's hand. "Trooper Redding," he said curtly.

"He's the one, Hunter," Kirk interrupted. "This *trooper* is the one who thinks I killed my wife! He thinks I killed Cassandra!"

Hunter turned a warning glare on Kirk. Even in his agitated state, Kirk recognized the look, pursed his lips, and stepped back.

Hunter still didn't trust his friend to maintain his cool very long in these circumstances. In his defense, most people wouldn't.

Hunter turned back to the trooper. "Aside from the obvious, can you tell me what's going on here?"

The trooper looked like a granite statue reading the weather report. "Well," he said, "near as we can tell, Mrs. Warren died a couple of hours after midnight, maybe two o'clock or so. Around eight-thirty this morning, EOC received a call from Mr. Warren. He claimed that he had just found her."

Hunter kept his face carefully impassive, but the answer startled him. How could Kirk have found her at eight-thirty if she had been dead for hours? "Did Mr. Warren tell you where he had been?"

Redding nodded. "Yes, sir. He said he spent the night on their yacht over at the State Resort Park Marina. Said he got here about eight-fifteen, eight-twenty. He called the victim's name several times and got no answer. He went into the bedroom and found her. Of course, she was long gone by the time he called EOC." Redding continued his rapid fire recitation as though he was preparing for cross-examination. "It appears Mr. and Mrs. Warren are separated and have been for some time."

Hunter's astonishment continued to grow. Why hadn't Kirk told him he and Cassandra were separated? An even more worrying possibility occurred. What if Kirk had told him and he had forgotten?

No, he wouldn't have forgotten *that*.

Would he?

Gathering his composure, he opened his palms and shrugged, feigning confusion. "Sounds reasonable enough. So why is the man in handcuffs?"

Redding sighed. They both knew Hunter already knew the answer to that question. "Mr. Cameron," he said, "whenever we have a homicide and the victim is estranged from his or her spouse, as is the case here, we immediately begin looking at the other spouse. Plus your client has no one to confirm his whereabouts or that he found the body or..." He didn't even bother with the rest. "We thought we should put a hold on him for now."

Hunter understood the rationale and, logically, he couldn't fault them for it. "Do you have anyone to confirm he was here at the time Mrs. Warren was allegedly murdered?"

Redding's lips thinned. "No, Counselor, we don't."

Counselor. A word intended to be a complimentary term for attorneys. Yet Hunter had never heard it said by anyone who meant it as anything other than a synonym for *asshole*.

"How was she killed?" he asked.

"Throat was slit. Sharp-bladed instrument."

Just like Eleanor Warren, Hunter thought, the shadow of an even deeper uneasiness creeping over him.

"Which bedroom?" he asked, already dreading the answer.

"The master bedroom," the trooper replied.

Hunter could no longer hide his mute horror as he gazed at the trooper. *Another Warren wife murdered, her throat slit. In the same bedroom, over forty years later?*

My God, he thought. *It really is happening again.*

He swallowed back his dread. "Do you have the weapon?"

Redding was reaching his limit. He stole a look at Kirk, who stood fidgeting nearby in the grip of the second trooper, then returned his steely gaze to Hunter. "No," he replied.

Hunter nodded. The police didn't have shit. Not yet anyway. Simply being the estranged husband of a murder victim was not nearly enough to even establish probable cause, the lowest standard of proof necessary for arrest. All well and good, Hunter thought, but it wouldn't do to have that particular debate. Not here. Not now. No, he would need someone with some ability to think objectively. Redding certainly didn't qualify.

That was when Hunter noticed a figure approaching from across the lawn. As the only person present wearing a navy blazer, tie, and khakis, Hunter quickly made him for a detective. His skin was a warm bronze, although it was impossible to tell if it was natural or from prolonged sun exposure. He wore the predictable aviator sunglasses and looked very fit. He stopped about twenty yards away to speak with a pair of loitering deputies. As one of them pointed to their little group, he made a gesture of thanks and walked toward Hunter and Redding.

"What's going on here, gentlemen?" he politely asked.

Hunter offered his hand. "I'm Hunter Cameron, Mr. Warren's attorney."

"Detective Anthony Newell, KSP." The man pulled a black leather folder from his pocket and briefly flashed his badge before tucking it back inside his jacket. Turning to Redding, he respectfully placed a hand on the trooper's shoulder. "Thanks Steve," he said, "I can take it from here."

Redding shot Hunter one last suspicious glare before nodding to the detective and walking away.

Newell offered Hunter a friendly smile. "I'm going to guess that your chat with Steve wasn't real chummy, Counselor."

"Nonsense," Hunter replied. "He and I were just deciding which one of us was going to buy the beer tonight."

Newell chuckled, stole a quick glance back at the house, then faced Hunter again. "So, Mr. Cameron, what's the deal with your client?"

"I was hoping you could tell me," Hunter replied. "Trooper Redding told me what happened to Cassandra. And I understand his point. They were apparently separated. But that along with the fact that he found her doesn't mean he should be taken into custody." Hunter kept his tone easy. This was no time to act outraged or indignant. "Redding also said there was no weapon found at the scene and no witnesses."

"Yeah, I know," Newell admitted. "The first officers to the scene probably jumped the gun when they realized your client was the estranged husband of the victim. Probably just some post-O.J. indigestion." The detective flashed a brief smile. Hunter was unaccustomed to such candor from law enforcement. Newell, he realized, was deliberately trying to disarm him.

"Does that mean that you're going to let him go?"

"Listen, Counselor. I've got a dead woman here. I know who she is and I know who your guy is." The words were matter-of-fact, not meant to either reassure or offend. "Under the circumstances—the separation, the fact that he found her—of course he's a suspect. He's the number *one* suspect, at least until we're able to investigate this case for a longer period of time than the two hours we've had so far. That's just our m.o." He grabbed a piece of Nicorette from his shirt pocket, popped it into his mouth, and continued. "But for right now, what we have isn't enough for probable cause to arrest and I know it."

Hunter was slightly taken aback by the casual manner in which this detective was handling the situation. Newell had a murder scene at a sizable home, flooded with law enforcement, with both the suspect and his attorney standing within five feet, yet he seemed perfectly comfortable with the situation. Odd, Hunter thought. Most cops in this situation would be either tough-guy arrogant, just looking for orders to bark out, or would be simply a nervous wreck, not knowing what to do first. Newell was neither. He seemed completely in his element.

"So, you're going to release him?" he asked.

"Looks that way," Newell replied. He motioned over the two troopers supervising Kirk. The bigger of the two quickly approached. Newell leaned over and said something in a hushed tone. The trooper nodded, then walked back over to Kirk and unlocked the handcuffs.

Turning back toward Hunter, Newell's expression became more serious. "I'm sure you know the drill by now, Counselor, but I'll repeat it. Your guy is still a suspect. I'd tell you that he shouldn't leave town, but you and I both know that I don't have the power to stop him, at least not for now. But," he continued, "I also don't have to tell you how bad it would look if he skipped out on the heels of his wife's murder. I don't have probable cause now, but I might then. Do we understand one another?"

Hunter nodded. Until there was another suspect, all eyes would be on Kirk. But that wasn't important right now. He needed to get Kirk away from the scene quickly before anyone changed their mind.

Hunter took out a business card and handed it to Newell.

"What are the odds your guy is willing to be interviewed?" Newell asked as he prepared to go back into the house.

"We'll see," Hunter said and shook Newell's hand.

Hunter turned and went to Kirk. Once the cuffs had been removed, he had gone from combustion to exhaustion. Despite his power, Kirk was still not much of an authority figure. He was able to survive in the boardroom because it was *his* company. But outside of that arena, he still looked like a small kid, easily bullied.

After rubbing his reddened wrists, he straightened his thick-rimmed glasses and ran his palms through the wisps of his remaining hair. He was clearly trying to regain his composure, but could not stop shaking.

"What did you say to them?" he demanded. "How did you get them to let me go?"

Hunter placed a steadying hand on Kirk's back. "It wasn't anything I did. They just don't have enough to arrest you."

"They damned sure thought they did a few minutes before you got here."

"Yeah, well," Hunter replied, "I suggest we don't stick around long enough to give them a chance to change their minds. Let's get the hell out of here."

Kirk nodded in agreement. "My vehicle's over there," he said, pointing toward the circular drive where his luxury SUV was parked.

"I think we'd better take mine, Kirk."

Kirk blinked at Hunter. "Why can't we take mine?"

Hunter reminded himself that not everyone knew how to act around a police investigation, particularly one in which they were the chief suspect.

"Kirk, you're a murder suspect. KSP has control of this entire scene, including your car. You won't be able to come back here until they're done with the investigation."

"And when will that be?"

Hunter turned and surveyed the goings-on around him. There

were at least six different police cars, all with their lights flashing, parked around the house. He and Kirk were the only two people here without a badge. There were at least five different crime techs walking around with their trusty kits. The whole scene left him feeling dazed and unsettled.

"It's going to be a while."

Chapter Thirty-Two

Kirk sat slumped on the leather couch in Hunter's home office with his hands folded in his lap, staring blankly at the pattern of the Oriental rug in front of him. Hunter sat behind his desk, gazing out the window at the woods that flanked his house.

"Kirk," he finally said, "I realize you must be in shock right now, but I need you to tell me what happened back there. I need to know everything."

"About what?" Kirk blinked at him, looking genuinely surprised. Hunter felt a flare of irritation that the wealthy—even the small and weak wealthy—seldom felt the need to answer other people's questions.

"Well, for starters, when did you and Cassandra separate? I'm supposed to be your best friend and I got the news from the state police."

Kirk ducked his head, going back to staring at the rug. "What was I going to say, Hunter? That Cassandra and I weren't getting along. That we *never* got along. Did I really need to tell you that? I mean, I gave you credit for figuring that one out on your own."

"A lot of people don't get along, Kirk."

"Yeah, and a lot of people separate, too."

"That's true. But they usually tell their best friend when they do. How long has it been?"

Kirk sighed and rubbed his face with both hands. "A couple of months, I guess."

"Jesus, Kirk," Hunter said, no longer trying to hide his anger or his hurt. "How many times have we talked during that time? How many times did we eat lunch together? Why didn't you say something?"

Kirk eased back against the couch, finally lifting his eyes to meet Hunter's gaze. "I guess I was embarrassed."

It was Hunter's turn to sigh. Maybe Kirk should be angry at *him*. After all, he was the one who had failed to notice his best friend's suffering.

"It's nothing to feel embarrassed about," he said, hating the platitude even as he uttered it.

"That's easy for you to say, Hunter. Katherine worships the ground you walk on. You've got your girls. Life is pretty good for you, the way it's been ever since I've known you." He paused, then continued. "You can't tell me you didn't know how things were between Cassie and me. Everyone had to know. When you saw the two of us together, didn't you ever wonder what in the hell a woman like that was doing with *me?*"

Refusing to let Kirk wallow in self-pity, Hunter said quietly, "No, Kirk. Quite often, I wondered the opposite."

Hunter had known Cassandra ever since she and Kirk began dating fifteen years ago. She was twelve years Kirk's junior and was, by anyone's standard, a knockout. The courtship was whirlwind, but the couple had appeared quite happy. There had never been any children, but Hunter had never known if that was because Cassandra couldn't...or wouldn't. What Hunter *was* sure of was that he had never completely warmed up to her.

He found her gaudy, a sort of redneck version of the *nouveau riche*. She hadn't come from much and before the echo of the wedding bells could fade, Cassandra began surrounding herself with the accoutrements of the wealthy. She maintained an umpteen-series BMW, seemingly buying a new one every few months. Her chest, already considerable, had been pumped full of silicone. She had double aerobic sessions almost daily so she could fit into clothing that was no doubt designed with someone a generation younger in mind. But it wasn't her questionable taste in clothing that put Hunter off. It was the way she treated Kirk.

During the early days of the marriage, she seemed attentive and loving to him, sometimes overly so, as though she was trying to convince everyone, especially herself, of her affections. Through the years, that affection had given way to indifference and finally to periodic displays of disgust. Hunter had been married long enough to know most spouses occasionally said dumb, hurtful things to one another. But with Cassandra there was something different: an undercurrent of disrespect in her words which only deepened when she'd had too much to drink. Hunter had never found the habit particularly becoming.

Kirk simply brushed off her comments. He was openly affectionate with his wife…when she would allow it. And when she wouldn't, he would laugh it off. Hunter had never seen him disagree with her in any fashion, let alone say "no" to virtually anything she wanted. He seemed content in her presence in the same way a freezing person is content to bask in a narrow ray of sunlight. That he was now a chief suspect in her murder was difficult to imagine.

"Yeah," Kirk said, interrupting Hunter's train of thought. "You never cared much for her, did you?"

The question was rhetorical, Hunter knew, so he was spared giving Kirk an honest answer. After all, the woman was his best friend's wife. And she was on her way to the coroner's office at that very moment.

"So," Kirk asked, "what do we do next?"

"Nothing we really can do until they finish their investigation at the house," Hunter replied. "And God only knows how long that will take."

"Oh, well. I've been staying on the boat anyway." Kirk heaved a deep sigh. "Besides, I really don't want to go back to the house. Not now. Maybe not ever."

"I understand. Kirk," Hunter said, no longer able to delay the inevitable question, "do you know who might possibly want to do this to Cassandra?"

Kirk spent a moment in thought, then shook his head. "I don't have any idea."

Well, you'd better get one soon," Hunter thought grimly. He decided to stop pushing for now. There would be plenty of time to develop a list of potential suspects. He only hoped the state police would be doing likewise, as opposed to merely focusing their investigation on Kirk. Not that he could blame them if they did, at least not initially.

He decided to take a different approach. "So where were you last night? Do you have an alibi?"

Kirk's reply was deadpan, as though he had already realized the ramifications of his answer. "I was on the boat."

"Alone?"

"Yep."

Hunter tried to hide his disappointment, but he knew the absence of an alibi witness in a case such as this one was damning.

"What made you go over to the house this morning?" he asked.

Kirk fidgeted, just long enough to make it clear that he didn't like the question, then said, "I had to talk to Cassie about something."

Hunter arched one eyebrow. "About what?"

Kirk began rocking back and forth on the sofa.

"Kirk," Hunter said, his irritation growing, "why did you go to the house this morning?"

Kirk went back to gazing at the rug. When he spoke, his voice was soft, as though he was afraid that he might break something with it. "I had to talk to her about the papers."

Hunter took a deep breath and rubbed his forehead, which was beginning to ache. *"What* papers?"

Kirk slowly raised his head and met Hunter's gaze. "Divorce papers. Cassie had me served with divorce papers."

Jesus, Hunter thought. *This just keeps getting worse.* "When did she have you served?"

Kirk looked down at his feet again. "Yesterday afternoon."

Chapter Thirty-Three

Detective Anthony Newell stood at the bow of the Warrens' massive yacht, gazing out across the harbor of Lake Barkley. Although it was only ten-thirty, the morning sun was already bearing down upon the forensics team working the scene. Sweat poured down foreheads and shirts stuck to backs. But Newell, navy blazer and all, seemed immune to the heat. He wasn't even sweating.

His Ray Bans thwarted any efforts to determine what, if anything, he was focused on in the distance. To the casual observer, he might have simply been daydreaming. But to those who knew Newell, and more particularly the power of his intuition and attention to detail, his quiet gaze was more indicative of confidence: the unspoken swagger of someone who knew he was about to find exactly what he was looking for.

As bubbles rose to the water's surface, the masked face of a diver emerged. The diver shook his head, clearing water from his face. Diving for clues in Lake Barkley was not nearly as glamorous as the expeditions on TV crime dramas. The lake was better known as a fertile ground for fishing than as a great place to swim. Its waters were a murky green and its floor a mixture of litter that rivaled the contents of any salvage yard in the area. Finding useful evidence in this water was a task almost as daunting as it was distasteful.

Newell looked down at the diver. "Any luck?"

"Not yet," the tech replied. "There's an awful lot of shit down there. A lot of aluminum, mostly beer cans. I could make a killing in recycling."

Newell offered a clipped grin in response. "Keep looking. We're looking for something shiny, but it'll be steel, not aluminum."

The diver nodded and wiped away the dirty water running down his face. "The problem is that with all of the shit down there, it's pretty damned difficult to tell what's what. It could take a hell of a long time just to look in about a fifty-foot radius."

Newell was either oblivious to the tech's frustration or unaffected by it. "That's okay," he said, smiling down at the man. "It just so happens I've got a hell of lot of time."

The tech snorted and shook his head. "Well, we don't have a hell of a lot of time," he replied. "We've got a shitload of cases we need to be working on right now. Cases where we have a snowball's chance of finding real evidence."

Newell's affable smile faded.

The tech, undaunted, decided to take a more direct approach. "Do you really believe this Warren guy would slit his wife's throat and then come here and dump the weapon off the edge of his yacht?"

"Well," Newell replied, a fresh edge to his words, "you haven't found anything yet, have you?"

"That's my point, detective," he said.

Newell returned his foot to the yacht's rail and went back to gazing across the water. "Then keep looking," he said.

Chapter Thirty-Four

Loren Gresham Owen, Jr. eased back in his mammoth executive's chair. Sturdy though the chair was, it whined as it absorbed his considerable weight, all but cursing its manufacturers for signing it up for a fight it could never win.

He looked across the top of his mahogany desk. His parents had bought it for him at an antique flea market twenty years ago after he had passed the bar exam and hung out a shingle in the back room of a run-down beauty salon, the only office space he could afford at the time. Since that day, the desk had gradually been sanded down and refinished, much like its owner. It had followed him all the way from the back of that salon to the Office of the Commonwealth's Attorney, where it now served him in his position as the chief prosecutor for Christian County.

Running his hand across the desk, he could feel the many layers of fine wood that defined the structure. It was not lost on him that the desk depicted him in many ways words could not: grand and intimidating in size and design, but beneath the surface warm and imminently reliable. The only thing about him that suggested brevity and restraint had been the merciful shortening of his name to its first two initials.

It was five o'clock and his office staff was in the process of evac-
uating *en masse*. L.G. waited patiently for the last *see you tomorrow*, the
last footstep in the hall, and the last closing of the back door. Once
reassured that the coast was clear, he rose from his desk and snuck—
in that inimitable way that only a six-foot six, three hundred-pound
man can sneak—across the hall and into the small kitchen located
directly across from his office. He found his trusty bottle of vodka in
the cabinet, then retrieved the grapefruit juice from the fridge and
mixed himself a Salty Dog, his drink of choice. He would allow
himself one, no more than two, on any given day. Never enough to
have a buzz when he finally went home to Jane and the kids.

Drink in hand, he strode back into his office and waited for the
call from the boat dock. Like the winds that precede a storm, he
knew it was coming. He had been prosecuting for far too long to
ignore the old adage of fire accompanying smoke.

Some prosecutors would envy the opportunity that would soon
be staring him in the face. A high-stakes, high-publicity murder trial
was a stepping stool for most prosecutors. Especially those with
visions of ascending to the great heights of a judicial seat. Or the
legislature. Perhaps even the governor's mansion.

But L.G. wasn't most prosecutors.

He was quite content with his current position and did not
aspire to a loftier one. When he prosecuted a case, he did so with
fervor. Not to enhance his reputation or his numbers, but because
he couldn't help himself. He was an emotional person, prone to
personal involvement with his cases and to explosive displays of
temperament when crossed by defense attorneys. In his more intro-
spective moments, he was willing to admit to himself that he
enjoyed playing the hero. He liked being the county's protector
against criminals. *I got big shoulders*, he'd say, his ample chest thrust
outward as if to prove it. He welcomed trials, not for the personal
attention, but because they sent a message that crime would not be
tolerated in Christian County. Not on his watch. And he wasn't
about to give up that watch just so he could take another perceived
step up the political ladder.

The Warren woman had been brutally murdered. On his watch.

And it was his responsibility to prosecute her killer. Even if that killer turned out to be the wealthiest man in the state. He knew the publicity would be overwhelming, especially for a small town.

That's all right, he assured himself. *I got big shoulders.*

He took another sip of his drink just as the light on his private phone line as it began to blink.

AT SIX-THIRTY THAT EVENING, Hunter received a phone call at the office. It was his direct line, a number to which only his family and staff were privy. That's why Hunter was surprised to hear L.G. Owen on the other end of the line. Although L.G.'s voice was congenial, Hunter knew the news would not be good.

"Hope you don't mind me calling on this line," L.G. said. "I called your house first, but Katherine said you were at the office and gave me the number."

"No problem," Hunter replied, still bracing himself for the proverbial other shoe to drop. "How can I help you?"

"I'm afraid I've got some bad news for your boy," L.G. replied.

Although he was currently defending a number of cases against L.G., Hunter never doubted for a moment who the *boy* was. He might have bristled at the term from another prosecutor. But experience had taught him that L.G. was different. Despite his job as prosecutor, the man had a heart as big as his waistline.

Hunter leaned back in his chair, readying himself for the inevitable. "Okay," he said. "Shoot."

"KSP just found a straight razor in the water about twenty yards off the deck of his yacht."

Hunter was glad L.G. wasn't there to see him flinch. His worst fears for his best friend were already coming to fruition. Keeping his voice carefully neutral, he said, "So?"

"It wasn't rusted, so it hadn't been there long at all."

"Anything else?" Hunter knew there was more. L.G. wouldn't have bothered to call if they had only found the razor.

"The medical reports aren't back yet, but we know the murder weapon was a smooth blade, not a serrated one. A straight razor would be consistent with that type of wound."

They both knew there were a dozen other sharp objects that could also be consistent with that type of wound. There was still absolutely nothing to tie this particular straight razor to Cassandra Warren. And barring where it was found, little to tie it to Kirk. "I hope you've got more than that," Hunter said, growing weary of L.G.'s leisurely tones.

"We do," L.G. admitted. "The blade was engraved with initials. It was also wrapped in a towel monogrammed with the same initials. '*CKW*'. Sound familiar?"

Hunter briefly squeezed his eyes shut.

L.G. gave him a moment to process the information before pointing out, "We've got enough for probable cause,"

Indeed you do, Hunter thought.

L.G. wasn't finished. "We're getting an arrest warrant signed by the judge right now. We're going to have to bring him in, Hunter."

Hunter propped his forehead on his hand. He couldn't decide what troubled him more: the incriminating evidence or the prospect of informing Kirk he was about to be taken into custody on the charge of murder.

L.G. sighed, no doubt knowing the toll his words were taking on Hunter. "So, can you bring him in or do I need to have him picked up?"

"I'll have him at the jail in a couple of hours."

Chapter Thirty-Five

C hristian County District Court was rumored to be the place where time went to die. If that was the case, time had chosen its tomb rather appropriately.

District Court was held in the cleverly-titled *Hall of Justice* in Hopkinsville. The building was only about twenty years old, but looked much older. The overhang had not been cleaned in nearly a decade, indicative of a rural county's lack of initiative, funds, or both. The peeling exterior paint hung lazily from the wall in random shreds, some of which tore off when the wind was strong enough and floated away like dead leaves in the fall.

The building housed two small courtrooms, the larger of which was used principally for misdemeanor criminal dockets and probate matters. The building also included tiny offices for each of the two District Court judges and a small area between for the secretary whom they shared. This area, accessible from the back of each courtroom, was important to the attorneys because this was where the secretary kept the coffee. Coffee was an indispensable tool in enduring the District Court criminal docket.

Hunter sipped his coffee from a white Styrofoam cup as he sat in

the tiny conference room. It was only eight-thirty on Friday morning, a good half-hour before court would begin, and a crowd of
public defenders, private attorneys, and police officers was already
forming inside the stuffy room.

Hunter had long ago learned not to schedule any appointments
or hearings to follow an appearance here. The majority of the criminal cases were misdemeanors, principally minor assaults, bad
checks in amounts under five hundred dollars, and minor dope
cases. However, in a felony case in which an arrest had been made
prior to the case having been heard by the county's Grand Jury—
which was the case about ninety-nine percent of the time—the
accused would be arraigned here in District Court and afforded the
opportunity for a preliminary hearing.

The purpose of the hearing was for the judge to determine,
after a bare-bones presentation of case evidence by the prosecution,
whether it appeared more likely than not that the accused
committed a crime; or using legal jargon, whether or not probable
cause existed for the police to make the arrest. Regardless of the
legal standard to which the prosecution was held, the practical standard was much, much lower. About as difficult as stepping over a
crack in the sidewalk, Hunter's dad had always said.

Reality dictated that a District Court judge, with forty to sixty
other cases on the day's docket, was almost never going to dismiss a
felony charge after hearing five to ten minutes of testimony from the
prosecution witness, usually the investigating officer. Granted, the
accused had the right to call his or her own witnesses at the hearing
and could even testify himself. However, given the likelihood that
the judge would make a finding of probable cause anyway, there
was little reason for the accused to provide the state with a not-so-
sneak preview of his or her defense. So the hearing was often
treated by local defense attorneys as a ministerial function.

In fact, the accused, on advice of the defense attorney, often
waived the hearing. This would put the case on the fast track to the
Grand Jury, where the return of an indictment was even more likely
than a finding of probable cause by the District Court. Once the
Grand Jury indicted the accused, the case would reach its ultimate

destination of Circuit Court. There the charges would either be resolved by agreement between the Defendant and the Commonwealth, or it would be scheduled for trial.

While Hunter didn't suffer under any delusions of getting felony charges dismissed at this level, it was nonetheless his normal practice *not* to waive the hearing. For him it was an exercise in obtaining simple answers to who, what, when, where, and why. It also gave the client a *Cliff's Notes* version of what was to come. Naturally, some of them had watched enough of *Court TV* to think that the preliminary hearings held in California, which apparently lasted for months, were the norm. Like the rest of the legal world outside California, Hunter couldn't help but wonder what the hell they were doing out there. He always informed each of his clients that this particular step of the criminal process was handled much more economically and decisively in Kentucky. Once the case was called, it would likely take no more than ten minutes before the case was whisked away to the Grand Jury. Unfortunately, what wasn't efficient about the process was the wait beforehand.

Hunter knew his client was unaccustomed to waiting for anything. Kirk was probably naively entertaining notions of prevailing at the preliminary hearing and getting his case dismissed. Given what little Hunter knew of the Commonwealth's case—and there was likely more to come—he had told Kirk he had a better chance of meeting God this morning than he did of seeing the judge make a finding of no probable cause.

The morning's docket was being covered by David Darnell, a young assistant prosecutor with the County Attorney's office.

After spending a couple of hours dealing with the public defender and her rash of cases, Darnell exhaled deeply and turned to Hunter. "Hey, Mr. Cameron," he said. "How're you this morning?"

Hunter felt compelled to tell Darnell to call him by his first name. Though Darnell was obviously just being respectful, Hunter was certain he had given him the same permission a couple of times before. *Or had he?*

"I'm not envying your caseload this morning," Hunter replied. "That's for certain."

"Yeah," he said. "I'm just muddling through another week. Going through the motions of handling this godforsaken docket."

Darnell was clearly in the latter stages of his tenure with the position. He had begun to make no secret of his opinion that his job was not to be an insurer of justice, but just to move things along.

He and Hunter made small talk about baseball as Darnell shuffled through the brown envelopes that covered the cheap, state-issued buffet table. Finally, he located the case file with the name WARREN, CHARLES KIRKLAND printed in all caps at the top. He pulled it from the pile and handed it to Hunter.

"I believe this one belongs to you," he said.

Hunter gave the cover of the file a perfunctory glance. He already knew it contained all of Kirk's personal information—address, date of birth, social security number—all in small type. Next to the line titled CHARGE were the words "Murder, First Degree". Hunter felt an icy shudder go through him as he read the words, almost as if it was the first time he had ever seen them. He had defended many murder cases and had earned acquittals in several of them. But if he was continuing to feel this much anxiety simply from looking at the case file cover, was he making a huge mistake by agreeing to defend his best friend on the charge of murder?

Darnell was already busy scribbling a note on another file. "Well," he said "I assume that you still want the preliminary."

"Yeah, I expect so," Hunter replied.

"Your guy's out, isn't he?"

"I got L.G. to agree to allow bond before he turned himself in."

"Let me see that file for a minute," Darnell said. He flipped through the guts of the file until he found the bond documents. He whistled when he saw the amount. "One million dollars." He turned an impressed look on Hunter. "That's the first seven figure bond I've actually seen someone make. Rank has its privileges, I guess."

Hunter nodded. In western Kentucky, it usually took several

days of scraping and borrowing from relatives and neighbors for a criminal defendant to post a cash bond of even ten thousand dollars. However, after L.G. had told him that an arrest warrant was being issued, he had told Kirk to give him a check in that amount to deposit in the law office trust account. When he went with Kirk to the police department, he had the bond check ready. Kirk had been booked and processed at the jail and they had walked out within two hours.

"Your officer here?" Hunter asked.

"I haven't seen him yet," Darnell said. "I'm sure he'll be around. This isn't one that he's likely to leave off his calendar."

"What do you know about Newell?" Hunter inquired.

The question might have been considered odd or even inappropriate in larger, more urban, court settings. But this was Hopkinsville and like other small towns, it carried little of the rigid formalities of big city law practice. It was not unusual for a defense lawyer to ask questions about particular police officers. Is this guy reasonable or is he a pain in the ass? How well does this guy testify? How does your officer feel about the case? And usually, the prosecutors would tell them what they thought. Darnell was no exception.

"To tell the truth," he said, "I don't know him that well." He stopped briefly to review a note he had just written on a file. "I've had a couple of prelims with him. No trials. He seems pretty sharp, though."

Hunter knew Darnell was telling the truth. Hunter had pretty much sized up Newell the same way during their initial encounter at the Warren lake house.

Darnell continued. "He hasn't been here that long. I hear he's got a pretty good rep in some of the other counties."

"You know where he's from?" Hunter asked.

"Not a clue."

"Wonder how he ended up here?"

"Hell if I know," Darnell said. "Maybe he likes to fish. Isn't that why everyone ends up here?"

Hunter smiled, then decided to move on to more practical

matters. "How long do you think we'll be until we get in front of the judge?"

"Not long," Darnell replied. "It looks like the P.D.'s going to be awhile. I can probably get the judge to go ahead and do this case first. It'll get all the damned cameras out of the courtroom."

Yes, it would, Hunter thought. He had left Kirk at his office for the express purpose of avoiding those cameras, at least for as long as he could. The office was only two blocks away from the courthouse. It would be easy to call him ten or fifteen minutes before the hearing. Kirk would not be testifying at the hearing so there were no last minute preparations to be done.

"Let me call Dispatch and find out how quickly Newell can get here," Darnell said.

"There's no need," Detective Newell said as he strolled through the doorway, wearing a friendly smile. Darnell rose and Newell shook the man's hand, then turned to Hunter, who was now standing as well. "Good to see you again, Mr. Cameron," he offered, still smiling.

"You, too," Hunter replied. He wondered just how long Newell had been standing in the doorway.

Newell looked the same as he had a few weeks earlier, Hunter thought. Only this time the Ray Bans were gone, revealing eyes of a peculiar greenish-brown hue, as though they were unwilling to commit to any particular color. Still, they were not unfriendly, especially when combined with Newell's warm smile. Something about them, however, gave Hunter the impression that this was a man who had seen more pain than most.

"So," Newell said, "are we having a prelim or does your guy want to waive?"

"Well, since we're all here," Hunter replied "may as well have the preliminary. It shouldn't take long."

"They never do." Newell took a small sip of his coffee. "It's usually the wait that kills."

"Not today," Darnell assured him. "I've already told Mr. Cameron we'd try and do this one early. Get rid of all those damned reporters in the courtroom. It'll make the judge happy." He stopped the file shuffling long enough to throw a sarcastic grin to Newell. "I assume you've got no objection to that, Detective?"

"None, whatsoever," Newell said as the three men headed for the courtroom.

Chapter Thirty-Six

The scowl on the face of the Honorable Richard Setchell as he presided on the District Court bench was indicative of the contempt with which he viewed his job. His scowl deepening, he yanked off his bifocals and peeled the hide off of a defendant who had not complied with court-ordered counseling of some sort. To the District Court regulars, Setchell minus bifocals could only mean one thing—he was pissed. These days, most of them swore the bifocals were off the vast majority of his time on the bench.

At fifty-eight, he had been on the District Court bench since the state legislature had created the position some thirty years before. He had run for the position following a brief and thoroughly dismal run at private law practice. The fact that no one had wanted the position at the time had not swayed him from seeking the appointment. It was his life raft. However, years on the District Court bench doing the legal equivalent of menial labor had taken their toll on the judge.

He was generally well-liked when the robe was off. However, when Setchell strode to the bench, a change would come over him. It was as though donning the robe confirmed that his youthful dreams of legal greatness—the ones all law students have—were nothing more than illusions of grandeur. In his mind, he was just a minor league judge presiding over a minor league courtroom. And he dealt with his own professional disappointment by using it as a weapon.

At best, he would mix learned rulings with acerbic commentary. At his worst, he was a bully who insulted both parties, and if the mood struck him, the attorneys and clerks, too. On the bright side, Setchell played no favorites. Neither prosecutors nor defense attorneys were safe from his wrath. He was, by all accounts, an equal opportunity asshole. He was set to retire at the end of his current term and it was generally believed that every morning at about eight-thirty, everyone who worked in Setchell's court—lawyers and clerks alike—took out black magic markers and marked another "X" on his or her calendar, counting down the days until Judge Setchell relieved the judicial establishment of the burden of his company.

The phalanx of reporters and cameras in the courtroom had done little to raise the judge's spirits. But Darnell's idea of doing the Warren preliminary hearing early in the docket was a good one. Darnell now stood at one of the two podiums that flanked the bench with Anthony Newell at his side. At the opposite podium stood Hunter with his client, Kirk Warren.

On cue, Darnell said, his voice ringing like a bell. "Your Honor, may we call the case of *Charles Kirkland Warren?*"

As the back of the courtroom rustled with reporters moving to get into position to watch the proceedings, Judge Setchell complied, rather eagerly by his standards, with the request. "The Court calls the case of *Commonwealth versus Charles Kirkland Warren.*"

Judge Setchell paused and looked at the docket for a moment, as though he needed to be reminded of the matter at hand. Looking up, he continued. "This case is scheduled for a preliminary hearing. Mr. Darnell, is the Commonwealth ready to proceed?"

"Yes, your Honor," Darnell replied.

The judge looked at Hunter. "Mr. Cameron, are you and your client ready to proceed?"

Hunter leaned inward to the podium's microphone, which was likely only turned on because of the anticipation of such a big crowd. "Yes, your Honor."

The judge turned back to Darnell. "How many witnesses for the Commonwealth?"

Darnell was in the middle of pulling the guts of the file from the envelope, looking for the warrant from which he would ask most of his questions. He looked up and replied, "Just one, your Honor."

The judge nodded. There was nothing unusual about this, given that the hearing was for the sole purpose of establishing probable cause and that hearsay was allowed in this limited instance.

"Very well," the judge said. "Mr. Darnell, you may call the Commonwealth's first witness."

"Your Honor, the Commonwealth calls Detective Anthony Newell."

Newell stepped forward from Darnell's side to stand in the small witness box immediately to the judge's left. He raised his right hand at the judge's request and was administered the obligatory oath.

"Would you state your name, please?" Darnell asked.

"Detective Anthony Newell."

"With whom are you employed?"

"I am a detective with the Kentucky State Police."

"Were you on duty on June 15 of this year?"

"Yes, sir."

"In the scope of your duty, did you obtain a warrant of arrest against a Charles Kirkland Warren?"

"Yes, sir. I did."

"Would you please explain to the court the facts and circumstances that led you to obtain this arrest warrant against the Defendant, Charles Kirkland Warren?"

Newell turned slightly to direct his answers to the judge. His voice was crisp and measured. He had no notes with him and it was clear he was completely at ease in the witness chair.

"On the morning of June 15, at approximately 8:35 am, E.O.C. received a call from the Warren residence. The caller said he had entered the home and found the victim dead in the bedroom."

Without any sort of prompting, Newell paused to allow Darnell to ask him the next question. Hunter was impressed. The guy was a pro.

Darnell played right along. "Do you know of the identity of the caller?"

Newell nodded. "Yes, sir. It was the Defendant. He identified himself immediately at the beginning of the call. He said that the victim was his wife."

Darnell nodded, as though this testimony was news to him. "What happened next?"

"Two cars were immediately dispatched to the scene, along with an ambulance," Newell said. "I wasn't in Christian County that morning, so it took me awhile to get there. I arrived at about 9:20 after the EMT's had arrived."

"What was the condition of the victim when you arrived?"

"She was dead," Newell responded. "Her throat had been slit, virtually ear to ear."

Hunter felt himself grimace upon hearing the words. Without being too obvious, he tried to send Kirk a reassuring glance. His friend's eyes were squeezed shut behind his thick glasses. Kirk was trying to put on a brave face, but Hunter could almost feel the anxiety radiating from him.

Darnell paused for a moment, letting Newell's words sink in before he continued. "Who was present at the scene when the police arrived?"

Newell nodded toward Kirk. "The Defendant was the only person present at the time law enforcement arrived. Their first job was to secure the crime scene. In this case, not just the bedroom, where the victim was found, but also the entire house and the imme-diate yard area."

Darnell realized that he had not quite connected the dots. "Was the bedroom where the victim was found?" The question was, Hunter knew, a leading one on direct examination, and technically, objectionable. But this was just a preliminary hearing and there was no benefit in needlessly angering a famously impatient judge.

"Yes," Newell answered.

"Okay," Darnell said as he moved back behind the podium. "How did you proceed next?"

"Once I arrived and was apprised of the situation, I questioned the Defendant about what had happened."

Darnell propped an elbow on the podium. He had hit his stride now and Newell had picked up the rhythm of the questioning as well. "What did the Defendant tell you?"

Once again, Newell took in the question and promptly turned to the judge to explain his answer. "At first, he was quite anxious, so it wasn't easy to get clear answers from him. I spent the first ten minutes or so just trying to calm him down. That's normal behavior for someone who just found a person dead—especially a loved one —so I didn't give it a great deal of significance at the time."

"In any event," Newell continued, "he told me that he had come into the bedroom around eight-fifteen and found the victim lying on the bed. He said that he could tell from all of the blood that he wouldn't be able to revive her himself, so he called 911."

"How long did it take for the EMT's to arrive?"

"Mrs. Warren lived out at the lake so it was about twenty to twenty-five minutes before they could get there."

"And she was dead by the time they arrived, correct?"

"That's correct."

"Now then," Darnell asked, "what was the relationship between the Defendant and the victim?"

"They were husband and wife," Newell replied.

"And I believe you testified earlier that the Defendant had told you he had come into the bedroom and found the body that morning?"

"That's correct."

"Did the Defendant tell you where he had been before he found his wife?"

Newell remained matter-of-fact with his tone and demeanor. "He said that he had come in that morning and called his wife's name, but got no answer. He said he thought she might still be in the bedroom so he went in there. That's when he said he found her."

"Did he say where he was coming from?""

Newell sat back in the witness chair. "Not at first."

Hunter was impressed with the exchange. He knew that both were probably too busy to have rehearsed a preliminary hearing. But they had a rapport and he was beginning to realize that it was more Newell leading Darnell than the other way around.

"What do you mean?" Darnell asked.

"Well," Newell responded, "when I asked him where he had been, he hedged for a few minutes and asked if he could have a drink of water. I had another officer get him a glass of water. He then told me that he had spent the night on his yacht at Lake Barkley Marina."

Darnell let his face take on a mock quizzical look. He knew the answer to his next question, but the actor in him could not let this go by. "Did the Defendant say *why* he had spent the night on the boat?"

Newell nodded. "He said that he occasionally spent the night there."

"That's all?" Darnell asked.

"Not exactly," Newell replied. "I thought it was a little strange for him to drive from his house to the boat to spend the night for no particular reason, so I asked him if he and his wife had been having any marital problems. After a few minutes, he admitted that they were separated. And that she had filed for divorce."

"Did the Defendant say when Mrs. Warren had filed for divorce?"

"Eventually. He had been served with the papers that afternoon."

"What afternoon?"

"The afternoon of June 14. The same day she was murdered."

Satisfied, Darnell shifted course. "Did the Defendant spend the night on the boat alone?"

"That was what he told me, yes."

"So he had no one to verify his whereabouts the evening of the murder?"

"Correct."

Darnell considered Newell's answer for a moment, allowing the Court to do the same. Finally, he asked Newell how he had proceeded next.

"We made a pretty thorough search of the house for the murder weapon, but were unable to find anything definitive. The wound was smooth and was clearly made with a sharp instrument without serrations. There were items in the house that fit that description and they were collected and sent to the lab. But there wasn't a 'smoking gun', so to speak."

Newell paused for a moment, trying to be careful not to over-whelm the judge with information. "Shortly afterward, Mr. Cameron arrived and asked if he could take the Defendant home. With no more evidence than I had at the time, I saw no reason to take the Defendant into custody. So I let him leave with his attorney and we continued to investigate the scene."

"What did you do next?" Darnell asked, knowing very well it was an open-ended question.

Newell took the cue. "As you may be aware," he continued "when we have a person murdered inside the home, the spouse, if there is one, is usually the first person we look at. Especially when, as in this case, we learn that they were separated. So as quickly as we could, we had an evidence tech search the Defendant's SUV. In the meantime, we decided to get a warrant for the boat."

"Did your evidence technician find any blood in the Defendant's SUV?"

"Yes, he did."

"What did you find on the boat?" Darnell asked.

"There was what appeared to be some blood on the bow. Two spots, to be exact. There were also some small stains on the interior —five, I believe—of what appeared to be blood. We collected those samples and sent them to the lab for identification. Still, there was no weapon inside the boat, which was not all that surprising. I decided to get some divers down here and search the immediate area around the boat on the off chance that they might find the weapon."

Hunter glanced at Setchell. It was apparent that the judge's interest was piqued.

"Did they find anything?" Darnell asked.

"Yes. One of the divers found a straight razor wrapped in a hand-towel approximately twenty yards from the bow of the boat."

"Why was that unusual?" Darnell asked.

"A couple of reasons. First, the blade on a straight-razor is smooth and would be consistent with the type of wound that the victim had. Second, it was not rusted, so the razor could not have been in the water for a very long period of time."

"Anything else?"

"Yes sir. As I said, the engraved razor was wrapped in a towel. More specifically, it was wrapped in a monogrammed bath towel. The letters on the towel were *C.K.W...*"

"And those are the Defendant's initials, correct?" Darnell said, clarifying the obvious.

"That's correct," Newell replied.

"Anything else?"

"Yes. The towel was so dirty from the lake water that we couldn't tell much from it at the time, aside from the monogramming. However, we sent it to the lab and it appears as though it too had blood on it."

"Did you have that blood tested?" he asked.

"Yes," Newell replied.

"What were the results of that testing?"

"It matched the blood collected from the boat."

Darnell turned away from Hunter and Kirk and turned his attention back to the witness stand. "Let me ask you another question, Detective. Did these matching blood samples match that of the victim, Cassandra Warren?"

Newell folded his hands, his composure absolute. "Yes, sir. They most certainly did."

Chapter Thirty-Seven

Before Hunter began his cross-examination of Detective Newell, he turned to Kirk and told him to relax and let him do his job. Of course, there wasn't much he could do at this stage. After hearing Newell's testimony, Hunter knew it was a foregone conclusion that the judge would make a finding of probable cause and send the case to the Grand Jury, where an indictment would surely follow. Therefore, there would be no need for courtroom histrionics or needless drama. He would simply try to get some elaboration on the *five W's*—who, what, when, where, and why —and get ready for the case to proceed in Circuit Court.

Hunter had with him a standard legal notepad on which to jot down notes during his cross-examination. He had not prepared a list of questions to ask the detective during the hearing. After all, he had participated in hundreds of prelims in the past thirty years and quit making notes long ago. There was no need.

Hunter greeted Detective Newell with a warm smile. *May as well keep it friendly,* he thought.

"Good morning, Detective," Hunter said.

Newell's tone was equally polite. "Mr. Cameron."

It was at that moment that Hunter began to feel the ground rise and fall beneath him.

As a child, he had on more than one occasion stood in a fishing boat on the lake, attempting to keep his balance. It was precisely that sensation he felt now. He grabbed both sides of the podium tightly and attempted to plant his feet on the moving floor. He stole a frantic glance around him. No one else was having trouble standing up in the courtroom.

That was where he was. Yes, he assured himself. The courtroom.

He looked at the two court clerks seated at the bench in front of him. He realized instinctively that he had known both of them for years, but suddenly he couldn't recall who they were.

To the clerks' right sat the judge. Of that, he was certain—the robe gave him away. Finally, Hunter looked at the dark-haired gentleman seated to the judge's right. Who was he?

"Mr. Cameron?" the judge snapped. Hunter looked up at the judge, but was unable to find the words he needed.

"Mr. Cameron," the judge repeated, more loudly this time.

Hunter still couldn't speak. If he were to speak, what would he say? He could feel beads of sweat begin to trickle between his shoulder blades and down his spine. Finally, perhaps only from instinct, he responded. "Yes, your Honor?"

Judge Setchell did not look amused by whatever it was he believed Hunter was pulling. His baritone was sharp and the redness of his scalp reflected his irritation. "*Well,*" he said, "are you going to ask Detective Newell any questions or are you just going to stand there and waste everyone's time?"

Even in his current fog, Hunter was taken back by the judge's vicious rebuke. He wanted to answer, but he had no idea who this Detective Newell was. He looked to his left and saw Kirk Warren standing next to him. He recognized Kirk, but thought he looked a lot older than when they were in college. *And just when was that?* he wondered. Kirk was staring back at him with a puzzled look similar to that of the judge's, but without the hostility. *What was it that they all wanted from him?*

"*Mr. Cameron!*" the judge thundered, banging his gavel down hard before pointing it straight at Hunter. "I'm going to ask you one more time, Mr. Cameron. If you don't answer me, not only will I be making a ruling on probable cause, but I will also be considering holding you in contempt of court." The judge paused to take a deep breath, but continued to glare at Hunter. "Now," he said, his voice softer, yet somehow even more dangerous, "do you have any questions for the detective?"

Hunter looked helplessly at the stranger on the witness stand. The man looked as bewildered as Hunter felt. Finally, Hunter answered the judge with the only words he could muster. "No, your Honor," he said.

Judge Setchell rolled his eyes in exasperation and sat back in his chair. The dreaded bifocals were off and held between his fingers. He clearly blamed Hunter for making a mockery of his courtroom —in front of the media, no less. After a moment, he angrily shoved the bifocals back on and began scribbling his findings on the court docket.

"The court makes a finding of probable cause that the charged offense did occur on the specified date and that the Defendant committed the offense. The case will be held over for the Christian County Grand Jury. Bond will remain the same."

After announcing that the Court would stand in recess for thirty minutes, Setchell rose and swiftly strode out the back door of the courtroom and into his chambers. Newell stepped down from the witness box, giving Hunter a quizzical look as he headed for the exit.

As the media converged around him and the rest of courtroom emptied, Hunter continued to stand at the podium, tightly gripping its sides as he waited for the floor to slowly quit rocking beneath him.

Chapter Thirty-Eight

On the short walk back from the courthouse to his office, the restraint Kirk had shown during the hearing disappeared. Hunter was walking briskly along the sidewalk, desperate to escape the courthouse, the crowd, the media, and even his client. Kirk was chasing him like a small dog nipping at his heels, his skinny arms flailing like a windmill.

"What in the hell happened back there?" he demanded, his voice also as high-pitched as a yapping terrier's.

Despite Kirk's near-hysteria, Hunter was actually glad he was along for the short walk back to his office. A few minutes earlier, he hadn't been certain he could find his way back. Now, he seemed to be regaining his senses. He knew they had been to the preliminary hearing and for some reason, he hadn't asked Detective Newell any questions. *What was happening to* him?

"Hunter," Kirk said, grabbing him by the shoulder. "Dammit, answer me!"

Hunter stopped. He slowly turned to look down at this friend. "What exactly is your question, Kirk?" He turned his head to give Kirk's hand on his shoulder a cool look.

Kirk, clearly surprised by his friend's turn of mood, lowered his hand and stepped back. "I thought you were going to ask that cop questions!"

Hunter continued to gaze down at him for a moment before answering. "I was." He then turned and resumed walking toward the office.

Kirk continued his pursuit, though he had dialed the histrionics down a notch. "Well?" he asked.

"Well what?" Hunter answered, not slowing down the pace of his walk.

"Why didn't you ask anything?"

That's a damned good question, Hunter thought. He could tell Kirk the truth he supposed, but he wasn't certain what the truth was. Now that he had his wits about him, Hunter decided to do what lawyers do best—rationalize.

"There really wasn't any need," he replied, keeping his voice measured, matter-of-fact.

Kirk recoiled, clearly aghast. "What do you mean *there was no need?*" His voice cracked as he spoke, making him sound like a middle-aged prepubescent.

Hunter stopped again and turned sharply on Kirk. Typically, he prided himself on being able to mask his emotions and dealing with any crisis in an objective fashion. But he was stressed and more than a little scared, for both himself and his friend.

"Look," he said. "I told you at the beginning there was no chance whatsoever that we would win the preliminary hearing. I told you it was a fairly routine matter that would get rubber-stamped by the judge and sent directly to the Grand Jury." Hunter could feel his face flushing with anger, anger Kirk truly didn't deserve. Anger which should have been turned toward himself.

"I told you that at the prelim I wouldn't be conducting a cross-examination like you would see on one of those damnable TV shows you love so much. This was a simple session of 'who, what, when, where, why.' Well in case you weren't listening, I got news for you, old friend. Detective Newell did a pretty damned good job of answering all of those questions. The only purpose of me repeating them would've been to preen in front of the TV cameras. That isn't my style and you know as well as I do that it doesn't play here, not in western Kentucky. If you want somebody who does shit like that, then get yourself another lawyer. I don't give a shit. Otherwise, keep your mouth shut and let me do my goddamned job!"

Kirk's eyes were bulging noticeably, even behind the thick lenses of his glasses. He'd never seen such a display of temper from Hunter. After swallowing hard, he asked sheepishly, "So what happens next?"

Hunter felt the anger drain from his head, leaving shame in its place. Whatever it was that was happening to him, he felt like a real horse's ass for turning on his best friend, however temporarily.

Hunter sighed, trying to shrug off his guilt long enough to answer the question. "The Grand Jury meets every Friday. Because of all the publicity, L.G. will want this one on the fast track. It usually takes at least a couple of weeks for them to get the case after the prelim."

Kirk listened intently before asking his burning question. "How long will it be?"

Though he was now inclined to be very gentle with Kirk, Hunter knew no other way to truthfully answer the question. "I expect that you'll be indicted by the end of this week."

———

HE STOOD outside the courthouse watching them.

Hunter Cameron and Kirk Warren were already across the street from the courthouse, heading for Cameron's office. Like everyone else in the courtroom, he didn't know what to think about Cameron's performance at the hearing. He had carefully studied Cameron for years and was well-aware of his reputation. He had even attended other preliminary hearings in which Cameron was the defense attorney and had walked away impressed.

So what had Cameron been up to today? He had appeared so— what was it—*confused* in the courtroom. Had Cameron figured out something? No, he couldn't have. There wasn't any way.

He had plotted everything out too carefully and had executed his plan as best he could under the circumstances. Still, the possibility of his plan being compromised yet again twisted his guts into a knot of anxiety and rage. He clenched his fists and caught himself grinding his teeth as he stared at Cameron and Warren, the two main characters in his plan. He felt the gun concealed beneath his jacket. They were close. *It* was close. So very close.

He felt breath quicken and exhaled deeply in an effort to maintain control. No, he wouldn't do it now. He would stick to the plan. Cameron didn't know anything. The courtroom drama, or lack of it, was all an act. Cameron had known the evidence against Warren was overwhelming, so he didn't ask anything. Of course the evidence was overwhelming, he thought. He had made certain it would be. It was all part of the plan.

The plan, he thought. *Stick to the plan.* He knew he could have taken out both Cameron and Warren at any point through the years. But that would have been too easy and they would've gone too quickly, without the requisite suffering. And they had to suffer. Both of them. Just as he had.

No, however hard it would be, he would stick to the plan. No matter what.

He had waited so long. It wouldn't be much longer now.

Chapter Thirty-Nine

Hunter walked into the foyer of his home, hung up his jacket, and tossed his keys on the small table near the front door. He took a deep breath and firmly ran both hands from the top of his forehead to the bottom of his chin, wishing that it would be so easy to wipe away the morning's events at the preliminary hearing.

As he trudged down the hallway, he could hear Katherine in the kitchen cooking dinner. He could also hear the voice of the anchorman for the local evening news station on the small kitchen TV. He was just concluding the story about the Warren case, stating that the judge had ordered the case held over for review by the grand jury. Perhaps mercifully, Hunter had missed any analysis of his performance, such as it had been. At least his knack for timing was still intact.

He was leaning against the entryway to the kitchen when Katherine rescued him from the burden of his thoughts.

"Hey, stranger," she said.

Hunter looked up. She was gazing at him from the stove with the same inviting smile he had fallen in love with all those years ago.

It was the only part of the day that had brought him comfort and he simply gazed at her for a moment, eager to soak in the badly needed reassurance.

"How'd it go today?"

Hunter's eyebrows twitched as he gave her a forced smile that pretty much answered her question. He walked over to the kitchen table and sat down. "I've had better performances."

"They said on the news that you didn't ask the detective any questions."

Great, Hunter thought. "Nope."

"That isn't what you usually do, is it?"

She wasn't being critical, Hunter knew, just curious. After all these years together, she had a pretty good idea of how he practiced law. But he didn't want to alert her to any problem.

"No," he said, "it isn't. But to be honest, that detective did a pretty good job of answering everything anyway." Hell, the excuse had worked on Kirk. If he kept using it, he might eventually believe it himself. Of course, Katherine was smarter than either he or Kirk and wouldn't be nearly as easily fooled.

He sighed, knowing she would require more. "Detective Newell is really an effective witness. Probably testified a couple hundred times or more. I damn sure wasn't going to shake him and I didn't see the need to let him repeat for all those reporters how guilty Kirk looks." Yeah, that was it. Didn't want to feed the greedy media or possibly poison potential jurors. It was a good strategy. Not what he had planned, but it was a sound result. He still knew what he was doing after all!

Katherine poured a glass of iced tea and handed it to him. "That bad, huh?"

"Afraid so."

Katherine resumed her cooking, seasoning crappie with Cajun spices so she could put them on the grill. He picked at the home-made hush puppies on the table, dipping them in cocktail sauce.

"Why didn't he tell you that they were separated?" she asked.

"He says that he was ashamed and he didn't know how to tell me."

Katherine turned to give him an incredulous look. "Don't you think that's a bit much? I mean, you're not his father."

"Thank God for that. No one is *that* big of an asshole."

Katherine gave him a look of mock disapproval. "That's not what I mean. Why would he be ashamed to tell you that they were separated? I mean, you didn't like Cassandra anyway. Why would you mind?"

"Maybe because it would confirm in some way or another that I was right about her," Hunter said, taking a bite of a hush puppy.

The look on Katherine's face made it clear she wasn't buying it. "I bet there was another man."

"I hope not," Hunter replied. "And if there was, I hope Kirk didn't know about it. And that the police don't figure it out if he did know."

"Have you asked him about it?"

"Not yet, but I guess I'll have to pretty soon." *I probably should've already*, Hunter thought. But it was an awkward thing to do, asking your best friend if his just-murdered wife was fooling around on him. Just another good reason not to be representing him in a case like this, Hunter thought, silently cursing himself.

"What does he say about the razor and the towel? Does he deny they're his?"

"Oh, they're his alright. He just doesn't know how they got to the bottom of the lake. Or how the towel got Cassandra's blood on it."

Katherine put a bowl full of tossed salad on the table and then went out on the deck to put the fish on to grill. When she came back, she picked right up where they had left off.

"You know, though," she said, taking a sip of her tea, "even with all of this evidence and the separation, all of that, I still have a hard time picturing him doing this. I mean, he's just so puny. And high-strung. Jesus," she said, "I don't think his nerves could take it."

"They're not holding up very well right now, either."

"I'm sure they're not. But can you really imagine someone that frail, physically and emotionally, having what it takes to cut his wife's throat? I just think he would collapse before he ever got to it."

Hunter had spent more than a little time in the last two weeks pondering that very issue. He had represented other accused killers, many of whom he knew were guilty. They came in all shapes and sizes, men and women, old and young. The clean-living and the career criminals. Simple thieves who killed in the act of robbery and God-fearers who killed in the heat of passion.

"No honey," he said softly, as though he was clinging to the same hope. "For the life of me, I just can't see Kirk hurting anyone, let alone Cassandra. Regardless of whether or not *we* liked her, the fact is he worshipped her."

Katherine gently placed her hand on his. He turned a haunted look on her. "Hunter," she said, her voice equally gentle, "what's wrong with you?"

"Nothing, really," he reassured her, knowing all the while that his smile felt more like a grimace. "I'm just tired from this case. I'll feel better tomorrow."

Katherine sat back in her chair. Hunter lowered his gaze, fumbling at his plate in an attempt to skirt her skeptical glare. "You know," she said, "Kirk hasn't even been indicted yet and you're already this tired. How bad do you think it will be when you're actually getting ready to go to trial?"

That got Hunter's attention. He returned his gaze to her face, bracing himself for what he knew was coming. "What do you mean?"

"I mean, have you considered what handling Kirk and this case is going to do to you?"

"I'll be fine."

"I'm not sure I believe you."

"I have a responsibility to Kirk."

Wrong answer. Hunter knew it as soon as the words left his lips. Katherine yanked her napkin from her lap and threw it down on the table. "What about your responsibility to *me?*"

Hunter sat back in his chair, uncertain how to react to his wife's rare display of anger. She had a good point and he knew it.

Finally, he asked, "What do you want me to do?"

Her response was immediate and unflinching. "I think you need to get out of this case. You're too close to Kirk—to this situation—to represent him. If you lose and he gets convicted, you'll never forgive yourself. I know you and you know I'm right."

Hunter couldn't disagree. However, she was missing one basic point.

"It has to be me." His voice was soft, almost inaudible.

"Oh, *bullshit*! Why, Hunter? Why does it have to be you? This isn't college," she continued. "You don't have to stick up for him against every person who tries to pick on him. He's not your child. He's a grown man! He's got enough money to hire a team of the best lawyers in the world. Why does it have to be *you?*"

Hunter wanted to tell her why. To give her a good reason. He was accustomed to giving answers. And he knew the answer now. But he knew it wouldn't be the answer she wanted to hear.

"It just has to."

He waited for a new explosion, but surprisingly it didn't come. Katherine leaned forward, resting her elbows on the table in defeat. She studied him for a long moment, then said, "I want you to go to the doctor. Get checked out."

Hunter's first instinct was to dismiss the suggestion. Like most men his age, he despised going to the doctor. But he sensed his wife was not to be trifled with at this moment. Plus, now that he thought about it, it might be a good idea to get a physical.

The doctor might have a simple explanation for his recent mental lapses. He probably just needed a prescription of some sort. Maybe some extra vitamins. And if the doctor could get him back on track, then he could really get down to business on Kirk's case.

Feeling better already, Hunter picked up his fork and began eating. "You know, I think you're right. I could probably use a check-up. I'll call Dr. Hampton tomorrow."

"Okay," Katherine said, clearly surprised by his easy surrender. "And you'll do whatever he tells you to do?"

"Of course I will. Why else would I go to see him?"

The doctor would cure what ailed him, Hunter thought, and

he'd be feeling more like himself in no time. He should have thought of this earlier. The day which had begun so poorly was now ending on a high note.

Yeah, he thought. *I'll go to the doctor.*

Everything will be fine.

Chapter Forty

The visit with the doctor did not go fine.

Hunter was sitting in his car outside a large office building in Nashville, Tennessee, a little over an hour's drive from his house. In Suite B-37—wherever the hell that was—of this building was the office of Dr. Colby Johnston, the neurologist to whom Hunter had been referred. Hunter was sitting in his car, procrastinating as long as possible before going in.

He was frustrated on a number of fronts. He was frustrated that he was here, getting ready to be poked and prodded by another doctor, one he'd never met before. He was frustrated that he wasn't in his office working on Kirk's case. He was frustrated with Dr. Hampton, who had examined him for all of twenty minutes before referring him to the neurologist.

First, because he had not been to Hampton's office in over a year, the receptionist had asked him to update his medical history. Katherine normally came with him and filled out forms like that, but she had an antique auction for her store today. He had honestly been relieved that she wasn't there. At least until he had to fill out that damned form.

After filling out his name and Katherine's the form had become, in his opinion, unnecessarily difficult. They wanted his date of birth and address, all of which had suddenly escaped him. Fortunately, he had remembered that his drivers' license would contain that information. He had pulled it out and, with some relief, copied the information from the card to the form.

The next questions required information about his health history. Had he ever had heart problems or cancer? Hunter started to write something down, but quickly realized that he didn't know exactly what he was writing. He pondered the question for a moment, but still couldn't come up with an answer. No problem, he thought. He'd just go on the next question.

Did he have high blood pressure? *There we go*, he thought, and smiled with relief as he checked the "no" box. But then the next questions threw him. Was he allergic to any medicines? If so, which ones? Had he had any surgeries?

Though he knew he should be able to answer those questions with ease, his mind had gone blank. He felt beads of sweat forming at the top of his hairline and in the palms of his hands. Finally, after twenty minutes of laboring over the questionnaire, the receptionist noticed he was having difficulty completing the form. Discreetly she came over and offered to help him. Hunter was embarrassed, but having no other choice, he accepted the offer with a sheepish nod. Fortunately, the only other people in the waiting area were an elderly couple, neither of whom seemed interested in his epic struggle with the questionnaire. As the receptionist finished filling out the form for him, Hunter wondered if the couple, both of whom were at least twenty years his senior, had fared any better than he had.

When Hampton entered the exam room, laptop in hand, he shook Hunter's hand warmly. Hampton was a hefty fellow in his early-thirties, his face softened with a bright smile. Sitting down to review Hunter's chart, he said cheerfully, "So...you've been having some problems with your memory?"

"Well, not bad really," Hunter said quickly. "Just here and there."

Hampton nodded as though he understood completely. "I see. Janie told me that she had to help you with your questionnaire."

"Yeah, just a little." Hunter ended the sentence with a forced snicker. "I never remember things like that."

Hampton asked Hunter to stand up and walk in a straight line. He checked his reflexes. After pulling out his ball-point flashlight and checking Hunter's eyes for involuntary twitching, he had Hunter stand on one leg with his arms outstretched and asked him to count backwards from one-hundred.

"Jesus, Doc," Hunter asked, "do you think I've been drinking and driving?"

"Very funny, Mr. Cameron," Hampton replied. "Now count." His tone had gone from affable to deadly serious.

Stinging from the reprimand, Hunter assumed the awkward stance and attempted to count as instructed.

"One-hundred, ninety-nine, ninety-eight, ninety-seven, ninety-six, ninety…" He paused for a moment. "Ninety…" After another awkward moment of silence, Hunter shook his head and laughed, as though he had just been the victim of a good-natured prank. "Sorry, Doc. I just couldn't help it. This all seems so ridiculous. I think it's just much ado about nothing."

Hampton simply lifted one eyebrow.

"All right. Fine," Hunter snapped. He'd just have to show Hampton he could pass the damned test. He resumed the stance and began counting all over again. He virtually fired out the numbers, insulted that he, a respected attorney, would be reduced to such childish exercises.

Then he stalled at eighty-six. A repeated effort got him to eighty-three. His last try stopped at eighty-nine.

Before Hunter left the office, Hampton had secured an appointment for the following morning with this Dr. Johnston, who had been a medical school chum of his. Hampton had advised him to consider having Katherine drive him to Johnston's office. Hunter had politely thanked him for the advice and then asked for written directions on how to get there. He wasn't ready to admit he had a problem to himself, much less to Katherine.

And now here he sat outside Dr. Johnston's office, getting ready to have God-knows-what done to him. At least he hadn't gotten lost on the way, he thought grimly.

When he entered the office and signed the registration sheet, Hunter was relieved to learn that Dr. Hampton's receptionist had faxed a copy of his medical history to Johnston's office. All he had to do was review the form and sign it. Hunter quickly complied. Hell, for all the trouble it saved him, he didn't care if it was accurate or not.

After a short wait in an exam room, Dr. Johnston walked in. Hunter was surprised he and Hampton had been in medical school at the same time. With his prematurely graying hair and wire-rimmed glasses, Johnston looked much older than the boyish Hampton. After a brief introduction, Johnston immediately got down to the business at hand.

The two of them discussed the problems Hunter had been having with his memory. Though Hunter again attempted to deflect some of the questions with humor, Johnston remained very personable. It didn't take Hunter long to realize Johnston was effectively pulling pertinent information on his condition from him, no matter how reluctant he might be to give it.

After the discussion of Hunter's symptoms, Johnston described in detail the series of neurological examinations and tests that would help determine the problem. He explained that Hunter would need an electroencephalogram, or *EEG*, an MRI, a CT brain scan, complete bloodwork, a chemical profile, and a spinal tap. His alarm growing along with the laundry list of diagnostic tests, Hunter could not help but ask, "Is it really *that* serious?"

Johnston paused a moment, then smiled. Hunter immediately recognized the smile. He had given it a thousand times himself, usually when a client asked him to assess a case before he knew the facts.

Johnston's voice remained measured and reassuring. "Mr. Cameron," he said, "I hope not. The tests may determine a problem, but they'll also allow us to eliminate other possible problems.

Either way, I don't want to offer any opinion until I see the test results."

Hunter was then ushered by a nurse to the main hospital at Vanderbilt. The first procedure was the EEG during which he sat in a darkened room, eyes closed, as waves of pulsating white lights were flashed in front of his face for several minutes. Next, he went to a different floor of the hospital for his MRI. It was late morning by the time the MRI and brain scan were completed and Hunter was ushered off for blood and chemical tests, as well as the spinal tap. He was assured that by early afternoon the EEG and MRI test results would be completed. Normally, a second appointment was scheduled to go over the results for all of the tests, but Johnston had made an exception for him and had agreed to meet with Hunter that same afternoon.

The nurse who had escorted him around the hospital offered to show him where the food court was, but with his stomach in knots over the tests, he wasn't hungry. Instead, he holed up in the waiting area of Johnston's office suite. He suddenly found himself incredibly fatigued from all the poking, prodding and imaging he had endured. He wasn't certain how long he had been dozing when he felt a gentle prodding on his shoulder and opened his eyes to the pleasant smile of the office receptionist.

"Mr. Cameron. Dr. Johnston will see you now."

Chapter Forty-One

Y*ou have suffered some damage to your cerebral vascular system.*
The words echoed inside Hunter's mind—his damaged mind—like a stone bouncing around a hollow cavern.

Dr. Johnston gave Hunter a moment to absorb the words. He tried to make eye contact, but Hunter continued to gaze at the wall.

Finally, the physician continued in a deliberately understated tone. "The damage was sustained as the result of what we call 'multi-infarct', which is a medical term for multiple breakdowns in the brain's blood vessels."

"How do we fix it?" Hunter asked. His voice was monotone and his gaze did not leave the wall.

"Your condition is progressive. I'm afraid there is no way to regain what you've lost." Johnston paused before saying gently, "There is no cure."

Hunter swallowed deeply and stood, turning his back to the doctor. He was trying to hold on to his senses, to be logical about his situation. In all of his years as a lawyer, logic had never failed him. But the seams of his legendary composure were beginning to unravel. "Am I losing my mind?"

"Even though your condition is progressive, there are certain drugs being tested right now that may very well slow the progress of the disease…"

"How long?" Hunter interrupted.

"Excuse me?"

"How long do I have?"

"How long do you have until what?"

Hunter finally turned around and faced the doctor. "To live?"

Johnston ran a hand through his hair. "Your condition isn't terminal. At least not in the traditional sense."

"What do you mean, in the *traditional sense*?"

"The average dementia patient lives eight to ten years following diagnosis, but it's very hard to predict. Many live fifteen to twenty years. Some longer."

Hunter struggled to assimilate this new information. *Okay*, he thought. *I'm not dying, per se.* Then, the next question sprang to mind. *What kind of life will I have? What about Katherine? The girls?* Then another question popped into his mind, one sprang from the seeds of denial.

"Aren't I too young to have Alzheimer's disease?"

"That's a good question," Johnston admitted. "Actually, we don't know that you have Alzheimer's disease. The only way Alzheimer's disease can be positively diagnosed is through an autopsy of the brain, and…"

"I'm not quite ready for that," Hunter finished wryly. He might be losing his mind, but he hadn't completely lost his sense of humor.

Johnston smiled faintly. "In any event, the brain scan results aren't back. It'll be a couple of days on those, but they may tell us something different."

He made another note on his chart. "Tell me, Hunter. Is there any history in your family of others suffering from something similar?"

"No," Hunter replied. "I'm pretty sure about that one. My mother died when I was a child. My father died of a heart attack about fifteen years ago. He was in his seventies, but sharp as a tack. Why?"

"There's a strong hereditary factor in these cases. If anyone in your family has suffered from multi-infarct dementia or Alzheimer's disease, it makes your chances of developing it three times as likely."

"Well, none of them did. So I guess I'm going to be the family pioneer."

"You could be wrong about that."

"Why is that?" Hunter asked.

"Dementia patients, despite their decreased capacity, are often quite resourceful when it comes to masking their problem."

Hunter considered this for a moment, then shook his head. "I don't think so. I would have noticed it."

"I'm not saying that someone in your family suffered from dementia," Johnston replied. "I'm just saying that you shouldn't dismiss the possibility solely on the basis that you didn't *notice* it. After all, how many of your family members have noticed yours?"

Touché.

Hunter did not bother to respond. He remained standing, arms crossed, stoking his chin between his right thumb and forefinger. He trying to be objective. Trying to figure out how to deal with the problem. It was how he had lived for the last thirty years. Hell, it was how he had lived his entire life. Only now the problem was his, not some client's.

"What can *I* do?"

"Well, you can start by living as happily and actively as you can. And you need, at all costs, to avoid stress."

An involuntary laugh escaped Hunter. Johnston just stared at him.

"That isn't going to be easy, Doc," he said. "I'm defending a murder case right now."

Johnston began shaking his head with a new sense of urgency. "It is my strong recommendation that you retire immediately."

"But Doc, I'm afraid you don't understand. I have a responsibility to my client."

Still shaking his head, Johnston rose from the stool and picked up his laptop. He clearly had more important things to do than argue with a hardheaded patient. "What you have, Mr. Cameron," he said, turning back in the doorway, "is a responsibility to yourself."

Chapter Forty-Two

"I afraid I can't represent you anymore."

The words hung between Hunter and Kirk like gnats hovering in front of their eyes. They stood in Hunter's office in a hastily scheduled meeting arranged via cell phone as Hunter had driven back from Nashville. He had told Kirk that he had to see him. Yes, that evening. Yes, as quickly as possible. And, no, it couldn't wait.

"What are you talking about?" Kirk said with an uncertain chuckle. "You're kidding, right?"

Hunter held his gaze, refusing to look away. "No. I'm afraid I'm not."

On the drive back from Nashville, he had rehearsed his lines several times, praying he could actually remember them once he arrived. He would tell Kirk that he was sick, but he wouldn't tell him exactly what the illness was. He wasn't ready for that—to lose his dignity along with his mind. It would be taken away from him soon enough.

"What the hell are you talking about?" Kirk asked.

Hunter exhaled deeply. "I went to a doctor today. I'm sick."

Kirk's expression quickly shifted from anger to concern. "What's wrong with you?"

"That's not really important." Hunter pushed himself away from the wall he had been leaning against and turned away, seeking to escape his friend's earnest gaze. Kirk knew him too damn well. "I've got a health issue so I'm retiring from the practice of law, effective immediately."

"Are you…" Kirk hesitated, "…dying?"

How do you say, "Well, sort of," Hunter wondered? "No," he said. "I'm not dying." *I'm just losing myself, one piece at a time, every minute of every day. That's all.*

"What is it then?" Kirk asked, his face ashen. "Do you have cancer?"

"No. I don't have cancer."

"Is it problems with your heart?"

"No." *It's my head. Not my heart.*

"Well, then, what's the problem?" Kirk demanded with a sigh of relief. "If you're not dying, then I don't see what the big deal is."

"I'm sorry, Kirk. I really can't say what it is. I'll help you find another attorney. I'll…"

"Another attorney?" Kirk was clearly growing more frustrated by the minute. And Hunter wasn't sure he blamed him. "Listen, Hunter. I don't know what the hell is going on with you, but I don't need this kind of shit right now."

Neither do I, Hunter thought. "Believe me, Kirk," he said. "I didn't ask for any of this."

The words were barely out of his mouth when Kirk hit back. "And I damned sure didn't ask for my best friend to turn his back on me just when I need him the most."

The words seared through Hunter's skin and hit his soul, exactly where they had been aimed. The doctor had been absolutely clear that he would have to avoid stress of all sorts and nothing was more stressful than a murder trial. And could he even function under those circumstances? He'd already frozen in front of the bench once. Did he have enough left in him to finish this trial? And that said nothing of the ethical dilemma he found himself in. He wouldn't need to call the *Lawyers' Ethics Hotline* to know that, at the very least, he had an obligation to advise his client of his condition. And even if Kirk *wanted* him to continue to represent him, Hunter still had a responsibility to drop the case if he believed he couldn't provide competent representation.

But Hunter couldn't bring the words *Alzheimer's disease* to the back of his throat, much less utter them. He felt fine, damn it. This couldn't be happening to him. He realized in that moment that Kirk wasn't the only one who wanted him to keep this case. *He wanted it himself.* His work would be finished soon enough. *Just one more,* he thought. *Just one more time. There's nobody who can try a case like this, in this town, in that courtroom, any better than I can. I can save him,* he thought. *I can save my best friend.*

And maybe, just maybe, a small piece of me…

He walked briskly to the other side of his desk and began making notes on a notepad.

"Hunter?" Kirk blinked, obviously taken back by the suddenness of Hunter's change in direction.

Hunter didn't answer his friend. He was writing furiously. He didn't want to give a single thought the chance to escape from his compromised mind without being put to paper first. Given how fast he was fading, the case would have to move quickly, much quicker than the downtrodden pace criminal cases normally kept. Fortunately, there was such a tool to move things along.

Motion for speedy trial, he wrote. Granted, because Kirk was out of jail, the judge might not give his client much priority in moving up in an already-saturated docket. Further, it was often the stance of defense attorneys that they should drag out a criminal case for as long as possible. Memories—even the strong ones—tended to fade with time and witnesses quickly become less certain of what they'd seen and heard. But Hunter could not wait for a trial that would take place a year or two from now. He would make this his only case and prepare for it like no other. Unfortunately, even if he wasn't handling any more cases, there would be much to do. He would need help.

Another lawyer? Co-counsel? He stared at his freshly-scrawled words for a moment, then crossed them out as quickly as he had written them. He had always been a lone wolf, as only children so often were. He had seldom worked with another lawyer on the same side of a case and had never enjoyed it when he did. As a solo practitioner his entire career, he was used to unfettered autonomy in handling a case and didn't see changing his style at this point.

Still, he feared his ability to do legal research would be greatly compromised by his disease, at least periodically. His secretary, Tess, was a talented woman, but she couldn't do research and draft pleadings. He needed someone with legal training. Not a lawyer, though. There weren't many true paralegals in the area, as they typically migrated to big cities like Nashville and Louisville, where the pay was better.

And then it hit him.

He opened a lower desk drawer and pulled out a file titled *Law School Resumes*. He wasn't certain why he had ever told Tess to open such a file. He had never hired an associate and had never entertained any notions of doing so. Still, he always wrote back to the sender, advising them that there were no positions open in his office, but he would keep their inquiry on file.

He flipped through the resumes, most of which were at least a couple of years old. He figured it was highly unlikely the senders were still looking for a job. And if they were, there was probably a good reason. Still, he was desperate. He had never been particularly good at delegation, trusting only himself to do something right. If he was going to see Kirk's case to conclusion, it was a habit he would have to change.

Finally, he came across one that was fairly recent. He saw a copy of the reply letter he neither remembered reading nor signing, but had nonetheless sent to the applicant.

The mailing address was in Mississippi.

Chapter Forty-Three

L ibby Masters wandered around her small, soon-to-be-former apartment, wondering what to move next. As was her nature, she had already boxed and labeled most of her personal belongings and had neatly stacked them in the living room. Most of the heavy furniture had been placed in the U-Haul truck parked in her spot in the complex, the work done by a couple of the many male admirers among her law school classmates. Thank God for them, she thought. It wasn't like there was a man in her life to help with practical matters such as these.

She picked at the small clip holding her straight, shoulder-length, blond hair back from her face. She hadn't put on any makeup and her petite, but very shapely, figure was dressed in a weathered sorority t-shirt and cut-off jeans. Underneath the right back pocket of the jeans was her tattoo, smack dab on her derriere, a lasting reminder of a drunken night during college at Western Kentucky University. She had chosen a four-leaf clover, she explained to her freshmen pledge sisters, because any male fortunate enough to see it would soon be getting lucky. Her hangover had faded with time, but the tattoo and the campus legend did not.

She had graduated from the Mississippi College School of Law just three weeks ago and unlike most of her classmates, wasn't quite certain where she'd be taking the bar exam, let alone where she would be working. She had grown up in Paducah, a city in far western Kentucky, but had moved to Jackson for law school. She had chosen Mississippi College not just because she had been offered a full scholarship, but to escape the shambles of what had once been her very normal life.

Libby had been a sophomore at Western when her mother was diagnosed with advanced breast cancer. An only child, she had moved back home and switched to night classes so she could care for her mother during the day while her father, a school teacher, worked. Her mother fought bravely, but succumbed before Thanksgiving of Libby's junior year, leaving Libby all alone to navigate the tenuous relationship she shared with her father.

She caught herself gazing down at a small portrait of what had once been her family on an otherwise empty kitchen countertop. The photo was now six years old, taken just before her mother had fallen ill. Despite his many faults, she had to admit her father was a handsome devil. His wavy dark brown hair was touched by just the right amount of gray. With his silvery-blue eyes and strong chin, his dark good looks contrasted perfectly with Libby's own fair beauty, like charcoal against a bright pastel. And appearances were just the starting point of the differences between father and daughter.

His strong appearance camouflaged his weaknesses. During her mother's illness, he had emotionally checked out, burying himself under a pile of imagined work duties and prescription meds. He taught at the local high school during the day and anesthetized himself from reality with pills and drinking every night. He left his daughter to care for his dying wife, although Libby knew he loved both of them dearly. He did it because he was weak. And because he loved himself more.

Libby had known her father was far too needy to be alone for very long. Jack had found and married her mother's replacement, Julia, within six months of the funeral. Libby was surprised it had taken that long. With her light, pretty features, Julia could have passed for her mother's sister. But the similarity ended there. Libby's

mother was a gentle soul to her last breath and Julia…
well…was not.

Julia wasted no time asserting herself after the wedding. Within
a short period of time all traces of Libby's mother had been swept
aside, permanently filed away in some attic, basement, box, or can.
But Jack's late wife was not Julia's only perceived rival. Julia objected
strongly to Jack paying Libby's tuition for her senior year at Western, despite the fact that he had done so during her first three years.
Julia insisted on being present every time Libby called or visited her
father, a virtual chaperone. Eventually, Libby's attempts to visit her
father were met with open hostility by Julia.

All the while, Jack turned a blind eye to it all. On one rare occasion when they were alone, Libby mentioned Julia's combativeness
to Jack. For a man who expected his daughter to take whatever steps
were necessary to make life easier for him, his response had been
predictable.

"Why don't you just try to work with her," he asked.

"You mean follow her rules," Libby said.

"Just try to get along with her. Julia just thinks you don't pay her
the respect she deserves as a parent."

Libby felt her temper rise. "She's *not* a parent, Dad. Not to me
or to anyone else."

"Well, she *is* your stepmother. And instead of making an effort
for my sake, you're trying to put me in the middle."

"I *have* tried," she retorted. "But there's no point. What you
don't realize is that her goal is to have you to herself and to control
your life. She doesn't *want* to get along with me. She just wants me
gone. Is that what you want, too?"

Jack had leaned toward her and gently patted her on the leg.
"Now, honey, you're being irrational. I want you to think about it. I
want you to think about how much easier you could make things
for me…"

And with that, Libby had realized her father was not only
content with the smothering type of attention paid to him by Julia;
he liked it. Reveled in it, in fact. He certainly wasn't going to risk his
happiness in order to stand up to Julia for his daughter's sake.

Recognizing the futility of the situation, Libby's visits to her child-hood home had slowly tapered off. Finally, tired of the turmoil with which Julia met every phone call, Libby had limited communication with her father to the obligatory cards sent for Christmas, birthdays, and, ironically, Father's Day.

Without any other living family, Libby had found herself alone. She hadn't seen her father since two weeks before her graduation from Western, which Julia had declared he couldn't attend for one reason or another. Now, three years later, Libby hadn't even wasted the stamp to send him an invitation to her law school graduation. As far as she was concerned, her mother was dead and her father had simply stopped living.

But now, with graduation past, Libby found herself once again at a crossroads. For reasons she could only begin to imagine, she had struggled her way through law school, lacking the academic focus that had always been her trademark. Her law school grades had been mediocre. She had graduated, she joked to friends, in the top *three-thirds* of her class. She had clerked for a small firm in Jackson and displayed a talent for research and writing. They had offered her a job on graduation, but Jackson didn't feel like the right place for her anymore. She had always assumed she would go back to Kentucky, even though there really wasn't anything left for her there.

Still, she felt herself drawn back to home. In an inspired weekend during her last semester, she had sent a blizzard of resumés to law firms all over western Kentucky, from Paducah to Hopkinsville. Not surprisingly, she hadn't received many replies. She had waited late in the game to be seeking employment and no job offers had been made. Now, in the beginning of June, with both the Mississippi and Kentucky bar exams looming less than two months away, she had no idea where she would be going. She only knew where she was. Eight hours from Paducah and a lifetime away from everything she had once known.

Shaking herself out of her malaise, she decided to get back to work. She had to get the truck loaded, despite the fact that she had no idea where she would be driving it. She grabbed a box and was headed out the door when her cell phone rang. She put the box down, grabbed her phone off the counter, and looked at the caller ID. It did not list the name of the caller, but she instantly recognized the area code prefix as western Kentucky.

Dad? she wondered for a moment before answering the phone.

"Hello?"

"Is this Libby Masters?" asked a warm voice that was not her father's.

"Yes," she replied, trying to hide a small sense of disappointment.

"Ms. Masters, my name is Hunter Cameron…"

Chapter Forty-Four

Libby sat nervously in the small lobby of Hunter Cameron's law office. Try though she might, she periodically caught herself clicking the back of her best heels against the graying laminate floor. She wondered if the secretary sitting on the other side of the wood-paneled partition could hear her tapping.

She had been stunned by Mr. Cameron's request for her to interview. Paducah was only an hour from Hopkinsville, so she had long known his name and reputation. He was one of the best-known criminal attorneys in the state. She had sent him a resumé simply because she had sent one to everyone else in the area, not because she thought he would actually agree to interview her. In fact, she had almost been flattered to receive his considerate letter in which he said his was a solo practice by design and no positions were available.

Obviously, as he had told her during their brief telephone conference, circumstances in his office had changed since then.

Now, in between fidgeting, she rehearsed her answers to the questions he would inevitably ask. And she attempted to organize her questions for him, should she summon the courage to ask.

"Miss Masters?" said the voice she remembered from the telephone, shaking her from her train of thought. She looked up and saw Hunter Cameron towering over her. She abruptly stood up, straightened her skirt, and proceeded to snap one of those best heels in the process. She stumbled forward into him, where he gently caught her. At barely five-foot two, she could have been in platforms and not even reached his broad shoulders.

"Whoa there, honey. I've got you. You're all right," he said, before steadying her on her one good heel.

Great, she thought. *Here I am broken-heeled and short-legged for the biggest interview of my life. What the hell,* she thought. *What do I have left to lose, other than a shot to find a place to unload all of my shit in that U-Haul? Do the best with what you have...*

Letting go of his arm, she reached down and yanked off both shoes. Holding both of them by the ankle straps, she offered her other hand to her prospective boss.

"They say 'break a leg'. Well, I broke a heel," she said, waving the wounded shoes in his direction. "I'm Libby Masters. I hope you don't mind interviewing a girl in bare feet."

———

HUNTER AND LIBBY sat across from one another, the large, well-aged desk between them. Hunter was already feeling optimistic about the interview. He had always believed the three most important qualities necessary to become a good lawyer were people skills, quick thinking, and the ability to research and write. If the glowing recommendation Libby had unknowingly received from her old boss in Mississippi had not been enough, her witty and graceful recovery from the heel-breaking incident in his lobby told him all he really needed to know about her. Given the deadlines, both professional and personal, he was facing, he had all but decided to hire her before they left the lobby. Still, he wanted to get to know the person with whom he would be handling the final case of his career.

They talked at length about her educational background and her work with the previous law firm. When he asked about her family she said she was an only child and her mother died when she was in college. She didn't mention her father and taking the hint, Hunter didn't push.

"So when will you be taking the bar? Late July?"

"July 27."

"Not a lot of time. Do you plan on working any during that time?"

"I'm going to have to. I've got to find a place to rent."

"Well, that actually suits me. I need help right away."

Hunter leaned forward and rested his arms on the desk. "Miss Masters, I should tell you this will probably be a different type of interview for you."

Libby tilted her head, her brow furrowing in confusion.

Hunter continued. "To be frank, until recently I had never so much as considered hiring an associate. I've been in solo practice since I graduated from law school, pretty much by design. However, recent circumstances have…well, they've dictated that I change my philosophy. I plan to retire in the very near future."

His words took Libby by surprise. Though she knew he was in his mid-fifties, Hunter Cameron looked ten years younger and remarkably fit, like he could go on forever. He just didn't look like the retiring sort.

"I never really thought about what I would do about my practice when I retired. Neither of my daughters ever had any interest in practicing law. I'm not interested in becoming *of counsel* to one of the larger firms, either. Large firms were never my style. I'd rather give it to someone who comes straight out of law school and wants to hang a shingle, so to speak."

Libby didn't know what to say. She had figured if she was lucky enough to get hired, she would be doing grunt work for the next several years, trying to earn her stripes. Instead, it sounded as though the general was about to hand her the keys to the tank before she was out of basic training.

She swallowed hard before she asked, "*Give?*"

"That's right," Hunter said. "If things work out, I would very much like for you to take over my practice."

Hunter could tell Libby was overwhelmed by his offer, just as he had wanted and needed her to be. He needed her to know that he wouldn't be in practice for very long and she would have to stand on her own quicker than most young attorneys do. He also wanted to see what her reaction would be. If she was the type to seize this as the golden opportunity that it was, then she was exactly what he was looking for. If she hedged, then well…

"How would I—" Libby started to ask. But Hunter raised his hand, politely interrupting her.

"Let me give you some of the details. I can probably answer most of your questions and alleviate your concerns fairly quickly. First, I would pay you twenty-five dollars an hour until you pass the bar. The going rate for clerks around here is around ten, but I want to make certain you're comfortable. Once you're licensed, I'll pay you an agreed upon salary for your first year. By the end of that year, I hope to have retired. Once I've retired, I'll turn the place over to you. I'll still own the building, which you would rent from me at whatever price you think is fair. I've been fortunate enough with my career that money is not a concern to me at this point."

Hunter paused for a moment and let all the information sink in.

"You'll be overwhelmed at first, as most young attorneys tend to be. I've been here for over thirty years and this office is reputable. I have a great deal of repeat business. These days, I turn down far more cases than I take. Those cases will all be referred to you and you'll have more business than you'll know what to do with. But I wouldn't be abandoning you. So long as I'm able," he said, with an emphasis on *able*, "I'll be around to answer your questions and you'll have a bunch."

Libby was flabbergasted at what she was hearing. It was incredible, overwhelming, frightening, and exciting, all in about five minutes. She had to clasp her hands together to hide her trembling.

"Oh, there's one other thing," Hunter said. "If you accept this offer and move here, give me a total for all of your rental and utility deposits and I'll take care of them. I know getting started isn't easy and I've got a lot riding on you. I want you to be comfortable, especially with the bar exam looming. You won't need to pay me back. We'll call it a signing bonus."

Libby's mind was racing. She had spent some of the lengthy drive from Jackson to Hopkinsville fretting about her deposits. Sleeping in her car hadn't been a particularly appealing thought so as a last resort, she had been planning on crashing with some college friends in Bowling Green. Hunter Cameron had just solved that problem. But still, here she was, twenty-six years old. Not licensed yet. Hadn't even cracked open her study materials for the bar exam, which was looming just around the corner. And she'd been asked to take over the practice of one of the most prominent lawyers in the state. She was doing her best not to quiver.

"So…what do you say?"

She broke into a huge grin, unable to stop herself.

Hunter cocked one eyebrow, a smile flirting with the corners of his own mouth. "I'll take that as a 'yes'?"

"Yes," she said, trying not to squeal in jubilation. "Yes, I accept your offer." She jumped to her feet and extended her small hand. He accepted it and they shook on the deal.

They sat back down, both clearly relieved.

"Now," Hunter continued, "as I said, I plan on retiring sooner rather than later. I'm only handling one case right now and I won't be taking on any new ones for the foreseeable future. When that case is finished, so am I. That's when you'll take over."

Libby was still too lost in her euphoria to catch the finality in his tone. Her knuckles were white from her squeezing her hands together in excitement. Still, she did her best to focus on what he was saying rather than do what she really wanted to do at that moment—stand in her chair and dance in her still-bare feet.

"What case is that?" she asked.

Hunter leaned back in his chair and exhaled. "The name of the case," he answered, "is *Commonwealth versus Charles Kirkland Warren.*"

Chapter Forty-Five

H unter and Kirk sat in the library/conference room of Hunter's office, cups of coffee in front of them. As intended, it was the most impressive room in the building. The usual array of a lawyer's unread law books and treatises lined shelves which had been hand-made nearly a century before and refinished by Hunter in the last decade.

Hunter had the documents provided by L.G. Owens's office spread out in front of him. Police reports, lists of evidentiary items that had been collected for testing at the KSP lab, the original citation, the indictment—all part of the documentation legally required to be given by the prosecution to a criminal defendant. They were now in the process of going over each one piece by piece.

Hunter was seated directly across from Kirk, scribbling various thoughts and lists on a yellow notebook. There were obviously no eye witnesses to the crime itself, so the case would be based purely on circumstantial evidence. The home belonged to Kirk, so there would be a multitude of physical evidence that would tie him to the crime scene. Much of which, Hunter knew, could be plausibly explained.

On the other hand, Kirk had found the body and called the

police, so there would be no problem, at least on the surface, for the prosecution to establish opportunity. That, standing alone, didn't go very far toward proving Kirk had been the killer.

The physical evidence was, at least initially, somewhat daunting. Traces of Cassandra's blood had been found in Kirk's Tahoe and both inside and outside the yacht. The interior traces could possibly be explained by the fact that Cassandra had been in both the truck and the boat on many occasions. Maybe she had been cut at some point while she was in either, hopefully both, of the two locations. Since Cassandra wasn't available to ask, Hunter asked the next best person.

"Do you remember any specific time recently when Cassandra was on the boat and might have cut herself or had an open wound of some sort?"

Kirk shook his head. "I don't, Hunter. That's just not the kind of thing most people keep on instant recall."

Fair enough, Hunter thought. They would have to check the autopsy report to see if there were any signs of recent minor cuts or abrasions unrelated to her murder. Even if Cassandra's body did have such marks on it, there was a decent chance the report wouldn't mention it. Hunter made a note to have their own medical expert look for them. It was, he knew, the kind of expert detail afforded only to the wealthy. Kirk would be able to buy the best experts in the world if need be. At least they had that going for them.

Of course, there was still the issue of Kirk's monogrammed razor blade having been found in the lake just off the front of the yacht, wrapped in the identically-monogrammed blood-soaked towel. This evidence was the most damaging part of the case. But, as Kirk had pointed out, it was almost *too* convenient, depending on your perspective.

"You couldn't think I'd be that damned stupid, do you Hunter? To murder"—he choked on the words for a moment—"to murder my wife and then put a monogrammed weapon in a monogrammed towel and throw it off the front of my boat?"

I'd hope to hell not, Hunter thought. He'd known plenty of dumb criminals. Dumb murderers, too. And he also knew that normal everyday people, when under extraordinary pressure, might do something they might not otherwise do. It wasn't exactly a scenario in which common sense prevailed.

"No, Kirk," he reassured his friend, "I don't believe you'd be that stupid. But it's still something we're going to have to deal with. It's the linchpin of their case." He paused briefly, then asked, "Any idea how your razor and towel got there?"

Kirk stared blankly at him. "Obviously," he replied, "I've been framed."

Great, Hunter mused. *Just what every jury wants to hear.* Still, there simply was no other plausible explanation. Unfortunately, Hunter knew whenever you point the finger, there had better be someone else standing at the end of it. This wasn't California. An unnamed, unknown slasher wasn't going to cut it, so to speak, in a western Kentucky courtroom.

"Any ideas on who would want to murder Cassandra? Did she have any enemies you knew about?"

Kirk's shoulders sagged even more than normal as he gazed down at his scuffed loafers. "She bickered with the women at the Country Club," he said, "but nothing that serious."

"We've got to do better than that," Hunter said. They weren't going to convince anyone that one of the tennis team gals had sneaked into Cassandra's house and murdered her because they were arguing over who had the best backhand."

Hunter decided to move to a different topic. "We're going to need a private investigator. I've got one in mind."

"I've already got one," Kirk replied.

"You do?"

"Yeah."

Hunter moved down the table, closer to Kirk.

"Kirk, why did you hire a private eye?" His friend's guilty expression made Hunter feel like a school principal questioning a student about the contents of his locker.

Kirk dropped his face into his hands, then swept them back over his forehead and through his wispy hair. "I hired him to investigate Cassandra."

"Why?"

"Look at her. Look at me." He said, as if the former was still an option. "Why do you think I was having her checked out?"

Hunter sat in silence for a moment, trying to figure out a diplomatic way to ask his next question. Kirk saved him the trouble.

"She was screwing around, Hunter. She was screwing around on me!" Kirk froze, almost as if the volume of his own shout had startled him. When he spoke again, his voice was barely a whisper. "My Cassandra was having an affair."

Chapter Forty-Six

L ibby Masters wandered around her small apartment, hoping to procrastinate for a little while before tackling the bar exam materials spread across the kitchen table. Hunter had called a client and helped Libby rent the family's vacant upstairs apartment. It was located in a picturesque Tudor-style house on Country Club Lane, just a couple of minutes from the downtown law office and within walking distance of Ft. Campbell Boulevard, which featured most of Hopkinsville's social opportunities, such as they were.

The apartment was clean and spacious, with dark hardwood floors that made even her ramshackle furniture look a tad more respectable. She had moved in, bought a few thrift-store decorative items, and even had some money left to spare.

For the first time in forever, Libby was excited about the future. She had a promising job, a great opportunity, the possibility of owning her own law practice sometime in the near future. Unfortunately, along with her good fortune came the realization that she had no one with whom to share it. Just as there hadn't been one single person present for her at her law school graduation. Both were painful reminders of the inescapable truth of her life—that she was indeed alone.

She looked at her cell phone, just as she had a thousand times before, and thought about calling her father. She picked up the phone and began to enter the number she hadn't called in years, but still knew by heart. She stopped before entering the last digit and quickly tossed the phone back on the table before her desire for her father to love her and be proud of her could tear down the emotional walls. Walls she had erected for the sole purpose of not allowing him to ever hurt her again.

She made her way over to the sofa and picked up the red-marked first draft of the *Motion for Speedy Trial* she had drafted. Hunter had, page by page, given his thoughts on the first work she had done for him. The corrections were few and far between, but she saw enough in them to realize he was not someone who simply glossed over work without reading it thoroughly. She was most pleased by the short note he had written at the top of the page.

Libby,

Excellent, excellent work. I know getting this granted is a long shot, but you've almost got me convinced that we could do it. Win or lose, this is a wonderful memo you've prepared. You are going to make a fine, fine lawyer.

Hunter

She read the words again. She was surprised and even somewhat embarrassed by how those words made her feel. She felt herself blush with pride and began to wonder exactly how long it had been since she had felt that way.

She remembered bringing home school papers as a child, eagerly running through the front door to show her mom and dad. She remembered feeling awash in the hugs and kisses, the candy, the rewards they would give her for what she had accomplished. But she had realized at an early age that it was their pride in her performance, not the performance itself, that had pleased her most. Her desire to receive those accolades had motivated her to do well. And now, so many years later, it was the memory of having once had her parent's love and approval, coupled with the knowledge that she could never have it again, that pierced her the most.

A tear trickled down her face and dropped down onto the draft motion, causing one of the red marks on the page to bleed. Libby read Hunter's note a third time and instantly felt a little better. Of course, she could never tell Hunter just what his words meant to her. He needed a mature young lawyer to help him defend his best friend on a capital murder case, not a heartbroken girl desperate for a surrogate father.

Still, she knew that, like a thick morning fog, the personal malaise that had plagued her academic life in law school following her mother's death and her father's desertion was finally lifting. Her number one priority was to do more good—no, make that *perfect*—work for Hunter. To make him proud of her yet again.

Libby got up, went to the kitchen, and grabbed a cold beer from the small refrigerator. As she took her first sip, she began to consider the prospects of the only other man she had met in Hopkinsville— Kirk Warren.

In their first meeting he had been polite, though somewhat reserved, with her. He was probably distrustful of a person her age, particularly a woman, playing what was sure to be a significant role in the battle of his life. For her part, she had been instantly struck by how weak a supposedly powerful person could look.

Like everyone else who had grown up in this end of the state, she had heard of the Warrens. But when she had stood nearly eye-to-eye with Kirk and shaken a bony hand no bigger than her own, all of her illusions about his powerful image had been shattered. Though she acknowledged the possibility that she had fallen into the young lawyers' trap of blindly believing in the innocence of her first real client, she found it terribly difficult to believe that this skinny little man could muster up the strength to step on a bug, much less slit his own wife's throat. *Hell*, she thought with a smirk, *I could kick his ass.*

She returned her attention to the case. She would finalize the motion in the morning and have it ready for Hunter to sign by lunch. Then, as they had agreed, she would come home and study for the bar exam in the afternoon. Hunter was adamant about her not letting work get in the way of her bar studies. She would not be nearly as much help to him, he said, if she had to sit on the sidelines come time for the trial. She was determined not to let that happen. So after reviewing the motion one last time, she put it aside and began to carefully organize her study materials. She worked into the late night hours, never realizing a hungry pair of eyes was watching her the entire time.

———

HE HAD PARKED his car at a church just off the boulevard and walked to the tree-filled front yard of the vacant house located directly across the street from Libby's apartment, skirting the tepid glow of the street lights. Still cloaked in shadows, he had climbed the largest of the trees and found a comfortable spot from which to conduct his surveillance.

He had been surprised when Cameron, a rather devout solo practitioner, had hired the young woman. Yet another thing, he mused, that had not gone as planned. Still, she was just a law clerk, though a very attractive one. She couldn't make a difference. Before the crime had even been committed—months before—he had made certain the case against Warren would be too strong, even with the missteps that had occurred afterward. The missteps had only served to fuel his hatred for both Warren and Cameron. Without even being aware of what he was doing, he snapped a branch from the tree and began to bend and ply it with his powerful hands.

He had made too many sacrifices and had planned for far too long. The moment was not far away now. Not far at all. He simply couldn't afford any more missteps. Even if it meant staying up until dawn, spying on some broad with a newly spit-shined law degree. Sleep had never meant anything to him before and it likely never would.

He didn't feel exhaustion. He didn't feel guilt.

He felt nothing.
Nothing but the rage.

Chapter Forty-Seven

T he repetitiveness of Kirk Warren's second arraignment, this one in Christian Circuit Court, Division I, did precious little to thin the phalanx of media that squeezed themselves into the courtroom. It was required procedure in the Commonwealth for a criminal defendant, once indicted by the Grand Jury, to appear in Circuit Court to have the indictment formally read by the Court and to set the matter for a pre-trial conference. Arraignments were, almost without exception, innocuous. This one however, might be a little different, Hunter thought. *These people might actually get their money's worth today.*

Once the arraignment date was set, Hunter immediately filed Libby's *Motion for Speedy Trial*. This was an unusual tactic. Defense motions were typically filed *after* the arraignment and were heard at the pre-trial conference. It was also unusual for a criminal defendant who was out of jail on bond to request a speedy trial.

Libby Masters sat with notepad in hand in the first pew of the courtroom with Kirk Warren seated next to her. She watched as Hunter mingled with the other attorneys who had gathered in the front of the courtroom for the criminal docket, all of them waiting for the judge to enter the courtroom. As planned, she had not followed him around for introductions, not because he was being rude or didn't want to introduce his lowly law clerk, but because he wanted her to sit with Kirk and keep him calm. It was a difficult job and one she would be undertaking on a regular basis for the foreseeable future.

Kirk fidgeted with his fingers and periodically asked questions that had been answered for him at least a dozen times before. She tried to be patient with him. Since she was still convinced of his innocence—of the little man's sheer inability to commit such a crime, physically or otherwise—she found herself feeling not only sorry for him, but strangely protective as well. She tolerated his questions in much the same way as she would have a small child asking repeatedly how they got the peanuts inside a candy bar. Or how Santa Claus could fit down the chimney.

Finally, Kirk excused himself to find the men's room. Libby sighed, feeling guilty for being so grateful for the respite. But she was not alone for long.

"Is anyone sitting here?"

Libby turned toward the side of the pew opposite from where Kirk had been sitting and nearly lost her breath when she saw the owner of that deep, smoky voice. He was tall, dark, and preposterously handsome. The lines at the corner of his eyes marked him as at least twenty years her senior, but the rest of him narrowed that gap considerably. He was dressed in khakis with a navy sport coat and tie, giving her the impression that he did more for the clothes than they did for him.

"N-No," she stammered, still struggling to catch her breath as she moved the expandable file Hunter had given to her. "It's all yours."

He thanked her and took his seat. She adjusted herself in her seat and tried vainly to look straight ahead, but found herself falling victim to both her peripheral vision and the man sitting next to her,

"So," he said, "you're working with Hunter Cameron?"

She glanced at him with a trace of surprise. "I am. How did you know that?"

"I've got a secret," he replied as he leaned forward toward her.

He ducked his chin and his eyebrows rose in synch with his devilish grin. Despite herself, Libby felt her pulse quicken.

"I saw you walk in with him and your client." He sat back against the bench, still smiling.

She rolled her eyes, wishing she felt as composed as she was trying to look. "How very observant of you."

"You a lawyer?" he asked.

"Hope to be."

"You still in school?" He didn't sound as though he was from here, she decided. In fact, he didn't sound like he was from anywhere.

"No," she said, pretending to rub out a wrinkle in her dark skirt. "Just graduated. Getting ready to take the bar exam." She realized she hadn't been this nervous while talking to a guy since middle school.

He nodded as though he understood completely and draped one arm over the back of the bench. Though his hand was still several inches from her shoulder, she could almost feel the electricity arcing between them.

The bailiff's voice broke her concentration. She rose to her feet along with the rest of the courthouse as Judge J. Richard Roberts rambled his way to the bench. At six-three, two-hundred-and-thirty pounds, the judge had the physical stature equal to his position in the profession. His thick, salt-and-pepper hair and the trendy glasses he had bought at his wife's behest perfectly complemented his well-deserved reputation for being an intellectual. He was known to have an affinity for underdogs, and despite an occasional show of temperament, was considered something of a sensitive soul.

After rumbling through the obligatory introduction of who he was and the purpose of the morning's docket, Roberts boomed out, "Commonwealth versus Charles Kirkland Warren, Jr."

"That's my case," Libby heard herself say to the man sitting beside her as she stood up and grabbed her file.

"Mine too," he said, rising as well. He smiled and held out his hand in a gentlemanly invitation for her to walk before him to the front of the courtroom. She obliged, wondering with every step just exactly who he was. She watched him walk around the empty jury box and join a husky fellow standing at the prosecution table whom she had already identified, based on Hunter's description, as L.G. Owen, the Commonwealth's Attorney.

Hunter met her about fifteen feet from the bench and took the file from her, offering her a reassuring smile. She returned to the bench and sat down. She barely noticed when Kirk Warren rushed past her on his return from the men's room and joined Hunter in front of the bench.

"Let the record reflect," the judge said, "that the Defendant is in court with his privately retained attorney, Hunter Cameron, and the Commonwealth is represented by the Commonwealth's Attorney, L.G. Owen."

The judge held up a single piece of paper. Several cameras in the courtroom flashed. "Mr. Warren, the Grand Jury of Christian County has returned an indictment against you for one count of Murder, First Degree. I am holding a copy of that indictment in my hand."

He then turned to Hunter. "Mr. Cameron, does your client wish to waive formal reading of the indictment?"

"Yes, your Honor. He does," Hunter replied. Though the waiving of the formal reading was ministerial in nature, designed purely to save everyone a lot of time, he couldn't help but wonder which one of the ham-handed reporters in the back of the court-room would report the waiver as being some sort of tactical blunder.

"Does your client wish to enter a plea of 'Not Guilty'?" the judge asked.

"Yes, your Honor."

"Very well then. This matter will be continued for a pre-trial conference on…"

"Excuse me, your Honor," Hunter interjected. "I'm very sorry to interrupt. But my client wishes to waive his pre-trial conference and proceed directly to trial."

Libby had known this moment was coming and Hunter had warned her how unusual their request was. But it was not until she saw the quizzical look on Judge Roberts' face that she appreciated just how right her boss had been.

"No pre-trial conference?" the judge repeated, apparently not certain he had heard it correctly the first time.

"That's correct, your Honor." Hunter's voice was authoritative and confident. "We wish to proceed immediately to trial, with the earliest date possible."

The judge turned his eye toward L.G. Owen, who seemed equally stumped. Despite the cordial relationship the prosecutor maintained with Hunter, it was evident from his stunned look his adversary hadn't shared his intentions with him.

"Your Honor," he said "the Commonwealth has no objection to the Defendant waiving his pre-trial conference and proceeding directly to trial."

The judge sighed and reached for his calendar. "Very well," he said as he thumbed through the pages. He studied first one month, then another. Occasionally, he shook his head in frustration as he attempted to find an open date on which to set the trial.

"We're full into next year," he said.

"Your Honor," Hunter said. "We have filed a *Motion for a Speedy Trial.*"

The judge glared at him over the top of his glasses. "I understand that, Mr. Cameron. But if you want to be first on the trial docket, and I assume that you do, the earliest this court can accommodate you is next year. L.G.," he snapped. "What about Commonwealth versus Wendell Allen in mid-April? Any idea where we are on that case?"

L.G. considered the question for a moment, then said, "I think that's a drug case, Judge."

"Is the Defendant in jail?"

L.G. pondered again before shaking his head. "I don't believe so."

"Well," the judge said, "I can set this case on that date and back it up with the Allen trial if you want." Despite his flare of irritation a few minutes before, he was clearly trying to be cooperative.

L.G. briefly studied his own trial calendar. "That's okay with us."

"That date is fine, your Honor."

Libby could feel the exasperation emanating from Kirk as Hunter agreed on the date. She could hardly blame him for not wanting to wait ten months to clear his name.

"I assume that with this being a murder trial, we will need a full week for the trial," the judge continued. Both Hunter and L.G. nodded.

"All right, then. This case is scheduled for trial on that date at nine o'clock," the judge said as he rose to leave the chamber. "Court will stand in recess for fifteen minutes"

Libby stood in the front row waiting for Hunter and Kirk. Hunter was smiling when he reached her, but Kirk was still glowering. They deftly avoided the media waiting outside the courtroom door and made a beeline for the office.

As they reached the steps of the courthouse, Libby was certain she could feel that energy again, the same energy she felt earlier in the courtroom. She glanced to her left and saw the man from the courtroom standing next to L.G. Owen beside the front door.

"Is that man an attorney?" she asked Hunter.

Hunter turned and looked at the man in a manner so blatant it made Libby blush, like a schoolgirl being ratted out for having a crush on a boy on the playground. Just as she had feared, the man noticed Hunter's scrutiny. As Hunter turned back to her, the man flashed her a wide grin and a wink.

Damn, Libby thought, rolling her eyes at her own stupidity.

"Who? Him? You ought to know him by now," Hunter said.

"Why is that?" she asked, glad no one was paying attention to the heat creeping up her neck.

"Because," Hunter replied, "you've read his reports about twenty times so far. That's the arresting officer in our case."

Libby froze in shock and then turned around and looked at the man. He was still watching her, a mischievous glint in his eye.

Hunter resumed walking toward his office. "Yep," he called over his shoulder. "That's Anthony Newell."

Chapter Forty-Eight

Hunter parked the car in his driveway and breathed a sigh of relief. He had gotten through another workday without incident, which these days was cause for celebration. Each day was like a game of keep-away. He did his best to behave normally as he kept everyone at arm's length, afraid to let anyone get too close lest they realize that he was not really Hunter Cameron at all; he was only playing him on TV.

For the most part, he had been successful. Of course, there had been a few misfires at the office. He frequently couldn't remember where to find a particular piece of office equipment, such as the copier or paper clips. He had on more than one occasion made silent searches for the same restroom he'd been using for over twenty years. He dreaded any out-of-office meetings, fearful of getting lost and needing directions to places he'd been a hundred times before.

But with all of his compensating at work, he still realized only half of his charade was done. He still had to keep the woman he'd loved all of his adult life in the dark. He had to fool Katherine.

She was standing in the yard watering her flowers when he climbed out of the car. He walked along the sidewalk up to her and kissed her on the cheek.

"How was your day?" she asked before returning her attention to the hose.

"Uneventful," he said, heading for the front door

Katherine shut off the water and followed him inside. She headed for the kitchen, where dinner was simmering on the stove. She was stirring the pasta when Hunter slipped his arms around her from behind and nuzzled his lips against the crook of her neck.

"Why don't we delay dinner for a while?" he asked.

"Aren't you hungry?"

"Not for food," he said. The husky note in his voice left little doubt as to his intentions.

"Oh honey," Katherine replied, stiffening in his arms. "I haven't seen you like this since we were newlyweds. It's been every night for the last two weeks. You're like a schoolboy."

Hunter wasn't so easily dissuaded. "Are you complaining?"

"I'm not complaining at all," she said with a sigh. "It's just that you've been insatiable lately."

Since she showed no sign of yielding, he finally let go of her and retreated to the dinner table. He could feel a trace of frustration building inside him and he had little doubt in which part of his anatomy it had begun.

In the recent weeks he had found himself with an ever-increasing libido. His sex drive was simply off the charts. Katherine was right. Though their love life had always, he thought, been very healthy—particularly given the length of their marriage—things had taken a decidedly accelerated turn. He simply couldn't get enough.

And it wasn't limited to Katherine. Though he never acted on it, Hunter found himself noticing and often being turned on by nearly every woman with whom he came into contact. Suddenly, he was noticing things about them he couldn't recall ever having noticed before—their curves and shapes, the delicate scents of their perfumes and lotions. He found himself flirting with them, however innocently. He felt like he had as a high schooler.

"Is that a problem?" he asked.

"No," she replied without turning around. "But I don't know

that I'm up for it again tonight, honey. I had a really long day. I got in a new shipment at the store and I'm awfully tired." She continued to slowly stir the pasta. "Maybe tomorrow I'll feel better."

Hunter felt his face flush with anger. He got up from the table and left the room without saying another word. She *never* seemed to want to when he did. Was she tired of him, he wondered? He certainly wasn't tired of her. Of that much he was certain.

Still, he figured he'd better ask Dr. Johnston about the recent spike in his libido during his next appointment.

———

AS HUNTER EXPLAINED HIS SITUATION, Johnston nodded as though he was hearing the same joke for the hundredth time.

"An increased sex drive is frequently seen in Alzheimer's patients, particularly for those in the early to moderate stages, as you are," Johnston said.

"Early to moderate," Hunter repeated. "That's just great." *Jesus,* he thought, running his fingers through his hair. *Here I am, losing my frigging mind. And I can't think about anything but sex.*

"Is your heightened sexual desire causing you frustration?" Johnston asked.

"Yes, it is," Hunter said, feeling his face heat. This was embarrassing as hell. He was approaching sixty years old and felt like he was discussing the damned *birds and the bees* with his father all over again.

"That's very common, too. Both for you and your spouse. Have you talked to her about it?"

"About what?"

"About the increase in your sex drive and the distinct likelihood that it is tied to your dementia?"

Hunter was silent for a moment. When he finally spoke, his voice was sheepish. "Not exactly."

Dr. Johnston couldn't quite hide his wince. "I see." His voice was quiet. "You haven't told her about your condition yet, have you?"

Hunter sighed, then nodded.

"How long do you think that you can keep this charade going, Mr. Cameron?"

"Until April," Hunter said, hearing the note of desperation deepen in his own voice. "I only need to keep it going until April."

"You're already showing signs of further deterioration. The stress of defending your friend on a murder charge while you're in this condition, along with not telling anyone about it is..." He paused. "None of this is helping you. In all likelihood, it's exacerbating your condition."

"Doctor, this isn't up for further discussion. Listen, I know there's no cure for what I have, but isn't there anything you can give me that can slow this down some? I need to buy myself some time. Once the trial is over, I'm all yours. And I'll come clean with Katherine. I promise. But I just have to do this one last thing first."

Johnston gazed at Hunter for a moment. "I'm going to refer you to a clinic. It's in Paducah, not far from you. It's called the Four Rivers Clinical Research Center. It's a clinical trials research center. They conduct trials for the prevention and treatment of a number of diseases, including Alzheimer's Disease and other dementias."

"You make it sound like I'm going to be living in some sort of lab, like a damned guinea pig."

Johnston offered him a faint smile. "Not at all. You simply go periodically and are given certain investigational medications and treatments. Your progress is monitored closely through follow-up appointments. This isn't voodoo, Hunter," he continued, clearly noticing the skeptical look on Hunter's face. "They'll keep me apprised of your condition. Four Rivers is overseen by pharmaceutical companies, the FDA, and other regulatory agencies. Their first priority is your health and welfare, not the promotion of an untested drug. If your goal is to buy some time, they may be able to help you. But for once, you *have* to do as I say."

Hunter pondered the physician's words for a moment. "Okay, okay. I'll go. Can you please get me set up there as soon as possible?"

"No problem," Johnston said. "I'll explain your rather *unique* situation and see if they can get you in immediately." Johnston made a note on his laptop and headed for the door.

"Dr. Johnston?" Hunter said. "Just one other thing."

"What's that?"

"Is there something you can give me for my, *umm...*" he paused for a moment. "My *urges?* I mean, I'm going crazy here."

Johnston shook his head, allowed himself a small, sad smile, and walked out the door.

Chapter Forty-Nine

L ibby sat in the booth of the small diner, her lunch special of chicken tenders and French fries left virtually untouched. If she still had her wits about her, she would have done whatever it took to not let her hands shake. Or to conceal the tears rolling down each side of her freckled face. She would have done anything to hide what he had done to her. Again.

The graduation card she had received listed no return address on the outside. It looked just like several others she had received from friends. When she had opened the card, it didn't contain any handwritten congratulations or well wishes. In fact, it wasn't signed at all. Rather, it contained a separate sheet of paper with a type-written message.

Libby,

I just saw the announcement of your graduation from law school in the local paper. I'm not foolish enough to think that your failure to send an invitation to me, your father, the man who gave you life and then loved and supported you afterward, was an oversight.

You have and continue to hurt me more than you could ever know. Or maybe you do know. Your Grandmother Masters would be proud of you for carrying on her legacy in that regard.

Love,
    Dad

Libby found herself re-reading the letter again and again. Possibly just to believe that she was actually seeing the words. The reference to her grandmother was both self-serving and typical. His dad's mother had been a small woman, but had more than made up for it with her overbearing, and often biting, personality. She had criticized him from the time he could walk and he often used the treatment he received as a child as justification for being conflict-adverse as an adult. Libby might have bought that part, but she knew her father's upbringing did not justify his evolution into a master manipulator.

Libby studied the letter for a moment, knowing beyond any doubt that although he had certainly read and signed the letter, it was her stepmother Julia who had written it. Above all else, she knew that when it came to writing a letter such as this one her father —the self-absorbed, manipulative bastard that he was—simply didn't have the balls.

She might have respected him more if he had.

Her father and Julia were the perfect match. He was weak and in need of someone to fight his self-made battles. And Julia was more than happy to oblige. They deserved one another.

Unfortunately, that insightful notion did little to comfort her.

Why can't she just leave me alone? Libby wondered. *She's gotten what she wanted. She has him all to herself. I'm not in the way anymore. Why can't they just leave me be?*

Libby could slowly feel the shock of the letter receding, pushed out by the anger rising within her. She grabbed the notebook she always carried with her, and with pen in trembling hand, began her first communication with her father in over two years. She wrote furiously, pressing so hard on the pen that the lines carved deeply into the thick tablet.

Dear Daddy,

I am in receipt of your "card". I guess I can always count on you to know just the right thing to say.

I don't know how you found my address, but it is certainly a shame that you went to such trouble in order to share with me the half-baked, illiterate bullshit spewed by that bitch you married.

As for my alleged ability to inflict pain, Daddy, if that's the case, then I certainly learned from the best. I'm sure that Grandmother would be equally proud knowing that her gift didn't skip a generation on its way to me...

"Excuse me, Miss?"

Libby felt a hand against her shoulder and was too embarrassed to look up. The kindly old waitress who was serving her had obviously seen her crying and was worried about her. *Oh shit,* she thought. *This is great. Dry your damned eyes and get a hold of yourself.* Maybe she could convince the waitress she just had a bad cold. She grabbed a napkin from the silver dispenser and swiped at her running mascara.

"I'm okay," she said, turning around.

It wasn't the waitress's hand on her shoulder. It was Anthony Newell's.

He was still as handsome as ever. But his smile wasn't the devilish one he had worn in court. This smile one was somehow warmer. More compassionate. She knew instantly that whatever bullshit she might throw him about a cold would be a waste of time.

"You all right?" he asked gently.

"I'm...um...I'm f-fine," she stammered.

Newell smiled again, this time with the knowing condescension of someone who was accustomed to being lied to.

"Do you mind if I sit with you?" he asked.

"No," she replied as she awkwardly tried to rearrange her notebook and the rest of her belongings spread across the table to hide her father's guide. "Not at all."

Newell smoothly slipped into the seat across from her. He folded his hands in front of him and studied her for a moment as she finished jamming papers into her leather bag. "I take it you're not having the best of days," he said.

"What are you talking about?" she said, deliberately feigning confusion.

"When I walked up, you were huddled over a piece of paper and you appeared to be upset. For a minute there, I thought you might even have been crying."

Libby sat back in her seat and folded her arms. *Damn it.* She wasn't going to let some older guy who hadn't even bothered introducing himself probe her soul that easily. No matter how hot he was.

She sighed, then picked up her drink coaster and began tearing little pieces from the cheap paper. "I don't know what gave you that idea," she replied, hoping her melted mascara hadn't left her looking like a raccoon.

With a smile, he silently gave up. "So," he asked, "what were you reading?"

It was her turn to smile now. "If you're going to sit here at my lunch booth asking me personal questions about my life, don't you think you could at least introduce yourself?"

He shrugged and leaned back against his seat. "Why should I bother? You already know who I am. Just like I know your name is Libby Masters."

She grinned, their little game making her feel better already. "What else do you know about me?"

"Not that much, really. I know you just graduated from law school and that you're working with Hunter Cameron."

"I told you that in court the other day," Libby pointed out.

"I know you just moved to town."

"Again. New girl in a new job. You're not making Holmes sweat about the competition."

"You're from Paducah."

Libby knew she should have been offended—or even alarmed—that a cop would have collected that much information about her. Somehow, with him it all seemed fine. Charming, in fact. Like he was just simply interested in knowing things about her.

"Go on," she said.

Newell obliged. "And I know that when I got here, you really were upset. But I don't know why."

He didn't back down from her challenging gaze as many men would have done. His eyes seemed like flat round saucers that could hold just a certain amount of emotion before it started to spill from them. The emotion they held now was empathy. Empathy for her. She wondered if anyone else had ever looked at her that way.

"Yeah, I was," she confessed as she continued to pick at the coaster. "I'm having problems with my dad. You ever have those?"

"Who, me? No. I don't," he responded, shaking his head. "Truth be told, I never got the chance. My father died when I was very young."

"I'm sorry."

"That's okay. I'm not here to talk about me anyway." His smile was back and even warmer than before.

Libby felt an odd bond between them, quite unlike anything she had ever known. Sure, she found him attractive, but it was more than just that. In the last couple of years, she had noticed her attraction toward older men. First, there was a law school professor with whom she'd had a couple of hush-hush dates. Then a married doctor back in Jackson had feverishly pursued her. She'd warded him off, but would have been lying to herself to deny that she had found him tempting. She knew young women estranged from their fathers frequently found older men desirable. But there was something more to what she was feeling for Newell.

"Did you come here to ask me about the case?" she asked, figuring it was better to find that out now.

"No. I'm not interested in the case."

"You're not?"

"At least not right now," he replied. "And even if I was, I

wouldn't come asking you for help. I'm not a lawyer, but I have a decent idea of how the attorney-client privilege works."

"Then why did you come here?"

"Because I like the food. I came in to get lunch and I saw you here, upset and alone. I thought maybe you could use someone to talk to."

"So you didn't come here just to hit on me?" she asked, unable to resist teasing him.

"No," he said with a restrained laugh. "I'm not quite that big of an ass. Yet." A brief moment of silence fell between them as they took stock of one another. "I will be getting around to it at some point though," he warned her as he pulled out a twenty for her check and handed it to the waitress. The cocky grin was back and Libby immediately realized she had missed seeing it.

"I'll be seeing you around," he said, topping it off with a wink.

As she watched him walk away, Libby's thoughts were not on her relationship with her father. Nor were they on the bar exam or, at least not directly, the Warren case. They were with the handsome stranger who had promised he wouldn't remain a stranger for much longer.

She looked at the pile of paper shreds, all that remained of her coaster, and contemplated just how complicated her life was about to become.

Chapter Fifty

————————————

Disgraced   former-sheriff-turned-private-investigator Thomas Dooley overwhelmed the chair in Hunter Cameron's office like a barge moored at a john-boat dock. He slurped hot coffee from a Styrofoam cup and occasionally, though not often enough, wiped the excess drippings from his bushy mustache with his thick callused hands.

The fallout following his statutory rape trial had not been pretty. Dooley was still likable, but re-electing a sheriff who, at the very least, was guilty of a tawdry affair with a teenager, exceeded the look-the-other-way hypocrisy limits of even his most fervent supporters. With surprising grace, he had voluntarily resigned from his position rather than get annihilated at the next election and set out his shingle as a private investigator. It turned out that luck was on Dooley's side. As PI's went, he was not only the only show in this town, but in the entire area. Dooley knew a lot of people and a lot of lawyers. Business had boomed quickly and he had hired first one staffer and then another. Soon he was picking and choosing his cases. His wife and children might be gone, but his career had been reborn in true American fashion.

Dooley had investigated Cassandra Warren for over a month

prior to her death and had been dogged in his pursuit. He had a small notebook in his hand and was reading notes back to Hunter from a myriad of different dates and times. Having caught a brief glimpse of Dooley's illegible scribbling, Hunter was grateful for his translation.

"She was definitely seeing someone," Dooley growled. "She was skipping things that she normally didn't miss...aerobics, social lunches, tennis. That sort of thing."

Hunter was listening and jotting notes at the same time. His head popped up briefly from the notepad. "But she could have missed those things for any number of reasons," he pointed out. "What makes you think that she was having an affair?"

Somewhere under that mustache, Dooley smiled. "Well, first off, she wasn't just changing plans. She was changing plans and then lying to Mr. Warren about it. Poor guy was none the wiser, until one of her tennis buddies—some gal named Lena Scotsdale—saw him at the marina one day and asked him if his wife was feeling better. When he asked why, the lady said that Mrs. Warren hadn't been to the weekly tennis match in almost a month. Some sort of knee injury. It was the first he'd heard of it."

Dooley leaned back in the creaking chair and proudly folded his chubby hands over his belly. "That's when Mr. Warren called me."

"So what else did you find out other than she wasn't following her normal weekly routine?"

"I tailed her almost daily for about a month. That woman sure wasn't much for sitting at home. Mr. Warren told me where she usually went and on what days, but at least for that month, she was definitely going by her own agenda."

Hunter felt his head beginning to hurt. He was already getting tired of having to jump through Dooley's hoops. "Where exactly was she going?"

"Hotels," Dooley replied, his voice concrete with certainty. "Every single time. She'd rent a room in her own name, pay cash, and then go to the room for a couple of hours. Then she'd leave. It was like that every time."

"Who was she with?"

"Now *that* is a good question," Dooley replied. "To tell you the truth, I really don't know."

Hunter's mouth dropped open. "You mean to tell me you followed Cassandra to and from hotels for three weeks straight and you never saw who she was meeting there?"

"I'm afraid so. This guy that she was seeing, assuming it was a guy..." Dooley paused a second to let his imagination run free. "Whoever he was, he was like Houdini. He could slip in and out like a ghost. I never even got a look at him."

"I mean," he continued, "I do this kind of shit—pardon my language, Counselor—all the time. I've seen men with plenty to lose who weren't nearly as careful as this guy. I've never seen anything like it. Her, on the other hand. She might not have had much regard for telling the truth, but she wasn't worth a shit at lying, either."

"What do you mean?" Hunter asked.

"She was as flighty as she could be," Dooley said. "She'd just hop in the car and zip right over to wherever. Her lies to her friends were transparent as hell. I can remember a time or two when I saw her wearing a hat and sunglasses as she got in the car. I laughed so hard, I nearly shit myself. I mean, she could wear a cute little disguise all she wanted to, but it usually ain't too hard to spot a gal who looks like that and drives a sixty-thousand dollar car. Not in these parts."

Hunter pondered Dooley's words. Knowing Cassandra as he did, there was no doubt Dooley was correct. Still, it did seem odd that Cassandra's presumed lover would be so painstakingly careful not to get caught, but at the same time would tolerate her ineptitude at hiding their affair. *Maybe the guy just assumed she was being careful*, he wondered. He quickly brushed away the thought. Any guy as deft as the person Dooley was describing wouldn't be able to miss Cassandra's complete lack of common sense. She had worn her shallowness like a badge of honor.

"You know what the funny part was?" Dooley asked.

"What's that?"

"The pattern of the location of the hotels. Look here." Dooley thumbed through his notebook with the haste he normally reserved only for menus. "I started trailing her on May 4. On May 9, she checked into the Holiday Inn in Murray around noon, left at about three-thirty. May 17, she visited the Shamrock Inn in Benton. Stayed for a couple of hours. On May 22, she went across the Tennessee line and stayed at Riverview Inn in Clarksville. All places out of town and a good thirty minutes to an hour away. Safe, right?"

Hunter nodded in agreement.

Dooley plodded forward. "But by early June, they were sticking their hands a lot closer to the fire. On June 9, she gets a room at the Little River Lodge. June 11, the Little River Lodge again. June 14, she got a room at the Holiday Inn on Ft. Campbell Boulevard. And the Riverdale Inn on Main Street in the afternoon on June 14. That was the day..."

"...that she was murdered," Hunter finished.

"My point," Dooley continued, "is that this guy of hers was extremely careful and particular. Even when he was here, I couldn't ever get a shot of him. But as careful as he was, he started out further away and then, slowly but surely, he got closer and closer. Until he was finally meeting her regularly in Hopkinsville. Right up until she was murdered. That seems to me, Counselor, to fly in the face of how this guy was operating."

Hunter leaned back in his chair, propping his chin between thumb and forefinger. "Maybe," he said, "or maybe not."

"What do you mean?" Dooley asked, his curiosity getting the better of him.

"Who's to say," Hunter replied, "that he didn't want to get caught? Or more precisely, who's to say that he didn't want *her* to get caught?"

Dooley looked perplexed, as only a man of his personal experience could. "Now why in the *hell* would a man ballin' another man's wife want her to get caught?" Dooley's scowl deepened. "If you ask me, Counselor, you should probably hope the police don't figure out any of this."

"Why is that?"

"It seems to me that Mr. Warren hiring me to follow his wife and learning that she's screwin' around on him gives him a pretty damned good motive." Dooley was making no secret of the fact that he believed Kirk had murdered Cassandra. Now he must be wondering if he had hand-delivered the motive as well. Knowing Dooley, Hunter doubted that would cause the man any sleepless nights.

"Of course," Hunter said, "if we can find out the identity of Cassandra's mystery lover, it would give us one other thing."

Dooley nodded. "Yep," he said grimly. "Another suspect."

Chapter Fifty-One

H e sat in the dark alone. A half-empty fifth of whiskey rested on the small table next to him, the requisite glass sitting beside it. A straight razor hung from his fingers, just inches from the cold hardwood floor.

Try though he might, he simply could not remember a time in his entire life when he had been as furious with himself as he was at this very moment.

Nothing was going as planned.

He had been disciplined his entire life. He wanted it, loved it. Had sought it out. His military training had brought moments of exhilaration, but it had also frequently been disappointing. Not because it was too harsh and disciplined, but because it wasn't harsh or disciplined *enough*. To compensate, he had taught himself certain tactics, certain rituals that forced him to be rigid and cold. To be disciplined. To be what he had to be to achieve the moment he'd been waiting for his entire life.

That moment was upon him now, towering over him like a brick wall backed up against the moonlight, overcoming him first by shadows and then in complete darkness. He swathed himself within that darkness, craving it like a drug. It had fueled him to get here, to this place and to this time. He was now on the cusp.

And yet he felt himself crumbling from the one place he had never dreamed his weakness would come. From the inside.

He had known, years before he met her, that Cassandra Warren would be a casualty of his war.

He had watched her from a distance for months ahead of time. He had known her likes and dislikes before he ever uttered a word to her. He had known she would want him. Her husband simply wasn't capable of giving her anything except money.

She would have gone with him after their first chance encounter. But he had made her wait. He had told her that he would find her again. And shortly thereafter, he did.

Their intimacy had swallowed her right up, overwhelming her. He had long ago programmed himself to separate himself from the act. To him it was just another task. Another step toward his ultimate goal. She was beautiful, yes…in a *faux* sort of way. Acrylic nails. Standard silicone enhancements. Ornamental, like a plastic Christmas tree. Certainly not the type of woman he could ever love. As if he could love anyone. After all, he didn't know *how* to love. He didn't know how to feel anything. Anything but *this*.

He thought he had accounted for her and for her demise. He thought he had accounted for everything. But he hadn't dreamed of the look on her face when she had told him the news. *Their* news. He hadn't accounted for such a scenario. In his entire life, he had never dreamed of the possibility of such a thing happening.

All at once, and for just an instant, he had felt himself wishing that the goal he was so close to accomplishing would never come to be. Had wished he could whisk her away and protect her from the fate that had been determined for her so long ago.

But he couldn't. The steps had been set in motion and now it was too late. There was nothing he could do to save her.

And there would be more casualties.

He thought he had prepared himself for this moment. He was *sure* of it. But he hadn't known it would feel this way to him. He had never dreamed that he would miss her. That he would miss the two of them, the one he had and the one he could only dream of having.

No, he thought. *No! I won't let this happen.* He brought his fist down, splintering the small table and shattering the whiskey bottle against the far wall. *My entire life has been dedicated to this moment. No matter what the losses are, I can't stop.*

I won't stop.

Still, he couldn't help but feel for her now. He decided she *would* be avenged. Just as he had ultimately caused her demise, he would exact her revenge, along with his own. The two of them—Cameron and Warren—would suffer because of what they had forced him to do.

He found himself on his feet, his fist tightly clenched. He no more felt the straight razor slice into his palm than he did the streams of tears that scorched their way down his cheeks.

Chapter Fifty-Two

"She was pregnant."

Hunter slapped the autopsy report down on the conference table in front of Kirk and waited for his friend's response.

Kirk sat quietly, his hands folded in his lap as he stared at the report.

Hunter began to pace around the room, his hands alternating between rubbing his face and resting on his hips. "Did you know about this?"

Kirk didn't answer.

"Did you know about this?" he repeated, his voice rising.

Nothing.

Hunter leaned over the table and planted his palms on both sides of the report until his face was just a few inches from Kirk's. He'd been choking back his anger at Kirk for most of his life; he no longer felt like it. "God damnit, Kirk! I asked you a question and I expect an answer!"

Kirk slowly lifted his head and met Hunter's gaze.

Hunter didn't budge an inch. "Did you know that she was *pregnant?*"

"No," Kirk said softly. "I didn't know."

Hunter straightened and resumed his pacing. He ran his fingers through his hair, muttering, "Jesus Christ!"

"What does this mean?" Kirk asked.

"Well, for starters, I'm pretty sure that you're going to be indicted for a second murder charge. This one for the baby."

"How can they do that?" Kirk asked, blinking helplessly behind his glasses. "I didn't even know there *was* a baby."

"All they need to do is prove there was a fetus," Hunter said, pointing to the report, "which the medical examiner appears perfectly willing to do."

Kirk's expression grew even more resigned. "What will it do to the trial?"

Hunter felt himself calming down. With his emotions subsiding, his mind started working again. "It won't move the trial date. The two crimes are about as connected as it gets so there's no reason to have separate trials. You'll most likely be indicted at the next meeting of the Grand Jury. They'll set the new charge on the same date with the other one."

Hunter caught himself using those terms—*charge* and *the other one*. They were no longer people to him. They were not a dead wife and her unborn child. They were now just numbers. Blurbs. They were nothing but cases, tragic figures in this battle for his friend's life —*his* final battle. But that was where he had to put them. If, in his compromised state, he was going to save Kirk, he wouldn't be able to expend any of his limited resources feeling pity for the victims. Their ghosts would just have to visit him in his dreams if they wanted to reach him.

A thought struck Hunter. "On the other hand," he said, "I suppose this rather unfortunate turn of events has a positive side. At least as far as your case goes."

Kirk snorted. "And just what would that be?"

"Well," Hunter replied, "if your wife was pregnant with your child, that gives you a significant motive to *not* want her dead." He nodded, and for the first time in weeks, actually felt some degree of optimism. "Getting a jury to believe you'd kill your wife is one thing.

But convincing them that you'd murder her when she was carrying your child is quite anoth—"

Kirk slowly raised his hand, interrupting Hunter. "That's just it."

"What's it?" Hunter asked, his optimism faltering before the expression on Kirk's face.

"Remember how you weren't convinced that Cassandra was necessarily having an affair? Just because old Dooley couldn't ever catch her with the guy? You said that you wanted to be able to argue that there wasn't any affair because, if there wasn't, they wouldn't have much in the way of motive?"

"Yeah."

"Well, my motive just got a lot better. For them."

"What do you mean?" Hunter asked as he sank into a chair.

"I mean this leaves no doubt that Cassie was having an affair. No doubt whatsoever." Kirk's voice gentled, almost as if he regretted dealing such a painful blow to his friend. "You see—I can't possibly be the father." Hunter's shoulders slumped as Kirk finished. "That's right, Hunter. I'm sterile."

Chapter Fifty-Three

Libby stood by the window of her apartment watching for headlights in the darkness of the driveway. She hadn't been this nervous before a date since she was fifteen.

And it was all because of that damned Anthony Newell.

She took a sip of her bottled water, completely unaware of the smile that crossed her face. She had been on her way home from taking the bar exam in Lexington when her cell phone had rang. Unlike many of her contemporaries, she had not been terribly nervous before or after the two-day exam. And unlike her days in law school, she had been actually focused on the task at hand. Preparation, she had determined with Hunter Cameron's help, was the best cure for nerves.

When she answered the phone, the voice on the other line was one indelibly etched in her memory, though she had heard it only a few times before.

"How'd the test go?" Newell had asked.

"Here's a better question," she replied. "How did you get this number?"

"I'm a cop," he replied. "I've got my ways." Libby could almost hear his cocky grin on the other end of the line.

"So," she said, hoping he wouldn't sense her pleasure at receiving his call, but suspecting he would. "What can I do for you?"

"I knew you'd be finished with the bar exam today. I thought you might want to go out and celebrate."

Her heart warmed under the heat of his courtesy, but she wasn't ready to let him know that. Not yet. "I would think a state police detective would have bigger things on his mind than going to the trouble to find out when my bar exam is over."

Newell ignored the comment. "Can I pick you up tomorrow night, say six o'clock?"

"Where are you planning on taking me?" The thought of declining the invitation never crossed Libby's mind, just as she knew the thought of her doing so had never crossed his.

"It's a surprise."

Somewhere not far from the surface of her mind, common sense and perhaps fear were waging an epic battle with temptation. "We really shouldn't."

"Why not?" Newell asked without a trace of doubt in his voice.

"Well," she stammered, "I don't think it's the best idea for us to be seen in public together under the circumstances."

"What circumstances?"

If nothing else, Libby thought, *he's damned good at faking cluelessness.* "We're on opposite sides," she said, trying to sound stern.

"Of what?"

"You know 'of what'. The Warren case."

"Oh, that again." He sighed. "Don't worry about it. I've got a plan. No one will see us."

"Why?" she asked, barely suppressing a laugh. "Are you going to take me parking on some country road?"

"Of course not. We'll be in a public setting, but let's just say I'll take my chances on anyone from Hopkinsville recognizing us."

"Fair enough. But what makes you think I'd want to go with you."

Newell's answer had been immediate. "What makes you think that you don't?"

Now, as she sat waiting for him to arrive, she was no closer to answering that question.

Headlights turned into the driveway and flashed through her window, interrupting her train of thought. As her heart began to beat faster in anticipation, there was a knock on her door.

When Libby opened the door and saw him, neatly pressed in a polo shirt, khakis, and loafers without socks, her mouth went dry.

"You look just as stunning as I thought you would," he said with a smile. "I'd love to spend more time telling you just *how* stunning"—he looked at his watch—"but we're going to be late."

They headed out of Hopkinsville in his '65 Mustang convertible on Highway 68/80 and were soon on I-24 headed northwest. It was not lost on Libby that this was the route she would take if she ever drove back home to Paducah. As if she ever would…

As they drove along the highway, they soon found themselves lost in conversation. The convertible top was down and the wind rustled Libby's hair. Still, they each heard every word the other spoke. Somehow, she felt completely at ease with this man she barely knew. And in some way, despite the vast openness of the rural summer evening, she felt a certain intimacy in the moment as though the two of them were the only people in the world. Or at least the only two that mattered.

Newell turned off the exit past Kentucky Dam and drove down a two-lane road, passing several fast food restaurants and gas stations. They were in Calvert City, just twenty minutes or so from her childhood home. The area was vaguely familiar to her and she was certain that she had been here before. Her brow furrowed as she looked around, trying to find the lost memory.

Newell turned right on another rural road and in less than a mile, Libby could see a line of cars extending from a field. Suddenly, she recognized where he was taking her. *No, it couldn't be.*

"Welcome to the Drive-In," Newell said, grinning at her as he eased the Mustang into the long line.

As the line progressed into the gravel drive, Libby could see the enormous screen on which previews were being shown. "I haven't been here in years," she said, unaware that she was smiling like a little girl. "What made you think of this place?"

"What girl doesn't like going to a drive-in movie in a convertible?"

"I feel like I should have on a cheerleader sweater and you should have on your varsity jacket," she said. "What's next? Are we going to drink the same milkshake with two straws?"

After paying their entrance, Newell drove to an unoccupied spot near the center of the crowded field. A teenage waitress quickly arrived and took their order of hamburgers, fries, and two oblig-atory milkshakes. After she left, they placed the removable speakers on the car doors.

"I remember my parents bringing me here when I was a kid," Libby said. "It's one of the few drive-ins left in the country. I had forgotten about it even being here until now." Not wanting to bore him with her reminiscing, she asked, "You don't have much of an accent. How did you end up in Kentucky?"

"When I was in the military I finished my enlistment at Fort Campbell. I liked the area so I decided to stay."

"Is that when you went to the State Police Academy?"

"Yeah. I always knew I wanted to be in law enforcement."

"How come?"

"Because of how my father died." Newell was quiet for a moment. "He was murdered when I was very young. It's why I became a cop."

"I...uh," Libby stammered. "I'm so sorry. I didn't mean to..."

He raised a hand, cutting her off. "That's okay. Really. I made it fine."

"Is your mother still alive?" Libby asked, surprised at how much she wanted, for him, the answer to be yes.

Newell shook his head. "She never really got over my father's murder. She died when I was ten. I found her in her bedroom. She looked as though she was just sleeping peacefully, but I knew some-thing was wrong."

Libby let the words settle, trying to show respect for their weight.

"My mother died a couple of years ago. My father seems to have rebounded nicely."

"Any brothers or sisters, or is it just you and your dad?"

"I'm an only child," she replied, deliberately ignoring the part about her dad. "What about you? Any siblings?"

"I have a younger sister," Newell replied as he fiddled with his straw. "We're not close though. She inherited our mother's weaknesses. She has a drug problem, or at least she did the last time I saw her."

"When was that?" Libby asked, finding herself genuinely interested in this stranger's family history. Interested perhaps so she could feel better about her own.

"About ten years ago. She was living in a dump in Las Vegas." He shook his head. "I asked her what she did for a living; she told me that I didn't want to know." He met Libby's sympathetic gaze with a frank one of his own. "I haven't seen her since."

"Oh," Libby replied, wishing she hadn't asked.

"Let's not dwell on that stuff," he said, rescuing her. "We're here to have fun."

They leaned back in their seats and eased back into conversation. Had they been able to break their attention from one another, they would have realized they didn't watch a single scene of the movie. Or of the second showing that followed it. They simply sat and talked. They listened, learned about one another, and laughed out loud. And at the end of the evening, as Newell pulled into her driveway and prepared to walk her to her door, Libby noticed something strange.

Sometime during the evening—she couldn't remember when— they had taken hold of one another's hand. Now at the date's end, she realized neither had ever let the other go.

Chapter Fifty-Four

Four Rivers Clinical Research Center was housed in a suite on the third floor of the Medical Arts Building, a mere blip in a morass of offices located throughout the building. Hunter sat in one of the chairs facing the large window in the Four Rivers' lobby, and surprisingly, found himself enjoying the view. Unlike so many medical buildings he had visited, this building was not cloaked in clinical coldness. A vast atrium dominated the first floor, creating a panoramic view from the third. The Research Center was nothing like he had envisioned. *My memory may be escaping me day after day,* he thought, *but the prejudices and preconceived notions are always the last to go.*

He nervously picked up a brochure from the small table next to his chair. Its cover was a collage of photos of men and women, both young and old, receiving all sorts of different treatments. At the top of the page a bold caption read *Four Rivers Clinical Research, Inc.— Putting The Future To The Test In the Heartland.* Hunter flipped to the first page and was reading the introduction when he heard his name being called.

"Mr. Cameron?" Hunter turned and accepted the thin hand being offered to him.

"My name is Janine Talcott," the woman said.

"It's nice to meet you," Hunter replied.

Wasting no time, she showed him down the hallway to her office. "Why don't you follow me back and we'll get started." She was very slight of build, no more than five feet or a hundred pounds or so. Her angular face told him she was close to his age. Her voice was soft, decidedly warmer than the contours of her features suggested.

Hunter followed her into the small office and sat where she instructed, in a chair next to a modern-looking desk. Talcott sat down at the desk, faced him, and folded her hands.

"Dr. Johnston has told me a lot about you," she said with a polite grin obviously meant to put him at ease.

"Should I be worried?"

"No, no, no," Talcott replied, opening a thin case file. "You do, however, have some rather *unique* circumstances."

"I hope you're not going to try to talk me to get out of my case," Hunter said. "Dr. Johnston already tried and it's not a matter that's open to debate." He knew he sounded defensive. He couldn't help it, though. He knew that this case, with the fate of his best friend hanging in the balance, would be his last taste of the life he had known. He wasn't about to let anyone take it from him.

To her credit Talcott was not taken aback by his words. "I understand, Mr. Cameron—"

"Please," he interrupted, "it's Hunter."

"Great," she replied. "I'm Janine." Her gentle, but direct, eye contact was clearly intended to make him feel more comfortable. Hunter could tell she was a pro at this.

"My job," she continued, "is not to convince you to do anything regarding the case. I understand from Dr. Johnston that you've made up your mind about that. While that may not be the optimal situation considering your condition, we will respect your decision. In the meantime, I want to assess exactly what stage of dementia you're in and attempt to treat it."

Hunter pondered this for a moment. "I thought that there was no cure for Alzheimer's."

"You're correct. Nothing can stop A.D.," she replied. "However, for some people in the early and middle stages of the disease, certain drugs may alleviate some of the cognitive symptoms."

"So, in other words, you may be able to buy me some time.

Talcott nodded slowly, as if she was reluctant to make any promises she might not be able to keep. "Some of our medicines also help to control behavioral symptoms of A.D., such as sleeplessness, agitation, anxiety, and depression. Treating these symptoms often makes patients more comfortable and makes taking care of them easier for their caregivers."

In other words, it isn't all about you, Hunter thought. Her reticence was understandable. This was a research center looking for cures, not a way for egotistical lawyers trying to get one last day in the sun before fading into the gloaming of their own oblivion.

"Why don't we begin by me asking you some questions?" she said, relieving Hunter of the burden of his own shame.

They quickly ran through the health history form, questions that should have been old hat to him by now. However, in his world, nothing was a given. Not anymore. With the benefit of faxed documents from Hunter's other physicians, Talcott never dwelled on his inability to answer a particular question about his own history, instead flipping through the pages until she found the answer she needed. The resulting comfort level eventually empowered Hunter to ask some questions of his own.

"What exactly is a 'clinical trial'?"

Talcott carefully laid down her pen, turned to him, and smiled warmly. He knew before a word passed her lips that it was an answer she'd given many times before.

"After a new drug has been tested on lab animals, they next conduct human 'clinical trials'," she explained, "on volunteers who then receive the new medication to establish how the drug is processed by the human body."

"After that," she continued, "individuals with the actual illness for which the medication is intended are recruited—again, on a volunteer basis—to participate in 'double blind' clinical trials to establish appropriate dosage levels. In these trials, the research medication is compared either to a placebo or to an already accepted effective medication to make sure that the new medication is also safe and effective."

"*Double blind?*"

Talcott chuckled. "Sounds bad, doesn't it? It just means that neither the clinical trial participant nor the physician conducting the study knows who receives the active medication and who receives the placebo. It assures that the clinical trials are done in an unbiased fashion.

"After completion of some double-blind tests, participants may have the opportunity to receive the actual medication. During this time the safety and effectiveness of the medication is still evaluated under the care of a physician."

"Whoa," Hunter said. "You mean that I've got to go through a series of tests with what may be sugar cubes before I can even try the real thing?"

"That's correct."

Hunter could feel his frustration growing. "But I need the prescription now. My time is limited. I'm losing more of myself every day."

Talcott shook her head sadly. "I'm afraid that's the only way."

She picked up a printout from her neatly arranged desk, then rose and moved to the chair next to his. "I'm going to ask you some questions," she said. Hunter reflexively began to roll his eyes. "And before you roll your eyes," she said more sternly, "there are no right or wrong answers. I want you to relax. This test is called a MMSE test. It stands for a 'Mini Mental State Examination' Test. It helps us determine what stage of the condition you're in and what drug to use to attempt to treat it."

Hunter sighed, then reluctantly shrugged, knowing his options were limited.

The test first began with a series of mundane questions: the day of the week, what year was last year, what is your street address, whose office are we in—a sort of cognitive foreplay.

Next, Talcott gave Hunter the name of three objects to remember: a table, a ball, and a stick. She then asked him to repeat names of the three items.

Then came the damnable task of counting backwards from fifty, only this time, it was by fives. Hunter's frustration must have been evident because shortly after this test began, she asked him to simply spell the word *dinner* backwards.

Just when he was feeling better about himself, Talcott asked him to recite, once again, the names of the three objects he was supposed to remember. Hunter could feel his blood pressure rising as Talcott next showed him an apple and a pair of scissors and asked him to identify them. Hunter felt like his basketball coach had yanked him from the free throw line and asked him to shoot layups. *Tear you down and build you back up,* he thought.

Talcott gave Hunter a piece of paper and told him that she would be asking him to carry out a three-step process. She told him to hold it, then fold it in half. Next, she stood up and asked him to place it in her chair. Hunter completed the tasks, smirked, and then felt a brief internal alarm at the notion of being proud for completing such a simple task.

Finally, Talcott handed him a new piece of paper and a pencil. She asked him to write a sentence on the piece of paper. Hunter unwittingly snorted. He had passed the test, damn it. Done everything she had wanted him to do. Write a sentence? *Give me a friggin' break,* he thought.

As he applied lead to the paper, he suddenly felt lost. He looked at the pencil in his hand. It didn't move. Not a word, not a single letter. He gritted his teeth and commanded himself to write the sentence. Any goddamned sentence. Just something.

He looked up at the lady standing over him, but he couldn't remember who she was. He felt drops of sweat begin to form at his widow's peak. Something began to burn inside of him and the room began to move.

Hunter put the pencil down and leaned back in his chair. "This is bullshit," he said, smiling. It was all he had to offer.

Talcott looked at him with an expression that he recognized

immediately. The look was one that he had given more than once himself and he now despised himself for being its recipient.

It was pity.

When he spoke, his voice trembled. "May I... May I try again?"

Talcott nodded. She watched him carefully as he leaned back over the desk and applied pencil to paper. Gradually the pencil began to move across the paper. The movements were slow, like a child first attempting to master the alphabet. After what seemed like an eternity Hunter put down his pencil and handed the paper to Talcott.

She had fought to hang on to her professional composure throughout their interview, but as she looked at him, then gently placed the paper on the desk, he could see the telltale mist of tears in her eyes.

Hunter could no longer remember what he had written, but if he could have seen the page from his seat he would have read a phrase that, in these, the darkest moments of his life, still brought him comfort. They were words that spoke of what he wanted most, and perhaps more accurately, of all he had left.

I love my wife.

Chapter Fifty-Five

Kirk Warren's yacht rocked gently under the smooth wake of the waters of Lake Barkley. The yacht was moored to the marina dock and only the most ardent of boaters would be willing to brave the shadows of night draped over the lake and the chill of the early winter.

Inside the boat, Kirk slept soundly, the serenity of the lake lulling him to sleep. He never even heard his nightmare, dressed head-to-toe in black, step from the dock and onto the boat. Never heard him pull out the smallest blade of his pocket knife and, with a skillful flick, unlatch the lock to the boat's living quarters. And Kirk certainly didn't hear that nightmare slip into his berth and stand over him, counting the breaths of his prey.

Kirk didn't hear a thing. Not until it was too late.

With an economy of movement that belied his fury, the intruder grabbed Kirk and rolled him over on his back. As Kirk's eyes flew open, a piece of duct tape was slapped firmly over his mouth, catching the scream about to be released. Just as quickly, he tossed Kirk back over on his stomach, pinned his hands behind his back, and secured them with duct another length of tape. With another flash of tape, Kirk's ankles were bound as well. It happened so quickly that Kirk never had the opportunity to resist, not that it would have mattered if he had.

Grabbing Kirk by the collar of his pajamas, the intruder yanked him out of the bed, whirled him around in a single motion, and slammed him against the bulkhead. Despite its size, the yacht shuddered and slowly teetered from side to side. Somehow Kirk maintained consciousness, though he immediately wished that he hadn't.

He felt himself lifted off his feet and held against the wall by what felt like only one hand. Though it was otherwise pitch black within the hull, a trace of moonlight shining through a hallway porthole caught the narrow glint of silver held just inches in front of his face. It vanished and Kirk felt a thin, sharp edge pressed against his jugular. He didn't have to guess what it was.

"Don't worry, you pathetic sniveling little shit," snarled the shadowy figure on the other side of that blade. "If I wanted to gut you myself, I would have done it years ago. No," he continued, "I've got bigger plans for you. *Much* bigger. And for Hunter Cameron."

Kirk felt a shudder of fear rise steadily up his spine, like cold air seeping through a cracked basement window.

"I've waited too long for this. Far too long. I didn't go to all of this trouble just to watch from the sidelines as you march toward your lethal injection. No," he said, making a *tsk*ing sound with his mouth, "that just wouldn't do.

"You see, I *want* you to know what's happening to you *while* it's happening. I've been waiting for this moment longer than you can possibly imagine. It's not enough that *I* watch your destruction. You and Cameron—you both have to watch it, too. I want you to see it coming."

Kirk felt the warm air of his attacker's breath as the voice on the other side of the blade moved closer to his own. "And you will realize it," the voice said. "Trust me, you *both* will."

The voice grew higher, the hoarse snarl morphing into a sing-song rhythm that was somehow more chilling than anything that had come before. Like a child's nursery rhyme from hell. "*First your mother, then your wife. Then you'll be the next to lose your life.*"

Kirk begin to whimper. For one mortifying moment, he was

afraid he was on the verge of losing control of his bladder or his bowels. Or both.

Suddenly, the pressure of the blade against his throat vanished. The hand released his collar and he crumpled to the floor, wincing as his temple struck the side of something, probably his dresser. Though he still could see nothing, his ear was pressed against the boat's deck. He could feel the vibration of footsteps traveling away from him. Then he heard the faint sound of the boat's front hatch being closed.

His tormentor was gone.

Kirk closed his eyes and sucked in a shuddering breath through his nose. The night was once again silent around him. The only thing Kirk could hear was the hoarse rasp of his own sobs.

Chapter Fifty-Six

Hunter's car skidded to a stop on the wet pavement of the parking lot at the Barkley Dam Marina. It had rained shortly before dawn and a residue of cold mist drifted over the lake. The morning was a somber black and white photo whose only beacons of color were the flashing lights atop the various police cars scattered like discarded toys around the dock's entrance. Hunter jumped out of the car and began running toward the slip where Kirk docked his yacht. Following her boss's cue, Libby Masters emerged from the passenger side of the car and trotted along behind him.

The boat was awash with law enforcement of all shapes and sizes. About a hundred feet from the boat, Hunter slowed to a brisk walk. *Too many weekend warriors in this bunch*, he thought. No need to startle them.

He scanned the front of the boat. Several cops were milling around outside the boat and from the looks of it, on the inside, too. Hunter stepped aboard and walked down into the living quarters. Two deputies were working there, searching beneath the cushions of the love seat and sofa. Another was looking through the cabinets in the galley. Hunter knew the guy was satisfying his curiosity more than the requirements of his job.

He walked up behind the deputy just as the man opened the pantry door and began to examine the top shelf. "Do you think you've got him cornered in there?" he asked loudly.

The deputy's head shot up, cracking hard on the shelf above him. "*Jesus Christ!*" he yelled as he spun around, instinctively reaching for his head with one hand and his holster with the other. His face was freckled and red.

"Got *who* cornered in there?" he asked, still rubbing at the knot forming in the middle of a pronounced bald spot at the back of his head.

Hunter lifted one eyebrow. "The intruder."

The deputy was not amused. "What in the hell do you think you're doing?"

The two sleuths in the sitting area immediately stopped their search and moved toward the galley.

"I was just about to ask you the same question," Hunter replied.

"Mister," the deputy said, "this is a crime scene. This boat was burglarized last night. You're interfering with our investigation."

"Really," Hunter said. "Burglarized, huh?" He scanned the room. "Is that why you're searching the galley? Because the intruder was just looking for a spectacular spice rack?"

"Listen here, you son of a—"

"Save it." Hunter turned his back on the man and peered down the hall. "I'm looking for whoever's in charge and you're clearly not it."

Leaving the man still fuming behind him, Hunter made his way to the back berth. A few steps from the door, he saw a uniformed trooper filling out some sort of report. Kirk was sitting on his bed with a blanket wrapped tightly around him. And standing over Kirk, questioning him, was Detective Anthony Newell.

"Excuse me, Detective," Hunter said. "Can you tell me just what the hell is going on here?"

Newell turned and smiled. "Good morning, Counselor. I guess

you heard that your client here had a break-in. No need to worry. He's fine."

Sparing Newell a skeptical look, Hunter sat down on the bed next to Kirk and put an arm around him. "You all right?"

Kirk merely nodded. He wasn't even fidgeting, but appeared to be in some sort of shock. Something had scared him and scared him badly.

Hunter rose and found himself face to face with Newell. "I'd like a word with you, Detective. Outside."

———

OUTSIDE, the wind had picked up on the lake, scattering the mist. Libby stood on the dock a few feet from the boat, almost wishing she hadn't quit smoking before being accepted at law school. She was wearing a thick overcoat on top of the wool sweater and jeans she had thrown on when Hunter's urgent call had jolted her from a sound sleep. And she was still freezing her ass off. The two deputies standing on the deck were ogling her openly, clearly missing the days when a catcall or two might not have been considered sexual harassment. Libby kept her hands in her pockets, fighting the temptation to expose her middle finger to the cold by waving it in their direction.

Suddenly, she saw Hunter's head pop out from below the deck. He walked above-board and was followed out by…Anthony. In spite of herself, she felt a warm sensation spreading through her chest, one that made her temporarily forget about the weather.

They had continued to see one another regularly, each experience better than the last. The had both agreed to keep relationship discreet. It simply had to be. Not only because of the age difference, but because of the Warren case. However much he liked her, Hunter could never allow her to give even the appearance of compromising his defense of Kirk. And if his superiors learned of their affair, Anthony's career could be damaged as well.

So the Warren case had become a wall, however thin, between them. At first, they didn't even discuss it. And then they began discussing how they never discussed it. Eventually, they acknowl-edged that though the case was a major part of each of their lives, they simply could not let it stop them from being together. Anthony had no one. And neither did she. If they had to be alone in the world, at least they could do it together.

Hunter and Newell's raised voices snapped her to attention.

"So why are you here with half the damned force if you don't believe that someone broke into the boat?" Hunter was yelling.

"Mr. Cameron, I didn't say that a crime hadn't been committed. But under the circumstances, it doesn't look like there's much here to back up your client's story."

"Oh, *bullshit!*" Hunter was talking with his hands now, some-thing he only did when he was stressed. "What do you think he did? Tied himself up with duct tape and split his head open just so we could create a mystery suspect for the trial?"

Anthony's deliberate shrug said it all. *Stranger things have happened.* Even from this distance, Libby had no trouble gauging his mood. Though Anthony was always professional to a fault, right now he was pissed.

"So if you don't think there's a crime, then what are you doing with all of these guys out here?" Hunter continued, waving a hand at the cast of officers who were beginning to surround the two of them. "You think you're going to find something else on the boat? Some other piece of incriminating evidence that just happens to magically appear on your watch?"

Newell moved a step closer to Hunter, his eyes narrowing. "Just what are you implying, Counselor?"

A shiver that had nothing to do with the cold ran through Libby and the trooper accompanying Newell put a hand on his shoulder. Newell shrugged it off.

"Just that if you boys aren't investigating what happened last night, then you really don't have any reason to be here." Hunter's normal tone had returned, as though something inside of him had reached out and snapped him back into reality.

Although his eyes never left Hunter's, Anthony also managed to regain his composure. "The man has a point," he called out to the other officers, "let's head out."

Turning away from Hunter, Anthony gracefully hopped off the deck of the boat and onto the dock, landing a few feet away from Libby. If he was surprised to see her, he hid it well, giving her nothing more than a discreet wink as he walked past. Libby bit back a smile.

Hunter motioned toward the boat. "Come on," he said, "we've got work to do. Besides, it's cold as hell out here."

———

KIRK WAS STILL SITTING on the bed, shivering beneath the coarse wool blanket. Hunter sat down next to him as Libby made coffee in the galley.

"Tell me what happened, Kirk." Hunter's voice was soft now, as though he was comforting one of his daughters after a bad dream when they had been little girls.

Slowly, Kirk described what had happened. How he had been awakened by having the tape slapped over his mouth. How he had been tied up and held against the wall, with the straight razor pressed against his throat. The straight razor was the only thing he had seen for sure. It was just like his. Just like the one the police claimed he had used to murder Cassandra.

And then, he told Hunter about the rhyme. That short little rhyme his attacker had recited with such horrifying delight. Hunter's arm fell away from Kirk and he slowly stood. He gazed blankly out the hallway porthole, staring at nothing at all for a long moment. Then it came to him.

He walked toward the galley where Libby was beginning to pour the coffee. "I need you to do me a favor."

Libby nodded, his grim expression making her hands tremble.

"I want you to call Dooley. Tell him to go to my house. You and Kirk can take Kirk's car and meet him over there. I'll call Katherine and tell her what happened. You'll all be safe there for now."

Libby nodded again, relieved that was all Hunter wanted. For once, having Dooley around sounded pretty good. "Where are you going?" she asked.

"To look at an old file," he replied.

"Why do you need to look at one of your old files?" she asked, still puzzled.

"It's not one of my old files."

Libby was thoroughly confused now.

Hunter didn't make her ask. "It was my father's."

Chapter Fifty-Seven

Hunter Cameron opened the back door to his office building and stepped inside. The hallway was pitch dark, but he didn't need the light to see his way. It was, after all, his father's building. The *Cameron & Cameron* law office. His playground as a little boy and even now, some might say, as a middle-aged adult. The morning's events aside, the echoes of his own footsteps on the aged hardwood floors always sounded eerie to him. He went to the first door on the right, drew in a deep breath, turned the knob, and walked inside.

James's office was in many ways, very much as he had been. The ceilings stood nearly twelve-feet high and the depth of the room, like that of its former occupant, was expansive. The built-in bookshelves were ornate, but the rest of the décor was large, heavy oak. Lived-in and comfortable, solid and of good repute. There were no brag walls bearing photos of James with local big-wigs, nor any framed certificates highlighting a lifetime of good deeds or momentous personal achievements. The only frames in the room were mostly reserved for pictures of Hunter. Scattered throughout the bookshelves, amidst now-outdated volumes of various law treatises, was a cadre of photos of Hunter. Sports activities, graduations, his wedding…his entire life.

James's desk was a large flat-top, propped up by four legs as large as posts. The surface was clear except for one item: a large black-and-white picture of Hunter's mother, Elizabeth, displayed prominently at the desk's right corner. Hunter guessed she had been about twenty-seven at the time the picture was taken, not much before his son's birth nor long before her death, and well before her only child could form any memory of her. On the credenza next to his desk were two baseballs. One was signed by Keith Hernandez, a prize James had bought at an auction some thirty years earlier. The other was the ball, the very same home run ball, that Hunter had hit off Big Chad when he was nine years old. The one and only *Ole Rumor*, itself. Forty-some-odd years later, Hunter still didn't know how James had gotten it.

In fact, nothing in this room had changed since James's death twenty-one years earlier. James had walked into the room that morning, removed his coat, and sat down with the intention of reading his mail before walking over to the courtroom to preside over a trial. When Ms. Polly had walked into the room at twenty minutes after nine to remind him to go to court, she had found him slumped over on the desk, his head facing Elizabeth's picture. The coroner would later say that James's hand had been touching the picture when they found him, as though in his last seconds he had reached out to meet her.

Hunter had taken over the office the next year, following his graduation from law school. His father had enjoyed a loyal following and business soon prospered. Still, no matter how many years had passed between then and now, this office had remained unaltered. It was regularly dusted and cleaned, of course, but the door stayed shut.

Most people went to cemeteries and gravesides to honor their dead, but it was here that Hunter always came to visit with his father. Standing in the doorway now, he realized it had been a long time since they had visited. He couldn't help but wonder how much longer he would even be able to remember his dad.

Hunter shook his head briefly, then walked across the room to one of the two closets. The first one, on the left of the bookshelves, was a coat closet. The one to the right was for storage. Hunter knew without bothering to touch the knob that the door was locked, just how James had always kept it. Hunter also knew without even looking inside, that the closet was almost empty. In fact, it held only one item: a file labeled *Commonwealth of Kentucky v. Javier Vazquez.*

Hunter had never spoken about the file with his father or about why, all the years after the soldier's electrocution, he had kept it locked in his office. He knew some people had a morbid desire to keep relics of their past pain nearby, like a wedding ring from a failed marriage or an old cast from a broken bone. But the *Vazquez* file was different for James.

Many times, even after his father had taken the bench, Hunter would innocently walk into this office and find his father sitting at his desk or on the couch with the box open and its contents strewn about as he pored over them, looking for something, anything, that he might have missed. His father had mourned for Hunter's mother every day that passed between her death and his own, but the Javier Vazquez case was the only thing that had ever truly broken his heart. Hunter returned to his father's desk and sank down in the old leather chair, feeling like a guilty child. He eased open the desk drawer. James had never kept the closet key anywhere else and though he had never used it himself, Hunter had known exactly where he would find it.

Hunter unlocked the closet. The door creaked as it swung open. He flicked on the light, but the bulb had burned out long ago. Looking down, he saw two jumbo banker's boxes resting in the floor. Each box had the name *Vazquez* written on both the top and the side, with one of them labeled *Box One* and the other *Box Two*. This did not surprise Hunter. What did surprise him, however, was the presence of a third, smaller box, marked *Personal—Do Not Open* in the shadowy back corner of the closet.

Ignoring the Vazquez files for a moment, Hunter knelt down and dragged the unfamiliar box into the light. Inside were several individual file folders, perhaps fifteen or twenty in all. None of the files was thick. In fact, none of them appeared to have much, if anything, in them. Hunter reached for one and pulled it out. On the file tab was the typewritten title *Lyon County Courthouse, Eddyville, Kentucky.* Thoroughly confused, Hunter opened the file. Inside was a thin sheet of typing paper, with a series of lines, each one numbered and double-spaced. Hunter began to read the lines, but could not believe what he was reading.

He threw down the file and grabbed another. It was marked *Christian County Jail.* Again, the file contained a sheet of typing paper with a similar set of numbered lines of text.

Hunter looked inside another file and then another, the content of each new one unsettling him more than the last. Finally, he came to the last file in the box. The tab simply read *Home.* In that file, just as in each of the others, there were typewritten directions. Only these were different.

They were directions for James to get from his office to his home. The very same home where he had lived since before Hunter had been born.

Chapter Fifty-
Eight

The Anverdale historical district of Hopkinsville, just a few blocks from downtown, had always evoked sheer comfort, grown into timeless maturity from the seeds of grace. The district had been there for decades, houses of all shapes and sizes, the personality of each as separate and distinct as any smattering of people walking down the street. The only common denominator was the neatness. Anverdale's historical homes were currently on one of their crests, considered by the town's young professionals as being full of character and worthy of renovation. In other words, trendy.

As he sat in Ms. Polly's driveway, his car's wipers fighting the rain, Hunter gazed up at the familiar blue house with the white trim where his father's secretary had lived for nearly fifty years. Her lawn and flowerbeds were still immaculately kept. Although he hadn't been aware of it at the time, his father and Polly had spent many an afternoon in the wicker swing hanging on the front porch.

What he did remember was the afternoons and evenings he'd spent here as a child, when his father had been busy at the office. Closing his eyes, he saw himself as a five-year old, sitting on the steps of the back porch with tears in his eyes as Ms. Polly applied merthiolate to the scrape on his knee and followed it up with peach cobbler and ice cream. He saw himself sitting at her kitchen table a few years later, studiously organizing his baseball cards by team and indexing them in a shoebox with labeled tabs she had typed for him. He saw himself at sixteen, putting up a picket fence that was as crooked as a child's first front teeth. Since Ms. Polly would never let anyone near it except for the occasional whitewashing, the fence was still there, as crooked as ever.

At each stage of his life, he saw her. He drew in a deep breath, as though he could somehow breathe in the impressions of those memories—the sting of the merthiolate, the cold and warmth of the ice cream and pie, the dazzling white of the first coat of paint he had put on that crooked fence.

As he gazed up at the house through the rain streaming down his car window, he felt another emotion stirring. One he had never before felt toward Ms. Polly.

Anger.

The drive over here had been short. Too short. His emotions were still raw from discovering the unmistakable evidence of his father's disease, the very same disease he now faced. The files with the typed directions sat in his passenger seat. There was only one person who could have prepared them for his father.

Drawing a deep breath, Hunter turned off the car. Ducking his head to shield his face from the rain, he hurried up the shrub-lined walkway to Ms. Polly's front door. The sound of her doorbell reminded him of the nervousness he had always felt as a boy, waiting for the door to swing open and for her smiling face to greet him. He had been certain she was the prettiest lady he'd ever seen.

As she opened the door, a familiar smile curved her thinning lips. "Hunter!" she exclaimed, "what a wonderful surprise!" She gave him a loving once-over that made him feel nine years old again. "Get in here out of that darned rain. Katherine will have my head if I send you home with a cold."

Hunter stepped inside the house. He slipped out of his overcoat and hung it on the oak rack behind the door, just as he had done hundreds of times before, then slowly turned to face Ms. Polly. Her

blond hair had gradually turned a snowy white without a trace of
the sallow tones that plagued many older women. Her face was
perfectly rounded, seemingly unaffected by the lines that had deli-
cately etched it through the years. Her eyes still appeared to dance
when they focused on him. Hunter had always wondered if her eyes
looked that way at everyone or if they only danced for him. At
nearly eighty years of age, Ms. Polly was still the prettiest lady he'd
ever seen.

"Do you have a hug for me?" she asked.

Hunter obliged, leaning down to gently peck her on the cheek.
When had she gotten so tiny? It was as if time was slowly shrinking
her.

"What have you got there?" she asking, pointing to the thin file
in his hand.

Hunter looked at the file as though he was seeing it for the first
time. "Just something I need to ask you about in a minute."

"Okay," she said, nodding at him. "I just made some hot tea.
Why don't you have a seat in the living room and I'll bring us a
couple of cups. You still like hot tea, don't you, honey?"

"Yes, ma'am. Thank you."

She gave him another warm smile. "I'll be just a second."

Her living room was decorated just the way Hunter remembered. A love seat and recliner were flanked by end tables and
squared off in front of a modest television, which was rarely turned
on. A built-in shelving unit held what seemed like dozens of pictures
of Hunter and his family. Katherine and the girls adored Ms. Polly
and she was a fixture at every family gathering. As grateful as he was
to have always had her in his life, Hunter wondered once again why
she had never had a family of her own. But perhaps he only needed
to turn his head away from the shelves and look to the right to see
the answer.

The picture of James Cameron was framed and matted, taken
of him in his judge's robe to be placed in the courthouse shortly
after he had assumed the bench. James had been in his early forties
at the time. After that day at Centre College when Hunter had
introduced his dad to Kirk, James had seemed to finally make peace

with the ghosts of the Vazquez case. He had stopped drinking himself to sleep every night and lost a little weight. The bags beneath his eyes no longer hung so heavy. In the photo, his thinning hair was parted to the side and neatly combed back. His grin was both modest and mischievous, the look of someone perhaps too young to be a judge, but determined to be a good one anyway. It was, Hunter knew, the smile that had grabbed Ms. Polly's heart decades before and had never let go.

Shortly after James's death, she had informed Hunter that she would be leaving the office. With James gone, her work was done. Hunter was disappointed, but didn't question the decision. He knew that she could never work for a lawyer other than James Cameron, just as she could never love a man other than James Cameron. Neither of them had ever discussed or even mentioned their relationship. It was simply understood. Even now, Hunter wondered how many quiet evenings she had spent in here, alone with a cup of tea or a glass of wine, gazing wistfully at that picture.

"He was a handsome devil, wasn't he?" Ms. Polly said.

Hunter turned around and saw her, holding a dainty tray with a white ceramic teapot and two steaming mugs. "That was what he liked to tell me, anyway," she said, answering her own question. "Especially as he got older."

She bent over and set the tray on the coffee table. She poured a cup and handed it to Hunter, then began to pour one for herself. "How are Katherine and my girls?"

"They're doing well."

"Are the girls enjoying school? I worry about Payton being up there near Chicago. That's so different from growing up here. I wish she had gone to Centre or someplace close like Alex did."

"I know," Hunter replied. "But theater's in her blood and Northwestern has an acclaimed drama department. She still calls every other day, but she seems to have really taken to the city."

Ms. Polly politely nodded. "So, what did you want to ask me about? Something to do with that?" She pointed at the file, which was resting on the end table where Hunter had placed it.

Hunter reluctantly picked up the file and walked over to join her on the love seat. It was often said that people feared the unknown. The reality, Hunter knew, was that the unknown was often preferable to the truth you knew but had yet to accept.

"I was looking around in Dad's office," he said. "More specifically, I was looking in his closet. His *storage* closet." He saw the sparkle fade from her eyes. "I found this,"—he held up the file —"and several more like it." He leaned over to offer it to her. When she didn't immediately reach for it, he gently rested it in her lap.

The file sat there for what seemed like an eternity. It was as if she thought touching it would somehow make the moment real. She finally looked up at him, her eyes now still and glassed over with tears.

"Why didn't you tell me?" he asked, his voice trembling more from heartbreak than anger.

"I...I...," she stammered, before taking a sip from her cup. The cup rattled against the saucer as she set it down. She stood up, turning her back to him, and hugged the file to her chest. It was clear she had no need to open it.

"I had hoped you would never have to know."

"Know *what*, exactly?" Hunter replied. He had to hear her say it.

She turned to face him, her cheeks now streaked with tears. It was the first time Hunter could ever remember her really looking *old*. "That he couldn't remember things anymore."

When Hunter said nothing, she walked over and sank back down on the love seat next to him. She reached to pat his hand, but stopped herself. "It began happening a couple of years before he died. First, it was missed appointments. He'd shrug them off, saying that he must have looked at the wrong date on his calendar. Then he missed his Tuesday docket one day. You know." She sighed. "The very same Tuesday docket he'd had for fifteen years. He just didn't show up." After a few seconds of silence, she continued on.

"He was terribly embarrassed. I asked him if he had been feeling well and suggested he go to the doctor. Well, you knew your daddy and doctors," she said, a smile flirting with the corners of her lips. "He dismissed that idea no sooner than it left my mouth. He began carrying his calendar with him everywhere he went. He would look at it over and over during the day, just so he wouldn't forget to be somewhere at a certain time. I had to keep a second one at the office and write the entries in both. Somehow, we made it work. For a while, it seemed like everything was back to normal."

"Then one night in the summer, probably the July before he died, I had just finished cleaning my kitchen. I had left him at the office that evening. He was reading some brief in one of his cases and said that he wouldn't be able to come over for dinner that night." At that, Ms. Polly's face flushed slightly. "Anyhow, it was after dark and I was out on the porch in the swing, reading a book by candlelight. Your father pulled up into the driveway. I...I was pleasantly surprised to see him. After all, he had told me he wasn't coming over that night. He got out of the car and walked up the steps. When I stood up to meet him, I was stunned at what I saw."

"His face was covered with sweat. His shirt collar was undone and his sleeves were rolled up, as though he'd been doing some sort of physical labor. His hair was a mess. I asked him what was wrong, if he was okay. When he looked at me, I noticed his eyes. I...I don't know. When I saw them, it was though some part of him was missing. Like it was just...gone. I began to get scared. I said 'James, what happened to you?' He said nothing. Finally, I got him to answer me. I can still hear the words coming out of his mouth."

Ms. Polly bowed her head. "*'Excuse me, ma'am,'* he said. *'I hate to bother you. But I seem to be lost. I can't find my way home.'*" Her lips were quivering now, "I knew your father for forty years, Hunter. It was the only time I ever saw the man scared."

Ms. Polly sank back against the love seat cushions. "After that, I made him go to the doctor. They didn't really seem that concerned. Just dismissed it as the forgetfulness that people go through as they get older. One doctor called it 'Old Timer's Disease'." She shook her head at the memory. "But I knew. I knew something wasn't right."

"Why didn't you tell me?"

Ms. Polly stared at him briefly, then nodded. "I should have. I wanted to. But James…your father, he…he made me promise not to."

"But why?" Hunter said. "Why would he want to keep such a thing…" He trailed off as the sheer hypocrisy of the question smacked him in the face. After all, who was he to criticize his father for concealing his illness?

Like father, like son.

The two of them sat there in silence for a moment before Ms. Polly said, "Hunter, I know this is painful for you and believe me, honey, I wish I could go back and make it different now. I promise that we can talk about this for as long as you'd like and I'll answer every single question that you have about your father. And your father and me, if you need to know. But first, I'd like to ask *you* a question."

"Yes, ma'am," he said, retreating once again into the polite patterns of their long acquaintance.

"Your father, God rest his soul, has been gone for so long. Why does this matter so much to you now?"

He turned to her, facing her squarely. She studied him, gazing deeply into his eyes. And that was when she saw it. Not what was in his eyes, but what was missing. What was never coming back.

Her hand flew to her mouth. "Oh, Hunter. My sweet boy…my sweet, sweet boy…"

Fighting back tears, she touched a hand to his cheek. Her palm felt just as he remembered it, soft and cool. It was the touch that used to make everything all right, and for just a moment, Hunter closed his eyes and allowed himself to believe that it was.

Chapter Fifty-Nine

Hunter squinted beneath the weight of his creased forehead as he worked furiously at his desk. Beads of sweat began to form in his hairline and stream down each side of his face. He never noticed and when he wiped it away with the sleeve of his dress shirt, it was an act of instinct rather than consciousness. The task at hand was what held his attention at the moment, something that simply had to be done. The insomnia that had plagued him for months was growing worse. He had told the staff that there were to be no distractions. Not until he had finished.

Suddenly his office door flew open and slammed loudly off the doorstop at the bottom of the wall. Hunter jumped out of his chair. Untrained fighter that he was, he drew back his fist, poised to strike.

Libby Masters stood in the doorway, one hand clasped over her mouth, the other holding a tri-folded piece of paper. "Hunter, I... I...," she stammered, "I'm so sorry. I didn't mean to startle you."

Hunter glared at her for a second, then plopped back down in his chair. "That's okay," he said, trying to hide his irritation. "I guess I'm a little jumpy." Without thinking, he placed the magic marker he had been holding on top of the large beige briefcase lying on its side in middle of his desk.

"Umm…am I interrupting you?"

"No," he lied, motioning with his hand. "Come on in."

"Good news," she said, handing him a piece of paper.

Hunter carefully unfolded it and began to read. When he did so too slowly, Libby could no longer contain herself.

"I passed," she said.

Hunter jumped up again, this time to hug her. "Congratulations," he said. "That's fantastic news! Just fantastic. We need to go out to lunch and celebrate. Where would you like to go?"

"We can't go to lunch," Libby replied, looking confused.

"Why not?"

"We're meeting with Mr. Warren and Dooley to discuss strategy."

Hunter blinked at her. "When?"

Libby walked over to the side of his desk. "They're waiting in the conference room. That was the other thing that I was coming to tell you and—" She stopped as she glanced down at the briefcase. On the side of the case, the phrase *HUNTER CAMERON—ATTORNEY AT LAW* had been written with magic marker. Not once, but twice, in bold capital letters. Her gaze traveled to the side of the case, where the phrase also appeared. Only this time it was underlined. She reached over and set the case upright. More of the same. At first glance, there were eleven different places in which the phrase appeared, some underlined and some not. All of them were in Hunter's handwriting.

She returned her gaze to Hunter, clearly trying to hide her bewilderment behind a tepid smile. "Scared someone's going to take your briefcase?"

Hunter glanced down at the briefcase for a moment, then quickly picked it up and shoved it under his desk and out of view. He grabbed the marker and threw it in the drawer. "I guess," he said, avoiding her eyes. Already despising the concern he knew he would find there. He reshuffled some already shuffled pages on his desk. "A lot of things have been turning up missing lately," he said. "It doesn't hurt to be careful."

"O-o-o-okay," Libby replied slowly. "Is there something you can't find?"

"Well, for starters, there was that Kentucky treatise on criminal law. I've had that thing for years, but I can't find it anywhere right now."

Libby's tone was respectful, but wary. "We found that book in the backseat of your car."

Hunter pursed his lips for a second. "What about my cell phone? I've had two of them stolen in the last month."

"We found both of those phones, too. You left one in a bookshelf at the law library at the courthouse. They found it and called us. The other one," she continued, "was found on the countertop at *Ferrell's*."

"See," Hunter said, "I told you someone stole it. I haven't been in *Ferrell's* in at least ten years."

"You took me there for lunch just the other day," Libby replied. "You told me that you had been going there since you were a kid and that they had the best hamburgers in western Kentucky."

"They are the best burgers. Wasn't I right?" he asked, hoping to distract her with a bright smile.

She folded her arms over her chest. "Don't you remember us going there?"

Hunter sat quietly for a moment. He felt the air around him beginning to compress. Once again, he felt perspiration, this time running between his shoulder blades. He wanted to speak, but nothing would come out. His tongue felt like a damp log. He looked at the girl in front of him. He knew her name, but it wasn't coming to him. She was looking at him sideways, like he had done something wrong, but she wasn't saying anything. Just on the other side of her, the room begin to sway.

The crackle of his intercom startled both of them. "Mr. Cameron?" the receptionist asked. Hunter was still looking helplessly at Libby

"Mr. Cameron?" the voice repeated.

Hunter suddenly sat up in his chair and pretended to clear his throat. "Yes," he replied in his strongest voice, still staring up at Libby.

"Mr. Warren and Mr. Dooley are here. They're waiting for you in the conference room."

Grateful for the reprieve, Hunter felt relief wash over him. He knew who Mr. Warren was. He was his best friend. Had been for most of his adult life. He stood up and grabbed a small stack of files from the desk, having no idea if they were the files he actually needed. He strode past Libby and headed for the door. "Come on, we've got a lot to do," he said, without the slightest clue as to whether or not this was actually the case.

Libby hesitated for a moment, then obediently followed him. When he suddenly stopped and turned at the door, she nearly ran into him.

"One more thing," he said.

"Yes, sir," she replied, no longer bothering to hide her confusion.

"Keep an eye on the cleaning lady," Hunter said, raising his finger for emphasis.

"The old lady? Mrs. Allen? Hasn't she been cleaning your office for, like, fifteen years?"

Hunter thought about that for a second. He would have sworn his father had just hired the woman.

"Keep an eye on her," he said, turning to head down the hallway. "I don't trust her. Things keep coming up missing when she's around."

Chapter Sixty

The Woodshed BBQ Restaurant on the west side of town was not constructed of wood but aluminum siding. Famous for its fine barbeque dining and conveniently located just a mile or so from downtown Hopkinsville, the restaurant cast a wide net over local businessmen, farmers, and mill-workers alike. Every day at lunchtime the place was full. In its unique way the Woodshed had torn down the walls between the county's classes in a way that sociologists would never be able to comprehend.

Several years earlier when President Bush had visited Fort Campbell to address the soldiers of the 101st Airborne prior to their deployment to Iraq, his motorcade had somehow found its way to the Woodshed. He had visited with the owner and employees as he wolfed down a hearty plate of pulled pork, slaw, and a slice of coconut pie, an event which had been memorialized by what seemed like a hundred framed photos hung awkwardly around the restaurant. Though he had never returned to the restaurant, it was rumored that whenever he had visited the area after that, a couple of dark suits wearing crew-cuts and dark sunglasses would discreetly stop by and pick up a barbeque plate for the Leader of the Free World.

Only in Hopkinsville…

On this day, however, President Bush's favorite barbeque joint was closed. Not for business, but for a private lunch gathering. Kirk Warren was among the most passionate of the Woodshed regulars. Craving the comfort of a barbeque pork sandwich with hot sauce and cole slaw, he was the one who had proposed the meeting. When Hunter had pointed out that they couldn't possibly discuss trial strategy in the madhouse that was the Woodshed at lunchtime, Kirk had picked up the phone and called the owner.

Knowing that Kirk could just as easily buy the place as rent it out for a couple of hours, the owner had quickly agreed to Kirk's request. When Kirk had arrived with Hunter, Libby, and Tommy Dooley in tow, Kirk had handed over a stack of bills that tripled what the Woodshed could earn on even the busiest of its lunch hours. Now the place was empty except for the cook and a waitress, both of whom had been instructed by the boss to keep their distance after taking the Warren party's orders.

Libby winced as she walked in the door. As a western Kentucky girl, she had been in barbeque joints more times than she could count, but she was still wary of any restaurant that posted its entire menu on a painted sign nailed to the wall. Predictably, everything on the menu was either barbequed or deep-fried. Thankfully, she spotted in small letters at the corner of the menu the words "chef salad", a phrase that had probably not been uttered inside these walls since Prohibition. She was sighing with relief when Dooley, who by all appearances had just been thrown into his favorite briar patch, elbowed her in the shoulder.

"You ever tried the burgoo here?" he asked with a wink.

Libby stared at him, her expression blank.

Dooley grinned, beaming with pride. "Smart girl like you, educated and all, you don't have no idea what burgoo is, do you?"

"Sounds like something you'd need a Kleenex for," she retorted.

As Dooley's face fell, Hunter and Kirk both struggled to keep from laughing.

They took their seats around the large dining table and began knocking around ideas on defense strategy, stopping only when lunch was served.

"So, the police ain't taking your claims about the intruder on the boat too seriously, huh?" Dooley asked in between bites of a massive pork sandwich.

Hunter, rifling through a file and ignoring his country-fried steak plate lunch, didn't bother to look up when he answered. "Nope."

Dooley mercifully wiped away the barbeque sauce that had formed a complete circle around his mouth. "Can't say that I blame 'em," he said, tossing away the now-saturated napkin.

"Why is that?" Kirk demanded.

"Look at it from their perspective," Dooley replied without missing a beat. "Here you are, accused of murdering your wife. Not another suspect in sight. And you come up with a story about some guy breaking into your boat, tying you up, and confessing he killed her just so you can get fried for it." Dooley paused just long enough to lick the greasy ends of his thumb and forefinger. "I probably wouldn't follow up on it, either."

"Well," Hunter said before Kirk could protest, "you *will* be following up on it. We need a list of people who hate Kirk. And not just people who only hate Kirk, but who quite possibly hate his family and are resourceful enough to find out exactly how his mother was murdered forty-five years ago and then turn around and reenact that crime with Cassandra as the target."

"We've already been through that," Dooley countered. "We went through a complete list of every employee who's been let go in the last twenty years. We've been through every Mom-and-Pop shop and family farm that's either been bought or put out of business by the Warrens since Kirk's dad was running things. I've had teams from four different agencies sort through every single one of them. They're all either dead, disinterested, or too pathetic to carry out somethin' like this."

"Then," Hunter replied, "we're obviously missing something."

"No shit," Dooley muttered.

"What about the blood tests?" Kirk asked. "Have those experts gotten anywhere on the blood the police found?"

Hunter had hired a leading forensic scientist, the Chief Emeritus of the Missouri State Police Forensic Science Laboratory, who had testified in over a hundred criminal trials. He was as talented in communications as he was in science and was considered among the best in the world at effectively relaying complex scientific terms and data to a jury. In short, he was extremely expensive. And Kirk hadn't even blinked at the cost.

"They're still working," Libby volunteered. "I talked to them yesterday. They say they may have found some inconsistencies and want to continue with some more tests."

"That's all well and good, but if we're going to sell this *he was framed* defense," Hunter said, "then I need to be able to point the finger at someone else."

"The *S.O.D.D.I.T.* defense," Dooley said with a nod.

"*S.O.D.*-what?" Kirk asked, obviously confused.

"*S.O.D.D.I.T.*," Libby repeated. "It's short for *some other dude did it.*"

"Ah," Kirk replied.

"That's right," Hunter said. "We can use our experts to pick apart the blood evidence and suggest that it was planted, but this isn't California. A Christian County jury is going to want to know exactly who we're pointing the finger at."

"It has to be the man she was seeing," Libby said.

"That's easy to say," Dooley replied. "But we still don't know who he was."

"You still can't find anything?" Kirk said. "There has to be something."

"Nada," Dooley replied, shaking her head. "Whoever he was, he was damned careful."

"Except about the pregnancy," Libby pointed out, deliberately avoiding Kirk's gaze. "Got to imagine that wasn't planned."

"See," Dooley said, "that's the beauty of their case. Victim number two—the baby—*is* their motive for victim number one. They don't even have to find the father and risk putting him on the stand in order to establish it. It's no wonder they're not turning over leaves to find him. Hell, they don't even want to find him."

"But we do," Hunter reminded him. "Badly."

They finished their meal, assigned various tasks, and began making their way out to the parking lot. On the way to the car Hunter handed his keys to Libby. "I want you to drive Kirk back to the office to get his car. I need to talk to Dooley for a minute."

He walked over to Dooley's Suburban. "Mind if I catch a ride back with you?"

"Sure thing," Dooley replied, looking both surprised and wary. "Hop in."

They had no more than pulled out of the parking lot when Hunter turned to confront him. "I need to know just what the hell your problem is."

Dooley glanced at him, feigning indignation. "What're you talking about? I ain't got no problem."

"I think you do."

"Oh yeah, why's that?"

"Because, at every turn, at every meeting, you're constantly reminding us of how bad a case this is."

"You ever consider that I might be right about that?"

"I've been through plenty of bad cases, Tommy. I don't need you to tell me every damned minute just how bad this one is. For that matter, neither does Kirk, who happens to be dropping eighty bucks an hour in exchange for those smartass comments you're shooting out like a damned Pez dispenser."

"Oh, I see. You got problems with my bill."

"No, I don't. I've got a problem with your attitude. What's your problem? Are you still too much of a cop to think that someone might actually be innocent?"

Dooley pulled the Suburban over to the side of the two-lane road. He hit the brakes hard and the car came to an abrupt stop. Ignoring the honking of the cars forced to maneuver around him, he turned sharply toward Hunter. "Tell me something, Hunter. Do you ever think that you're so close to Kirk you're not seeing the case clearly?"

"No," Hunter said. "But clearly you do."

"Damned right I do."

If he wanted to get on with the case, Hunter knew he had no choice but to hear Dooley out. "All right then, Tommy. Enlighten me. Tell me what I'm missing."

"It's right in front of your nose, Hunter, about to smack you in the damn face. There's all the physical evidence in the world tying Kirk to the murder. Murder weapon. Blood traces. You name it. He found the body and had no alibi for the night before, so he had opportunity. Plus, God knows he had all the motive in the world for wanting her dead. Hell, if I was him I probably would have killed the bitch myself." Dooley's voice softened, losing its usual bluster. "Have you ever considered the possibility that he might have actually done it?"

Hunter stared out of the windshield for what felt like an eternity before answering. "All the questions you're asking me now," he said, "I've already asked myself. Over and over. I wake up at night and walk the floor and wonder all of that evidence could have gotten there...in his car, in his boat. The razor blade. The monogrammed towel..."

"You know me, Tommy. Hell, I've represented more murderers than I could count. I know they come in all shapes and sizes, from all walks of life. A lot of the time there's no rhyme or reason to it. There's no set pattern or criteria, no real way that you can ever tell for certain who among us could take someone else's life." Hunter shook his head. "But I know Kirk Warren and I'll never be convinced that he could kill anyone, let alone Cassandra."

Dooley heaved a thick sigh and turned back toward his steering wheel, shifting the Suburban back into Drive. "I hear you, Hunter. But we used to have a saying in the Sheriff's Department. There ain't no such thing as a coincidence. Put another way," he said as he pulled the car back on to the road, "where there's smoke, there's pretty much always fire."

Hunter gazed out his passenger side window at the fast food restaurants and convenience marts streaming past them. "I'm glad, then," he muttered.

Dooley just barely heard him. "Glad about what?"

"Glad the jury didn't see the smoke when we were trying your rape case."

Chapter Sixty-One

For many brand new law school graduates, getting sworn in to the practice of law was the reward for all of their hard work. The shining conclusion to three years of getting through school, followed by a summer of arduous study for the bar exam. If law school graduation is the wedding ceremony, then getting sworn in by the Chief Justice of the state Supreme Court, along with the other members of your class in front of family and friends was the wedding reception, the grand send-off for the life and, more importantly, the career that lay ahead.

For Libby Masters, whose boss needed her to be a real lawyer practicing real law as quickly as possible for the murder trial that would begin in a matter of weeks, and whose family members were either dead or indifferent, there would be no swearing-in at the state capitol in Frankfort. To save the Warren defense team valuable time, she would be sworn in by an Associate Justice of the Supreme Court, an old law school classmate of Hunter's, in his office in Paducah. It was, Libby mused, the equivalent of being married at the courthouse with passers-by serving as witnesses and skipping the honeymoon because the baby was due any day.

As he always did when driving to Paducah, Hunter took the exit off Interstate 24 at Lake City, for the express purpose of driving across Highway 62, and across Kentucky Dam. Kentucky Dam offered a more spectacular view of the water than did Barkley Dam. He never missed a chance to take this route. Not just because he wanted to see the lake, but because he liked to visit what came after it. Between the dam and Paducah was the profoundly stereotypical Possum Trot.

Hunter had always found Possum Trot to be uniquely charming. It certainly wasn't for its beauty. The community was largely comprised of mobile homes built in the seventies with pickup trucks dwarfing them as they sat in small gravel parking spaces. Mutts of all shapes and sizes occupied the small yards, each of them chained either to a wooden porch or to a tree that, invariably, had a satellite dish attached to it.

No, Hunter liked Possum Trot because he saw it as being devoid of progress. There was no McDonald's, no Wal-Mart, none of the chain-driven establishments so closely associated with rural Americana. Instead, there were a few mom-and-pop stores and a couple of gas stations with pumps still running on tickers. There was a country diner or two and some bait shops, one of which distinguished itself by advertising the sale of fifty-pound bags of ice.

"Is your father coming over to see you sworn in?" he asked Libby as he navigated the narrow two-lane road.

Libby had always prided herself in being resilient, but she could feel her pulse start to race at Hunter's innocent question. "No. He's out of town on business. He felt bad," she added, hating herself even more for lying, "but it was unavoidable."

Hunter slanted her a glance he'd probably given to more than one client, making her wonder if he knew she was lying.

They made their way through Reidland and drove toward downtown Paducah, which was cradled by the east bank of the Ohio River. The area had made a serious comeback in the last twenty years and its old buildings were now populated with banks, restaurants, law and accounting firms, fine clothing stores, and a variety of other small businesses. She had expected the associate justice to have taken up office space in one of the more distinguished old buildings. But when Hunter pulled into the empty parking space right in front of the man's office, Libby couldn't believe what she was seeing.

Robert L. Rose, Associate Justice of the Kentucky Supreme Court, practiced law from a strip mall. A new, but nonetheless unimpressive, strip mall located a couple of blocks from the downtown riverfront. The only feature that distinguished it from the insurance agencies and finance companies that shared the building was the official seal of the Commonwealth expertly transfixed on the glass door of the office.

Libby followed Hunter, who entered the office as though it were his own. He greeted the receptionist by her first name and introduced her to Libby. She smiled and quickly whisked them back to Justice Rose's office.

Like the rest of the office, the judge's private chambers were nondescript. The walls were fresh sheetrock. Justice Rose stood up from his desk, removed his gold-framed bifocals, and quickly made his way around to greet them.

Justice Rose was warm and kindly, his raspy voice bouncing with pride as though this were the first time he had sworn in a new attorney. Libby laid her purse in a chair and at the justice's request, raised her right hand and repeated his words. Something or another about solemn vows, obeying the laws of the Commonwealth, never having fought in a duel, etcetera. The justice closed his law book, shook her hand, and the ceremony was over almost before it had begun. Hunter thanked his old friend and then he and Libby rushed out, eager to get back to Hopkinsville and the landslide of tasks that awaited them.

"Shit," Libby exclaimed just as she climbed into the passenger's seat.

"What's wrong?" Hunter asked, his key already turning in the ignition.

"I must have left my purse in Justice Rose's office."

Hunter sighed. "That's okay. I'll wait," he said, as though he had any other options.

Libby hurried back into the office, cursing herself with every step. Unfortunately, the receptionist explained, Justice Rose was on some sort of important conference call and could not be interrupted.

Libby paced back and forth in the small lobby, waiting for the red light on the receptionist's multi-line phone to fade to black. When it finally did, the receptionist rose from her desk, offering to fetch the purse for her.

After what seemed like an eternity, the woman returned with Libby's purse. Libby thanked her and raced for the door, already bracing herself to face Hunter's irritation.

But when she reached the parking space, her apprehension was replaced by shock.

Hunter's car was gone.

Chapter Sixty-Two

L ibby Masters raced from the sidewalk to the end of the small parking lot, desperately searching for Hunter's car. But this wasn't a mall. There weren't more than thirty spaces and less than half of those were filled.

The car wasn't there. And neither was he.

In another place and time, she might have thought he was playing a practical joke on her. Or that he'd grown bored and decided to go get a newspaper or a latte from some nearby Starbucks. But after the attack on Kirk and the threats the intruder had made against Hunter himself, there was only one thought that coursed through her mind. And with it came waves of panic.

She grabbed her phone from her purse and called his cell phone number. Predictably, since he preferred to check messages at his own pace instead of turning his damn ringer up, it immediately rolled over to his voicemail. Libby left him a frantic message.

Her mind raced, her thoughts ricocheting around like BBs shot into a coffee can. She ran back inside Justice Rose's office and explained to the receptionist what had happened.

The woman just shrugged, apparently unmoved by Libby's panic. "He likes to eat at the Kountry Kastle over on the beltline whenever he's in town," she said. "Justice Rose sometimes meets him over there."

"He wouldn't have left without me," Libby insisted. "May I speak to the judge? Maybe he'd know—"

"I'm sorry,"—Gladys held up her hand, having clearly reached the end of her patience with Libby's interruptions—"but *Justice* Rose is busy working on an important ruling and can't be disturbed."

Gritting her teeth in frustration, Libby left the office on foot and walked a couple of blocks to Broadway, then made her way toward the river. She recalled that one of her sorority sisters still worked at Shandies, a high-end restaurant a block from the murky waters of the Ohio. Luckily, her friend was on-duty and volunteered to drive Libby back to Hopkinsville as soon as the lunch crowd dispersed.

As they drove, Libby searched frantically through the contacts on her phone for anyone who might be able to help her. She called Hunter's office, but his staff had assumed he was with her and were just as confused as she was. She asked them to call L.G. Owen's office and tell him that Hunter was missing. The burly prosecutor was fond of Hunter and might be able to get the state police to help. She called Dooley, but got his voicemail. She knew Kirk was too high-strung to be of any help and would only make matters worse. She debated calling Katherine Cameron, but decided to wait. There was no sense worrying her for nothing. Maybe there was a perfectly good explanation for why he had disappeared from the parking lot. Maybe he was okay.

The drive from Paducah to Hopkinsville seemed endless. Libby periodically checked in with the office. L.G. had sounded concerned, they said, and quickly agreed to call the KSP Post. Libby briefly considered calling Anthony, but again decided against it. The line they had drawn between their professional lives had served their personal ones very well. She was reluctant to blur that line, even in this situation.

As her sorority sister dropped her off at the office, Libby scanned the parking lot. Her heart sank when she didn't see

Hunter's car. After a brief check inside to make sure his staff hadn't heard anything new, she ran to her car.

She headed for Hunter's house at the lake. It was time to tell Katherine that Hunter was missing and she wasn't about to do it over the phone. If Katherine wasn't home, Libby would simply have to wait for her.

Libby sped over the winding roads of the lake subdivision, driving well above the speed limit. She pulled to an abrupt halt in front of the house and jumped out of the car. She ran a couple of steps toward the driveway and then stopped in her tracks, gaping at the open garage.

There was Hunter's car, parked neatly inside.

Like most lake houses in the area, the Cameron home sat lower than the road, with the driveway starting at the top of the hill and descending to the garage. Libby carefully made her way down the concrete slope, slowly approaching the car. She stepped inside the garage, walked around to the driver's side, and looked inside the car. Hunter's marked-up briefcase lay in the backseat with several yellow legal pads stacked neatly on top of it. There was no sign of a struggle.

She walked to the front of the car and rested her hand on the hood. It was still warm, but not warm enough to have just arrived from a seventy-mile drive from Paducah. The car had been here for a while, at least a half-hour or so.

That's when she noticed the door leading from the garage into the laundry room was open. She took one step toward the door and began to wonder if Hunter was in there alone. Was it so inconceivable that Kirk's intruder could have kidnapped him and brought him back here? After all, the man had attacked Kirk inside of his own house boat while he was sleeping. The thought chilled her, though not nearly as much as the unmistakable sound of footsteps walking across the tile of the laundry room.

Instinctively, Libby ducked down next to the car, keeping out of sight. She heard the sound of someone walking down the steps and over to the car to place something on the car hood. Her heart pounding in her ears, she dropped to all fours and peered under the car. From that vantage point, she could see a pair of well-worn work boots standing at the front of the car. The boots slowly began to move toward the driver's side where she was hiding. It was too late to flee. She slowly lifted her head, wondering if the face she was about to see would be her last.

Hunter Cameron was standing over her.

He reached down and gently helped her up. He was dressed in a flannel work shirt and old jeans. He smiled warmly at her, but the look in his eyes was one she had seen only one time before. On the day they had met.

"Are you okay, miss?" he asked.

"Oh, I'm fine," she snapped, her hands trembling with both relief and anger as she dusted off her skirt. "Just freaking dandy. And how the hell are you?" She was so pissed that in that moment she didn't even care if he fired her.

Before he could answer, she saw what he had placed on the hood of the car. It was a blue plastic bucket with a thick sponge and several plastic spray bottles containing soap concentrate, wax, and Armor All. Libby's mouth dropped open. The son of a bitch had stranded her in Paducah, scared her half to death—and set off a state police manhunt—all so he could wash his damned car.

"What is this?" she demanded, jabbing a finger at the car wash supplies.

He stared at her as if she was speaking a foreign language.

"What the hell is this?" she asked again.

Nothing.

Libby went around the car and grabbed the bucket. "Do you know what I've been through in the last three hours? Do you have any idea? You *left* me, Hunter. You left me in Paducah with no way to get home. I thought that…that you'd been kidnapped for God's sake. Kidnapped by that psychopath who attacked Kirk. I called L.G. The state police are out looking for you. I came out here to tell Katherine that you were missing. *What in the hell were you thinking?"*

Hunter just stared at her.

Flabbergasted, Libby threw the bucket out into the driveway. The bottles bounced and scattered, rolled back toward the front of the garage. The noise did nothing to dissuade Libby. She wasn't just angry at Hunter; she was angry at herself for caring so much. She had sworn she wouldn't let him replace her father in her heart, yet that was exactly what she had done.

"I said answer me, dammit!" She'd have thrown something else had anything been within her reach.

Hunter stood in silence, only this time his expression was different. He wasn't just stunned. He was scared.

Libby had seen that look before. But not on Hunter. Never on Hunter.

One summer her sorority had volunteered to go to an assisted living center in Lexington to play bingo with the residents. Many of them were very sharp mentally, sharp enough that they often got the better of her when playing various board games. But there were others whose facial expressions said it all. That they had lost forever the person and the mind behind the expression, the memories that both had held, leaving behind nothing but an empty shell.

That was precisely the look she saw now on Hunter's face.

Libby looked down into the car and saw the legal pads. She quickly opened the door and grabbed one of them from the top of the stack. Reaching into her jacket, she pulled out a pen and marched back toward Hunter. She had to know. And she had to know now.

She thrust the pen and pad in front of him. "Write something," she ordered.

Hunter stared at the pad for a second, then slowly took it. He looked back at her, his face awash with confusion.

Libby wasn't budging. "Write something," she said again.

Hunter looked back down at the paper and studied it.

"Please, Hunter," she whispered, tears beginning to slowly roll down her cheeks. "Write something. It can be anything. Your name. My name. The date. Whatever. But, please," she begged, "write something."

Sighing, Hunter set the pad down on the car hood and very deliberately began to write. He did so without faltering, as if he had written those very same words before.

When he was done, he set the pen on the pad, and looked at the girl. This time his eyes were filled with hope instead of fear. Hope that he had done the right thing. That she, whoever she was, would be pleased with his efforts.

Libby picked up the pad, her hand trembling. She slowly lifted her head to meet Hunter's hopeful gaze. She didn't even hear the smooth purr of an approaching motor or notice when the pad fell from her hand and landed on the garage floor.

On the first page, in Hunter's indelible scrawl, was a single handwritten sentence.

I love my wife.

Chapter Sixty-Three

B y arriving when she did, Katherine Cameron had rescued them.

She did this simply by turning into the driveway and pulling into the garage of the home where she had lived for so many years. She climbed out of her convertible and gave Libby a cheery greeting and the same warm hug she'd given her the first time they'd met. Libby mumbled a few pleasantries she wouldn't remember later as Katherine walked over to Hunter, who still stood silent in his work clothes and boots, and gently kissed him on the cheek.

Libby swiped at her face, praying Katherine hadn't noticed the tears tracks on her cheeks. She knew the scene had played out thousands of times before and that Hunter, at least at this moment, probably didn't remember even one of them. Katherine turned to go into the house and Hunter instinctively followed her, leaving Libby standing all alone in the garage.

Libby walked slowly up the driveway to her own car, the yellow pad with Hunter's message tucked safely inside of her jacket. She realized then that Katherine hadn't really saved them. She had just given them a reprieve.

Now, fifteen hours later, Libby and Hunter sat in his office. He was seated at his desk. She was seated in the chair in front of it. He was showered and immaculate, once again the man with the razor-sharp intellect who had hired her.

"Have you told Katherine?" Libby asked him.

He bowed his head, toying with the fountain pen on his desk, which was answer enough.

"How has she not figured it out?"

Sighing, he lifted his head to meet her gaze. "I don't know. I ask myself that same question every day. I mean, you figured it out quick enough and Katherine is certainly nobody's fool."

"Maybe you never left her stranded in Paducah," Libby muttered. "So…what do we do now?" she asked, beating him to the punch.

"We have a case to try," he replied. "So we try it." There was no trace of the doubt or fear that had plagued him in that driveway. His voice was calm and resolute, as though he had never considered any other alternative.

Libby was far less certain. The thought of serving as co-counsel on a death penalty case, knowing that her client's lead attorney was attempting to try the case while suffering from Alzheimer's Disease or some other form of dementia, conjured up all sorts of profes-sional and moral dilemmas. She was certain that the rules of profes-sional conduct would require her to advise the client, and quite possibly the court, of Hunter's illness. Her law license was only slightly older than the dilemma itself. She didn't want to lose it before trying her first case.

"Does Kirk know about it?" she asked.

"No." Hunter stood up, slid his hands in his pockets, and wandered over to gaze out the window, his back to her. "Not exactly. I told him that I was having some health problems and that I should probably turn his case over to someone else. But you know Kirk. He doesn't want anyone but me. There was nothing I could do."

"You could have told him the truth!" Libby felt bad the minute the words left her mouth. But her guilt faded as another realization sank in. "This is why you brought me in, wasn't it? Why you made me the offer…to let me take over your practice. This is why you're closing your practice."

Hunter didn't waste his breath confirming her suspicions.

Libby sank back in her chair. She hadn't believed she could feel any worse; she'd been wrong. She had been used, brought here to prop up Hunter with her legal work, like a screenwriter feeding lines to a great, but aging, actor. She'd been hired to save him.

But when she looked back to her life before Hunter—the cramped apartment in Mississippi, the lack of job prospects, the shattered family—she couldn't help but wonder who had saved who.

Swallowing both her pride and her misgivings, she asked, "Do you really think you can try the case?" *In your condition.* She didn't say the words, but knew he heard them anyway.

He turned to face her, his hands still in his pockets. "I've thought a lot about it. I think I can handle most of it. You'll handle all the witness preparations and we'll have to prepare written questions for each witness. The biggest problem I have is that I never know when I'm going to have a…a lapse.

"So you're going to have to prepare," he continued, "as though you're going to be the one doing the examination of the witness. It could happen at any time, just like it did at the preliminary hearing."

Libby pondered his words, her loyalty to him dueling with her common sense. She had turned her back on her real father for his betrayals. Could she really turn her back on Hunter when he needed her the most?

And what about her client? Kirk was pitiful. Extraordinarily wealthy, yes, but still pitiful. Granted, he could hire an army of lawyers, the best of the best, and have them descend on the steps of the Christian County Justice Center first thing on Monday morning. But this wasn't Los Angeles or New York. It wasn't an urban metropolis where celebrity lawyers could wax eloquent in front of awe-inspired jurors and where an acquittal could be assured simply by the size of the retainer paid and the talent bought.

No, Kirk's jury would be one made up of local citizens. Farmers, factory workers, whites, African-Americans, blue-collars, and shitkickers separated more by their shapes and sizes than the landscapes of their respective backgrounds. And there was no lawyer in this country who, at one-hundred percent capacity, could talk to such a diverse group of people like Hunter Cameron could.

Even half of Hunter was better than a whole of most other lawyer on earth. At least in front of a Christian County jury. Libby decided to cling to that belief. She would give everything she had to help Hunter, to save Kirk, and to somehow, in the middle of all the chaos, save herself. Maybe they would all find salvation together.

But somewhere in the back of her mind, there was another consideration. A consideration beyond Kirk's trial, Hunter's health…even the future of her career.

She didn't want to leave *him*.

Part Four

The Trial

Chapter Sixty-Four

H unter Cameron pulled his car into a parking spot at the Christian County Justice Center. Daylight Savings Time had just kicked in, heralding the arrival of spring, so even at six-thirty in the morning it was not quite daylight. His was the only car in the parking lot, but as a respected member of the local bar, he had a key to the building. He climbed out of the car, shivering in the cold breeze. By tomorrow it was just as likely to be unseasonably warm. *If you don't like the weather in Kentucky,* the saying went, *just stick around. It'll change soon.*

He gathered up his old beaten-up briefcase—the one that now bore his name written in permanent marker in about twenty places —and made his way to the front door. He was expecting Libby and Dooley around eight o'clock with the files containing the documents they planned to use during the trial. The jury pool would begin filtering in around eight-thirty. Until then, he would be alone in the courtroom. *His* courtroom.

One last visit with an old friend.

It was in the quiet hours before a trial began that he always gathered his thoughts. The facts of the case would finally be fully categorized in his mind, available instantly for recall. He would stand at the defense table and rehearse in his mind the steps he would take toward or away from the witness stand during a particular line of questioning. The glances he would make at the jury, the subtle expressions of whatever emotion—disbelief, anger, surprise, or *I told you so*—he needed to convey to his audience to prove his case. To guarantee he would see those same expressions mirrored on the face of the jurors. That had always been his gift—to make the rehearsed seem natural. With his power of recall, learning his lines had always been easy. It was his delivery that made them special.

Until now.

Hunter had spent the last few weeks rehearsing his opening statement over and over. He had worked tirelessly on the questions for the examinations of both the prosecution and defense witnesses. But on some days, his words simply disappeared like dead leaves scattered by a hard autumn wind. He slipped into the deserted courtroom, walked to the lectern next to the defense table, and placed a series of cards in the precise order in which Libby had numbered them.

Note cards. For the first time in over thirty years of trying cases, he was relying upon goddamned *note cards* in order to talk to a jury.

What in the hell was he doing here, trying a capital murder case in his condition? It wasn't a new question, of course. His doctors had asked him. Libby had asked him. He had asked himself more times than he could remember, as if *that* was any sort of reliable barometer. It still wasn't too late, he told himself. He could back out. He could ask to approach the bench with L.G.. He could see it playing out in his mind...

"Your Honor, if it pleases the court, I'm going to have to request a continuance of this trial so my client can obtain new counsel."

The judge and L.G. would exchange befuddled looks. "What are you talking about, Mr. Cameron?"

"Well, Judge, in all candor, I have Alzheimer's Disease. More to the point, more plaque is caking on my brain cells each and every day. As a result, well, I often can't remember shit. I never know if I'm going to remember my way home. Or what my name is. Or, with all due respect, your Honor, what your name is. When we adjourn at the end of the day, there's a fair to middlin' chance I won't

remember how to get back to my office. As such, I don't believe that I can provide my client with the adequate defense assured to him by the Constitution of the United States of America."

What would they say? What *could* they say? Judge Roberts might yell at him. He might sanction him. He could even report him to the Bar Association. But then, what would the Bar Association do? Take his license? Deprive him of the opportunity to represent other unsuspecting clients while he had, at best, half his mind?

Hunter heard sounds behind him. The courtroom doors had officially opened and members of the jury pool began to trickle in. They were, just as they were supposed to be, a random sampling of the population of Christian County. There were retirees and twenty-somethings. Oxfords and t-shirts. Long-dresses and denim mini-skirts. White and African-American. Some of them knew one another and made small talk as they made their way down the pews.

Libby and Dooley pushed through the doors, she with a brief-case on rollers, he with a dolly carrying several banker's boxes full of documents. Libby confidently walked up to the table, smiled at Hunter, and began to expertly unload the contents from her brief-case. Conversely, Dooley was sweaty and nervous, even more so than usual. He hadn't been in a courtroom since his statutory rape trial. Avoiding the curious gazes of the jury pool, he unloaded the boxes, nodded to Hunter, then scurried back out the door with surprising speed. Hunter was biting back a smile when he felt a light tap on his shoulder.

It was Kirk.

By his standards, Kirk looked fairly presentable. His dark suit was probably expensive, but not overtly so. Naturally, it still looked as though he had slept in it. His tie was tied too long and his pants were pulled up too high, making him look like a circus clown. His hair, though freshly cut, stood up in places and whipped from side to side whenever he turned his head. He had dropped close to fifteen pounds since the attack on the yacht, which was fifteen more than he had to give. All in all, he looked like what he was—a piddly, albeit fantastically wealthy, little man who seemed no more likely to marry a woman who looked like Cassandra Warren than he was to murder her. For that exact reason, Hunter had made no effort to spruce him up. For once in his life, Kirkland Warren's unimpressive appearance would work to his advantage.

Kirk reached out and Hunter enveloped Kirk's hand with his own. "Well, it's here, isn't it?" Kirk said. He actually seemed to be making an effort to control his nerves.

Hunter nodded. "Afraid so."

"I'm not afraid," Kirk said, clearly lying. "I've got you. They don't. The way I see it, that puts me in the catbird's seat." He forced a thin-lipped grin.

That familiar smile shook Hunter. He might not be able to remember where he lived half the time, but he could remember all of the times he had seen that smile. Like that night back at Centre, when Kirk had talked Hunter into accepting the invitation to the Kappa Sig party, thinking that they would both get bids to join the fraternity. And after the fight with the football player, Hunter could have sworn he saw it again. And then again at Kirk's wedding to Cassandra. The smile had never been meant as an expression of happiness to the world. Rather it was a question directed only to his best friend. In every one of those instances, the thin-lipped smile was Kirk's way of asking Hunter if everything was going to be okay. And if things were okay, it was only because Kirk knew Hunter was by his side.

The double-doors opened one last time and L.G. Owen lumbered into the courtroom, toting his hard-side briefcase in his hand like a child's lunchbox. As always, the neatness of his appearance seemed ill-suited to his grizzly physique. His double-breasted suit, equal in size to a large tent, was well-pressed. His tie was conservative and knotted precisely and his shoes had been thoroughly shined. He had celebrated when his thick curly hair had gone gray, and then nearly white, believing it made him more credible as a prosecutor. He was right. People loved him, and it was people, of course, who comprised juries. It was with good reason that L.G. seldom lost at trial.

L.G. walked up to Hunter and offered his hand. The two of them had engaged in little communication in the months leading up to the trial. Hunter knew L.G. would have offered Kirk life without parole on a guilty plea, but Hunter had had no intention of letting that happen.

As L.G. moved to the prosecution table, Hunter reached deep into his briefcase and pulled out his trademark. The bag of Red Man tobacco was the same one he had put on top of the counsel table during Dooley's trial and many more before it. He set it on the far right corner of the table, displayed prominently for all the jury to see.

Looking across the courtroom, Hunter caught L.G. watching him with a knowing grin. Without taking his eyes off of Hunter, he reached into his briefcase and pulled out a pouch of his own—Beechnut, no less. He opened the pouch as though he were, undoubtedly for the first time, about to pull out a plug and stick it in his cheek. Instead, he drew a deep inhale from the bag, closed it, and placed it at the corner of the table nearest to the jury pool. He put both hands on the table and leaned forward, the grin reappearing on his face.

The battle was on.

Chapter Sixty-Five

Much was made in legal circles about the jury selection process. Many of the TV legal experts, some of whom were gracing Christian County Circuit Court with their presence to cover the case for their respective networks, droned on tirelessly about *voir dire*, the French word for the jury selection, being the be all-end-all of trial practice. What type of jurors should each side be looking for? Men or women? Young or old? Blacks or whites? Professionals or blue-collar workers? There were lawyers who did nothing more than advise other lawyers on juror selection during trials. Soon psychologists and other alleged experts on human behavior had jumped into the fray. A virtual cottage industry had sprung up nationally in the supposed area of *jury consultants*.

Hunter Cameron thought it was all a bunch of bullshit.

Any halfway educated individual could take a look at a completed questionnaire and gamble on whether or not a particular juror would be favorable in a trial. To Hunter, it was a case of taking supposedly objective criteria and applying it to a subjective question. People's lives, faiths, opinions, and behavior simply could not be ascertained from a couple of sheets of paper. He might not know much about juries in places like New York or Los Angeles, but hiring a jury consultant to help him pick a jury in western Kentucky was like getting Beethoven to teach you how to play *Chopsticks*.

Hunter's rule was simple: he liked folks who paid attention. And those folks had no certain age, gender, or profession. He'd seen high school dropouts who hung on every last word and college professors who couldn't stay awake during the trial of a mass murderer.

He preferred to ask the jury pool routine questions and watch rather than listen as they replied.

Judge Roberts took the bench and immediately dispensed with formalities. Eighteen names were selected by random drawing and each of them took their seats in the jury box. The judge introduced both sides and asked if anyone knew either the parties or the attorneys. Naturally, in a small town, several of the potential jurors did. Questions were asked about whether knowing the parties would allow the jurors to be fair and impartial to both sides. Most said no; a few said yes and were dismissed. After an expertly-given lecture on the prosecution's burden of proof beyond a reasonable doubt in criminal cases, L.G. and Hunter, in that order, were each given an opportunity to address the jury pool and to ask questions geared to determine the impartiality—or rather, its favorability—to their respective sides. By lunch, the jury of seven men and five women was seated and each side was ready to proceed.

"Mr. Owen," asked the judge, "do you care to make an opening statement to the jury?"

"Yes, your Honor," L.G. Owen said, rising to his feet. He treaded heavily to his lectern, grasped it with a hand on each side, and rolled it a few feet until it stood facing the center of the jury box. He didn't let go of the lectern. Instead, he stood locked to it for a moment, his gaze measured and his bottom lip pursed, a preacher looking over his faithful congregation.

L.G. again introduced himself, explaining that he was the Commonwealth's Attorney, which was really the people's attorney. *Their* attorney. He explained, without any noticeable trace of egotism, that in this capacity it was his sworn duty to prosecute crimes that were committed against the Commonwealth and against the citizens of Christian County. It was an old L.G. tact, Hunter knew, and a very effective one. Though he had heard the same spiel countless times before, he still found himself waiting for Coach John Calipari and the UK basketball team to come bursting through the courtroom doors, followed by the school marching band as it played *My Old Kentucky Home.*

From there L.G. quickly turned to the matter at hand. His voice was powerful, but unlike many prosecutors, it was without indignation. The Commonwealth, he told them, treated all its citizens the same, regardless of race, gender, or social standing. No matter how wealthy you are, if you commit a crime in the Commonwealth you should be called to answer for it. Today was the day when Charles Kirkland Warren II, one of the wealthiest men in the state, would begin to answer for his. And this was not just any crime. Rather, it was perhaps the most brutal, most heinous crime imaginable. To murder his wife by slitting her throat while she slept. And by doing so, murdering her unborn child as well. For these crimes, he should face the ultimate penalty imaginable—death.

The Commonwealth, he continued, would not only prove each and every element of two counts of Murder in the First Degree, but would do so beyond a reasonable doubt. After all, that was the standard to which it was held, and the one to which it should be held. If he, as *their* Commonwealth Attorney, did not believe that there was evidence to meet this burden, then he wouldn't be wasting their time. This comment, Hunter knew, was argumentative, and therefore improper at trial. Still, it was an unwritten rule of trial practice that unless your opponent went completely overboard during opening statements, it was frowned upon by judges for one to object. Hunter trusted he would be given similar leeway when his time came.

The jury would hear, L.G. continued, about how the Warren marriage had been a troubled one; so troubled in fact, that Cassandra Warren had filed for divorce. They would hear from the constable who had served Kirk with the divorce papers that he was visibly upset upon receiving them. They would also hear from the constable that he had served the papers on June 14 at approximately three-fifteen in the afternoon, and less than twenty-four hours later, Cassandra was dead.

Hunter intently studied the faces of the jury as L.G. continued. It was clear that they were beginning to assimilate information, to put faces with the names that before now, had just been headlines. They had begun to feel the weight of the responsibility that had been placed upon them. Sitting straight as planks in their chairs, each of them seemed ready to accept it.

L.G. next talked about the opportunity that Kirk had to commit the murder; that he had been the one to call the police after allegedly "finding" Cassandra's body. Naturally, as the estranged spouse of the murder victim, he had become a suspect. He discussed at length the damning forensic evidence against Kirk. Of course, his DNA had been found all over the house; after all, it was *his* house. But what about Cassandra's blood being found in his utility vehicle? What about her blood that was found in the yacht, where Kirk had been staying while they were separated? And then, what about the straight razor, wrapped in a towel stained with Cassandra's blood and monogrammed with Kirk's initials, found in Lake Barkley such a short distance from where the yacht was moored?

These were all questions that led to only one conclusion. And once the Commonwealth presented its evidence, they too, would not be able to deny that conclusion. Not just beyond a reasonable doubt, but beyond *any* possible doubt.

Kirk Warren was guilty of murder.

Chapter Sixty-Six

T he time that passed between the end of L.G. Owens's opening statement and the moment when Hunter rose to make the opening statement for the defense seemed interminable.

Hunter stole a glance at the jury.

They had been visibly shaken by the Commonwealth's description of what had been done to Cassandra Warren, along with L.G.'s matter-of-fact recitation of the evidence pointing to Kirk's guilt. Despite the presumption of innocence, Hunter knew that the burden of proof now rested squarely on the shoulders of the defense. It would be his job to remove it and to put it back where it belonged. Until he could do so, the jury would convict Kirk and anyone else who got in their way.

He glanced down at his note cards, so painstakingly prepared by Libby. Kirk's life hung in the balance. There could be no mistakes. They simply could not afford to have Hunter draw a blank in front of the jury during his opening statement.

He took one last long look at the jury, which still looked ready to avenge Cassandra's death with their own hands if necessary. Drawing in a deep breath, he made his way to the jury box.

And left the cards resting on the table.

He went to the lectern and carefully moved it aside, wanting nothing to stand between him and his audience. He stood in front of the jury, hands in his pockets, and took them in. Just as he had all those times before. For the first time in what seemed like forever, he felt like all of himself again.

"I agree with L.G. on a couple of things," he began. "Clearly and tragically, Cassandra Warren was murdered. So too, was her unborn child. I can think of nothing worse than the manner in which she was murdered...other than perhaps to have been her widower and to have been accused of being the one who murdered both her and the baby she was carrying." Hunter knew he had to tread carefully. He had to acknowledge the crime's brutality to give himself credibility with them, while at the same time distancing Kirk from the act itself.

"These crimes are among the most heinous acts I have ever seen or even heard about. When I arrived at the scene and saw what had happened, I responded in a way that I reckon most people would respond. I wanted to find who was responsible and..." He paused for effect. "Well, let's just say that I wanted to make sure that person was held accountable for those acts.

"One of our frailties as human beings is our, well, *human* reaction to seeing horrible things. So often our initial inclination is to do whatever we can, as quickly as we can, to fix it, to clean it up. To get it out of our sight. And if we react quickly enough, then maybe either the problem will be solved or at least it will be put away, and we won't have to remember what we saw." Hunter was beginning to find a comfort zone with the jury now, as though he was sliding down into a warm bath.

"The problem," he continued, "with such a notion is that frequently, in our haste, our desire to *fix* such a horror, it, we attempt to do so in a manner that throws caution to the wind. Sort of like my father used to say, we occasionally do things just for the sake of doing them, whether or not they're wrong."

"I submit to you, ladies and gentlemen, that the evidence will show that this is precisely what happened in this case. This case is about a rush to judgment made by the Commonwealth. You see, it is the job of the police, even in the face of unspeakable tragedy, to step up and take charge. In that respect, they are to be better than the rest of us. They must come in, free of bias or preconception, and conduct a thorough and comprehensive investigation of the case. Perhaps most importantly, it is their job to *objectively* investigate the case. To follow every available lead, to explore every avenue. You see, it is not only the job of the police to solve crimes, but also, through thorough police work, to protect the innocent from suspicion of having committed those crimes. It is only after such an investigation has taken place that they should attempt to draw concrete conclusions." Hunter moved closer to the jury now, resting his hand on the box. "Because to do anything else is to rush to judgment."

Hunter studied the jurors' faces, looking for any sign that their fundamental notion of fairness was returning. He wondered if they would realize that, by discussing the rush to judgment made by the police, he was subtly challenging them to not make the same mistake.

"The evidence in this case will show that there is not one witness, not one single solitary soul, who saw Kirkland Warren at his home that night. The evidence will further show that Mrs. Warren had been dead for several hours prior to the police arriving. Kirk told them that he had arrived at the home that morning, found Mrs. Warren's body, and immediately called the police. The Commonwealth will not produce any proof to the contrary."

"Unfortunately, the Commonwealth does not have any witnesses to the crime itself. As a substitute, it will ask you to consider certain *alleged* physical and forensic evidence that was *allegedly* found at the scene and in Kirk's truck and yacht. This is called 'circumstantial evidence'. That's a lawyer's fancy way of saying 'we didn't see who did it, but here's some evidence and you all can draw your own conclusions from it.' Well, all I ask you to do as you receive the items the Commonwealth claims as evidence of a crime is that you do *not* do as the police did. I ask that you question if there are alternative explanations for this alleged evidence, explanations that seem consistent with everyday life rather than being indicative of guilt for murder." Hunter paused, half expecting an objection from L.G., as he had treaded well into the area of argument. However, L.G. must have realized that Hunter had afforded him a similar courtesy during his own opening and kept silent.

"Finally, we can talk about motive. The Commonwealth has already brought to your attention the fact that the Warrens' marriage was troubled and that Cassandra had filed for divorce. We cannot take issue with any of those facts. They are what they are. However, we do take issue with the Commonwealth's position that a rocky marriage and looming divorce are concrete motives for murder. Particularly in this case."

"As you probably know, Kirk Warren comes from a very wealthy family. Wealthy enough that, no matter the amount of money Cassandra might have demanded as her fair share from the divorce, it wouldn't have made a dent in the family fortune. Therefore, we submit that the evidence will show that money was *not* a motive."

Hunter paused for a moment, then lowered his voice to address the last, and certainly the most sensitive, of the issues at hand. "Finally, we turn to the issue of the unborn child. The evidence will show, unequivocally, that Kirk was not the father of this child. Specifically, the evidence will show that he *could not* be the father of the child. You see, ladies and gentlemen—and my client takes no joy in admitting publicly such a private and painful fact—he is sterile. Therefore, because he could not be the father of this child, the simple fact is that someone else must be."

"Now," he continued, "some of you may think that this is the beginning of a trial in which the victim's character will be put on trial. That we will endeavor to demean and insult Cassandra Warren in an attempt to convince you that she somehow deserved her fate. Let me assure you that this will *not* be the case." He shook his head at the jury. "Because no one—not Cassandra Warren, or anyone else—deserves to die in the manner in which she died.

"Rather, I mention this fact to you simply to point out that there was someone else besides Kirk with whom she shared an intimate life. Someone with whom she had conceived a child. Who is that person, you ask? The answer is, all these months after Cassandra's death, we simply don't know who the father of her child was. The evidence will show that the police don't know, either. But their lack of knowledge is not the most damning part of their case. Rather, it is their lack of interest in finding the identity of Cassandra Warren's lover that is most regrettable.

"The identity of this man took a backseat from the very outset in this case. Why, you ask? Because the police focused their efforts on Kirk Warren and no one else. The evidence will support this. And in so doing, the police turned their back on significant questions. Did Cassandra's lover know about the baby? Was he happy about it? Was he, too, married? If so, what would a baby mean for his marriage?"

"All of these questions, ladies and gentlemen, are relevant as to motive. The bottom line is that Cassandra's pregnancy may have created a motive for murder for the child's father, whoever he may be. And because the police rushed to judgment in determining that Kirk Warren was the guilty party, we may never learn who this man was.

"Of course, I'm sure you're wondering about the effect of the pregnancy on Kirk Warren. After all, how would any man react to the news that his wife was carrying another man's child? And, as the Commonwealth suggests, wouldn't that in itself be motive for murder?"

"The answer, ladies and gentlemen, is yes. *But,*" Hunter said, "the fact is, and the evidence will show, that Kirk *didn't even know about the child.* He didn't find out Cassandra was pregnant until *after* she had died."

Confident that he now had the jury's rapt attention, Hunter turned away, walked a couple of steps, and then slowly turned back toward the jury. It was time for the big finish.

"The Commonwealth argues that my client had the motive, opportunity, and incentive to murder his wife. But, standing alone, do these things really make him a murderer? It is just such a leap of faith, a rush to judgment, that has been made by the Commonwealth.

"I ask that you not make this same mistake. I ask that you take the evidence and consider it not with the tunnel vision that has plagued the Commonwealth from the moment Cassandra Warren was found, but with your common sense.

"What I'm really asking, ladies and gentlemen, is that you *not* rush to judgment. If you keep an open mind as you hear the evidence, I am confident that, at the end of the case, you will have no other choice than to find my client not guilty of these crimes."

Thanking the jury with a nod, Hunter retreated to his counsel table. Kirk was gazing up at him with gratitude shining in his eyes while Libby gave him a look of open-mouthed astonishment. He spared them both a hedged smile and sat down. Immediately, he gathered all of the note cards he had abandoned at the table a short time before and triumphantly shoved them back into his briefcase.

Kirk and Libby both had to lean forward to catch the words he muttered under his breath.

"I'm not dead yet."

Chapter Sixty-Seven

D r. Karen Nolan was a study in perpetual motion. An addicted runner, she ran several marathons each year and had finished in the top ten percent of women finishers in each of the Boston, Chicago, and New York City marathons for the last several years. She stood five-feet-one on her tiptoes, boasted a stylish haircut, and never seemed to stop smiling. Her personality made her welcome in even the most finicky of crowds.

She was also the Commonwealth's Chief Medical Examiner and its leading expert on forensic pathology. Hunter had cross-examined her in perhaps fifteen or twenty trials and could never quite equate the notion of someone who was so alive serving as the last voice for the dead.

"Dr. Nolan," L.G. asked, "where did you receive your medical training?"

She listened patiently as each question was asked and then turned to face the jury before answering, making certain that they understood that she was responding to the prosecutor, but speaking to them. "I graduated from the University of Louisville School of Medicine in 1992. I completed an Internship in Internal Medicine at the Medical School in 1993. From 1993-1997, I did my residency in Anatomic Pathology, again at the U of L Medical School. Finally, I completed my fellowship in Forensic Pathology at the Medical School in 1998."

"Are you Board Certified?"

"Yes, sir. I am certified by the Board of American Boards of Anatomic and Forensic Pathology."

"How long have you served as the Chief Medical Examiner for the Commonwealth of Kentucky?"

"Since 2008."

"In that capacity, approximately how many autopsies have you conducted?"

Dr. Nolan thought for a minute, though Hunter was certain the number was readily waiting at the tip of her tongue. "About twenty-five hundred, give or take."

"In addition to your duties as the Chief Medical Examiner for the Commonwealth, do you serve in any instructional or teaching capacities in your field?"

"Yes. I serve as a consultant to the FBI's National Center for the Analysis of Violent Crime and Child Abduction and Serial Murder Investigative Resources Center. I also frequently teach courses in forensic pathology at the FBI Academy in Quantico."

"Anything else?" L.G. asked with a smile.

"Yes. I'm also a Professor of Clinical Pathology at the University of Louisville School of Medicine," she said, ending with a teasing smile. "If you all can't tell, I'm partial to U of L."

"Your Honor," L.G. said, "I ask that Dr. Nolan be acknowledged as an expert in the field of Forensic and Anatomic Pathology."

Judge Roberts turned to Hunter. "Any objection, Mr. Cameron?"

Hunter rose from his seat. He had, of course, offered to stipulate to Dr. Nolan's credentials as an expert rather than have them paraded in front of the jury. L.G. had wisely declined, choosing instead to let the jury hear just how qualified she was. In another case, the Medical Examiner's office may well have sent a very competent medical examiner. However, given the profile and resources of the accused, L.G. had asked for and received the biggest gun that the Commonwealth had. In addition to her impeccable credentials, Nolan was attractive and personable, the polar opposite of the stereotypical medical examiner. The jury already loved her. If the cause of death were to be an issue in the case, she would be a powerful enemy. As it was, there wasn't going to be much bickering over what had caused Cassandra's death, so it could be worse.

"No, your Honor."

"Very well," replied the judge. "The jury shall consider Dr. Nolan as an expert in the fields of Anatomic and Forensic Pathology. You may continue, Mr. Owen."

"Dr. Nolan, in your capacity as Chief Medical Examiner, did you conduct an autopsy on the decedent, Cassandra Warren?"

"I did."

L.G. slowly waved a hand toward the jury. "Dr. Nolan, will you please share with the ladies and gentlemen of the jury your findings from that autopsy?"

Again, Nolan turned to the jury. "I performed the autopsy on Mrs. Warren on June 15. Her only injury appeared to be an incised wound to the neck."

At this point, L.G. asked Nolan to identify pictures that were taken from the autopsy. During pretrial motions, Hunter had objected to the pictures on the basis that their graphic nature would unduly prejudice the jury. In truth, he had been amazed, given the horrific nature of Cassandra's murder, that the pictures weren't even *more* gruesome. Cassandra's face was actually peaceful, as if she were simply sleeping. Hunter's objection had been overruled and the pictures were displayed prominently on a diagram board a few feet from the jury box. At L.G.'s direction, Dr. Nolan left the witness stand and stood next to the board, where she could more easily make reference to the pictures.

"The incised wound of the neck is gaping," she said, pointing to a large photograph in the top right corner of the board. "It exposes the larynx and the cervical vertebral column. The wound measures five inches by one inch in length and was found at the level of the superior border of the larynx." Nolan then described, in wrenching detail as she was instructed to do, the various muscles and membranes through which the weapon had sliced before getting to the epiglottis. "From there," she continued, "the weapon passes into the body of the third cervical vertebra where it incised into the bone."

"The vertebra is a bone, correct, Dr. Nolan?"

"Yes."

"And the weapon cut into it?"

"Yes."

"About how far did the weapon cut into Cassandra Warren's vertebra?"

"Approximately one-quarter of an inch."

L.G. looked at the jury and nodded slightly. He noticed that several of the jurors were wincing. Giving them a second to let the grimaces ease, he asked Nolan to continue.

She described how the wound had apparently started on the left side, just shy of the ear, and then continued across the throat before becoming more superficial by tapering off close to the right earlobe. In short, this was no random cut. It had been made ear-to-ear.

"The right common carotid artery was transected," she continued, "with a hemorrhage in the surrounding carotid sheath. On the left side, the left common carotid artery is transected with hemorrhaging in the surrounding carotid sheath and the left internal jugular vein is largely transected with only a thin strand of tissue remaining intact."

L.G. again let these terms sink in before asking the obvious question. "Doctor, based upon these findings, what was your opinion as to the cause of death of Cassandra Warren?"

By now, Nolan had resumed her seat in the witness box. "The wound was fatal. It severed the left and right carotid arteries and the internal jugular veins in the victim's neck. In short," she said, "she bled to death."

L.G. ran his hands through his thick, white hair as though he, too, was trying to come to grips with what he had heard. He drew a deep breath, as if steeling himself to continue.

"Were there any other findings that you were able to make from the autopsy you conducted on Mrs. Warren?"

"Yes. She was pregnant."

L.G. hands held firm to the lectern and he allowed his head to drop only a fraction. "How far along was she?"

"Based upon our calculations, approximately fifteen weeks."

"So Mrs. Warren was in the second trimester of her pregnancy."

"That's correct."

"At that point in a pregnancy, how far along would the baby be in development?"

"In terms of size, she was approximately six inches long, and weighed a little less than four ounces."

L.G.'s face took on a look of surprise. "You say *she…*"

"Yes. Mrs. Warren's baby was a girl."

"What happened to the baby," L.G. asked, careful to avoid the more clinical term *fetus*, "following the fatal injury to Mrs. Warren?"

Nolan exhaled slightly. To the trained eye, it was clear that despite her professional demeanor, she, too, was not immune to the horrific nature of this crime. "In layman's terms, once Mrs. Warren died as a result of blood loss, the baby was deprived of essential supplies of both blood and air."

The next question, Hunter knew, legitimately hurt L.G. to ask. But he had no choice. "Based on your medical training and experience, how long did it take for the baby to die?"

Nolan swallowed hard, in spite of herself. "Once Mrs. Warren's heart stopped, I would say within no more than a couple of minutes."

"So," L.G. asked, "in your professional opinion, was the death of the baby caused by the fatal injury sustained by Cassandra Warren?"

"Absolutely."

Chapter Sixty-Eight

L ibby Masters rested her chin on a closed fist, trying for all the world to appear attentive in front of the jury as they assembled in the jury box. She took a sip of her caramel macchiato, thanking her good fortune—and not for the first time— that even a rural town like Hopkinsville boasted a Starbucks. Without her daily jolt of caffeine and sugar, she didn't think she could have survived the rigorous trial prep, much less the trial.

Unfortunately, coffee wasn't the only thing she was craving.

She and Anthony had decided it was best they avoid one another during the trial. Actually, it had been her suggestion on the Saturday night before the trial began. Since Anthony was the Commonwealth's chief witness and a state detective to boot, she had feared the temptation to discuss the case—a temptation they had successfully avoided since the beginning of their affair—might be too much for either of them. After all, the trial was only scheduled to last for a week.

She had almost been disappointed when Anthony had politely agreed to her suggestion. Although she would have sworn she saw a trace of hurt in his eyes.

They were now in Day Two of the trial and Day Four of their

separation. Though she longed for him, the time apart had provided her with some perspective. In all these months, their physical passion for one another hadn't cooled in the least. But in the quiet, breathless moments after making love, when other couples might have been trading confidences, the two of them routinely fell silent. When Libby had mentioned that to him one night after too many glasses of wine, his response had been uncharacteristically passionate.

"Do you really think that you're in any position to talk about someone else being guarded?" The fact that it was a dead-on observation had pissed her off even more.

She *wanted* to talk to him, to give him more of herself. Much more than she'd ever given anyone else. It was like she had given him eighty percent of her. The superficial, cute, spunky part. The part that everyone saw and loved. But she couldn't seem to open up and give him the rest. If her own father knew her better than anyone else and didn't love her, how could she expect another man —even a man as amazing as Anthony Newell—to do so?

God, she needed a shrink.

But that was for after the trial. Right now, she needed to focus all of her attention on the prosecution's latest witness.

Hank O'Bryan sat in the witness box with a mischievous smile cemented on his face. Those who knew him knew that he couldn't help the smile—it was literally how his face was made. His thick mustache appeared to dance whenever he smiled, which was almost every minute of every hour he was awake. He was thirty-eight years old, short and pudgy, with coarse wavy hair that on court days like today, he would fruitlessly try to comb down.

And yet he still had the look of the rooster with the key to the hen house. Not an ideal prosecution witness, for certain. But then, Hank's daddy had been chief of police way back when, and though he'd been retired for fifteen years, he somehow still swung enough weight to keep his dim-witted son on the force. That Hank had been the first officer at the scene of what was now the most publicized crime in the history of the state was an indicator that the ball always did have a way of finding the worst player in the field.

The formalities of Hank's initial testimony were interesting simply because no one ever knew what he was going to say. This morning, however, Hank answered the introductory questions with surprising efficiency. There were those in the courtroom who would later say that they could hear L.G. sigh with relief after every such answer.

"How long have you been with the Hopkinsville Police Department?" he asked.

Hank took a minute to look toward the ceiling and count. "About...about nine years I'd say now," he replied and then looked back toward the ceiling to check his math. Once he was done, the shit-eating grin, which had briefly ducked behind a cloud while he spoke, was back on full-beam.

"Where did you receive your police training?"

"At the Academy at Eastern Kentucky University."

"In the course of your training, did you receive any training in the preservation of crime scenes?"

Hank sat back in his seat and thought for a moment. "I wouldn't really call it *training*."

"What exactly, would you call it?"

"Well, they kind of gloss over it."

L.G. was aghast and tried not to look to the jury for help. He had, of course, worked on preparing Hank to testify, but the preparation had been focused on the specifics of the crime scene, not Hank's training to have been there in the first place.

"Have you received any on-the-job training for the preservation of crime scenes?" he asked.

"Yes, sir."

"What sort of on-the-job training have you received in that regard?" L.G. asked, wiping beads of sweat from his brow.

"When I first started with HPD, I was assigned to a supervising officer. They tell you what to do to set up a crime scene. Identification, preserving evidence...all of it."

"In your nine years on the force, how many crime scenes have you had to preserve?"

Hank looked once more at the ceiling, as if searching for divine guidance. "I'd say thereabouts of forty to fifty."

L.G. again breathed easy, then looked closely at his notes to get back on track.

"Now, were you on duty in the early morning of June 14 of last year?"

"Yes, sir."

"Were you assigned to patrol the lake area near the Palisades subdivision?"

"Yes, sir."

"In the scope of your duty, were you directed to a residence in that area?"

"Yes, sir."

"Would you please describe to the ladies and gentlemen of the jury what happened after you were sent to that home?" L.G. stepped back from his lectern and briefly eyed the jury as if to say *he's all yours now.*

"As I arrived at the scene, Mr. Warren was standing in the driveway, sort of jumping up and down. He flagged me down and I stopped the car. He told me that he had found his wife and that she had been murdered."

"And after he told you that, what did you do?"

"I drew my weapon and told him to stay outside. I went inside the house and began to look for her. It's an extremely big house, so it took me a few minutes to find her. I stepped inside the bedroom and sure enough, she was laying right there." For once, the grin actually faded from his face.

"What did you do next?" L.G. asked.

"I walked over to her body and checked her wrist for a pulse. She was dead. So I went back to my car and requested a supervisor, additional units, and an ambulance. I then began to speak to Mr. Warren."

"What was the condition of the bedroom as you found it?"

Hank blinked at him for a minute, as though he didn't understand the question. "Oh, yeah," he finally said, "it was pretty neat actually. No signs of any struggle."

"Can you describe the amount of blood that you saw?"

"Yes, sir. There was a bunch, as you'd probably imagine. The sheets were satin and it had pooled up and then run off into the floor. The floor was hardwood—teak, I think it's called."

"And in the blood did you see any patterns?"

"Yes, sir, I saw what appeared to be a heel print from a shoe."

L.G. approached Hank and handed him a picture, which Hank quickly identified as being one he had taken at the scene. "Do you see that footprint anywhere in this picture?"

"Yes, sir. It's right there," Hank replied, holding up the picture and pointing to the heel mark for the jury.

"Did you find any more footprints?"

"Yes, sir. There were several more that led to the porch. The porch has a stairway exit down the side of the house. The footprints continued all the way down the steps and to the ground."

"Officer O'Bryan," L.G. rumbled, "did you at any time step in the blood that was around the body?"

Poor Hank looked like someone had just cursed his mother. His answer was emphatic. "*No, sir.*"

"What about when you walked down the stairs from the porch? Did you step in any of the blood on those steps?"

Hank's blood pressure was coming back down now. "No, sir."

L.G. turned away from Hank and wandered back toward his lectern. "Let's go back to the time that you entered the house. Did you look to see if there was any sign of forced entry?"

"I did. There was no sign of that."

"Did you see any signs of blood anywhere else in the house?"

"No, sir."

"Did you touch any of the evidence at the scene?"

"No, sir."

"Why not?"

"I was trying to preserve the integrity of the crime scene, sir."

"What did you do next?"

"The state police and Detective Newell arrived at that point and took responsibility for the crime scene."

"What did you do then?"

"I went over to my car and stood next to it."

"While you were at the crime scene, did anyone enter through the tape who was not authorized to do so?"

"No, sir."

L.G. turned to the judge. "No further questions, your Honor."

As he retreated, Hunter rose and walked with deliberation toward the witness stand. Hank sat up even straighter.

"Officer O'Bryan," Hunter asked, "you're a patrol officer, correct?"

"Yes," he replied. The *sir* had apparently been reserved for the Commonwealth Attorney only.

"Who was your immediate supervisor at the crime scene?"

"Detective Newell, once he arrived."

"Now you told Mr. Owen a few minutes ago that at the Academy you all just sort of 'glossed over'"—Hunter held up his hands to hang quotes on Hank's words—"this crime scene maintenance and training. Is that correct?"

Hank raised an eyebrow, his grin back in full force. "Yes."

"Then much of what you have learned about crime scenes is what you've learned on the job, while you're in the field. Is that correct?"

Hank again looked at Hunter and then at the jury as if they could help him. "Yes," he said tentatively.

"Have you had any training—formal or otherwise—in the sensitivity of DNA or blood evidence?"

"No."

"You've told the jury about how you went to great lengths during your investigation of the crime scene not to walk through any of the blood or any of these alleged footprints, correct?"

"Yes."

"And that was because you knew that it was very important to try and preserve the integrity of the crime scene, correct?"

"Yes."

Hunter walked over to the defense table where Libby, right on cue, handed him a single sheet of paper. He turned around and walked back toward Hank.

"Now, you wrote out a statement containing your observations on that particular morning, correct?"

"Yes."

"And in writing out that statement, you attempted to be as accurate as you could, correct?"

"I wrote out what actions I took," he responded. "I didn't write out every single thing that happened that morning."

Hunter let that answer float around the courtroom for a minute. Hank was growing more fidgety by the second.

Hunter continued to hold Hank's statement in his hand. "Now, Mr. Owen asked you several questions about the crime scene. Police officers were free to come and go through the crime scene as they pleased, correct?"

This caught Hank off guard. He had to think about it for a minute. Finally, he said, "No."

Now it was Hunter's turn to look confused. "The police officers couldn't walk through the crime scene whenever they wanted?"

"No, sir."

"And there wasn't a large number of other police officers who were walking through the scene?"

"No," Hank said, growing a little more adamant with each response.

Hunter again returned to the defense table where this time, Libby handed him several photographs. Hunter shuffled through them as he approached and then, his timing perfect, he whipped out the one he wanted and held it out just in front of Hank's face.

"Officer O'Bryan, these were the pictures of the crime scene that you identified for Mr. Owen this morning. Specifically, this is the bedroom where Cassandra Warren was found and where all of the blood was located."

Hank looked up at Hunter. "Yeah, what's your point?"

Hunter studied the picture closely for a second. "My point is, who exactly is *that?*" He pointed to a thick fellow dressed in khaki-pants and a dark-brown button-down shirt with a sheriff's badge pinned to it. He had a crew-cut, an unkempt goatee, and some gaudy convenience-store sunglasses

Hank studied the photo for a minute. "He's a deputy sheriff. New kid, I think. I'm not sure what his name is."

Hunter raised his eyebrows and turned toward the jury. "Now, Officer O'Bryan," he continued, with his back to Hank. "Isn't the job of a sheriff's deputy at a crime scene merely to stand on the periphery and make certain that no one who shouldn't be there gets in?"

"That's my understanding, yes."

"Is this deputy standing on the periphery of the crime scene?"

Hank's shoulders slumped. "No, I don't suppose he is."

"In fact," Hunter said, still facing the jury, "he's standing smack dab in the *middle* of the crime scene, isn't he?"

"Yes," Hank muttered.

"Did this deputy have on plastic booties or anything else that might have protected his shoes and the evidence at the time he was walking through the area?"

Hank took another look at the picture. It didn't lie and neither could he. "No."

"In truth, *none* of the officers who were at that scene were wearing booties on their shoes that morning, were they?"

This time, Hank's "no" was barely audible.

"Were any of the officers using gloves that morning, Officer O'Bryan?"

"Some were, some weren't. I know I saw Detective Newell wearing gloves."

Hunter turned slowly to face Hank. "Now, you said that when you were following the alleged footprints, you walked all the way out onto the porch, and then down the outside stairwell, and down to the ground. Is that correct?"

"Yes."

"And you were careful to step over these footprints as you followed them, correct?"

"Yes."

Hunter handed him another of the pictures in his hand. "This is the ground at the bottom of the steps, correct?"

"Yes."

"And the ground is merely mud and grass, with a line of cement footstones placed a foot or so apart, leading around the house and to the driveway, correct?"

"Yes."

"And it is on this footstone and this footstone," he said, pointing to the stones to which he was referring, "that you claim you found bloody footprints?"

Hank didn't even bother to glance at the picture this time. "Yes."

"It had rained basically all night the night before, hadn't it? And quit sometime in the early morning? Is that correct, Officer O'Bryan?"

"Yes."

"And the ground was still very wet from the heavy rainfall the night before, correct?"

Hank clearly wasn't sure where Hunter was going with this. "Yes," he answered again.

Hunter pretended to ponder before asking the next question. "There isn't enough room for you to step on these footstones and still avoid the alleged footprint, is there?"

"Well, no," Hank replied with a snicker.

"So you *had* to step on the wet ground when you were following this alleged trail of footprints, correct?"

"Yes."

"How did you get back in the house after you went to the bottom of the steps and took these photos?"

"Well, I went back up the steps," Hank replied, as though there couldn't possibly have been any other way.

"Did you take any photos of the steps on your way back up?"

"Yes."

"Did you take them from the bottom to the top after you had stepped on the previous step?"

"Yes."

"Hmm... That makes me wonder..." Hunter trailed off, inviting Hank to take the bait.

Hank was only too eager to oblige. "Wonder what?"

"It makes me wonder," Hunter said, as he turned and placed the last of Hank's pictures, an all-encompassing view of the stairs, some of which clearly had bloody footprints on them, "why we don't see *your* muddy footprints on the stairs from your trip back up."

Hunter turned back toward Hank. The man's smile had finally vanished.

Chapter Sixty-Nine

Valerie Delcambre was more than just Cassandra Warren's older sister. She was a tragic glimpse into a future Cassandra would never have. Valerie *was* Cassandra, only seven years older, with seven more years of silicone, fillers, Botox, designer shopping, aerobic classes, and tennis matches.

Hunter watched Valerie stride into courtroom as if she owned it. She was very attractive in her own right, with dark hair, well-sculpted features, and a figure, like Cassandra's, that could easily draw the eye of every man in the room.

Valerie also had the perpetual look of someone who had just finished her third cocktail, even when she wasn't drinking. She had never been willing to negotiate with life. Everything had to be done on her terms and when life refused to surrender to those terms, she came out swinging. She still bore the scars and rigid layers of resentment from those battles, evident to anyone who took the time to look.

Valerie's fifth husband, Stanley, had dropped dead of a heart attack just months before Cassandra's death. That marriage had lasted six years, making it the longest of her unions as well as the only one that didn't end in divorce.

Valerie was still living comfortably from the life insurance money, though she was no doubt already searching for her next wealthy mate. They'd barely finished patting down the dirt on Cassandra's grave when Valerie had hired a Louisville attorney to represent her, as Cassandra's only living relative and the administrator of her estate, in a wrongful death suit against Kirk. *Her* attorney was sitting on the front pew, diligently taking notes. He was probably ten years older than his client, well-coifed, and *sans* wedding ring, making him an excellent candidate for Husband Number Six…whether he knew it yet or not.

L.G. had tried to clean up the mess left by Hank O'Bryan's disastrous testimony by calling two evidence techs who had methodically described the blood evidence found at the house and testified that it had not been contaminated in any way. Hunter had sparred with them for a while, but had not made much of a dent. Now it was time for L.G. to appeal to the heart. As Cassandra's only living relative, Valerie was being called to personalize Cassandra. To give her a face. Given how much they looked alike, Valerie was virtually giving her a voice, too. Like she was talking to the jury from the grave. L.G. undoubtedly knew about his witness's past and the risks associated with calling her to the stand. That he was willing to assume those risks was an indicator of how significant her testimony would be.

Valerie took the stand and was sworn in. She sat down and immediately turned an icy glare on Kirk. Surprisingly, and to his credit, Kirk refused to avert his gaze. Hunter already knew the two of them had never gotten along. This was probably not their first staredown. But instead of hostility, Kirk's gaze conveyed only confusion and pity. She had seen the look before and it pissed her off even more. Her skin tightened over her surgically enhanced cheekbones like the skin of a drum. L.G. noted it and acted quickly to gain her attention.

"Miss Delcambre, are you related to Cassandra Warren?"

"Yes, I am."

"How?"

"She is—she *was*," Valerie corrected herself, "my baby sister."

"Did the two of you have any other brothers and sisters?"

"No."

"Are either of your parents still living?"

Valerie sat up a little straighter in her chair. "I don't know."

L.G. gave her a confused look, though he had prepped her and certainly knew what her answer would be. "Why don't you know?"

"My father abandoned us when I was ten and Cassandra was three. We never heard from him again, so I have no idea whether he's alive or dead. We had a stepfather who died, oh, I don't know, maybe fifteen years ago. Our mother passed away five years ago come September."

"So, with Cassandra dead, you have no other living relatives?"

Valerie shot Kirk another venomous glare. "No."

Well played, L.G., Hunter thought. The jury members were looking at Kirk like he had herded Cassandra's entire family into a death camp and personally gassed them.

L.G. pointed at Kirk. "Do you know the Defendant seated over there at the counsel table?"

"I do."

"He's your brother-in-law?"

Valerie rolled her eyes before responding. "Yes, he is."

"When did you first meet the Defendant?"

"Just a few months before my sister married him."

"Did you attend the wedding?"

"Yes. I was the matron of honor."

Hunter could still recall the wedding day. He had been Kirk's best man.

"Did you buy your sister a wedding gift?"

"I did."

"Did you also buy the Defendant, at that time your brother-in-law to-be, a wedding gift?"

"Yes."

L.G. plodded over to the prosecution table. His paralegal handed him a bag with a white cloth inside. The item had, of course, been listed in the exhibit list that had been furnished to the defense, but Hunter and Libby collectively held their breath anyway.

L.G. took the cloth out of the bag and handed it to Valerie. She clenched it tightly, her perfectly manicured blood-red nails disappearing in the folds.

"Do you recognize this?"

Valerie looked up from the towel. "Yes."

"What is it?"

"It's one of the towels I bought for him for the wedding."

L.G. feigned confusion again. "Well, Mrs. Delcambre, I have to ask...how would you remember one in a set of towels that you bought for someone seventeen years ago?"

Just as she had no doubt been coached to do, Valerie whipped the towel open to its full length. "Because I had it monogrammed in navy with his initials. They're here," she said, pointing to the embroidered Edwardian letters at the bottom of the towel.

After asking the Court to admit the towel into evidence, L.G. proceeded. "Did you say that this towel was part of a set?"

"Yes."

He walked over to Valerie and retrieved the towel. He held it out from his body with the monogrammed emblem facing the jury, like a matador presenting his cape for a bull. "Was there another hand towel in the set?" he asked her.

"Yes. There were two of them."

L.G. neatly folded the towel and handed it to the court clerk. "No further questions."

Hunter stood up and gently approached Valerie. He had been prepared for a more personal testimony from her—some story of Kirk abusing or demeaning Cassandra. He had been prepared to cross her on the credibility of her testimony. To show that Valerie had been ecstatic over her sister's good fortune in marrying a near-billionaire. That to appease Cassandra, Kirk had been willing to finance the dismal business ventures proposed by Valerie's third, fourth, and fifth husbands. And that when he had refused to throw money to the late Stanley so he could purchase some legacy racehorse, Valerie had called and cursed Kirk out over the phone. And later, that she had allowed Kirk to attend Stanley's funeral only because Cassandra had begged her to.

But L.G. had never given him the chance.

Knowing his witness's vulnerability, L.G. had asked what is quite frequently a lawyer's best question—the one that isn't asked at all.

And, now, all that was left for the defense were towels.

"Good afternoon, Mrs. Delcambre," Hunter said, deliberately using the French pronunciation her late husband had preferred. She looked at him with the same affection she would a nurse about to draw her blood.

"Mr. Cameron," she demurred.

"You claim that you remember purchasing these monogrammed towels that were taken from Mr. Warren's yacht. And that you bought them seven—was it really *seventeen* years ago?"

"Yes," she said, not bothering to hide her disgust. "I do."

"Tell me," he said, thrusting his hands in his pockets as he walked back and forth in front of her, "how many weddings have you attended in the last seventeen years?"

Clearly caught off guard by the question, Valerie sent the jury an uncertain glance. "I...I don't know."

"Please," Hunter replied with a light smile, "estimate."

"I don't know," she repeated, but when she saw that everyone was still waiting for her answer, she shrugged. "Maybe twenty or thirty?"

How many of them were your own? Hunter wanted to ask. "Okay," he said instead, "of those twenty to thirty weddings you claim to have attended in the last seventeen years, how many required the purchase of a wedding gift?"

"None that involved my little sister," Valerie fired back.

Touché, Hunter thought, but not good enough. "Your Honor," he said, "we respectfully ask that the witness answer the question."

Judge Roberts turned to Valerie and directed her to do so.

"I don't know," she said, her irritation growing.

"You don't know," Hunter echoed. "Hmm... On another topic, you testified that you've known Kirk"—he waved a hand toward his client—"for around, what, seventeen or eighteen years. Is that correct?"

"Yes," Valerie replied, clearly relieved to answer a question with a concrete answer.

"During those years, you spent a fair amount of time in the presence of both Kirk and Cassandra, correct?"

"Yes," she replied.

"And, in all of those seventeen or eighteen years," Hunter continued, "you never once saw Kirk Warren strike your sister, did you?"

Valerie sighed deeply. "No," she admitted.

"You never saw him push her, either, did you?"

"No."

"You never heard him threaten her, physically or otherwise, did you?"

Valerie opened her mouth, and for a worrying moment, Hunter thought she was about to lie. But her common sense prevailed. "No."

"So," he summarized for her, "you have nothing, nothing *whatsoever,* to offer to this jury regarding the circumstances surrounding your sister's death. Isn't that correct, Ms. Delcambre?"

Valerie glared at him as if, given the chance, she might just commit a murder of her own. "I suppose not."

Hunter turned to the judge. "No further questions, your Honor."

Valerie's stiletto heels clicked against the hardwood floor as she stormed away from the witness stand. Hunter could only hope the jurors were too distracted by her dramatic exit to notice him as he bent over the defense table and exhaled a sigh of relief. By daring to bring up a possible history of violence or threats by Kirk against Cassandra, he had committed the well-publicized sin of asking an adverse witness questions to which he did not know the answer.

But his gamble had paid off. At least for today.

Now all he had to worry about was L.G. introducing the jury to the matching—and very bloody—hand towel.

Chapter Seventy

H e weaved with deliberate care through the packed hallway outside the courtroom It was his way of trying to avoid the bumping, backslapping, body odor, and bull-shit. Most of all he wanted to avoid the gossip. The Hopkinsville hicks musing about how the murder had happened. As if any of them had a clue—a *single fucking clue*—as to what had *really* happened the night Cassandra Warren was murdered.

None of them had anything better to do with their miserable lives than to cram their fat asses into those burled pews, watch the trial for a couple of hours, and then spew their worthless theories to one another. The thought made him want to grab the staccato blade hidden in the heel of his boot, grab the next idiot who crossed his path, and carve a half-moon across his jugular.

At least it would a swift end to a meaningless existence. In some ways, he would be doing them a favor. The only thing that stopped him was knowing it would prevent his own plan from coming to completion.

Breaking away from them, he made his way to the front of the courthouse and finally outside. The spring had been a violent one, with lots of rain and thunderstorms and the occasional threat of a tornado. He had stood outside in the most serious storms, welcoming their rage without shelter of any kind. He admired them. The calm, the control that came before, and then, at precisely the right moment, the release of a fury that could only be crafted by God. The kinship he felt to them was logical. The storms were everything he had trained himself to be.

He took a pull his own hand-rolled cigarette and considered how the pieces of the chessboard he had created were being played. The case was proceeding well, he mused as he exhaled a perfect smoke ring. The footprint evidence had been very effective, just as he had known it would be, even before he had planted it.

It had almost been too easy.

Despite the fact that he was much bigger than Kirk Warren, their shoe size was almost exactly the same. He had simply grabbed a pair of Kirk's shoes from the yacht and put them on once he got to Cassandra's house. Later, when he was finished with them, he had put them back on the boat, where they were found. He hadn't wanted to make it too obvious, so he had washed the blood from the shoes. Still, as one of the techs had pointed out earlier in the trial, the grooves in the sole matched perfectly with the foot prints, just as he had planned. The only problem had been that dumbass O'Bryan who had nearly fouled up everything by letting everyone and their goddamned brother muddle through the crime scene. That was, he knew, the problem with any plan. Just when you think that you've devised a foolproof plan, God decides to build a better fucking idiot.

Still, the plan was working. The defense was scrambling, though he had to admit that Cameron was everything that he was supposed to be. The strange behavior from the preliminary hearing had disappeared and he had managed to punch holes in the testimony of not only O'Bryan, but the whore sister-in-law, too. But the case was still strong because he had made certain that it would be.

And the best was yet to come.

In the end Warren, despite all of his money and his resources, would fry. And then, Cameron would fry, too, just not at the hand of the state. The prospect made his pulse race. He closed his eyes and envisioned a day when his war would finally be over. When he would finally have peace. He opened his eyes, troubled by a new thought. When that time came, would he even recognize that peace? Or would it be just another stranger that passed him on the street, aloof, disinterested, and unaware of him.

The problem with climbing the mountain, he knew, was that at struggle's end, there was often nothing left on the other side. Once his prey was gone, would there be anything left in *his* life? And if not, would that life still be worth living?

Warren and Cameron had been his life's work. Once they were gone, maybe his life should be gone, too. He liked the symmetry of it. It all made sense now and he wondered why he had never thought of it before.

Maybe then he would finally find peace.

Chapter Seventy-One

At six-feet seven inches tall and just a tic over two-hundred pounds, Luther Boyd was loose-limbed and gangly, so much so that when he walked, his arms flapped like hanging flags in a stiff breeze. He was extremely bow-legged, and from the front or the back, appeared to be a wishbone with a torso. As he took his seat next to the judge, the jury members waited to hear the sound of his kneecaps banging into the hard underbelly of the witness box. They weren't disappointed.

His face was long and banana-shaped, like the ramp to a water-slide. His unruly thatch of hair bore a ring from the black cowboy hat he had taken off as he entered the courtroom. The hat now rested in his lap. Jeans and boots, paired with a dark sportscoat, completed the ensemble. The look stood out even in Kentucky, where—contrary to stereotype—the rednecks preferred farm hats and work boots to Stetsons and shitkickers. Libby might have been tempted to dismiss him because of his Roy Rogers get-up, but the intelligence glinting in his steely eyes made her wonder if Ol' Luther might not be more than he appeared.

"Mr. Boyd," L.G. asked, "what is your occupation and assignment?"

"I am a criminalist employed by the Kentucky State Police." Boyd's voice did not match his person. Libby had expected a baritone, maybe even a bass. Instead, his drawl poured over the courtroom like liquid velvet. When L.G. asked his next question—what exactly was it that a criminalist did—she found herself leaning forward in her seat just so she could hear him speak again.

"A criminalist," Boyd replied, "is someone who uses the principles of science to identify, document, preserve, and analyze evidence related to a crime."

"How long have you been a criminalist with the state police?"

"Since 2005."

"Approximately how many crime scenes have you investigated during that time?"

"Oh," Boyd said, leaning back in the chair to reflect, "around five hundred or thereabouts."

"On June 15 of last year, were you responsible for collecting certain evidence at the Indian Hills subdivision and the Lake Barkley Marina, both here in Christian County?"

"I was."

"After you received the call advising that there had been a homicide, where did you go first?"

"To the decedent's home on the lake."

"After you arrived at the lake house, what did you do first?"

"I was met by Detective Newell. He briefed me as to what had been found inside the house and how he wanted me to proceed. He gave me a walk-through of the bedroom where the body was located and then showed a trail of what appeared to be bloody footprints leading from in there to the front deck and down an adjoining stairway." Boyd leaned forward and placed the black cowboy hat on the top corner of the witness stand. He was very relaxed, as though he could just as easily be having this conversation over a cup of coffee in a diner as he could in a court of law.

"What condition did the footprints appear to be in?"

"They appeared to be fresh."

"Did you collect samples from the prints?"

"I did."

"Did you eventually receive a sample of the decedent's blood for purposes of comparison?"

"Yes."

"Were you able to make a determination from your comparison of the sample of the decedent's blood to the sample you collected from the bloody footprints?"

"Yes." He looked to the jury. "The blood from the footprints was an exact match to that of the decedent."

"Did you examine the footprints in any other manner?"

"Yes. I measured the size of the footprints."

"Did you make any determination of the size of the footprints?"

"Yes. I determined that it was a men's size ten and a half."

Hunter rose from the table. "Objection, your Honor. Mr. Boyd here is not an expert as to men's shoes."

L.G.'s smile was kind, though a tad condescending. "Your Honor, it isn't necessary for someone to be a shoe salesman to measure the length of a shoe. Any reasonable person can do that."

Judge Roberts pondered the issue for a second, then nodded in agreement. "Overruled."

"Was the Defendant's utility vehicle at the lake house when you arrived?"

"Yes."

"Did you examine it?"

"Yes."

"What evidence did you find inside the vehicle?"

Boyd turned his face slightly to the jury. "I saw what appeared to be reddish stains in the interior portion of the vehicle."

L.G.'s expression became quizzical, as though this was breaking news to him. "Where did you find these stains?"

"They were on the console and in and around the driver's side floorboard."

"Did you collect samples from these stains?"

"Yes."

"And did you compare them to the samples of Cassandra Warren's blood that you described earlier?"

"Yes," Boyd replied, allowing himself a brief glance at Kirk, before looking back toward the jury. "They also matched."

"After you left the lake house, where did you go next?"

"To the Defendant's yacht at the Lake Barkley Marina."

"Were you alone?"

"No, I was accompanied to the scene by Detective Newell. After we got there, he again gave me a walk-through of the scene."

"By 'scene', you mean the Defendant's yacht?"

"Yes."

"Did you find any evidence at the Defendant's yacht?"

"Yes. I found some more reddish stains. There were a couple of small, but noticeable, stains on the deck. The floor on the deck is white, so they were fairly easy to see." Boyd paused to take a long drink of water from the glass that had been provided for him. "I also found a series of small reddish stains on the carpet in the hull, between the front door and the back bedroom closet."

"Did you collect samples from those stains?"

"Yes. I compared them to the blood samples from the house, the utility vehicle and, of course, the victim. "

"And?"

"They all matched. The blood found at each of those locations belonged to the victim, Cassandra Warren."

"No further questions, your Honor."

Hunter was out of his seat before L.G. could take his own. He spoke as he walked toward the witness. "Would you agree, Mr. Boyd, that it is a principle of crime scene contamination to first protect the scene?"

"Yes, sir. No doubt about it."

Hunter already had the picture—the same one he had used on Hank O'Bryan—in his hand. He approached Boyd and handed him the photo. "Mr. Boyd," he said, "based on your experience, is this not an unusually large collection of officers to be present inside a crime scene, in this case the bedroom of the decedent?"

Boyd studied the picture for a long moment, then nodded candidly as he handed it back to Hunter. "Yes, sir. I'd have to say that it was."

"Was this the same number of people you witnessed at the crime scene at the time you were conducting your investigation?"

"No, they must have been there either before I arrived or after I left."

Hunter held the picture in front of Boyd and pointed to the digital time stamp in the corner. "It says here that the picture was taken at nine-thirty-five in the morning. Was that before or after you arrived at the scene?"

"I didn't arrive until eleven, so it was definitely before."

"If you had been at the scene and saw a person or people standing in the crime scene who shouldn't be there, would you object to them being there?"

"Yes, I would."

"And,"—Hunter shifted his weight so that he partially faced the jury—"would the basis for that objection be that their presence might impair the integrity of the very evidence that you were there to collect?"

Boyd sighed. "That would be correct."

Hunter turned away, his satisfaction with the answer evident and returned the picture to the clerk. "Now, Mr. Boyd," he said as he walked to the middle of the floor just in front of the jury box, "let's talk about your arrival time to the scene. You said that you arrived at the scene at eleven. At what time did you receive the call?"

"I believe that it was just before nine that morning."

Hunter considered this for a moment. "Is there any requirement or regulation that the criminalists should arrive at the crime scene within a specific period of time?"

"Yes," Boyd confirmed. "Once we receive a call, we try to arrive at the scene within an hour, if possible."

"And your response time to the lake house was nearly two hours, correct?"

Another sigh. "That's correct."

Hunter could have asked why Boyd had taken so long to arrive. Libby knew that he had decided against it because it was clear that the jury liked Boyd and his western affability. He had made his point and was ready to move on.

"Was the victim's body at the scene at the time you arrived?"

"Yes, it was."

"At the time you arrived at the scene, someone from the coroner's office had already placed a blanket over the decedent's body, hadn't they?"

"Yes." Boyd's long face grew even longer, as though the answer stuck in his craw.

"In fact," Hunter continued, "that's why they advise the criminalists to get to the crime scene before the coroner arrives. So you can examine the body before they do anything with it, correct?"

"That's true," Boyd admitted.

"Did you later find out that the blanket had belonged to the Warrens and had come from inside the home?"

"I did."

"And you are aware, are you not, that the home belonged to Mr. Warren, too, and that he had resided there?"

"That's my understanding, yes."

"And since he lived in the house, isn't it possible, even likely, that at some point Mr. Warren had come into contact with that blanket, Mr. Boyd?"

"It's certainly possible."

"In terms of contaminating the crime scene, was it not a critical error for that blanket to be thrown over the body? If Mr. Warren had come into contact with that blanket at any time, would that not be a likely source of cross-contamination of hairs and fibers?"

"It might be, depending on how clean the blanket was prior to being placed over the victim…"

"But," Hunter interjected, "that's something we'll never know, will we?"

Boyd gave a faint smile. "I suppose not. But then, since we knew Mr. Warren had *once* lived there," he emphasized, "I focused less on hairs and fibers found in the home and more so on the blood evidence that I found."

"Let's talk about the blood for a minute," Hunter said, ignoring that smoking gun. "Based upon what you saw at the lake house in terms of the footprints that led out of the bedroom, down the steps from the deck, and then the traces which you claim to have found in the utility vehicle, you wouldn't expect to find even more blood from shoeprints on Mr. Warren's house boat, would you?"

"I wouldn't expect to, no. But it's not impossible."

"But it's also not very likely, is it, Mr. Boyd?"

Boyd shifted in his seat. The point of the question was obvious, but it had been framed in such a way that he could not wiggle out of the answer.

"I'd say it was unusual."

"*Unusual,*" Hunter repeated the word slowly, letting it resonate over the jury and seep into their minds, like fertilizer spread over a planted crop. An admiring smile touched Libby's lips. From those seeds, she knew, would spring the notion of reasonable doubt.

Chapter Seventy-Two

As Anthony Newell strode confidently through the courtroom doors and toward the witness stand, Libby, as usual, could not take her eyes off of him. But this time it was not because he was the most handsome man she had ever seen; it was because of his phone call to her the night before and how it had ended.

The defense had just finished yet another long evening at Hunter's office preparing for the next day of court. But somehow, this session seemed different. Though the Commonwealth's lengthy list of witnesses contained the usual array of red herrings, it was clear to all of them that L.G. would be concluding his case the next day with the one person who could tie it all together—Newell. After that, it would be the defense team's turn and they had very little from which to work.

Despite Hunter's success in pointing out the sloppiness of the investigation, the fact remained that a brutal murder had been committed and that every last piece of evidence pointed at Kirk. Their only defense was that Kirk had been framed, a defense that always raised eyebrows and seldom resulted in acquittal. Pointing the finger and having no one at the end of it was courting doom and they all knew it.

Even Kirk, who had taken an active and occasionally even helpful role in his defense, had now lapsed into hopeless silence. Dooley was still out with his rented troops, chasing leads on the identity of Cassandra's boyfriend that had come in through a reward hotline Kirk had established several months ago. Thousands of calls had been made, but none had turned up anything of any value. When Libby left the office just ahead of the others, she was not going home so much as escaping the pall that had fallen over all of them. Her cell phone rang just before she opened her car door.

Newell didn't bother with a greeting. "I need to see you."

Libby felt herself shiver and didn't know if it came from the spring chill in the air or from what the smoky purr of his voice always did to her. "You know I can't."

"Why not?"

"Let's see...I'm representing a man accused of murder and you're the chief witness for the prosecution, set to testify first thing in the morning. I really don't think hooking up tonight is the best idea."

"That's not what I meant."

"Where are you?" she asked.

"A couple of hundred yards behind you, parked diagonally in front of the old bank building."

Libby turned and looked. A state-issued Crown Vic was parked in front of the building that had once held the old Hopkinsville Federal Bank. Its windows were tinted and its lights turned off. From a distance, she would have assumed it was empty.

"Where's the Mustang? I've never seen you in the state car."

"What, you don't like the Crown Vic?"

She shook her head. "Too generic. It doesn't suit you at all."

He laughed. "Just what every guy wants to hear his girlfriend say, that his car is generic."

"Is that what I am?" she retorted. "Your girlfriend?"

To his credit, Newell didn't hesitate. "You're a hell of a lot more than that. I really need you tonight."

She sighed, frustrated by their impossible situation. "We talked about this. You know I can't. Not while the trial is going on."

"*You* can't," he said in a rare display of emotion. "In all these months, I can't remember a time, a single goddamned time when it *wasn't* about you and what you could or couldn't do. I got news for you, Libby…this trial isn't just about you. In fact," he reminded her, "it'll be my happy ass up there on the hot seat tomorrow, not yours."

Her home screen reappeared, leaving her staring down at her cell phone in disbelief. The bastard had hung up on her.

Now, as he walked down the courtroom aisle and past her table, he didn't even bother to look at her, which wouldn't have hurt so badly if she had been able to take her eyes off of him. The other women in the courtroom were looking at him as well. In his perfectly pressed khakis and navy sport coat, Newell looked like a sexy college professor beloved by all the coeds.

He stood rod-straight to take the oath, then claimed his seat on the witness stand. He respectfully nodded at the judge, then offered the jury a smile so polite it was returned by nearly all of them. He even gave L.G. a friendly wink. He seemed to be greeting everyone in the courtroom. *Everyone but me,* Libby thought, *the one who loves him the most.*

L.G. efficiently dispatched the formalities of Newell's testimony so he could get to the crux of his case. "At what time did you arrive at the lake house?"

"At approximately eight-forty that morning."

"Did Deputy O'Bryan brief you on the situation when you arrived?"

"Yes. Deputy O'Bryan explained that there was a homicide at the location." Newell's authoritative voice lent O'Bryan some much-needed credibility. "He had searched the home for the perpetrator and believed it to be empty at the time. I asked him to give me a brief walk-through of the house so I could acclimate myself to the crime scene."

"Did you go into the bedroom?"

"Yes."

"And it was there that you saw Cassandra Warren's dead body?"

Newell nodded regretfully, then remembered he needed to answer out loud. "Yes."

"Did Deputy O'Bryan point out anything in the victim's bedroom at that time?"

"He did," Newell replied, visibly brightening. "He showed me the bloody shoeprints that led from the bedroom out onto the deck, and then down the stairwell that goes toward the driveway."

"How did you proceed next?"

"By that time the evidence techs were arriving and I was satisfied that the crime scene was secure for the purpose of collecting evidence. Deputy O'Bryan had already advised me of the fact that the Defendant was the one who had found the body and that he had been detained for questioning. During that time, I was also advised that the Defendant and Mrs. Warren were separated and that he had been served with divorce papers the day before." There was nothing to object to on this point, Libby knew. The divorce, along with the pregnancy, formed Kirk's motive. The deputy who had served him with the divorce petition had testified on the trial's first day. On the bright side, he had acknowledged under Hunter's cross that Kirk had not reacted with any sort of temperamental outburst when he was handed the papers. In fact, the deputy had acknowledged, he didn't say a single word.

"At that point," Newell continued, "the Defendant became a serious suspect. I learned he had been staying on a yacht at the Lake Barkley Marina and proceeded over to the marina to see what, if any, evidence I could find."

L.G. pursed his lips and furrowed his brow. Libby saw Hunter visibly brace himself for the coming blow. "What did you find at the marina?" L.G. asked.

"At first, nothing." Newell adjusted himself in his chair, not because he was nervous, but so he could get comfortable. He seemed to be settling in for the duration. "The workers at the Marina had already washed off the fish-blood that had accumulated the day before, so the dock walkway to the boat was clean when I arrived.

"But," he continued, with a narrator's timing, "they didn't wash off the decks of the boats."

"When I arrived at the Defendant's yacht, I saw what appeared to be a couple of blood spots on the bow of the boat."

"This was on the *outside* of the boat," L.G. asked, careful to make the point to the jury that Newell had not gone inside Kirk's yacht without a warrant.

"Yes."

"Please continue," L.G. said, satisfied.

"Given the nature of the crime scene, it occurred to me that someone had carried something that was dripping with blood onto the boat. I walked around the bow and found two more spots in front of the door to the boat's living quarters."

"What did you do at that point?"

"I radioed back over to the lake house and told them what I'd found. At that point, we had a search warrant prepared and issued for the lake house, the boat, and the Defendant's utility vehicle."

"What did you do while you waited for the search warrant to be issued?"

"Well, on the way over to the marina, it occurred to me that if the Defendant had indeed murdered Mrs. Warren and then retreated to his yacht, the lake would be an awfully convenient place to dispose of the murder weapon." Newell paused, allowing L.G. to give him the assist.

"So?"

"So," Newell continued, "since I knew I would be waiting awhile at the boat for the warrant, I thought we could get a head start on looking in the lake. So I called the post at Madisonville and asked for a diver."

The diver had testified yesterday, and through him the Commonwealth had admitted both the bloody monogrammed towel and the engraved razor blade, each bearing Kirk's initials. A lab technician from KSP had later testified that the blood on the towel had been Cassandra's. Now those items sat on the counter next to the court clerk like forgotten toys left by a child. It was through Newell that these items would be rediscovered and brought back to life for the jury.

L.G. took the bagged towel and razor in his hand, walked over to Newell, and handed them to him. Newell quickly acknowledged that they were the very items that had been dredged up from the murkiness of Lake Barkley by the diver.

"After the warrant arrived, how did you proceed?"

"By then, Specialist Boyd had arrived. He found additional blood stains in the hallway carpet that led to the Defendant's cabin closet."

"Did you find anything else?"

"When we looked in the Defendant's closet we found shoes belonging to the Defendant that matched, in both size and sole, the bloody prints found at the lake house."

L.G. promptly retrieved the shoes from the clerk and had Newell identify them so he could enter them into evidence. The matter of the shoes, of course, had been the subject of a heated evidentiary hearing. After an FBI expert had verified that the shoes were indeed a match, Hunter had decided to stipulate to the identification. There was, after all, only so much questioning of blatant evidence that he could do and still maintain any semblance of credibility with the jury.

"Anything else?" L.G. asked, with a sidelong glance toward the jury that clearly said, *How much more do you need?*

"Yes," Newell responded. "We looked in the bathroom—I think boaters call it the *head*—and found monogrammed towels."

By this time L.G. was already standing by the clerk, who obediently handed him the towel that had been introduced by Valerie Delcambre. He quickly handed it off to Newell. "Is this the towel you found?"

Newell made a play of studying the towel, like it was an artifact he had just unearthed as part of some archaeological dig. "Yes, it is."

"Detective Newell," L.G. asked in summary fashion, "I'm going to ask you to take the towel you found in the closet of Kirk Warren's yacht and the one found in the lake, wrapped around a razor blade, and hold them both up for the jury to see."

Newell stood, holding up both towels. One was laundry-fresh, white and clean; the other had been stained light brown by the filthy lake water and was heavily marked by larger dark brown spots. But their size and the letters *CKW* boldly emblazoned at the bottom of each towel identified them as mates.

Libby dragged her gaze away from Newell and stole a look at the jury. What she saw there scared her more than anything she had ever known. It was in their expressions as they looked at the towel. *That* towel. The one that had sopped up Cassandra Warren's blood and then been submerged in the lake. Though it was dry now, Libby could almost see those crimson drops of blood falling anew. Only this time it wasn't Cassandra's life seeping away.

It was Kirk's.

Chapter Seventy-Three

As he readied himself to begin his cross-examination of Detective Newell, Hunter rose slowly from his chair. In stark contrast to the aggressive manner in which he had approached several of the prosecution witnesses, his steps around the defense table were measured, as though he felt the need to approach this particular opponent with caution and respect. Newell offered Hunter the same pleasant look he had given everyone else that day.

"At what point in your investigation, Detective," Hunter began, "did you realize that Cassandra Warren was pregnant?"

Newell didn't blink or hesitate. "I was notified by the state medical examiner after she completed the autopsy."

"And at what time did you learn that, because he was sterile, Mr. Warren could not be the father of the child?"

"That would be shortly after Mr. Owen notified you of the pregnancy and you apparently informed him that Mr. Warren could not be the father. Mr. Owen told me afterward."

"So how long was that after Mrs. Warren's death?"

"A couple of days," Newell replied. "Less than a week."

"And, because Mr. Warren could not be the father of this child, you then realized, of course, short of history's second recorded instance of immaculate conception, someone else must be, correct?"

"We reached that same conclusion, Mr. Cameron," Newell replied, refusing to crack a smile at the tepid jest.

"What impact, if any, did the knowledge that Mrs. Warren was pregnant by a man other than her husband have on your investigation?"

"We considered it a motive for murder."

Hunter arched one eyebrow. "A motive? For *whom?*"

Newell cocked his head slightly. "I'm not sure that I follow you."

"Okay," Hunter said, as he began to slowly pace the area between Newell and the jury. "You have a married woman who is pregnant by another man and is subsequently found murdered. Don't you think that if her pregnancy is a motive for the husband to have committed the murder, it might be just as strong a motive for the baby's father? Maybe even a stronger one?"

Libby noticed Newell's expression shade a bit, as though a thin cloud had passed in front of the sun. "Perhaps," he said, recovering quickly. "But then, we didn't find any evidence connecting the murder to any other person."

"Did you ever bother to look?"

"No. We didn't need to."

"It's been nearly a year since Cassandra Warren's death. In all that time, have you been able to determine the identity of the father of her baby?"

Newell breathed an audible sigh. Libby could tell that his patience was expiring. "No."

"Will you please tell the ladies and gentlemen of this jury what, if any, steps the police undertook to find the father of Mrs. Warren's baby?" Hunter held out an arm toward the jury, as if he was welcoming Newell into the circle of truth.

"We asked a few of her friends if she'd been seeing someone. No one knew anything."

Hunter's face became awash with feigned surprise. "That's it?"

Newell's lips tightened.

Hunter asked again, only a tic louder. "That's it?"

Again, no answer.

Hunter looked toward the jury, as though they could give him the response, any response, to his question. "In the ten months since Mrs. Warren's death, the only effort that the Kentucky State Police made to determine the identity of her baby's father was to ask her friends if they knew anything?"

The question hung in the silence. "So," Hunter continued, "since you don't know the identity of the baby's father, you don't know whether or not he was happy about the pregnancy, do you, Detective?"

Newell leaned his head to the other side. "No."

"Or whether or not he, too, was married?"

"No."

"Or whether or not he was so angry over the pregnancy and the inconvenience that it might cause to his life that he might have wanted Cassandra Warren dead?"

"Objection!" L.G. thundered, leaping to his feet. His broad face had gone beet red. "That question calls for speculation. In fact, this entire line of questioning does."

"Sustained," Judge Roberts said calmly. "Move along, Mr. Cameron."

Libby had to bite back a proud smile as Hunter approached the defense table. Knowing exactly what he he was looking for, she held out a document. She was amazed by his performance. He was such a brilliant lawyer. Maybe, somehow, he could pull this off.

Maybe he wasn't as sick as the doctors thought.

Maybe...

Hunter was gazing down at her. Or was it *through* her? Libby felt a hush descend over the courtroom. It was as if she and Hunter were the only ones there. She recognized Hunter's blank expression. She had seen it before.

Hunter didn't know where he was.

"Mr. Cameron?" Judge Roberts's voice startled her. Libby's gaze jerked to the bench as Hunter slowly turned around. The judge peered at him with a slightly quizzical look. "Do you have any further questions for Detective Newell?"

Hunter stared at the judge for a moment, then turned back to Libby. She stood up and fumbled for her list of questions. She felt her heart race as panic began to settle in.

Then Hunter's hand come down gently over hers. She looked up at him. *It's okay,* he mouthed silently.

"Mr. Cameron?" the judge asked, this time sounding more concerned.

Hunter whirled around quickly. "Sorry, judge. Just gathering my thoughts." He walked briskly to the lectern, as though he were trying to leave something unpleasant behind.

The judge smiled warmly and seemed satisfied. "Very well, Mr. Cameron. Proceed."

"Just so I'm clear, Detective," Hunter asked, "was there any blood trail leading away from where the utility vehicle was parked at the marina?"

Clearly growing weary at this continued line of questioning, Newell frowned. "The utility vehicle was found at the lake house, not the marina."

"So, you didn't look for blood drops in the marina parking lot?"

Newell settled back in his chair. "Yes, we did."

Hunter leaned his elbow on the lectern. "Did you find any blood in the parking lot?"

"No," Newell replied, "but it also rained early that morning."

"That's true," Hunter agreed. He nodded slightly, his expression that of someone who is reluctantly facing an unavoidable fact. "Tell me, Detective, Mr. Warren's yacht is not docked under a canopy, correct?"

Newell hesitated for a second. "That's correct. It's not."

"And is the front of Mr. Warren's boat, the bow…is it covered by any overhang from the boat?"

"No."

"I can't help but wonder then…" Hunter said, followed by a deliberate pause that had everyone in the courtroom, including the jury, moving closer to the edge of their seats. "I can't help but wonder how you can sit up there and say that rain would have washed away any blood that would have been in the marina parking lot, that the workers washed away any blood on the walkway when they hosed it down that morning, but the blood you allegedly found on the uncovered bow of Mr. Warren's boat after a rainy dawn somehow managed to stay intact, just waiting for one of you to find it."

There was a lengthy silence as the question filtered through the courtroom. Finally, and far too late, L.G. rose and said, "Your Honor, I don't believe that there was a question in there anywhere. I'll have to object to Mr. Cameron's comments as being argumentative."

The judge sustained the motion, but it was too late to close the barn door. Hunter's common sense observation, for which there seemed to be no readily available explanation, had resonated with the jury.

"No further questions, your Honor," Hunter said as he returned to his chair.

The judge looked at L.G., who rose yet again from his chair. For the first time since the trial had begun, he looked fatigued.

"The Commonwealth rests, your Honor."

Chapter Seventy-Four

The whiskey seared a trail down the inside of his throat. It was still burning when he took another, longer, pull from the bottle.

Things were not going well. In fact, everything—his plan, the case against Kirk Warren that he had created, his revenge, *everything* —now seemed to be slipping away from him. He paced the floor of his room, salving his simmering fury with another swig from the fifth of Jack Daniels he carried by the neck.

There was no denying that Cameron had been brilliant in court. Newell had been the key to the case, the one testimony that would be unshakeable. But somehow Cameron had found the soft underbelly in the prosecution's case—the inconsistency of the blood evidence and where it was found—and had poked holes in it. The fact that he was the one who had planted the blood evidence on the boat infuriated him all the more.

Another long pull from the bottle did little to soothe him. This was what happened when plans go awry, he knew. And the plan, *his* plan, the one he had devised and gradually implemented over the course of years, had gotten away from him the night that Cassandra Warren was murdered. Her murder, of course, had been part of his plan. The problem was not that she had been murdered. It was that she had been murdered too soon.

That and the damned rain.

In the pre-dawn hours after Cassandra had taken her last breath, he had seen a distant flash of lightning. Had heard the warning rumble of thunder as he was walking in Kirk Warren's blood-tinged shoes down the stairwell from the bedroom deck at the lake house, when he strategically placed drops of blood on the inside of the utility vehicle, when he left several drops in the marina parking lot, and down the walkway to the boat. It was only after he had placed the bloodstains on the bow of the boat that it had happened.

In a particularly dry and uncomfortably hot summer, one that hadn't seen so much as a sprinkle, it had begun to rain.

The bloody footprints on the lake house's outside stairs were thick enough and sufficiently protected by the roof overhang and surrounding trees to survive the downpour with only some runs.

But the blood on the bow of the boat had washed away. He had watched it, and when the rain had slackened, he had applied it again. Then it had started to rain even harder, washing away the *evidence* a second time.

He had taken refuge in the deepest shadows of the dock, his pulse racing, and waited for what felt like months, silently pleading for the rain to stop. He might have even dared to pray had God not given up on him long ago.

By the time the rain finally slowed, daylight was beginning to break. He had quickly planted the blood on the bow for a third time, wrapped the blade inside the towel he had stolen from the Warren house months before and hurled it from the bow of the boat into the murky waters of the lake

He had hurried back up the ramp and toward the parking lot, careful not to step in any of the drops of blood he had planted. It would be much later that he would learn one of the idiot marina boys had washed them away while spraying the ramp with a hose. Through his research, he had learned that the kid washed the ramp a couple of times a week. He had even known the days on which it would be done. What he hadn't known was that the kid was taking the next day off and would decide to spray off the ramp a day early.

When he had reached the parking lot, he had realized the blood trail he had left to the walkway was now gone, yet another victim of the summer shower. Even worse, he had no way to replace it. The bloody towel was now resting at the bottom of the dirty lake. Plus, daylight was breaking and he couldn't afford to be seen at the marina. He would simply have to hope Hunter Cameron would not pick up on the missing blood.

That hope had made him a fool.

Maybe Cameron hadn't done enough damage to create reasonable doubt, but he had certainly created a lot of uncertainty. And while the jury might not find that uncertainty enough for an acquittal, they might not be able to ignore it long enough to sentence Warren to death. The thought of Warren avoiding the fate he deserved laced his body with rage. He drained the rest of the whiskey, his hand shaking violently.

His revenge had taken too long. There had been too much sacrificed, too much lost, to give up on it now. The death penalty had always been his goal—the only goal. And the only thing that could make him whole again. A life sentence for Warren—even without the possibility of parole—could never satisfy him.

If Warren went to prison instead of directly to hell, he'd never be able to get to him. Never be able to make him suffer enough.

He jerked up his head, the empty bottle falling from his fingertips to land on the carpet. If Warren was acquitted, he could still exact his revenge. It wouldn't be the same as the image that had driven him all these years—Warren waiting on death row, the endless days of infinite misery stacking one on top of the other like the piles of dirt they would eventually throw on his grave. But, he acknowledged to himself, it just might have to do.

He couldn't risk a conviction with a life sentence. His current plan might have gone awry on the night Cassandra had died, but like any good soldier, he would just have to adapt.

Chapter Seventy-Five

Despite the day's success with Anthony Newell, Hunter's team spent the evening at the office, still scrambling for the defense they would have to muster the next day. The wraps and paninis from the Corner Coffeehouse sat mostly untouched, with the notable exception of Dooley's 3-Cheese Grilled Cheese, which was scarfed down in two enormous bites as he ran out the office, chasing down another lead that had come in on his cell phone. A few months ago, such a call would have stirred unbridled optimism, particularly from Kirk and Libby. Now they were met with jaded indifference.

Still, they dug in. Libby was typing furiously on her laptop as she prepared to meet with their forensic expert in an hour, fine-tuning the questions Hunter had already rehearsed with the man a dozen times before. Hunter was poring through the expert's reports, making sure he understood the terms well enough to be able to effectively argue them to the jury.

Kirk sat across from him, diligently studying each page after Hunter had finished with it. "So," he said, "explain to me again what happens in the morning."

Hunter was too focused on the reports to lift his head. "We'll ask the judge to dismiss the case on the basis that the Commonwealth hasn't met its burden of proof beyond a reasonable doubt."

"And you believe there's no way he'll grant the motion?"

"Not a chance," Hunter replied.

"Why not?" Kirk asked. "You ripped that detective apart on the stand today."

Hunter lowered the report. Kirk looked like a dog begging for a treat. Hunter swallowed his own frustration. As grueling as this trial was for him, it wasn't his life on the line. Just his ass.

"Because, Kirk, it's just not going to happen. We pointed out several problems with the evidence scene and raised some real questions about why there was blood on the boat even though it had rained early that morning. But that still doesn't give us an out for the razor blade and the towel with Cassandra's blood on it."

"They were planted," Kirk retorted.

"I know that, Kirk. And I believe it. I really do. But like I've tried to tell you a dozen times, if we're going to allege that you've been framed—and we have no other choice than to do so—we need someone to point the finger at. Right now," he paused to shake his head, "we just don't have that person."

He gave Kirk time to absorb his words before continuing. "Listen, the razor and towel alone give L.G. enough ammunition to get this case out of the judge's hands and into the jury's. Plus, since this is the high-profile trial of a wealthy defendant, Judge Roberts isn't about to dismiss the case and take shit for favoring the rich. I'd like to tell you differently, Kirk," he said, picking up the report, "but I can't. I'm afraid this case is going to be decided by the jury."

Kirk lowered his head in begrudging acceptance. "So how long will the forensic guy take?"

Hunter sighed heavily and leaned back in his chair. "I'd say he'll be up there all day tomorrow, maybe into the second day. Depends on how much L.G. wants to tussle with him."

"Then who will we call next?"

"Good question. We'll have done all we can do with the physical evidence. We don't have an alibi, so there won't be any alibi witnesses. Unless we pull a rabbit out of a hat and find Cassandra's lover, then there'll only be one witness left to call." Hunter gave Kirk a long look. "You."

"Me? That quickly?" Kirk immediately began fidgeting as though someone was holding a lit match underneath his seat. "I thought you said you'd probably call me last."

"I did. There isn't anyone else."

They were both silent for several minutes. Hunter didn't return to the reports, however badly he might have needed to. Instead, he kept his wary gaze on Kirk, knowing how fragile his friend was when it came to this kind of stress.

"Kirk?" he said gently. When his friend looked up in response, Hunter saw that he was trembling. He reached across the table and put his hand on Kirk's shoulder, trying to reassure him. "Kirk," he said, more firmly this time, "we have to get you ready to testify."

Chapter Seventy-Six

Libby had never met a real forensic scientist before the Warren case. Stereotypes being what they are, she had always pictured them as looking like rats wearing white lab coats. Thin and bespectacled, slump-shouldered, hair all awry—typical geeks. She shot Kirk a sidelong glance, realizing she had just described their client. Dr. Howard Neiswander, perhaps the country's most noted criminal forensic scientist, didn't look anything like that.

As the bailiff swore him in, he looked more like one of those dashing, middle-aged models peddling Ralph Lauren cologne in a magazine ad. He was tall and athletic with classic features accentuated by his finely tailored navy pinstripe suit. Streaks of silver shot through the thick waves of his hair, blending nicely with his sterling silk tie. The only feature that wasn't quite perfect was a mouth that seemed slightly too small for his perfectly whitened teeth. Not that any of the women in the courtroom, Libby included, seemed to mind.

"Dr. Neiswander," Hunter asked, "what current position do you hold?"

The doctor turned slightly to face the jury and smiled before answering. "I'm the chief criminalist for the state of Missouri. I'm also the laboratory director for the Missouri state police forensic laboratory."

"Just so we're clear, Doctor," Hunter continued, "are you here today in that capacity?"

"No," he replied, still holding on to that smile. "I'm here as an independent consultant."

"Do you testify frequently?"

"Yes. Several times each month."

"And in terms of which side you're usually on in a criminal case, how often would you say you testify for the prosecution and how often for the defense?"

"In terms of percentages, I'd say about ninety percent of the time for the prosecution and the remaining ten for the defense."

"Can you give us your educational background?"

"Yes. I received my Bachelor's Degree in Forensic Science from the John Jay College of Criminal Justice in New York, and my Master's Degree and Doctorate in Biochemistry from Washington University in St. Louis, where I am adjunct professor."

"Are you a member of any professional associations?"

"Yes, about twenty or so."

"Have you published any books on forensic science?"

"Yes. I have written or co-written sixteen books on forensic science and have published another two hundred or so articles in professional journals covering crime scene investigation and recon-struction, trace evidence, bloodstain pattern analysis, chemistry, and instrumental analysis."

Dr. Neiswander made rattling off his qualifications seem modest, as though he was unfazed by it all and they should be, too. However impressive he might look and sound, he was still just a guy there to tell about the way he saw things in this case. It was no wonder that he was renowned almost as much for his jury appeal as he was for his scientific brilliance.

"Dr. Neiswander, how were you brought into this case?"

The doctor crossed his long legs. "You called me last summer, shortly after the crime occurred."

"And what tasks did I ask you to perform for Mr. Warren's defense?"

"You asked me to study the crime scene and the boat. You also asked me to look at the crime scene photographs, as well as the bloodstain analysis."

After getting permission from the judge, Hunter approached Dr. Neiswander and handed him a bottle of red ink and paper. "Doctor," he said, stepping back from the witness stand, "using the ink and paper I've just handed you, can you please demonstrate for the jury the different kinds of bloodstain patterns?"

"Yes." He continued to speak as he spread out the paper across the top of the stand and then temporarily placed the inkbottle on top of it. "As you all probably know, our human circulation system is what carries the nutrients from oxygen throughout the body. If this system is interrupted, then the blood will come up."

He paused and then picked up the inkbottle. "For example, if an artery is severed, the blood will gush out. This is called 'arterial spurting' or 'arterial gushing.'" He removed the dropper from the bottle and holding it in his hand, gently snapped it forward, as though he was casting a short line with a rod and reel. Red ink scattered over the paper. "The blood splatter would appear, at least generally, like this," he said pausing to hold up the paper.

Hunter handed him a clean sheet of paper and took away the first one. The doctor continued without the need for further instruction. "If a capillary was cut, then the blood would simply drip out, like so." Again, he held the dropper over the paper. Only this time he merely squeezed its top, allowing several random drops to fall on to the paper. He held the paper up for the jury, and then, like clockwork, Hunter retrieved the paper from him and gave him another clean sheet.

"What if a vein were to be cut?" Hunter asked.

"In that case, the blood would pour out like this." Dr. Neiswander carefully tipped the bottle to its side and allowed a sufficient amount of ink to pour onto the page before turning it upright and screwing the top back on.

"Have you read the autopsy report?"

"I have."

"Was it Mrs. Warren's veins or arteries that were cut?"

"Actually," Neiswander replied, "they both were."

"So then, there would have been both arterial spray," Hunter said, holding up the first sheet of paper peppered with ink spots, "and—for lack of a better phrase—a blood spill." In his other hand, he held up the second sheet that was now nearly completely red from the ink poured on it by the doctor.

"Yes. That's correct."

"Have you examined photos of the murder scene?" Hunter continued, as he put the sheets down on the defense table.

"I have."

"Based upon those photos, what happened with the blood after it left Cassandra Warren's body?"

"The blood first deposited onto the surface of the bed on which she was lying. However, because the blood flow was running at a speed greater than the ability of the satin sheets to absorb it, it pooled and eventually ran off the side of the mattress and onto the next lowest surface, which was the floor next to the bed."

"Doctor, is it possible to measure bloodstain patterns and correlate them to the source of the target?"

"Yes, it is."

"How is this done?"

"We do an estimation, based upon the size of the drop and the substrata, that is, the surface of the area where it fell."

"So when the crime scene is being documented and preserved, is it important to try to make a reasonable estimate by measuring the vertical drop with respect to where the source was?"

"If we know the parameters," Neiswander replied, "then we can make an educated estimate."

"Therefore, it is important to document the size of the drops at the crime scene."

"Yes. It certainly is."

"And did any of the photographs of the crime scene that you've reviewed contain rulers so that these measurements could be made?"

"No," the doctor replied. "They did not."

"Okay, let me ask you this: in a closed environment such as the Warrens' bedroom, and with a wound like the one suffered by Mrs. Warren, with 'arterial spurts' as you termed them, do you have an opinion as to whether or not the assailant would be covered with blood from the struggle?"

"Yes, I do."

"And what is that opinion, Doctor?"

"Both the right and left carotid arteries were severed, so the arterial spurting would have been massive. In short, it would be difficult to imagine that there wouldn't have been some blood on the attacker's clothing."

"And was there any blood found on any clothing owned by Mr. Warren, other than his shoes?"

"It is my understanding from the police reports that there was not."

"Okay," Hunter said, "let's talk then about the bloodstain that was found on the bow of Mr. Warren's boat." He walked over to the clerk and shuffled through the previously admitted photographs until he found the ones he wanted. He delivered them to Neiswander and then stepped toward the jury box while the Doctor reviewed them.

"Have you reviewed those photographs?"

"Yes, I have."

"Have you also familiarized yourself with the weather on the morning that Mrs. Warren was found, and perhaps more specifically, when the blood was found on the bow of the boat?"

"I have," he replied. "You received quite a bit of rain between two-thirty and six that morning. About three inches' worth, according to the National Weather Center report for that day."

"And, according to the autopsy, wasn't Mrs. Warren's approximate time of death between eleven p.m. and one a.m. the night before?"

"Yes, it was."

"Tell me, Doctor Neiswander, how is it possible for a bloodstain located on a hard fiberglass surface like the bow on Mr. Warren's yacht to withstand a rainfall hard enough to produce three inches of accumulation in less than three hours?"

"Very simple, Mr. Cameron," Neiswander replied without hesitation, "it's not. The blood had to have come into contact with the surface *after* the rain had stopped."

Chapter Seventy-Seven

D r. Neiswander's direct examination had taken the entire day on Thursday and L.G. was prepared to begin his cross-examination of the scientist on Friday morning. The doctor was back in the courtroom, resplendent in a charcoal gray suit with a perfectly knotted burgundy tie. Libby stood next to Kirk, whose spirits seemed to be lifted from the impact of Neiswander's testimony. Judge Roberts sat patiently at the bench, looking over calendar entries on last week's docket. L.G. had his documents in order and looked ready to go. In fact, everyone looked ready go. There was only one problem.

Hunter wasn't there. Not in the courtroom. Not in the court-house. In fact, no one had seen him this morning. No one at all. Libby had started getting worried when he didn't make it to the office for the planned morning session to help Neiswander prepare for L.G.'s cross. She had immediately called Hunter's house, but got no answer. His cell phone went to voice mail on the first ring.

Judge Roberts had already asked where Hunter was. Libby had risen and, with the first words she had ever uttered on the record in a court of law, lied to the judge and told him Hunter was consulting with a crucial witness for the defense. She knew it was only the judge's respect for Hunter that prompted him to put the court in recess for thirty minutes. By her watch, that was exactly twenty-one minutes ago.

Libby felt a tug at her sleeve. She turned. With her heels on, she stood eye-to-eye with Kirk.

"Where *is* he?" Kirk demanded furiously.

She paused, trying to formulate an answer. There were only two possibilities. One, he'd had another episode and had no idea where he was. The second possibility was that Kirk's attacker had made good on his threat to deal not only with Kirk, but with Hunter, too.

As she stood in that courtroom as her client's only means of defense, she couldn't decide which of the two possibilities scared her the most.

———

HE PACED OUTSIDE THE COURTHOUSE, toking hard on his hand-rolled cigarette. He needed it to soothe his nerves before the judge reconvened the trial. *What in the fuck was Cameron doing?* he wondered. Things had gotten away from him, he knew. Too damn far away. He couldn't leave his life's destiny in the hands of a jury. Not anymore. He was going to have to take action immediately, if not sooner.

He felt an unexpected tap on his shoulder and his training took over. He whirled around with one fist pulled back and ready to strike. His other hand snaked behind his waist, ready to whip out his hidden blade if the circumstances called for it.

He found himself gazing up into the face of Hunter Cameron. He would have expected anyone to look frightened by his stance. But Hunter Cameron looked terrified. Of something even more significant than him. Ignoring every combat technique he had ever been taught, he slowly lowered his fist.

"Excuse me, sir," Cameron said. "I'm afraid that I'm a little lost. I was wondering if you could maybe tell me how to get to this place." Cameron handed him a folded piece of paper, torn from a stenographer's notepad.

He looked first over one shoulder and then his other. Surely this was some sort of trick.

When he saw nothing out of the ordinary, he slowly unfolded the note. On it, in bold block letters, were written the words *Christian Circuit Court, Judge Roberts's courtroom.*

———

"MISS MASTERS," Judge Roberts said, clearly growing more exasperated by the minute. "Have we heard from Mr. Cameron?"

Libby rose from her seat, so nervous she felt like she was on roller skates. "No, y-your Honor," she stammered. "He must still be with that witness."

Judge Roberts inhaled deeply through his nose, yet another sign of his irritation. "Well, Miss Masters," he said, exhaling on a sigh, "I'm afraid that we're going to have to get started without him. I can't ask these jurors to wait here all day while he's out interviewing witnesses." Shaking his head with regret, he instructed the bailiff to bring in the jury.

They had just been seated when the courtroom doors swung open. The entire courtroom turned around and saw Hunter Cameron walk through the doors.

Libby's knees went weak with relief. Hunter looked fine. Great, in fact. He was, as always, clean-shaven and neatly dressed. But when she saw the look on his face, her relief melted into fear.

Spotting her, he headed her way just like a man lost at sea might head for a familiar shoreline.

"Mr. Cameron," the judge said, "I'm so glad that you decided to join us."

Hunter glanced up at the bench more because of the sharp note in the judge's voice than because he recognized his name. Libby hurried to meet him, pretending to whisper something in his ear as she guided him to the defense table.

"Is the Commonwealth ready to proceed?" the judge asked.

L.G. rose from his table, shooting a puzzled look in Hunter's direction. "Yes, your Honor. We are."

———

HE WAITED a few minutes after Cameron went into the courtroom before entering himself. Frankly, he had needed the time to try to make sense out of what had just happened.

Cameron's behavior had been beyond bizarre. He had seen a lot of drunks and junkies in his day and he was positive this hadn't been an act. The more he thought about it, it was an awful lot like what Cameron had done at the preliminary hearing all those months ago. Only this time, there had been no courtroom to influence. Maybe it was some lawyer trick, but he couldn't imagine what value a lawyer's incoherence would have to a jury.

He couldn't let it, whatever *it* was, affect him now.

Whatever was up with him, Cameron would go down. Had they not been standing in front of the fucking courthouse, he would have taken him then. But the timing wasn't right. Not yet.

Not quite yet.

———

AS HUNTER SANK DOWN in the chair, he could have sworn that he was at the bottom of a pool and the rest of the world was swimming around him.

The large man to his right was standing and asking questions of the well-dressed man sitting in the raised chair in front of him. They both seemed to know what they were talking about, but he didn't understand any of it. For a while, he asked questions about rulers and measuring blood. Then he asked some questions about blood on the front of a boat and something about rain. Then he started asking about something else.

"Doctor Neiswander, are you familiar with an article entitled 'The Absence of Evidence is Not Evidence'?"

The man who must be named Neiswander nodded. "I am."

"And do you generally agree with the crux of that article, which is that you really can't deduce that a person didn't participate in a bloody crime simply because that person didn't have blood on their person or on their clothing?"

The man in the chair nodded again. He spoke more friendly to the large man than the large man did to him. "That depends on the situation," he said. "If you kill someone from a long distance away, as with a gun, then it's entirely possible that you wouldn't get blood on your person. If you shoot them at close range, it's highly likely that you would."

Hunter could feel himself relaxing. He felt comfortable in this room, as though he was supposed to be here. But for the life of him, he couldn't remember why. And whatever it was these two guys were talking about made absolutely no sense to him.

"If someone were standing on the left of someone, reached over to the right, and slit that person's throat, and blood spurted to the right, would you expect that assailant to be covered in blood?"

The pretty girl sitting to his left stood up and spoke.

"Objection, your Honor," she said. "The question assumes facts not in evidence."

Another large man, this one wearing a robe, spoke this time. "Overruled. The witness may answer the question."

"Under the facts you're giving," the well-dressed man said, "I'd have to say probably not."

The large man without the robe looked at a couple of sheets on his desk. Finally, he looked up. "No further questions, your Honor."

The man in the robe turned toward Hunter's table and asked if they had any questions. The pretty young girl stood up again. "No, your Honor," she said. He looked down at her legs and saw that her knees were shaking as she spoke. "Your Honor, it's already eleven o'clock. If it pleases the court, the defense requests a recess until one."

Hunter watched as the man in the robe looked toward the people sitting on the side of the room in the large box. They looked tired and some of them were moving their heads up and down.

"Very well," he said. "Court is adjourned until one o'clock."

Chapter Seventy-Eight

Libby needed a drink. Since she was now, by default, lead counsel in the capital murder trial of the wealthiest man in the state, she would have to settle for a strong cup of coffee.

The secretaries were trying to keep Kirk calm. Their only advantage in the battle was that they were both bigger than he was. Libby had called Dooley for help, but he was talking up a lead. He said he would get there as soon as he could.

Hunter was lying on the couch in his office. He hadn't said anything on the way from the courthouse to the office. He hadn't needed to. Sadly enough, they had planned for this.

Libby called the number he had given her, the one for Four Rivers Clinical Research Center in Paducah. His nurse there, Mrs. Talcott, had generously agreed to be at his beck and call this week. She picked up the phone on its second ring. Though she and Libby had never met, Talcott knew her name and didn't waste time with pleasantries.

"What happened?"

Libby explained what she knew. He looked fine, she said, so he must have been all right when he dressed that morning. It was as though between getting ready for court and arriving there, the fabric of his reality had torn loose.

"He's been so incredible in court all this time," Libby said, feeling her throat tighten around the words. "I thought maybe the medicine was curing him."

"It can't cure him," Talcott said, her voice gentle and compassionate. "It's merely experimental. The researchers think that it might help slow the progress of the disease, but even they don't know for certain that it will, and even if it does, for how long."

"But he's been doing so well," Libby said, swiping at her nose with the back of her hand without realizing it. "You wouldn't have known anything was wrong with him."

"He's been on what we call a *plateau*. It's a holding pattern. A period of time when the disease doesn't appear to progress."

"Why did it stop?"

"I don't know. *We* don't know. This may sound crass, but think of it like cancer. It affects different people in different ways. With some people, cancer stays dormant or in remission for many years. With others, it eats them alive within months or even weeks. It's the same thing with dementia. Some don't show much deterioration for many years. There are others who get the very same treatments who become invalids within a year."

"What do we do now?"

Libby felt the weight of Talcott's sigh. "The stress of the trial hasn't helped. Where is he now?"

"On the couch in his office."

"He can't go back to court. He needs to go home. Send someone with him if you have to, but under no circumstances should you let him *not* let him go alone."

Libby hung up the phone. She called in Tess, told her Hunter wasn't feeling well, and asked her to drive him home. Though the request was way out of the norm for one of Hunter's secretaries, Tess didn't bat an eyelash. It occurred to Libby that in the months since she had learned about Hunter's disease, she had fallen victim to the naïve idea that no one else in his life had noticed his lapses. She had been just as foolish as he was. But at least he had an excuse.

Libby knew she had to tell Kirk what was going on with Hunter. Under the circumstances, Judge Roberts would probably grant them a mistrial, though she hoped he wouldn't question her about how much she knew about Hunter's condition—or how long she had known about it. She was getting her files together when Dooley stormed into her office.

"We got to talk, honey," he said, his chest and belly unfurling like sails on a boat. "Where's Hunter?"

She swallowed. Hard. "I'm afraid he's not going to be in court this afternoon."

"Just who's going to be the attorney, then?"

Libby shoved the last file in her case, then lifted her head to meet his gaze squarely. "You're looking at her."

"*You?* You can't be serious."

"Screw you, Dooley."

Dooley waved off her insult with a hand as big as a catcher's mitt. "We don't have time for this shit. Listen," he said, "I've found someone you need to talk to."

"Who?" Libby asked, knowing they didn't have time for any unnecessary drama. "And where are they?"

"He's here. In the lobby. Let me go get him."

Dooley brought the new witness into her office and the three of them talked. Libby asked him all the same questions Dooley had asked him and then asked him several more. In the end, she was satisfied. Grabbing her briefcase, she told Dooley to retrieve Kirk and meet her at the courthouse, and then strode out of the office, her walk brisk with resolve.

She needed to walk alone, she had told them. To gather her thoughts.

And so none of them, especially the man whose life now rested in her hands, would see the tears stinging her eyes.

Chapter Seventy-Nine

Tad Ramey was embarrassed to be wearing his ripped jeans and threadbare work boots in court and was grateful the jurors couldn't see either as he sat in the witness stand. At twenty years old, he was barely old enough to be on a jury, let alone testifying before one.

His skin was a deep bronze, even though it was just the middle of spring. His tan had been gained from toiling in the heat of the sun rather than basking in its glow. His blond hair was matted down from the *Lake Barkley Marina* cap he had been wearing before he entered the courtroom. He had wanted to change out of his work clothes before coming, but that big Dooley fella, who was apparently in good with his boss at the marina, had said that there wasn't time.

Libby and L.G. filed out of the judge's chambers, followed by the judge and bailiff. They had been in the chambers since just after Tad had been called as a witness. L.G. had objected immediately, claiming that Tad was not on the witness list. Libby had explained that the witness had just been located and that the value of his testimony would outweigh any prejudice to the Commonwealth. L.G. had continued to grumble until the judge had been forced to move the argument outside of the jury's earshot and into his chambers.

After a few minutes of heated discussion, they were now back in the courtroom had ready to proceed.

"I have heard the objection of the Commonwealth," Judge Roberts announced, "and it is hereby overruled. Miss Masters, you may proceed."

Libby turned to the witness and smiled. She wondered which of them was more nervous. "Will you state your name, please?"

"Joseph Tad Ramey, but everyone calls me Tad."

"All right, Tad. Where are you employed?"

"Lake Barkley Marina. Been out there, what," he paused to count in his head, "four years now. Except for six months this past year. I went to work on a barge. But I didn't like it much so I came home and went back to the marina."

"When did you leave the marina to go work on the barge?"

"I remember it exactly. July 4th of last summer." Tad perked up momentarily, pleased with the precision of his answer.

"When did you come back to the marina?" Libby asked.

"Just last week. They were kind enough to give me my old job back."

"Have you been working there today?"

"Yes, ma'am," Tad replied. "That's why I'm dressed like this." He looked down at himself, blushing beneath the tan, then looked up at the judge. "I sure am sorry about my appearance."

Judge Roberts gave the kid an encouraging smile. "That's quite all right, Mr. Ramey. We all understand that you were working and didn't know you'd be called here today." Several members of the jury were smiling as well.

Libby struggled to regain her train of thought. There were no prepared notes for this one, forcing her to wing it. *Funny,* she thought, *I sort of like the freedom.* "Do you know why you're here today?"

Tad nodded. "Yes, ma'am. They told me that this was about the police thinkin' that Mr. Warren killed his wife."

"Before today, has anyone ever talked to you about anything you might have seen last summer relevant to this case?"

"No, ma'am."

"Did you ever try to talk to the police about this case?"

"No, ma'am."

"Why not?" Libby asked.

"Well, ma'am, I really didn't think I had anything to tell. I really didn't think anything about what I saw. Not until now."

"Mr. Ramey," Libby continued, "are you aware that this case has received an awful lot of publicity? That it's been in the newspapers and on the news?"

"No, ma'am."

Libby feigned incredulousness. "How did you miss the coverage of this case in the newspapers and on TV?"

Tad winced. "I suppose this is a bad thing to say, but I really don't read the newspaper. I reckon that I've never once read it. Don't watch the news, either. I guess I had too much going on, being on the barge and all, to worry 'bout what else is going on in the world. Besides, when you're down the river on a barge with a bunch of roughnecks from all over, you pretty much forget about what's going on in Hopkinsville."

"So, Mr. Ramey," Libby continued, "when did you find out about Mr. Warren's arrest for the murder of his wife?"

"Today. Sure sorry to hear it. Mr. Warren was always nice to me."

Libby decided to shift gears away from any intimation that Tad was here because he liked Kirk. "What do you do out at the marina?"

"All sorts of things, really. Pump gas. Wash people's boats when they ask me to. I work the cash register some, but only when we're short-handed. I prefer to be outside."

"Do you have any other duties outside?"

"Oh, yes, ma'am. I usually open the gates in the morning and check them at night. I do a lot of cleaning up around the marina and the dock area where all the boats are kept. Just a lot of things, I guess."

"Were you working on June 15 of last year?"

"Was that the date all the police came and searched Mr. Warren's yacht?"

Libby took a quick look at L.G., who was watching Tad closely, no doubt looking for any opportunity to insert an objection.

"Yes, it was," she replied.

"Then, yes, ma'am, I was working that day."

"What time did you arrive?"

"When I'm opening the marina, I get there before dawn. The sun wasn't up yet and I remember that it was raining. I'd say it was four-thirty or so."

"Can you tell the jury what you remember happening that morning."

"Well, ma'am, it's like I told you earlier…"

Tad pulled his decrepit Ford Ranger around the long bend of the roadway that led to the marina parking lot. It wasn't even four-thirty and he was already pissed off. It was raining in sheets and he had three boats to wash down today. The owners were the big spenders, too. No boat washing meant no tips. Oh well, he thought, at least the rain will wash some of the dust off my truck.

He had his lights on and needed them to see even twenty feet ahead of him, what with the rain and all. As he pulled toward the walkway, he drove at about a quarter the speed he usually drove at, scared he would hit one of the cars parked in the marina lot. Fortunately, only a few people spent the night on their boats during the week so the lot was virtually empty. He pulled into his usual employee spot, close to the gate. He fumbled with his keys, trying to find his gate key so he could make a run for it once he got outside. It was then, right before he got out of the car, that he noticed a black car, parked one spot over to his right. He might not have noticed it, but it was parked in another employee parking space.

"Did you happen to notice," Libby asked, "the make and model of the car?"

Tad shook his head. "No, ma'am. I just sort of saw it and shrugged. I knew I was the only employee there because the office was still dark. I got out of my car, ran to the gate, opened it, and ran down to the marina so I could get out of the rain."

"What did you do next?"

Tad made it inside the store area of the marina. He found an old towel and dried off. He hadn't spent thirty seconds outside, but was soaked down to his drawers. He ate a bag of peanuts, drank a Coke, and then put in his second dip of the day. With both his caffeine and nicotine fixes firmly in place, he set about restocking the food shelves and checked to see if the minnow supply needed to be refilled. It did and he was lugging them from the back storage room to the store tanks when he noticed the rain letting up.

Tad looked outside, out toward the yacht dock. The clouds were separating. The rain had slowed to a light sprinkle. He grinned. Looks like I'll be washin' those big boys after all, he mused.

Tad finished pouring the minnows, washed his hands, and decided to wander down to Dock C, where Mr. McDaniels kept his houseboat. He wanted to look the boat over, see how big a job cleaning it would be. Mr. McD's boat was usually the dirtiest of the boats and he liked to get the worst of them out of the way as quickly as possible.

"It was then that I noticed him."

"Noticed who?" Libby asked.

"I don't know the guy's name. I just know it was a guy. He was pretty good size, too big to be a girl."

"What did this guy, this *man*, that you saw…what did he look like?"

"That was part of what I noticed. There it was, middle of the damn…uh…middle of the darned summer, and there was some fool dressed all in black. Black winter hat. Everything."

"Did you get a look at his face?"

"Not a good one," Tad admitted. "He appeared to be a little dark skinned, but I couldn't tell you any more than that."

Libby's face took on a look of great interest. "Where was this man, dressed in black, when you saw him?"

"He was standing over at the end of Dock B, where the yachts are."

"About how far was that from where you were standing?"

Tad took a deep breath as he contemplated her question. "Maybe sixty or seventy yards."

"You could see him. Was it possible for him to see you?"

"I don't see how. Mr. McD's slip is in the middle of Dock A. I doubt he could have seen me because I was in between several of the boats. On the other hand, he was standing at the end of that dock, next to the yacht that's moored there. There's several empty slips over there because not many people have yachts."

"So did you have any problem seeing him?"

Tad again shook his head. "None at all, ma'am."

"Tad, if you would, please tell the ladies and gentlemen of the jury, whose yacht this man dressed in black was standing next to."

"That would be Mr. Warren's boat."

"Are you sure?"

"Yes, ma'am. I know that boat well."

"How's that?"

"Mr. Warren has me clean it a time or two a month." For the first time, Tad turned and looked straight at the jury, as though he was about to tell them something of staggering importance. "You get a tip like the ones Mr. Warren gives, you'll for darn sure remember that boat." The entire courtroom, judge and jury included, struggled to suppress a collective laugh.

Libby, on the other hand, was all business. "I take it, then, that you know Mr. Warren."

"Oh, yes, ma'am." Tad gave Kirk a small wave. Kirk returned it with a feeble smile.

"Is it possible that the man you saw dressed in black was Mr. Warren?"

"Noooo, ma'am," Tad exclaimed, clearly incredulous at the very idea.

"How can you be so sure?"

"Like I said, Miss Masters, this guy was a little ways away from me, but I could tell that he was pretty good size. Probably six feet or better. He also looked pretty stout. Now," he continued, "no offense to Mr. Warren or anything, but he ain't exactly the biggest dude you're ever going to see."

"So you're telling the ladies and gentlemen of this jury that there is no possibility whatsoever that Kirk Warren was the man you saw that morning."

"No, ma'am. No chance whatsoever."

"Okay," Libby said, satisfied that her point was made. "What did you see the man dressed in black do in front of Mr. Warren's yacht?"

Tad couldn't believe that fool. Granted, it was morning and it had just rained, but damn, the humidity was still awful. He couldn't imagine being in that get-up. He tried to turn his attention to the boat, but he just couldn't keep from looking at that idiot in those clothes. The guy would look at the water, then glare up at the sky. Tad didn't know if he was checking to see if the rain had stopped or what. He seemed to stand there for several minutes, and then, finally, he knelt down and reached into a bag that was sitting next to him.

Tad strained to see what he was doing with the bag, but the man's body was in the way. Suddenly, the man pulled out a large plastic bag. It looked like it was full of something red. At first glance, Tad thought maybe the freak had some pillow stuck in there. The man held the bag out away from him and over the water as he removed what appeared to be a small cloth of some sort, maybe a dish towel. He then stepped lightly on to the front bow of the boat, and with one hand continued to hold the splotchy cloth out from his body. After a few seconds, he moved to the very front of the boat and held the cloth over the water. He then pulled a shiny object of some sort, Tad couldn't tell what, and tightly knotted the cloth around it. He then stepped off the boat and back on to the dock.

Tad found himself transfixed by the guy, trying to figure out just what the hell he was doing. The man, at least for a moment, ignored the bag on the dock and took a few steps back up the dock walkway, as though he was leaving, the balled-up cloth still in his hand. Then he turned around, appeared to measure his steps, and ambled slowly toward the front of the dock, as though he was getting ready to throw a Hail Mary pass. He heaved the cloth a pretty fair distance, maybe twenty-five yards or so. Tad was impressed by the guy's arm.

"That's another way I know it was a guy," Tad said. "Ain't no girl gonna heave something that far."

"What happened next?"

"He grabbed his bag and started to high-tail it back up the walkway to the front gate. At first," he continued, "I began to walk up the walkway to my dock, too. They tell us at work that if we see someone littering and throwing stuff in the lake to tell them not to."

"Was that what you told him to do?"

"No, ma'am. You see, his dock is a lot closer to the main walkway that leads out to the parking lot. The marina likes to make it easier on the rich folks. Anyway, he had a lot shorter distance to the parking lot than I did and, like I said, he was high-tailing it pretty good."

"So you couldn't catch up to him?"

"No, ma'am. By the time I got midway up the walkway to the parking lot, he was already in his car and was pulling away." Tad paused. "I saw his license plate, though."

"Do you remember the number?" Libby asked.

"No, ma'am. But I know who it belonged to."

"How do you know that if you don't know the number."

"Because, Miss Masters, you been pulled over as many times for speedin' as I have, you know what a state police license plate looks like."

Libby did her best to look disbelieving, even though her heart was being flayed by his testimony. "It was a Kentucky State Police car that the man in black was driving?"

"Yes, ma'am," Tad replied. "Stake my life on it."

"Was it a marked car?" she somehow found the strength to ask.

"No, ma'am. Remember how I said when I got to the marina and it was rainin', I saw that car parked a space over from me? How I told you it was dark and rainin' so hard then that I couldn't make out what kind of car it was?"

"I remember," Libby replied.

"Well, with the sun out, I could see the car." Tad turned to the jury, nodding for emphasis. "It was one of them black Crown Victorias."

Chapter Eighty

"The Defense recalls Detective Anthony Newell to the stand."

After she said the words, Libby's insides felt as though they were being brought to a slow boil. She was asking the court to call her lover to the stand so she could cross-examine him about his whereabouts on the morning that the murder was committed. Kirk wasn't at the boat that morning, just as he had said. Someone from KSP, however, was. They finally had someone at whom to point the finger, and the knowledge of who it was—that the man she loved had planted evidence in a capital murder case—left her heart in shards.

The bailiff wandered out to the hallway to tell Newell he had been recalled. The doors stayed closed behind him for a long time. Libby was so lost in her own personal thoughts that she didn't realize how long he had been gone. Finally, he came back in, approached the bench and whispered something to the judge. The judge then summoned L.G. and Libby to the bench.

"Mr. Owen," Judge Roberts said under his breath as he pressed a button to stop the audio recording of the proceedings, "do you know where Detective Newell is?"

L.G. didn't bother to try to hide his confusion. "I assumed that

he was out in the hallway or in one of the witness rooms. The officers all know to stay in the area because they might be recalled."

"And they're all out there. All of them except Detective Newell."

"Did you call the Madisonville post?" L.G. asked.

The bailiff nodded. "Yes, sir, we sure did. They tried his phone a
couple of times and then his squad car. Nothing."

"Did you try the 911 center?" the judge inquired.

"Yes, your Honor. No luck."

The judge stewed on it for a moment, then turned to Libby.
"Miss Masters, it appears as though Detective Newell is unavailable.
How do you wish to proceed? Do you wish to call another witness?"

"Your Honor," Libby replied, "in light of Mr. Ramey's testimony about what he saw on the dock, we believe that it is absolutely
essential that we get Detective Newell back in here and find out
where he was that morning."

"The kid didn't say it was Detective Newell he saw," L.G.
interjected.

Libby turned on L.G. "No, but the fact that the man at the dock
is the same approximate size, build, and complexion of Newell,
along with the fact that whoever threw the towel into the lake was
also driving a KSP-issue Crown Vic, the question bears asking."

Even if I know what the answer will do to me.

Another deputy came into the courtroom and motioned for the
bailiff. He whispered in the bailiff's ear. The bailiff nodded several
times. After a few seconds, he tapped the deputy on the shoulder
and returned to the bench. He, too, kept his voice low, mindful of
the jurors. But his volume did little to quell the fears of those who
heard what he had to say.

"KSP just called," he whispered. "They have a way to break
through on any employee's phone and can tell if they're on another
call or if the phone was simply left on. They tried to break in to
Newell's line, to tell him that he was needed here in court."

"What happened?" the judge asked, his anticipation and frustration clearly running neck and neck.

"The breakthrough didn't take, meaning that the phone was
turned off. The state police are instructed to have that phone turned

on at all times while they're on duty. So KSP ran a trace on the phone and got a location."

"Where was it?" L.G. demanded.

"It was lying on one of the grass medians here in the courthouse parking lot. Someone must have tossed it there."

The bailiff looked around at all of them, knowing what he was about to say, and knowing that none of them, himself included, knew what it meant.

"Detective Newell is gone."

Chapter Eighty-One

Hunter Cameron paced around his living room, watching through the front window as Katherine eased her car down their driveway and into the garage. It had been a couple of hours since he had gotten his bearings and dismissed Tess from her caretaking duties. It had been an hour since Libby had called to check on him. She was pissed when he told her that he had sent Tess home and threatened to come out there and tell Katherine about his illness herself if he didn't.

This time, he didn't argue with her. It was time—way beyond time, frankly—for his wife to know.

He dreaded telling her. Dreaded the questions she would inevitably have and the shameful answers he would have to give. Dreaded the hurt he would cause her. But most of all, and this was the most selfish part, he hated that it was over. He had managed—somehow, some way—for all of these months to keep those in his public and private lives in the dark. Until this day, he had still been the man he had always been to them. And now he would never be that man again.

He heard the sounds of her car shutting off, the back door opening, and the click of her heels as she came through the kitchen and into the living room.

"Hey," she said, as she laid a couple of bags on the couch and made her way around to him. He reflexively lowered his head so she could drop a kiss on his cheek. She looked up at him and smiled as she affectionately rubbed his chest, then turned and wandered back toward the kitchen.

"How'd the trial go today?" she called over her shoulder.

"Real well," Hunter said, as though he had actually been there. After scolding him during their phone call, Libby had let him know what had happened. That Neiswander had fared well under L.G.'s cross and what had happened with Tad. That Newell had disappeared. Even if his mind was clear, he would have had trouble believing that Newell had been the one who planted the evidence. He just didn't seem the type.

"I guess the trial will carry over into next week," Katherine said with a sigh. "I'm sure I won't be seeing you again this weekend. Frankly, I'm surprised that I'm seeing you tonight."

"No," Hunter said. "There won't be any court next week."

Katherine turned, giving him a puzzled look.

"That's right," he confirmed. "No court next week. At least not for me."

"Why not? I didn't think you were finished with your case."

"We're not," he said, "at least from what I understand."

"From what *you* understand?" she repeated, her bewilderment shifting to concern. "Hunter, what's going on with you?"

"I need you to come in here. We need to talk."

Hunter despised using those words, knowing they would do nothing but heighten her anxiety. He despised the words she would hear next even worse.

Katherine slowly returned to the living room, walking as if there was broken glass beneath her feet. She lowered herself onto the couch, never taking her eyes off of him. Hunter swallowed hard and moved toward the sliding glass door, which he always kept open in the spring months so they could enjoy the breeze coming off the lake.

"Do you remember last summer and fall when I wasn't feeling so well and you insisted I go to the doctor?"

Katherine nodded.

"And you know I went, right?"

Another nod.

"Do you remember what I told you he said?"

Katherine's brow furrowed in a frown as she struggled to remember. "That you just needed to rest more. That you were working too hard."

"Well," Hunter replied, "that's true. He did say that."

"Did he say something else?"

He sighed. "Yes."

She stood and he could tell that was seeing not her life, nor his, but their life together passing before her eyes. With palpable trepidation, she began to move toward him. "Hunter, please, you're scaring me." Tears began to trickle down her cheeks. She rested her hands on his shoulders. "If there's something wrong, you've got to tell me."

"I...I don't know where to begin," he stammered. He felt his own eyes beginning to well with tears. He couldn't remember the last time he had cried, but, hell, he couldn't remember a lot of things.

That was when he saw it.

The reflection of movement in her eyes.

If they weren't so beautiful and glimmering with tears, he might have reacted sooner. He might have whirled around and faced his intruder and given the two of them a fighting chance.

But they were and he didn't.

A blunt object jabbed against the small of his back, followed by a jolt of pure shock. His failure to save his wife was his last thought as he crumpled to the ground, his mind descending into darkness.

Chapter Eighty-Two

She had never been to his apartment.

Not once, in all of these months and in all the time they had spent together, had she ever been to Anthony Newell's apartment.

As she drove there now, the realization bothered her. Not so much because she had never been there, but because the fact was just now occurring to her.

Had she been so wrapped up in him she had never bothered to look even an inch below the surface? Had his looks, his charm, his strength, his worldliness simply reduced her to another starry-eyed female, the very thing she had always hated and never wanted to be? Or, even worse, had she grown addicted to the idea of an older man finding her worth his time? Worth his regard? Had she given herself to a man simply because he made her feel better about the fact that her father didn't love her?

Was she really that damned *needy?*

She was still knee-deep in self-loathing when she pulled into his driveway. His address was near the north side of Hopkinsville, more than five miles from her own. It wasn't an apartment, which was what he had told her he had, but a small house. Small, old, and in obvious need of repair, but a house nonetheless. And another lie. Had anything he had told her—especially the complimentary things he had whispered in her ear while they were making love—contained even a morsel of truth?

She parked her car and got out. His Mustang was parked in the driveway, but there was no sign of the Crown Vic. The wind was beginning to whip as one of Kentucky's frequent spring storms toyed with the atmosphere. Soon there would be rain and likely a lot of it.

She walked toward the front door of the house. She might have felt better with a gun in her hand, but she didn't know how to do anything but point it anyway.

When she got to the door, she lifted her hand to knock only to discover it was already cracked open. It gave way easily beneath the pressure of one finger, and with a long creak, begrudgingly welcomed her inside.

The interior was sparsely furnished, but that didn't surprise her. What did surprise her was the ashtray full of cigarette butts, right next to a pouch of tobacco and rolling papers, all of them sitting on a coffee table in the living room. She had never once seen Anthony smoke, but he spent a lot of time bitching about smokers. But at that moment, his hypocrisy was the least of her worries.

She made her way into the kitchen. The garbage can was over-flowing with an array of empty microwave meal boxes. The only items on the counter were a shriveled plant and a bottle of Jack Daniels that, judging from its content level, had received significant play at some point or another.

She walked back through the living room and into the bedroom. It was the antithesis of Anthony. Nothing was kept or orderly. The bed and blankets were strewn about, not like someone had slept there, but like someone had been unable to. At the bedside table was another overflowing ashtray and an empty fifth of Jack. A cheap digital clock was flashing twelve o'clock, giving the distinct impression that its owner didn't give a damn what time it was here or anywhere else.

Libby could hear the wind pressing against the windows and the first drops of rain beginning to jab at the cheap roof. She was scared and the fact that she could be so scared to be in the home of a man she had thought she had loved scared her even more.

Even though she had come to confront him, she was almost relieved he wasn't there. Maybe he was gone for good. Maybe it would be easier for her that way. After all, she knew what to do with men who disappeared on her, emotionally or physically.

She was on her way out of the bedroom when she glanced over at the dresser and saw the wallet-sized photo wedged in the top right corner of the mirror. All she wanted to do was escape, but she found herself walking over to the mirror and pulling the photo from its crease between the glass and the cheap pressed wood that framed it.

The picture was clearly military. It depicted Anthony as a young soldier, maybe twenty-five or so. That would have been close to twenty years ago, she guessed, but who could say? He'd been vague about his age, too.

Despite herself, she couldn't help admiring the picture. He was so handsome then and even more so now. She gently ran her finger down the picture, touching his face for what would certainly be the last time.

That was when she noticed it.

There was something funny about the picture. Something that seemed out of place. The Anthony in this picture was serious and proud. And though he had been a pillar of strength in her moments of weakness, she could not recall ever having seen such an expression on his face. Nor could she imagine him ever having worn such an expression, regardless of how long ago the photo was taken.

Libby slowly turned the photo over, not even sure herself what she was looking for.

There was nothing significant about the name she saw written on the back of the photo, at least not at first glance. It sounded vaguely familiar, but she had come across a lot of names during her studies in law school. It was only when she saw the date written below the name that the realization struck her.

The man in the photo wasn't Anthony, either.

A flood of panic rushed through her. She now recognized the name on the back of the photo and knew the identity of the man in the photo.

More precisely, she knew the identity of his son.

Chapter Eighty-Three

H unter was back in the old Christian County Circuit Courtroom. He was sitting in that same pew, right next to the nice old lady who had made room for him, but he wasn't certain how long he had been there.

He looked toward the front of the courtroom and saw his father sitting at the large table right next to the young soldier, his back to the crowd. The prosecutor with the slicked-back hair and the large bald spot was up there, too. The hard oak benches were still stuffed with onlookers, all of them watching as a heavy-set man wearing overalls handed the piece of paper to the old bailiff. In turn, the old bailiff delivered the piece of paper to the judge.

The judge held the paper in front of him. His lips were moving, but no sound was coming out. His lips stopped moving and he banged his wooden hammer. Somehow, Hunter knew that the room was about to explode. And it did, just as it had before.

All of the adults lunged to their feet and began talking loudly and shaking hands.

The prosecutor was standing and shaking hands, too. The thick, powerful man with the dark suit and tie towered over the prosecutor, and once again, Hunter felt himself tremble at the sight of him.

Hunter saw his father's arm draped across the soldier's back and knew his dad was trying to comfort the man.

Again, he saw the soldier's wife, who had been sitting in the front pew with the soldier's son—the five-year-old—jump to her feet and start screaming. Only this time he didn't have to cover his ears because there was no sound. He saw her jump over the railing and run toward the twelve people who were leaving the wooden box in the front of the courtroom.

Again, he saw the bailiffs grab her and pull her to the ground.

Again, he saw the soldier break away from James and run to help her. Again, he saw the bailiffs hit the soldier in the head with the butt of a gun, handcuff him, and drag him away.

And once again, he looked at the soldier's son, the young boy sitting in that front row, right next to the space vacated by his mother. The boy was no longer looking at the scene being played out right in front of him. Instead, he had turned around and was looking straight at Hunter.

The smell of ammonia shot through Hunter's nasal passages, stinging everything it touched. His head kicked back and his eyes flew open. He was awake and his dream was over. But when he looked up, a pair of eyes was gazing into his. Even now, they looked no different than they had when focused on him more than forty years ago in that ramshackle courtroom. And in his dream just a few seconds before.

Hunter was staring into the eyes of the boy once known as Michael Vazquez. And the man now known as Detective Anthony Newell.

Newell smiled and slowly rose from his kneeling position. "Glad you're awake, Counselor," he said as he walked out of Hunter's line of vision.

Adrenaline immediately lifted Hunter from his fog. He tried to raise his hands to defend himself, but he couldn't. He looked down. They were bound with thick leather straps to the arms of the wooden chair in which he was sitting. The back of the chair was high and extended far beyond the top of his head. Two other thick straps were fastened around his torso and his chest and his ankles had been bound to the stout legs of the chair. The legs of his slacks had been cut off above the knee. Other than his head, which was not yet secured by a strap, he literally could not move.

Katherine? Where in the hell was Katherine? His heart began to race, doubling its rate again when he saw her lying on a couch next to an enormous sliding-glass door. She was lying on her side with her hands and feet bound and her mouth gagged. Relief swamped him when he saw her chest rising and falling slightly. If she were dead, there would have been no need for Newell to have tied her up.

Hunter scanned the room the best he could from his position, then frowned in confusion. He knew this room, but couldn't quite place it. It was a bedroom, with furniture as large and ornate as its setting. He was facing the sliding glass doors and could just make out the glowing trail left across the lake by the moon. The gigantic bed that rested between his chair and the double doors also looked familiar. Not because he had ever been in it, but because of a vivid memory of who had.

This was Cassandra Warren's bedroom, he realized with a start of shock. At the lake house. Kirk's lake house.

And, looking to his left, there was Kirk. He, too, was strapped in a ponderous wooden chair, his feet not quite making it flat to the ground. His pant legs were also cut off just above the knees. His chin rested against his chest. Somehow, his glasses had managed to stay in place.

Hunter looked a little closer. Though Kirk's hair was already thin, he could see a spot, maybe a couple of inches in diameter, on the top of Kirk's head that appeared to have been shaved. Instinctively, he wondered if there was a similar spot on the top of his head. There was no way he could tell for sure.

Newell sauntered back into the room. Hunter noticed for the first time that he was dressed in military camouflage. He was carrying a large bowl containing what appeared to be hot water along with a bag of salt. A good-sized sponge was floating in the water. He set the items down on the dresser. He then moved a small desk from the far corner of the room to within about twenty feet of where Hunter and Kirk were sitting.

"Newell," Hunter demanded, hardly recognizing the hoarse rasp of his own voice. "What the hell do you think you're doing?"

Newell raised an index finger, silently instructing him to hold on, as though he'd be right with him in a minute. He left the room, and within seconds, was back again, this time carrying a large wooden box that had wires protruding from it. He sat the box on the desk and began to assemble the items inside.

"You were saying," he said, his voice polite though he didn't look up from his task.

"I asked you what you think you're doing? Why in the hell have you kidnapped us? Tied us up?"

Newell's eyes remained focused on the box. He was rapidly plugging cords into slots. He clearly knew exactly how to do whatever it was that he was doing. "You're the smart lawyer," he replied. "I'd assumed that you'd have figured it out by now."

"Figured out what? That you're Javier Vazquez's son?"

He finally looked up. "That's right, Counselor. I am *Michael Vazquez*," he said, his dormant Hispanic accent suddenly becoming much more pronounced. "However," he continued, his more neutral dialect returning, "I haven't been known by that name in a very, very long time."

"And this is, what, some sort of revenge?"

"Not exactly the way I had planned it, but it's going to have to do."

"You've got a twisted sense of justice then," Hunter retorted. "The two of us had absolutely nothing to do with the death of your father."

"*The sins of the father shall be visited on the sons*," Newell said, as though he was reeling off the answer to a *Jeopardy* question.

Hunter stared at him in disbelief. "You're blaming *our* fathers for *your* father's death?"

Newell finished with the box and began to run another set of wires from the box to the chairs. "You mean my father's *murder*, don't you, Counselor?" he asked as he worked. "Tell me, is there someone else I *should* blame?"

"Maybe you should start with your dad," Hunter spat, rapidly growing sick of this game. "If he was the one who murdered—"

Newell whirled around and caught Hunter's face flush with the back of his hand. The blow jarred Hunter's head, and his body, held tightly by the straps, snapped back to the base of his spine. He was just beginning to taste the blood in his mouth when he saw Newell's face hovering just inches above his own.

"Don't you *ever* say that about him," Newell growled. "Do you understand me? Or I swear I'll make this experience even more painful than I had planned to."

Hunter shook his head, trying to get his bearings. Next to him, he heard Kirk starting to stir.

"My father did everything in his power to save your father's life," Hunter ground out, swallowing the blood trickling down his throat.

Newell's icy calm returned as he resumed his task. "Your father was incompetent. Hell, if he was half as good an attorney as you are, none of this ever would have happened. After all, did you ever have an innocent client get the death penalty?"

At Hunter's stony expression, Newell said, "I didn't think so" with a knowing half-smile. Turning away, he moved to the doorway to retrieve what appeared to be some sort of helmet sitting on the floor. Until that point, Hunter hadn't even noticed it.

"And just what is this *experience* you have planned for us?" Hunter asked.

Newell set the helmet down on the floor in front of Hunter, went to get the bowl of hot water, and came back. "Let's just say, I'm a big believer in the notion of *an eye for an eye.*"

Hunter blinked at him with real confusion. Then it hit him. The chairs. The hot box. The salt water and sponges. He'd seen it all before, just never anywhere but in movies and at the state penitentiary at Eddyville.

The very same place where Javier Vazquez had been put to death in the electric chair.

He swallowed hard. The state had decommissioned "Old Sparky" since Vazquez's sentence had been carried out. The last Kentucky inmate put to death by electrocution had been in 1997. Both inmates executed since 1997 had been killed by the far more humane lethal injection. But being *humane* was clearly not Newell's first concern.

Newell poured the salt into the hot water. Then he submerged the sponge, his hand apparently impervious to the heat. He pulled it out, sopping wet, and set it inside the helmet, which was sitting upside-down. He picked up the helmet and placed it on top of Kirk's head, fastening it beneath Kirk's chin with a Velcro strap.

Water poured down the sides of Kirk's face and neck, finally rousing him from his stupor. Kirk shook his head violently. "Hunter," he sputtered, spewing out a mouthful of water, "what... what's happening?"

"You're about to die," Newell said matter-of-factly. He grabbed another set of wires, some of which, Hunter noticed with increasing alarm, contained electrodes, and began to fasten them to the strap on Kirk's right leg. He then fastened what appeared to be lead wires to the electrodes and walked back over to the desk where the control box was sitting.

"What's he t-t-talking about, Hunter?" Kirk stammered, vainly trying to pull his bony arms loose from their bonds.

Hunter gritted his teeth, trying desperately to keep his wits about him. "It turns out that Detective Newell here is really Michael Vazquez."

Kirk was still lost. "Who's Michael Vazquez?" he squealed.

Hunter braced himself for Newell's reaction to the slight. Unfortunately, Kirk did not.

Newell was on him in a flash. His hand shot across Kirk's face almost as soon as the words left Kirk's mouth. The blow snapped Kirk's glasses and one of the pieces nicked the skin above his left eyebrow. Almost immediately, blood began to trickle from the wound. Kirk's chin dropped toward his chest as he faded back toward unconsciousness.

"I'm the son of Javier Vazquez, you weak little piece of shit," Newell shouted. "The man *your* father murdered."

"Speaking of murder," Hunter retorted, trying to distract Newell from doing any more damage to Kirk, "you murdered

Cassandra Warren and her unborn child. Let me guess—you think they had something to do with your father's execution, too."

"Cassandra and *our* unborn child," Newell corrected. For just a moment, he stopped fooling with the box. The words seemed to have pierced him, Hunter realized. If he didn't know better, he could have sworn that some piece on the inside of Newell had just broken off and dropped down into a chasm.

Newell raised his to glare at Hunter. "I suppose, in a way, I did murder Cassie."

"So *you* were the other man? Cassandra's lover?"

"She was a casualty of this war," Newell replied. "This process was set in motion decades ago. Once it was started, there was no way I could stop it. Not for Cassie or for anyone else. Cassie was necessary. I cared for her, but she was expendable. Nothing but collateral damage."

"*Expendable?* She was a human being, Newell. Jesus, you're as bad, if not worse than your father, or Kirk's father, or whoever the hell you believe murdered Kirk's mother."

Newell shot a speared hand at Hunter's throat, connecting squarely. Hunter's body wanted to spasm and convulse, anything to find air without pain, but the straps held his body upright. He choked and gagged violently.

"I've heard enough of your bullshit, Cameron." Newell went back over to the box and began adjusting the knobs.

"They'll know you did this," Hunter croaked in between desperate breaths. "They'll find you. You won't be able to run."

When he looked up from the control box this time, Newell's expression made Hunter's blood run cold. He looked like a man on the verge of finding some long sought-after state of bliss.

"Who said I was I going to run?"

Chapter Eighty-Four

When she saw Newell strike Hunter, Libby felt her own scream brush up against the inside of her mouth. She ducked back behind the corner of the balcony, right next to those famous bloody steps she had climbed to get up here, and tried desperately not to let that scream escape.

The picture she had found at Newell's had made it all clear for her. She had first called Kirk's cell to warn him, but no one had answered. She had tried Hunter's cell next, but voice mail had picked up. Though there were any number of logical reasons why neither of them would answer the phone, her desperation had mounted. She remembered the threats that Kirk's attacker, whom she now knew to be Anthony, had made when he broke into the boat. Those threats, coupled with Newell's disappearance, had led her to an inescapable conclusion:

They were in unimaginable danger.

She had sped out to the marina and walked out to Kirk's yacht. The boat was dark and no one appeared to be aboard. However, Kirk's new car was parked in the parking lot. She knew he kept a spare key under one of the exterior cushions and had started to walk across the bow to get it when she noticed that the hatch was slightly ajar.

She slowly crept inside the front salon and saw no sign of life. She walked into the galley and turned on a light. A plastic cup lay on its side and what looked like Coke was spilled all over the top of the table. Nothing else seemed out of order. If there had been a struggle, she realized, it hadn't been much of one.

She had rushed out of the yacht and made a beeline for her car. She tried to call Hunter's home phone and got his answering machine. Her anxiety mounting, she called 911. When she explained who she was and what had happened, the dispatcher was dubious. After all, Detective Newell was not a wanted man, at least not yet. All Libby had so far were some unanswered phone calls and a spilled cup of Coke. The dispatcher said she would check with the police who were out and about and see if one of them would do a drive-by of the Camerons' home. Only after she hung up had it occurred to Libby that if Anthony Newell had indeed done something with Hunter and Kirk, he wouldn't take them to Hunter's home.

No. He would return to the scene of the crime. And the scene of his father's crime, too. Nearly out of options, she had called Dooley's cell phone. She ignored Dooley's obnoxious greeting message and left a rambling message, telling him what had happened and begging him to call her.

When she had arrived at the lake house and saw the black Crown Vic parked along the side, she had felt a cold sheen of sweat envelop her skin. She could tell that the master bedroom light was on. *Cassandra's* bedroom.

She had removed her heels and soundlessly crept up the outside stairs, heading toward the bedroom. She stepped around the corner and took a quick glance inside. The sight that greeted her nearly made her retch.

Anthony was dressed in military combat fatigues and Kirk and Anthony were each strapped in some sort of homemade electric chair. There were wires running from them both and Kirk was wearing some sort of helmet on his head. His clothes were drenched from the water leaking from the helmet and down his face and neck.

Hunter said something to Newell, but Libby couldn't hear the words through the glass. Newell, with breathtaking speed, took two steps and punched Hunter in the throat. Hunter's head had lolled from side-to-side, spittle seeping from both sides of his mouth.

Libby peeled back around the corner and pulled out her phone. The service out near the lake was often dismal, but she had to try. She called 911 again and this time was placed on hold. She couldn't wait any longer. She had no one left to call.

She was trying to figure out what to do next when an arm corded with muscle wrapped around her neck. A merciless palm captured her scream before she could get it out. With brutal efficiency, she was lifted off of her feet and carried into Cassandra Warren's bedroom. She was placed, gently but firmly, face down on her stomach. Her hands and feet were quickly taped together. She caught a quick glimpse of the strip of duct tape just before it went over her mouth. She hadn't seen the face of her abductor, but she didn't have to. She had felt those same powerful hands on her body too many times before.

Anthony rolled her over. "You shouldn't have come here, Libby."

She wanted to scream at him, to beat at his chest with her fists, as if he could feel it. As if he could feel anything.

He took her chin gently between his thumb and forefinger. "I want you to listen to me. You can answer me by nodding. Do you understand?"

Libby just glared at him.

"Is there anyone with you?" he demanded.

No nod. No nothing.

"Answer me, Libby!" His powerful fingers dug into her shoulders. "Is there anyone with you?"

Nada.

Gritting his teeth in frustration, he hauled Libby up and set her down inside the walk-in closet, slamming the door behind her. The closet light was on so she wasn't in complete darkness. He grabbed what she assumed must be the desk chair and propped it against the doorknob. She pressed against the door from the inside, but it wouldn't budge.

All she could do was listen.

"What are you going to do with Katherine and Libby?" she heard Hunter ask.

"I have no issue with either of them. After I take care of the two of you, and then myself, the police will find them unharmed." Newell sounded farther away to her, like he was standing at the desk where his control box was located.

"I've waited my whole life for this moment," he said, his voice rising. "To give my father's life meaning. To finally restore to him the honor that he deserved, the honor your fathers stole from him, leaving him to die in disgrace."

She heard a click and then a slow buzzing sound. Something was happening.

"*No!*" Hunter yelled, "*Stop, damn you!*"

The buzzing grew louder and the light in the closet began to flicker. Libby could hear the sound of wood rattling, as though it was being shaken. Hot tears trickled down her face, but with her hands bound she could do nothing to wipe them away.

Then came a scream. It was a scream unlike any she had ever heard before. A scream that could only come from a man who was dying.

When the buzzing, rattling, and screaming came to an abrupt stop, she slumped in relief. She was so grateful she didn't even realize that two gunshots had been fired just before the sounds had ceased.

She struggled frantically to sit up. She could hear heavy foot-steps approaching the closet door. They were coming toward her. Coming *for* her. Anthony had clearly changed his mind about killing her. And why wouldn't he? He couldn't afford to leave any witnesses alive after the atrocity he had just committed. She shoved her feet against the door, trying to squirm farther away from it now, trying to do something, anything at all, to get away. The knob slowly turned; the door swung open.

Tommy Dooley reached down and gently picked her up, cradling her in his massive arms. He carried her out of the closet, murmuring to her all the way, "It's okay now, honey. It's okay…it's all over now."

Chapter Eighty-Five

Dooley carried her around the chairs where Hunter and Kirk were still sitting. Hunter's head was moving and she heard him asking Kirk if he was all right. Kirk's head was hanging forward and he was groaning softly. Katherine, too, was beginning to stir.

She didn't see Newell anywhere.

Dooley rested her on the bed, then took out his pocketknife and quickly cut through the tape binding her hands and feet. She immediately ripped the tape away from her mouth, dragging in a desperate breath.

"Where is he?" she gasped. "Where's Newell?"

Dooley pointed toward the other side of the bed. "The sum bitch is on the floor over there, either dead or dyin'. I can promise you he ain't goin' nowhere or hurtin' anyone else." He turned his attention to Hunter and began to unbuckle the straps holding him to the chair.

Libby stood up, her legs still trembling with reaction, and cautiously made her way around the bed. Even before she saw Anthony, she heard him drowning in his own blood.

She rounded the end of the bed. The man she had believed she loved was sprawled on the floor next to the bed. The bed where Cassandra Warren had died. And Eleanor Warren before her.

The bullet entry wounds on the left side of Newell's chest looked like nothing more than small red paint blots on his camouflage, as though he had been tagged in one of those weekend competitions. The blood streaming from his mouth, however, was a different matter. The fog of pain in his eyes cleared as they focused on her. He used what little remaining strength he had to reach for her. And just as she hadn't been able to deny him the first time he had reached for her, she couldn't do it now.

She took his hand and knelt next to him. She cradled the back of his head in her other hand, lifting it up. "Oh, Anthony," she whispered, fresh tears streaming down her cheeks, "what have you done?"

"I...I'm...s-s-so s-sorry," he stuttered, his breathing pattern all over the place, "S-s-sorry."

She leaned closer to him, lowering her voice so the others wouldn't hear. "It's okay, baby. I'm here."

"Y-y-you n-n-need to kn-kn-know..."

"I need to know what, Anthony."

"I...I..." Squeezing her hand, he drew another jagged breath. "I didn't..."

"You didn't what, Anthony?"

Footsteps were rapidly approaching from outside the bedroom. It was probably the police, the paramedics, or both.

"I d-didn't..."

Then a sound came from his lips, like wind being sucked back up a chimney. And when the wind stopped, Anthony Newell, Michael Vazquez, and whoever else he may have been, was gone.

Chapter Eighty-Six

Libby and Dooley stood next to the paramedics as they loaded Kirk into one of the ambulances. Newell had indeed begun to electrocute him, but in his haste had crossed a couple of the wires incorrectly. Also, the helmet he'd placed on Kirk's head was simply too large. As a result of those two mistakes, Kirk had not taken nearly the amount of voltage intended for him. It had been a hell of a shock, but not enough to send him into cardiac arrest. Except for a few scattered scars from his burns, he would make a full recovery.

Hunter and Katherine sat on the bumper of one of the ambulances with blankets wrapped around them. Hunter had shown no ill effects from the taser blast Newell had used to knock him out and Katherine, who had been chloroformed, was only suffering from some nausea. Physically, they were both fine.

"Hunter," Katherine said, "I know we've been through a lot tonight. Things that it will take months to even begin to understand."

He just looked at her.

"But I need to know," she continued, "what you were getting

ready to tell me before that man"—an involuntary shudder coursed through her—"that *awful* man, attacked us."

Hunter continued to gaze at her.

"Hunter," she repeated, "is something wrong?"

He was quiet for a minute. "I don't remember."

"You know—you were getting ready to tell me something about having gone to the doctor."

"I…I'm sorry. I don't remember."

She looked at him strangely. The paramedics had assured her that he was fine and didn't need any further attention.

Hunter pointed at Dooley. "He saved us, didn't he? I suppose I should thank him." Before Katherine could reply, he stood up, placed the blanket in the back of the ambulance and began to walk toward Dooley. Katherine pitched her blanket aside and followed him, her concern edging toward panic.

As Hunter approached, Dooley turned to face him. The two men had known one another for twenty years and, counting the Warren trial, had just gone through their second major battle together in the last twelve months. They sized one another up, then Dooley leaned over and enveloped Hunter in a huge bear hug. Katherine and Libby both looked on and, despite the horror of the night's events, they couldn't help but smile.

Dooley released Hunter, which meant basically setting him back down on the ground.

"By the way," Hunter said with a smile, "I don't think we've ever been formally introduced." He extended a hand to Dooley.

"My name is Hunter Cameron."

Epilogue

Libby Masters sat at her desk, the one previously used by her former boss, Hunter Cameron. She was studying the uniform citation for Nathan Watson, whose grandfather, Orvis, had retained her to represent his ne'er-do-well grandson. This time, Nathan had been nabbed for marijuana possession. The pretrial conference was that afternoon in District Court. The charge wouldn't have been a major concern if the twenty-two year old Nathan wasn't already a preferred customer of the office of Probation and Parole due to a past conviction for possession of cocaine. Now he was staring at five years in the penitentiary if convicted of this new charge. Nathan needed a good lawyer, Orvis had said, and he had heard that Mr. Cameron was the best.

After Libby had told him that Mr. Cameron was retired and she would be the one handling the case, he had been a tad reluctant. The prospective clients who walked through the door of *Cameron & Masters* still wanted the legendary Hunter Cameron, not his young protégé. However, once those same clients realized that *she* was the one who had gotten the charges against Kirk Warren dismissed, their misgivings melted away. Both Libby's reputation and practice were beginning to boom and she had all of the work she could say grace over.

As she was reading the citation and making notes, Libby's bulging stomach rubbed up against the desk. She was reminded that in less than two months' time her personal life, much like her professional one, would be in a state of upheaval. With his usual impeccable timing, Anthony Newell's unborn son gave her one of his patented kicks, reminding her of the challenges that lay ahead for her.

She would be a never-married, single mother in one of the most visible professions in the county. Small-minded people would whisper as she went into the clerk's office or when she stepped into court. Or even when she turned the aisle in the grocery store. They would wonder why such a pretty girl with such a bright future could end up in such a predicament. Why, some had even heard she had a tattoo—and on her backside, no less! They might also wonder why such a fine man as Hunter Cameron would associate professionally with such trash.

Oh well. She had never really wanted to be one of them anyway.

No one knew that Anthony was her baby's father and it was likely no one ever would. Of course, she knew she would someday have to talk to her son about his father. What would she say? That he was an angry man who had harbored a desire for revenge so strong that he had plotted it for decades? That he was almost certainly a murderer who had tried to take two more lives before getting killed himself?

No...she would never say any of those words to her precious son. He would only need to know that his father was dead and that she had briefly loved him while he lived. And maybe in some small corner of his damaged heart, he had loved her, too. She placed her hand on her stomach, cherishing the fluttering feel of their child's tiny kicks.

Still, every boy needed a man in his life. She wished that man could have been Hunter Cameron. He would have made a wonderful surrogate grandfather for her son. She knew it might take her a long time to find a man like Hunter. A man who made her believe in herself, made her believe she was worthy of being loved, something her own father had never done. But at least, thanks to him, she now knew such men existed and she was no longer willing to settle for anything less than what Katherine Cameron had found.

Tess buzzed into her office and reminded her that she had court in fifteen minutes. Libby thanked her, but didn't rise to rush out the door as she normally would have. She slowly pulled out the desk drawer and found the graduation card her father had sent her. She was careful to hold it away from herself when she read it, so her tears wouldn't fall on it and smudge the ink.

If Hunter's long-standing relationship with Kirk Warren had taught her anything, it was that he was a man who believed in forgiveness, in giving those he loved more than one chance to redeem themselves, even if it meant waiting a lifetime.

Instead of tucking the card back into the desk as she usually did, she left it open and sitting on her desk. Then, drawing in a deep breath, she reached for her phone.

———

HUNTER CAMERON SAT in his favorite rocking chair on the screened-in porch, his empty gaze fixed on his beloved lake. He was dressed warmly in jeans and a designer sweatshirt, perhaps a little more clothing than most people would wear on a sunny day when it was seventy-five degrees, but he seemed to get cold so easily now. The chair moved slowly back and forth, creaking slightly with each motion. The act was habit, as Hunter no longer had the capacity to do virtually anything with conscious intent.

A small radio sat on the table next to him, playing the afternoon broadcast of the Cardinal game. Mike Shannon's throaty voice was no longer familiar to Hunter. However, to Katherine, the view of her husband looking across the water and listening to the game was a fond remembrance of better times. She set up this scene for nearly every game. Most caregivers, who seldom have time to grieve during the descent of their loved ones into the darkness, try to hang on to any memory of their previous lives. Katherine Cameron was no different.

Most of Hunter's days now were like this one. Though his disease had stalled in the months leading up to the Warren trial, it had made up for lost time afterward. Its assault on his brilliant mind had been quick and vicious. He had gone from asking the same question over and over to blurting out partial sentences to absolute silence. Katherine's prompting of him to perform even the simplest of tasks had become fruitless. He had recently become unable to feed himself, but on most days he would still swallow when Katherine gave him small spoonfuls of pureed food. She had managed to keep his weight from declining too much, but it hadn't been easy.

Katherine had closed the antique shop almost immediately after the trial, when it became apparent Hunter could no longer be left alone. Luckily, their finances had allowed her to hire home health aides to assist her with bathing and dressing him. She had managed to convince the girls not to give up their own lives to come home. Payton had finished college and was living in Nashville, attending graduate school at Vanderbilt. She still came home almost every weekend. Alexandria remained at Northwestern, but came home once a month. Both girls seemed desperate to spend as much time with their father as they could, even if he didn't seem to realize they were there.

From the beginning, Hunter's visitors had been extremely few. The same pride and ego that had made him such a stellar lawyer had also prompted him to withdraw from public life almost entirely after the Warren trial. When he had still been able, he had sternly directed Katherine to limit his visitors to a chosen few. Knowing his relative youth and otherwise good health would keep his body alive long after his dignity had died, he simply hadn't wanted anyone to see him like this.

Kirkland Warren was the exception to that rule, just as he'd always been the exception to every rule in Hunter's life. Now he stood in the frame of the open sliding glass door, gazing with a mix of sadness and amazement at his best friend, or rather, what was left of him.

It was the first time Kirk had come to visit Hunter in several months and Hunter's rapid decline stunned him. Kirk had finally appointed a CEO for the company and escaped the family business, probably for good. He spent a great deal of time traveling abroad and had just returned from South America. He had purchased a large condominium in Antigua, where he planned to spend most of his time, and was shopping for a new yacht. He was no longer comfortable in western Kentucky and, truth be told, probably never had been.

He sank down in the cushioned patio chair to Hunter's right. Together they stared at the water as they had so many times before. Of course, during those times they'd shared their thoughts about business and baseball, along with their fond memories of their college days at Centre. Now the awkwardness of their silence hung like a heavy noose around Kirk's neck.

Finally, Kirk broke the silence, telling Hunter in detail about his year's travels. About the condo and the new boat and the deeply tanned skin and white bikini favored by the female companion he had found in Cabo. She was using him for his money, he knew. But that was no worse, he admitted, than how he was using her. It was a little sad, he guessed, but there were worse fates.

As he rambled on to his friend, he realized that although Hunter was unresponsive, he was doing what he had always done for Kirk— he was listening. Hunter had always listened to him, he thought. He was the only one who ever had. Hunter had never mocked his mousy appearance and demeanor. Had never behaved as thought Kirk was not worthy of his family's wealth or social status. Hunter had always listened. Even now, in his incredibly diminished capacity, he was still listening.

"You know Hunter, it occurs to me that I never really thanked you for what you did for me."

Kirk paused and took a sip of the iced tea Katherine had served upon his arrival. He instinctively waited for Hunter to turn toward him with a quizzical look, as if to ask him what the hell he was talking about.

"No, seriously," he continued. "I mean, when I think about what you went through trying to defend me. I'm sure that you did some of it for yourself—trying to make up for what happened with your father, enjoying one last moment in the sun as the best damn lawyer in the state—I get all that. But it took its toll on you. I know now how hard it was for you. And somehow you won. It almost got you killed, but you still won because here I sit on your porch instead of wasting away on death row."

Kirk turned to the lake, vainly searching for that spot in the far distance that apparently Hunter could see.

"You were always there for me. You, more than anyone else. Other than my father, you were the only person in my life who never let me down. You were loyal to me.

"After all," he added, "you never even asked me if I was guilty."

Kirk took another sip of his tea, now watered down from the melted ice. His focus was narrowing, though not at anything within his sight. It was though he was on the verge of finding something he'd lost a long time ago. Or maybe never had.

"Cassandra had been distant for a long, long time. Not being able to have kids probably had something to do with it, but she never would have admitted that it bothered her. She just saw it as another inadequacy of mine. She'd probably been screwing around for years. There were times when I was suspicious, but I never tried to hire a private eye or anything. I guess I was too self-conscious. I didn't want to have to admit to anyone that my wife would screw around on me. After all, I'm a *Warren*," he said, with no small amount of self-mockery.

"But then Cassandra became careless. I don't know if it was because she wanted me to find out or if she was just at the point in our relationship where she no longer gave a damn." He paused for a moment, as though he was amazed he was actually saying these words out loud. The moment was becoming less a visit to a fallen friend than it was a visit to a confessional. Only Hunter couldn't grant him absolution and wouldn't even if he could.

The only sound coming from Hunter was the steady creak of his rocking chair.

"Knowing what we know now about Newell, he was really quite smart. He seduced her, which, knowing Cassandra, probably wasn't hard to do for a man like him. He would have the affair with Cassandra, make certain I knew about it to create the motive for murder, kill her himself, and make certain that I took the fall for it.

"But as smart as he was, I guess he never considered the possibility that I would kill her myself before he ever got the chance."

————

AFTER KATHERINE HAD BROUGHT him a fresh glass of iced tea and retreated back to the house, Kirk picked up where he had left off with a sigh. "I was slow to realize it," he said. "Her taste for other men. I guess I wanted to believe that she loved me. That I could satisfy her." Kirk was engrossed in his story now, so engrossed he didn't notice that the pained creaking had begun to pick up its pace.

"I didn't know who her lover was. I didn't really care who he was. I only knew who she was supposed to be. *What* she was supposed to be. She was my wife. She was supposed to be loyal to me. To the vows that she took. The life I gave her. But it meant nothing to her. She threw it all away for a roll in the sheets with a stranger." His voice, so controlled only moments before, had begun to escape in clipped syllables through nearly clenched teeth.

"When she served me with the divorce papers, I knew what I had to do."

"That night, I remember going and getting my straight razor. It was my favorite and I always kept it sharp, even though I didn't even use it for shaving anymore."

"Cassandra was just standing there gazing out the moon, waiting for her precious lover. She didn't even have time to fight me. I just put the blade against her throat and pulled. I swear"—he shook his head in amazement—"the cut was so smooth she didn't even grab her throat immediately. She gasped a couple of times and then just stared up at me as I laid her back on the bed. It was like she was trying to say with her eyes what she couldn't say with her voice. I watched her draw her last breath, Hunter. I had to. I mean, given how needy she'd always been, I couldn't let her die alone."

Hunter's steady rocking continued.

"It must have been after I left that night that Newell arrived. Maybe he showed up that night to kill her, too. I guess we'll never know. But what we do know is that he then set about framing me for her murder. I bet he never planned on framing a guilty man. That poor, sad, son-of-a-bitch," he said, chuckling as he shook his head.

"Before I left, I went outside, took the hose and rinsed myself off, along with the razor. It was getting ready to rain. I had a change of clothes in the truck and changed in the shadows of the driveway. I also had a self-addressed packaged envelope in the truck. I put the razor inside of it. I drove with my lights off, figuring that I wouldn't meet any traffic at that time of night. Then I drove down the interstate to Clarksville. The first thing I did was go to the post office. I knew the mail from Tennessee to Hopkinsville takes an extra day and sometimes two. I dropped the package off. Since it was already Friday morning, I figured they'd be done searching my boat by the time it arrived at the marina. I found a Waffle House, dropped my bloody clothes in a dumpster out back, and hung out there for a couple of hours until I thought it would be safe to go back to the house and call the police.

"But when I got back to the house and saw the bloody footprints on the outside steps, I knew they weren't mine. I had gone out the front door, not the outside steps.

"The kicker was the whole razor blade and bloody towel thing. Newell must have slipped onto the boat and stolen another razor from my collection and the towel right before he went to Cassandra's." Kirk shook his head again, this time in disgust. "It's hard to imagine that even Newell believed he'd be able to convince you or anyone else I'd be so damned stupid as to throw the weapon and a bloody towel in the lake right in front of my boat.

"It was obvious that someone was framing me and I knew that exploiting it was my only chance at freedom. That's where you came in, my friend," he said as he placed his hand warmly on Hunter's shoulder. It did nothing to slow the rocking of Hunter's chair. "I knew you'd figure something out."

"Still," Kirk admitted, "when we got to trial and we still didn't know who had framed me, I was getting pretty damned nervous. I never told you, but the thought of testifying just about sent me over the edge. I'm not good at speaking in front of people. Never have been, you know that. Trying to get up there and get by with some sort of cockamamie story would have been a disaster. They would have finished me.

"Fortunately, it never got to that point."

Another thought crossed his mind, and for a second, he actually looked guilty. "I hope that you won't feel bad...you know, over getting a guilty man off. You've always had that damned moral code, the same one your father had. I can understand why he was pissed when Javier Vazquez got fried for something he didn't do. Other than fucking my mother, of course. But Newell...he was one sick son-of-a-bitch. Think of it this way," he said, giving Hunter's shoulder another pat. "If I hadn't killed her, he would have."

"So you see, my friend—he really got what he deserved."

Hunter, of course, could not agree or disagree. He continued to rock in his chair, his pace slowly but steadily increasing.

Kirk was silent for a long time, as though taking stock of what he'd said and, maybe, what he had left to say. Finally, he ended the silence with a slight snicker.

"Somewhere along the line, I remember being told that men tend to marry women like their mothers." He paused, soaking up the wisdom in the statement. "Can you imagine," he asked, "the irony of marrying a woman who was just like the mother that you killed?"

———

"'LOYALTY IS to a man's traits what gold is to his eye,'" Kirk continued. "That's what my father always said."

"He was, as you probably know, a quiet man. He didn't relate to other people so much as he imposed his will upon them. But to me, he exuded loyalty. So as long as I was loyal to him, I would always be good enough for him, no matter how else I failed."

"That was Mother's failure, you know. She was incapable of loyalty. She was never loyal to me. She sure as hell was never loyal to my father. She could only be loyal to herself and her own wants and needs. She had a family, unbelievable wealth, social stature—everything. But she just couldn't stop herself." Kirk's voice had hardened along with his face.

"My father never talked about it, you know. Her infidelity. He never said anything about it, before or after. But he knew, he always knew. I could see it in his face. Even as a small boy, I could see it. I could see it on his face when she would walk into a room, even when she would put her arm around him or kiss him on the cheek. It was like watching a house from the street as the people inside turned the lights off at night. I knew the look and I knew what it meant. But I didn't know why.

"And then I saw her. With him."

"She didn't even have the sense of decency to realize I might be home from school. I wasn't early that day. It was the same time that I always came home. So, it wasn't that she had forgotten something. *It was that she just didn't care.* She brought that soldier into our house. Into the bed that she shared with my father."

"The servants weren't home. My father was in Frankfort overnight for business. I had gone in the bedroom to ask her to come with me down to the pool. She had even left the door cracked. I just stood at the door and watched. It was as though she and that soldier were the only two people who existed in the world. Or the only two people who mattered."

"He was on top of her. I heard her talking to him, begging him for *more*. I could see his back moving across her; his head buried in her neck; and her face—the look on her face. The *pleasure* she was getting from screwing another man in my father's bed..." His voice trailed off, momentarily.

"I knew then why my father looked at her the way that he did. And I knew then what I had to do.

"I remember her trying to make idle chit-chat with me that night, as though she had spent the entire day at home being the perfect wife and mother. *'How was school?'*" he mocked. "Can you imagine? She was even concerned that I was being too quiet." His face was a mask of amazement and disgust, as though his mother had just walked out on the deck with them to ask those very questions.

"I had always been fascinated with straight razors," he continued. "I used to sneak into the bathroom and watch my father shave with one. I remember being amazed that he could shave without slitting his throat. He would sharpen the blade almost daily. He always kept them sharp, I knew.

"Sharp enough to split a hair."

Hunter's face remained impassive. His rocking continued, the pace double what it had been when Kirk arrived. It would have been impossible to tell if he could see Kirk pulling the velvet wrap from his jacket pocket and removing the thin metallic object from inside.

The old straight razor was, indeed, in pristine condition. The blade still gleamed from its daily polishings. Kirk turned it over, clearly comfortable with the familiar weight of its handle in his hand.

"She was sleeping so soundly that night. She always did. She didn't hear me come into the master bedroom. I knew which drawer my father kept the blades in. I walked to her side of the bed. She was on her back, her head rolled toward me. I remember how odd it was that she was sleeping on just one side of the bed even though my father wasn't there." His laugh was bitter. "I mean, she didn't care where she was in the bed just a few hours before.

"I never hesitated. I simply reached across her and drew the razor across her throat. I was amazed at how physically easy the actual act was. It was like pulling a zipper up.

"She looked up at me, reaching for her throat. I remember wondering if she was disappointed in me, the same way that I was in her. I wondered if I would see the shame in her face, the way I had always felt shame when I had been punished for doing something wrong. And I remember seeing no shame in her face, only surprise that she had been caught.

"Your father, God bless him, went to his grave certain that my father had, in some way, killed my mother. But my father was out of town that night. The perfect alibi—a genuine one. And he never considered me." Kirk shrugged. "I mean, who could blame him? Who would have guessed a twelve-year-old boy could slit his mother's throat while she slept?"

"But my father knew. Just as he knew how my mother had lived, he knew how she had died. We never discussed it, of course. But he knew. He approached me at the funeral and looked down at me. He put his hand on my shoulder. He saw that there were no tears in my eyes that day, just as there were none in his, and he *knew*. Neither of us ever mentioned my mother's name again."

Kirk paused, waiting for his friend to either agree with him or tell him that he was full of shit. But the only sound coming from Hunter was that damned creaking from his rocking chair.

Kirk sighed. He wasn't going to get any response from his friend. Not now. Not ever. He gazed out over the water, making one last effort to see whatever Hunter's empty eyes were seeing. Then, he slowly rose and walked around to the back of Hunter's rocking chair. He reached around Hunter. A fond smile curved his lips as he used one hand to gently drape the light-weight quilt that had been resting on the opposite arm of the chair over Hunter's legs. "Here you go, my friend. You must be getting chilly or you wouldn't be rocking so hard."

With the quilt now in place, Kirk affectionately patted his friend on the shoulder. "I guess I'll let you get back to what you were doing. I hate that I had to tell you all of this today, but I couldn't leave without thanking you. You're a damned good friend—my best friend—and you always will be."

When he reached the sliding glass door, he stopped and turned around, taking one last look at the view.

As the gentle breeze dried the single tear that had trickled down Hunter's cheek, his chair was still rocking. And it would continue to rock into the night, until this memory, like all the rest, faded into oblivion.

The straight razor still dangled from Kirk's fingers. He expertly flicked it in the air, then caught it safely by its handle. He ran the flat edge of the razor across his tongue and tasted the familiar combination of cold steel and tart blood.

Snapping it shut, he pocketed the blade, and with a rueful smirk, Cassandra and Eleanor Warren's killer turned and walked away.

The End

Author's Note

As anyone who reads this novel and is familiar with western Kentucky will instantly realize, I took the liberty of consolidating the city of Hopkinsville with its neighboring city of Cadiz, which sits about twenty-five minutes away, town-proper to town-proper, cumulatively referring to both as "Hopkinsville". Cadiz, resting in Trigg County, encompasses one shoreline of the beautiful Lake Barkley, which is an essential setting of the story. Hopkinsville is a downtown area in which Hunter's office and the courthouse are both set.

Both of these towns are wonderful in and of themselves and certainly don't require some wiseacre writer to use one to augment the other. But for the sake of "literary convenience", or, perhaps less likely, the convenience of the reader, I decided to combine the two. I encourage anyone who reads this book and is interested in visiting either or both to do so. Any failure of this novel to accurately depict either setting as anything other than a warm and charming community rests solely at the feet of its author.

Lastly, this book was inspired by my late father's diagnosis of Alzheimer's Disease. Most, if not all, of the scenes regarding Hunter's diagnosis, treatment, and struggles are directly derived from those experiences with my Dad during his own war with this wretched disease. Some of them were tragic, some of them were frustrating...and some of them were even humorous. Alzheimer's, like all forms of dementia, is often the longest of goodbyes. If any reader has a loved one suffering from the effects of Alzheimer's, or any other form of dementia, or is at the onset of it themselves, please consider contacting the Alzheimer's Association at www. alz.org. It's my experience that wonderful people doing wonderful things are good folks toward whom to gravitate when things go south. The folks at the Alzheimer's Association fall succinctly within that category.

Thank you so very much for reading.

JH
    June 2019

About the Author

Jason Holland is an attorney practicing in western Kentucky. He lives with his wife and daughter and their pets—Payton, Gabby, and Pearl. In his spare time he dedicates himself to cheerleading their daughter as she cheerleads (awkwardly, as only a middle-aged dad can), participates in local theater, plays tennis, struggles with golf, and obsesses to an unhealthy degree over his beloved Chicago Bears. He is currently working on the sequel to *Honor Thy Father*.

Photo Credit: Tony Kirves

CPSIA information can be obtained
at www.ICGtesting.com
Printed in the USA
BVHW032224031019
560214BV00001B/32/P